The first tendril of fog snaked its way around his body, thick, cold, and wet. Thunder rumbled and the wind howled as the air temperature dropped about fifteen degrees in a matter of seconds. Whatever he had on the end of his line was now pulling hard enough to drag his boat through the waves.

The fog fully enveloped him, a phantom of mist that draped everything around him, obscuring his surroundings, isolating him in the middle of a never-ending thick grayness. He couldn't see more than three feet in any direction, and he felt the hair rise on the back of his neck.

The lake water began to roil crazily, bubbling and churning in a way he'd never seen. When he looked over the side, he saw two gleaming eyes rapidly rising from the depths toward him. He braced himself as terror flooded his veins.

A Death
in Door County

Annelise Ryan

BERKLEY PRIME CRIME • NEW YORK

BERKLEY PRIME CRIME
Published by Berkley
An imprint of Penguin Random House LLC
penguinrandomhouse.com

ISBN: 9780593441596

The Library of Congress has cataloged the Berkley Prime Crime
hardcover edition of this book as follows:

Names: Ryan, Annelise, author.
Title: A death in door county / Annelise Ryan.
Description: New York : Berkley Prime Crime, [2022] |
Series: A Monster Hunter Mystery; 1
Identifiers: LCCN 2022014344 (print) | LCCN 2022014345 (ebook) |
ISBN 9780593441572 (hardcover) | ISBN 9780593441589 (ebook)
Classification: LCC PS3568.Y2614 D45 2022 (print) |
LCC PS3568.Y2614 (ebook) | DDC 813/.54—dc23
LC record available at https://lccn.loc.gov/2022014344
LC ebook record available at https://lccn.loc.gov/2022014345

Berkley Prime Crime hardcover edition / September 2022
Berkley Prime Crime trade paperback edition / July 2023

Printed in the United States of America
3rd Printing

Book design by Elke Sigal

*This book is dedicated to all the brave sailors of the world
who have given their lives over to a watery grave.
May your souls rest in peace.*

A DEATH IN DOOR COUNTY

PROLOGUE

—

He shut down the motor and let the boat drift, one hand on his pole, the other grabbing his nearly empty beer. The late-afternoon sun warmed his face and sparkled on the waves as the craft bobbed gently, nearly lulling him to sleep. He tossed his empty beer can on the floor, leaned back in his seat, closed his eyes, and let his body relax. This tiny slice of bliss was why he came to Door County whenever he could. It restored his soul.

There had been reports of people catching some good-sized salmon in this part of Lake Michigan recently, and he recalled the eighteen-pounder he'd caught last summer. Visions of a repeat performance excited him, but even if he didn't get a single bite, it was always worth the trip.

As if the thought of a bite had sent a message into the deep, he felt a tug on his pole, hard enough that it nearly slipped from his hand. Adrenaline flooded his veins and he bolted up in his seat, tightening his grip automatically as he went to set the hook. But the line had gone limp. Disappointed but also rejuvenated by the fact that he'd come so close, he settled back into his seat, popped open another beer, and waited.

An hour later he jerked awake, surprised that he'd dozed off. His pole was on the floor of the boat, and he picked it up, figuring it was time to give up and head in. It was getting late; the sun would be setting in another hour, and he didn't want to be out on Lake Michigan after dark in this sixteen-foot skiff with no lights, the only rental he'd been able to get on such short notice. Not to mention that there was a bank of fog off in the distance that looked like it was headed his way, pushed along by a roiling bank of dark, menacing storm clouds. He realized the boat had drifted while he dozed, and it took a minute or two of studying the nearest landmarks before he guessed where he was.

He started to reel in his line, but after only a few cranks, it went taut, zipping off the reel as something on the other end took the hook and made a run for it. Adrenaline shot through him, and he braced himself with his feet against the metal seat in front of him and let the line spin out, fearful it would break if he tried to stop it. Whatever was on the other end would tire soon enough, hopefully before the line ran out. Maybe he wouldn't go home empty-handed after all.

The wind gusted, whipping his hair into his eyes and sculpting the waves into treacherous hills and valleys of froth and foam. When he glanced over his shoulder, he was alarmed to see how much closer the fog and clouds had come in just the last minute or two. He decided to risk a grab for the spinning handle on his reel to try to stop the line, but it rapped his knuckles so hard that the skin split open on one of them, making him bleed. The boat bucked wildly as waves threatened to wash over the side, and he realized he was turned the wrong way.

He grabbed for the reel handle again, succeeding in holding it that time, but the line continued stripping off the reel as he struggled to adjust the tension.

Seconds later, the first tendril of fog snaked its way around his body, thick, cold, and wet. Thunder rumbled and the wind howled as the air temperature dropped about fifteen degrees in a matter of seconds. Whatever he had on the end of his line was now pulling hard enough to drag his boat through the waves.

The fog fully enveloped him, a phantom of mist that draped everything around him, obscuring his surroundings, isolating him in the middle of a never-ending thick grayness. He couldn't see more than three feet in any direction, and he felt the hair rise on the back of his neck. Panic kicked in and he glanced around for his flotation vest, saw it back by the motor. Cursing, he reached into his pocket and took out his Swiss Army knife, using it to cut the fishing line. He tossed the pole into the bottom of the boat just as a huge wave washed over the side, nearly knocking him into the water. Fear and desperation caused another release of adrenaline, making his hands shake. He knew he had to reposition himself quickly so that the bow faced into the waves. Another big wave over the side like that last one would scuttle the boat, leaving him stranded out there in deadly waters. Grabbing the oars, he frantically tried to maneuver the boat into a better position to give himself time to crawl back to the motor and start it.

The lake water began to roil crazily, bubbling and churning in a way he'd never seen. When he looked over the side, he saw two gleaming eyes rapidly rising from the depths toward him. He braced himself as terror flooded his veins.

Something hit the boat hard from beneath and he was tossed over the side, into the water. He thrashed about for a few seconds, trying to reach the surface, and when he did, he sucked in a panicked breath and looked around desperately for his boat. Waves crashed and broke over his head, seeming to come at him from every direction at once. He couldn't see his boat anywhere and he tried to swim, not caring or knowing which way he was going as the waves tossed him about. Then a huge wave crashed over him, dragging him under. He struggled to get back to the surface, to air, but something grabbed his arm and pulled him down.

His frantic efforts to break free drained away the last of the fight in him, and as he sank down into darkness, those two glowing eyes were the last, terrifying things he saw.

CHAPTER 1

⸺

I had just wiped some dust from Henry's hat (dusting him was a regular Saturday chore) and was cursing my decision to move his corpse closer to the entrance when the bell over the door tinkled. A man—blond, fair skinned, and blue eyed, though a deep, dark blue rather than a pale, almost gray blue like my own eyes—entered my bookstore, bringing a new crop of Wisconsin late-summer dust in with him. He stopped a few feet in, staring at Henry's mummified body with horrified fascination.

"Is that real?" he asked.

"It is. Welcome to Odds and Ends," I said. "What oddity, mystery, or bit of magic can I find for you today?"

I can often tell a lot about a person based simply on appearance, but this fellow was a bit of a puzzle. He looked to be around my age—early to mid-thirties—and of average build. His hair was cut short and there was a slightly rigid, military bearing about him. He had on slacks, a dress shirt, and a tie, unusually formal apparel for mid-August. It was the height of tourist season here in Door County and most of our customers arrived kicked back, relaxed, and dressed in summer casual.

"I'm looking for a woman named Morgan Carter," he said, still staring at Henry. I liked his voice. It was even and mellow, though it lacked any discernible accent.

"That would be me. How can I help?"

He managed to tear his gaze from Henry and aimed a disconcerting level of scrutiny my way. "I . . . um . . . I've been told that you are something of an authority on strange things. Is that true?"

He glanced at Henry again and I imagine he realized how silly that question was under the circumstances.

"What sort of strangeness did you have in mind?" I asked with a chuckle. "Our store has a varied inventory."

"I see that." His gaze shifted, breezing over the mystery books and settling on a nearby jewelry display.

"Can I interest you in a necklace or perhaps a tie clip?" I suggested. I walked over and pointed to a pair of cuff links. "These are made from pig bone and there's a matching tie clip to go with them."

"Uh, no, thank you," he said with a look of distaste. He turned back to Henry and stared at him. "Can I ask . . ."

He let the question hang there, but I knew what he wanted.

"Sure, allow me to introduce you to Henry," I said with an arm flourish. "Rumor has it he was part of the Klondike gold rush at the end of the nineteenth century, heading up toward what's now Alaska in hopes of striking it rich. Instead, he fell into a crevasse and died there. Decades later, some indigenous folks came upon his mummified body still wearing the tatters of his mining clothes, and rather than leave him there or bury him, they carried him back to their community and sat him outside the entrance to one of their trading posts as an attraction. Kind of a reverse version of a cigar store Indian, I suppose. At some point, the body was treated with something that preserved it, but only after bits of it had fallen away. That's why he has no nose. Eventually, he was relegated to the dark corners of someone's attic until my dad found him on one of his trips to Alaska. He paid a ridiculous sum of money for the fellow, named him Henry, and brought him back here to the store, where he's been a mascot ever since."

"Hunh," the fellow said, still staring at Henry. After a few seconds he looked at me and said, "Is there somewhere private we can talk?"

"Private" made me nervous. My shop isn't your typical mystery bookstore, though I do have a vast collection of those, everything from the latest releases to some antique, valuable first editions. But I also sell all manner of peculiar, obscure, and eccentric items that sometimes appeal to folks of questionable character.

I looked around for my employee, Rita Bosworth, who is generally easy to find because she's nearly six feet tall, always wears her white hair piled atop her head in a messy bun, and her glasses are attached to a chain of sparkling rhinestones that catch and reflect the overhead lights. The last time I had seen her, she had been shelving books, but she wasn't there any longer. I spotted her over in the creepy-critters area, chatting with a customer near the skull collections. She must have sensed my unease because she looked my way and gave me a little nod, letting me know she'd keep an eye on me. Plus, I had Newt.

I turned back to the man and that was when I saw the badge. He must have pulled it out of a pocket when I was looking for Rita. I eyed it closely to see if it was legit because last year I'd had a collection of antique police badges that had sold like hotcakes. The fact that he held it out for me to scrutinize until I was thoroughly satisfied reassured me.

"We can chat in my office," I said, leading him to the room under the stairs that served that purpose.

The space was small, and by the time the two of us and my dog, Newt, squeezed in there, it was uncomfortably close. There was a chair against the wall, and I gestured toward it while I scooted around behind my desk. Once the cop was seated, Newt positioned himself about two feet away and stared at him.

"He's really big," the cop said, eyeing Newt uneasily. "Is he friendly?"

"He's friendly if you are. He likes to analyze people and situations. That's what he's doing now, deciding if you're a good cop or a bad one."

The fellow stared back at Newt, the furrows in his brow deepening.

"Oh, and he doesn't like direct eye contact," I added.

The cop quickly looked away, shifting nervously in his chair.

I laughed. "I'm kidding. His name is Newt and he's a sweetie pie."

"Newt?" the cop said, and I couldn't tell if he was talking to the dog or questioning his name.

"Yeah, short for Newton because he just dropped in on me one day, kind of like Newton's apple. Plus, he's wicked smart."

"Does he always stare at people like that?"

"He does. It's because he can't see well. His other senses are incredibly keen, though. There are times when he stares at me, and I swear he's reading my mind. When he first showed up here, he was thin as a rail, bedraggled, and bloodied. I think someone tried to use him in an illegal dogfight, thinking he'd be tough because of his size, but he doesn't have the temperament for it. He really is a sweetheart. I had his DNA tested and it turns out he's Labrador retriever, Saint Bernard, and golden retriever with a tiny bit of Anatolian shepherd thrown into the mix."

The cop relaxed some and gave me an awkward smile, though he kept giving Newt a nervous side-eye every few seconds. I can't say I blamed him; Newt's stare can be quite disconcerting.

"Now you know my dog's name as well as mine," I said. "Might you return the favor?"

"Oh, geez, right. Sorry," he said, looking contrite. "I suppose I should have led with that. My name is Jon Flanders. I'm the chief of police on Washington Island."

I didn't know if he expected me to be impressed with his title, but I wasn't much. Washington Island had a police force of three. One of them had to be the chief.

"What can I do for you, Chief Flanders?"

"I've been told you're a cryptozoologist."

I paused for a beat and then said, "I am."

"I confess, I didn't know that was a real occupation until recently."

"You're not alone. And it can be a bit of a grab bag," I admitted. "However, unlike the many con artists out there who are eager to take money from gullible people, I consider myself a professional. I have degrees in both biology and zoology, as well as minors in religions and mysticism. I'm also a professional skeptic. While I'm certain there are lots of interesting things in the world that we have yet to discover, I'd need absolute proof before I'd believe in the existence of a cryptid."

"A cryptid?"

"A creature that people say exists even though no definitive proof bears that out. Like the Loch Ness Monster or Bigfoot."

"Oh, right. Yes. That's exactly what we need," he said. "A skeptic."

This piqued my curiosity. The folks who hire me as a consultant cryptozoologist are typically looking for validation, not skepticism. "Who is this *we* you're referring to?"

Flanders shrugged. "A political figure, a couple of business owners, law enforcement, the DNR."

It seemed an odd combo to me, particularly the inclusion of the Department of Natural Resources. "What is it you want from me?"

"We're hoping you can help us determine what happened to a body we have in the morgue."

"Isn't that what an autopsy is for?"

"The official word out there right now is that our victim drowned in a boating accident. But the medical examiner in Milwaukee is a bit stymied because this fellow's injuries are . . . unusual."

"I'm no expert on forensic pathology," I told him.

"That's not what we're looking for." He sighed, giving Newt another side-eye glance. "We need someone who thinks . . . outside the box."

"Okay," I said. "Where was this man when he died and sustained these unusual injuries?"

"We aren't sure. Based on what he told the boat rental shop, he was planning on fishing between Gills Rock and Washington Island."

"Porte des Morts," I said with an appreciative nod. "Death's Door."

Death's Door is a strait that connects Green Bay to Lake Michigan, a waterway that's prone to crazy weather, hidden shoals, and bizarre currents. It used to be an extremely busy shipping canal because Green Bay was once the biggest lake port in Wisconsin. As a result, the lake bottom through Death's Door is also the final resting place for many a wrecked ship and the souls that went down with them. In fact, it's purported to have more shipwrecks than any other body of fresh water in the world.

"He might have changed his mind," Flanders went on. "The shop told him there were some nice-sized salmon that had been caught north of Washington Island and he seemed interested in that. We found his boat floating off the western coast of Washington Island. Two days later his body turned up on a small strip of beach on the eastern side of Boyer Bluff."

I shrugged. "A drowning, while tragic, isn't exactly unheard-of in these parts. In fact, wasn't there also one back in June?"

"There was."

He said that in a way that made me think there was more to that story, but after waiting a beat without any further clarification, I said, "I don't see where I fit in."

He sighed, ran his hands down his thighs, and cast another wary glance at Newt. "We're hoping you can provide an explanation for the bite marks we found on the body."

"Bite marks?" I said, surprised. And yes, intrigued, though I tried not to show it.

Before Flanders could answer, there was a knock on the door, and it opened to reveal Rita on the other side. She quickly surveyed our situation and then said, "Sorry to interrupt, but there's a lady out here who's looking for a couple of those hair balls from cows' stomachs. Didn't we get some in recently?"

We had several of these hair balls on the shelf and I knew Rita not only knew that but knew where they were. She was just using the question as a ruse to make sure I was okay.

"I put them on the shelf below the buffalo and moose skulls," I told her.

I smiled to let her know I was fine, and she backed away, shutting the door.

Flanders grimaced. "Hair balls?"

"Do you really want to know?"

He considered the question, and then shook his head.

"Back to this death," I said, eager to hear more. "Are you telling me that something tried to eat this man whose body you found?"

Flanders bobbed his head from side to side, an equivocal expression on his face. "Not exactly," he said. "The skin wasn't broken, just bruised. But you can see tooth impressions. There was one on his arm and a much larger bite on the torso."

"How much larger?"

"Nearly twelve inches wide. Organs on the bite side of his body were crushed."

"Did he drown or did the crush injuries kill him?"

"He drowned." He sighed. "But the crush injuries occurred at or close to the time of death. I'm sure you can understand why certain folks in our area would prefer not to have word get out about this. The tourist industry is too critical to folks' survival."

"You underestimate the lure of the cryptids," I said. "A rumor of one might attract people."

"Not the kind we want," Flanders countered.

Fair enough. "How did you come to know about what I do? I consult only part-time, and my clients thus far have all been out of state."

Flanders hesitated, wincing. His cheeks flushed red. "Karl Swenson is my uncle," he said finally.

The name made my hackles rise. "You mean, Karl Swenson, the detective in New Jersey?"

He nodded and waited for me to say something more, but that wasn't a topic I wanted to discuss. I needed to slap the lid back on that can of worms right away.

"You know," I said, "if you hadn't told me the truth about your dead man, I never would have questioned the public reports of his death. Why not just sweep it under the rug? If I start looking into things, it might draw unwanted attention."

"I know," Flanders said. "But I don't think we can ignore it any longer."

"Why is that?"

"Because a kayaker we found dead back in June had nearly identical injuries."

Okay, definitely intrigued now. I thought for a moment and then said, "If I find a creature that's responsible for these deaths, what will happen to it?"

He shook his head but said nothing. To his credit, though, he held my gaze and didn't look away.

"They want it dead," I said.

"And kept under wraps."

At least he was honest. I thrust that issue aside, figuring I could deal with it later if, and when, the time came.

"Okay," I said. "I'll need a thousand-dollar retainer up front, and I charge one hundred bucks an hour for my time. Plus, reimbursement for any equipment I might need to rent."

"That's fine, but check with me first to see if I already have the equipment."

Government people never let go of money that easily, and I'd purposely given him a number that was prohibitively high. His quick capitulation told me how desperate he was. To be honest, I was willing to help him for free and didn't need the money, but charging fees is a good way to weed out the crazies and test how serious someone is.

"I can start first thing tomorrow morning, if that suits you."

"It does."

"I'm assuming you have access to a boat?"

"Sure. I can arrange for a patrol boat."

"Great. Tell me when and where to meet you in the morning and we'll be there."

"We?" Flanders asked, eyebrows raised.

"Me and Newt," I said. "I don't go anywhere without my dog."

CHAPTER 2

fter informing Rita that I wouldn't be in the store the next morning, I called Devon Thibodeaux, my other employee, and made sure he'd be able to work the full open hours with Rita. Devon, a Louisiana Creole with an interest in voodoo, has been with the store for four years, ever since he graduated with a degree in computer science and realized that jobs in IT were so boring, they made him feel like one of the zombies that so fascinated him. I'd inherited both Devon and Rita along with the store upon the deaths of my parents two years earlier. Rita has been there for nearly six years. She and her husband had owned a rare-books store in Milwaukee for thirty-four years, and when her husband died unexpectedly of a heart attack, Rita discovered his accounting skills had been a bit sketchy. The store was heavily in debt and Rita had been forced to sell it—or, more accurately, give it away. My parents had snatched up some of her inventory and offered her a job, knowing her book knowledge would be invaluable.

The following morning, confident the store would be in good hands, I put Newt's flotation vest on him and we set out at seven thirty, driving twenty minutes to a boat launch in Baileys Harbor, where Flanders had said he would meet me. It was a beautiful morning, with clear blue skies as far as the eye could see and only a light breeze to provide a reprieve from the heat that would come later. That also meant the waters of Death's Door would be relatively calm for the day, though I knew that could change in the blink of an eye.

Flanders was dressed more like a tourist today, in shorts and a polo shirt, and after greeting me and handing me an envelope, he gave Newt a nervous pat on the head.

"Thanks for doing this," he said.

"No need to thank me."

I peered inside the envelope at ten one-hundred-dollar bills, thinking, *Cash. Interesting. He doesn't want a paper trail.*

"You're paying me well," I added as I stuffed the envelope into my pocket.

Flanders checked his watch and looked out at the harbor. "The boat should be here soon."

The two of us stood there quietly gazing out at the water. I was content to maintain the silence, but Flanders appeared nervous, rocking back and forth on his feet and glancing over at me every few seconds.

"Morgan is an interesting name," he said after a minute of nervous rocking. "Are you named after King Arthur's half sister, the sorceress?"

"Nothing so mystical, I'm afraid," I told him, mildly impressed that he knew the reference.

He shrugged and said, "She's often depicted with long, wavy dark hair like yours. And with all that stuff you have in your store, I thought maybe . . ." His words drifted off, and he fidgeted with his shirt.

"You thought I might be whipping up an elixir made from toe of frog and eye of newt in my spare time?" Newt whined beside me, and I gave him a reassuring pat on the head, adding, "Not that kind of Newt."

Flanders flushed and looked embarrassed. "No, of course not."

His voice was convincing; his expression was not. I felt sorry for him and decided to ease the tension a little. "In the Welsh language, 'Morgan' means 'sea-born.' I was born aboard a boat in the middle of Loch Ness when my parents were on a search mission for Nessie."

"Really?" Flanders said, looking skeptical.

"Really."

He seemed to consider this for a moment, and then said, "Did they find anything?"

I found it interesting that this was his next question, rather than anything about the circumstances surrounding my birth. Maybe Flanders wasn't as straight an arrow as I'd originally thought.

"No, they didn't," I told him. "But that didn't stop them from looking. I went on several other expeditions to Loch Ness with them when I was a kid. None of those trips panned out either, but my parents passed down their love of the hunt to me. It's what attracted me to cryptozoology."

"Interesting."

I studied his expression for a few seconds, trying to tell if he really did find this interesting, but for the moment, his face was placid, giving away nothing.

We were back to awkward silence and staring out at the water. I think we both breathed a sigh of relief when we finally saw the boat approaching. The pilot docked the vessel neatly and Flanders sur-prised me with his handling of the mooring lines. Then again, he worked and presumably lived on an island, a fact of life that often re-quires some level of boating knowledge.

This boat was a thirty-eight-foot aluminum patrol craft rigged with three outboard motors, sonar, radar, Wi-Fi, floodlights, a winch, a small dinghy, and the worst coffee I've ever tasted. Our pilot was a thin, wiry fellow whose face looked like old tanned leather. Flan-ders introduced him as Haggerty—that was all I was given, just Haggerty—and the fellow acknowledged me with a nod.

Flanders waved a manila folder at me. "Before we head out, there are some things I want to show you. Let's sit."

We settled in at a small table inside the pilothouse while Hag-gerty leaned against a side window and watched us, sipping the crap he called coffee. Newt walked over and sniffed Haggerty's free hand, sat down beside him, and stared up at his face. Haggerty stared back for a second, smiled to reveal several missing teeth, and then reached down and scratched behind Newt's ears like he'd been doing it for years. No hesitation. Newt chuffed his approval, and just like that, Haggerty made it onto my good-guy list.

Flanders, who was still giving Newt the occasional side-eye, slid his folder across the table toward me, but when I went to grab it, he flattened his hand on it and said, "This contains some written re-ports, but it also includes autopsy photos. They're quite graphic."

"I'll be fine," I assured him. He lifted his hand, and I pulled the folder to me.

The first thing in it was information on a twenty-nine-year-old man from Green Bay by the name of Oliver Sykes, who had been re-ported missing by his friends back in mid-June. There was a photo of Oliver clipped to the inside of the front of the folder—probably a driver's license picture—and I stared at it for a moment, thinking the fellow looked vaguely familiar. I couldn't place him, however, and he had the generic blond-haired, blue-eyed look of thousands of other men in this part of the country, so I moved on to the next thing: a narrative report.

Oliver Sykes had been part of a group of six guys who had rented a house on Washington Island for a week. All of them were avid kayakers. According to the report, Oliver had told his friends he was going to kayak out from Schoolhouse Beach and run along the northern coast of Washington Island, after declining to head toward the peninsula with the others, who had some sightseeing planned. Oliver was a far more experienced kayaker than the other guys, so none of them worried about him going out on his own.

Oliver Sykes was never seen alive again. His kayak was spotted the following morning floating upside down half a mile out on the western bay side of Washington Island. A search was initiated, and Oliver's body was found the next day, still in his wet suit, on a small bit of beach on the bay side of Boyer Bluff, a jutting tower of tree-topped cliff on the northwest corner of Washington Island that rises seven hundred feet from the water. He wasn't wearing any type of flotation device, like a life jacket, and one never turned up.

Behind the report summary were some autopsy photos. It was easy to spot the bite mark once the wet suit had been removed, because discoloration on the flesh made the outline of the teeth stand out on the pale skin of the chest and abdomen. The autopsy report said Sykes had died by drowning, but that his organs had been crushed at or around the time of death by an unknown force.

Next in the folder was another report, that one for the second, more recent victim, a thirty-two-year-old man named Will Stokstad. Like Oliver, there was a headshot of him included—brown hair and eyes, all in all rather nondescript. Unlike Oliver, Will had come there on his own. An avid fisherman, he would come up to Door County from Madison whenever he could for a few days of fishing, while his wife, Janelle, who apparently didn't share his passion for the sport, stayed at home with their two kids. That most recent trip had been a last-minute, spur-of-the-moment thing that Will, who was a self-employed electrician, had decided on when a job canceled at the last moment. Janelle had reported Will missing after trying to call him numerous times during the last day of his scheduled stay without ever getting an answer or a call back.

There was some confusion as to where Stokstad had gone in his boat. The shop he rented it from was located on the northeast corner of Washington Island, not far from Rock Island, and he'd indicated to the shop owner that he planned to head east toward a spot known as Fisherman Shoal. But then he was told about the salmon that had been caught in the Rock Island Passage a couple weeks back and he seemed interested in that.

Stokstad's body had also turned up on a narrow strip of beach, this time on the eastern side of Boyer Bluff, though his boat was found floating in Death's Door, near Hedgehog Harbor on the north coast of the peninsula. Like Oliver, Will wasn't wearing a life vest or other flotation device when his body was found though, unlike Oliver, he'd been wearing clothes: jeans, shirt, and one purple-and-orange sneaker, the colors bright fluorescent shades that looked like they could have glowed in the dark. Both men, according to their friends and family, were strong swimmers. So what had happened?

Will's autopsy photos resembled Oliver's, though he also had a gash on the knuckle of a finger on his right hand and what appeared to be a tooth impression on his right arm. According to the ME's notes, Will, like Oliver, had drowned and had crush injuries to his chest and abdomen that were inflicted at or around the time of death. Unlike Oliver, Will also had a crush injury to his right arm.

There were more pictures at the back of the folder, and I pulled them out to examine them. Two were shots of the bodies of the men exactly where and how they'd been found: Will fully clothed with that purple-and-orange sneaker on his left foot acting like a beacon; and Oliver, barefoot and dressed in his wet suit. The wet suit made sense; many kayakers wore them, particularly if they were going to paddle in the lake waters as opposed to Green Bay. Even when the air temperatures were as warm as they had been back in mid-June, when Oliver Sykes had disappeared, the lake would have been chilly. Rarely did the temperature get above seventy, and that early in the season, it would have been closer to the high fifties or low sixties. The lack of shoes bothered me, but I shoved that thought aside for now.

Will had drowned in late July, when the water temperature would have been closer to seventy, maybe even a few degrees above. It had been a hot summer so far. It was now mid-August and I'd heard a report the other day that said the water temperature in Lake Michigan had hit a balmy seventy-five.

The last two photographs in the folder puzzled me at first, but when I looked closer, I saw why they'd been included. I closed the folder, looked at Flanders, and said, "You and these people you're working with think there's some kind of Loch Ness Monster in the waters here, don't you?"

Flanders appeared flustered and he stuttered for a few seconds before spitting out, "I don't. They don't exist." Then he squeamishly added, "Do they?"

I smiled at him. "Let's go and find out, shall we?"

CHAPTER 3

⌒

I'd like to see the spots where the bodies were found," I told Flanders.

"Can do," he said, giving me an exaggerated salute.

As Haggerty started the engine, Flanders went outside to undo the moorings, and moments later, we were underway.

I left the cabin area and went to sit on one of the bench seats at the back of the boat. Newt followed me and curled up at my feet. After a brief chat with Haggerty, Flanders joined us, settling on the bench opposite mine.

"Don't you have to return to the island?" I asked as we motored out of Baileys Harbor.

"I have a full-time officer on staff who can cover for now."

"Does one of you have to be on duty and patrolling all the time?"

Flanders shook his head. "No, but one of us is on call all the time.

Fortunately, the crime rate on the island is low, even now with all the tourists."

Once we left the harbor, Haggerty steered us around the Northport pier that served the ferry to Washington Island. This put us squarely in Porte des Morts, or Death's Door, where the waters of Green Bay and Lake Michigan mingled, sometimes with deadly results. Off to the east, I could see the southern tip of Detroit Island extending out from behind Plum Island, and another tiny spot of land that I knew was Pilot Island.

At one time, Pilot Island had been covered with healthy, leafy trees and bushes, and the lighthouse had been manned by a keeper who lived in the decent-sized house. But as has been the case with many lighthouses, it eventually became automated and no longer needed a keeper. Once humans left the island, it was taken over by cormorants, large black fishing birds that arrived by the thousands. Their guano proved to be so toxic, it killed off all the trees and other greenery on the island. What is left now is a creepy and desolate bit of rock, sand, and scrub, with dead tree trunks, a lighthouse near the center of the island, and a crumbling foghorn building at one end. The lighthouse is maintained at a minimum level to keep the light functioning and the walls from crumbling, but the workers who provide the maintenance need to wear respirators and other protective equipment. Even divers who have been in the waters surrounding the island have been known to get sick.

The closest island to Northport pier is Plum Island, once home to a Coast Guard station and still home to the Plum Island Range Lights, a pair of lighthouses 1,650 feet apart with a line of sight that directs ships through the narrow portion of Lake Michigan that leads into the Death's Door passage. There were hundreds of shipwrecks around

Plum Island, and during this time of the year, ferries passed it on their way to Washington Island nearly every half hour.

Haggerty patrolled a parallel path along the northern coastline of the peninsula, keeping our speed at a reasonable pace, monitoring our progress, and watching for deadly shallows and shoals on his radar and sonar. These hazards, combined with the highly unpredictable weather, were how Death's Door had earned its name. There are well over two hundred fifty shipwrecks in the area, so many that some of them are on top of others. The combination of fresh water and cold temperatures preserves many of the wrecks in the pristine waters. There are places where the wooden hulls and decks of sunken ships more than a hundred fifty years old can be seen so clearly that even the wooden pegs can be visualized. Scattered about the mainland and Washington Island are historical markers that tell bits and pieces of the area's tragic history, some of them displaying literal bits and pieces from the ships that created that history. Navigating these waters without knowledge of how treacherous they can be is a fool's errand. Judging from the way Haggerty kept a keen eye on everything around him, I could tell he was no fool.

Another tale of how Death's Door got its name has to do with a legendary battle rumored to have taken place between the Potawatomi and Winnebago tribes in the seventeenth century. There are several iterations of this tale, making the truth elusive, but most people agree that a deadly battle of some type occurred. Yet another claim states that the French named the passage merely to scare others away from the profitable fur trade that ran through it. Regardless of how Porte des Morts came by its name, there is no denying the many wrecks and the number of men who have lost their lives there.

As we cleared the Death's Door passage and rounded the western side of Washington Island, Flanders stared down into the water, which ranged from ninety to one hundred twenty feet deep in this area.

"Do you believe in Nessie?" he asked me.

"I believe in the possibility of Nessie."

He looked over at me with a doubtful expression.

"I'll tell you why," I went on. "There's a fish called a coelacanth that was presumed extinct sixty-five million years ago. We knew of it only through fossils until a live one was recovered off the coast of South Africa in 1938. Since then, more have been discovered and we've learned that they tend to congregate in deep underwater caves several hundred feet down during the day, and come out and swim up into shallower waters at night to feed. Could there be a Nessie-type creature that lives deep down in some waters and is rarely seen? A creature that, like the coelacanth, has remained largely hidden for millions of years? Sure. But is it likely?"

I shrugged. "There are reports of such creatures all around the world, all bearing a striking resemblance to one another. In Okanagan Lake in British Columbia, the First Nations indigenous people have Ogopogo. In Lake Champlain in upstate New York there's Champ. In the Chesapeake Bay area, the creature is called Chessie. Many of these reports describe an animal that looks much like a plesiosaur, a creature that was known to exist eighty million years ago. Maybe, like the coelacanth, it never really went extinct, but went into hiding instead."

Flanders considered that. "Have there been rumors or sightings of these creatures in the Great Lakes?"

"Oh, yes. There are stories going back more than a century about Bessie, the Lake Erie serpent with the head of a dog. In Lake Huron, the Ojibwa talked of a great lynxlike creature. The one in Lake Ontario is rumored to be able to fly and breathe fire. And Lake Superior is probably the most prolific and varied of them all, with reports of everything from a dragon to a giant snake with a turtle head that possesses supernatural powers. The sinking of the *Edmund Fitzgerald* has even been blamed on a lake monster by some."

I paused as Flanders stared at me, wide-eyed.

"Interestingly," I went on, "Lake Michigan has had the least number of sightings of all the Great Lakes even though it's had the most drownings. But that's because of longshore currents, not lake monsters."

Flanders broke his stare and shook his head. "Surely all these stories are merely figments of people's vivid imaginations. I'd have to see something like this to believe in it."

"Why?"

He gave me a puzzled look. "Because that would be proof. Seeing is believing and seeing it with my own eyes is the only way I could be convinced."

I nodded thoughtfully. Then I asked him, "Do you believe in oxygen?"

"What?"

I felt certain he'd heard me and that his question was a reflexive one designed to give him a beat to figure out where I was going. So I didn't repeat myself. I just waited.

"It's not the same," Flanders muttered finally, confirming my suspicions.

"Isn't it? We believe in all kinds of things that we can't see . . . some that we can't prove or don't understand. Faith, not scientific proof, is the basis of all religions. Faith is the thing that allows people who have no concept of aerodynamics to confidently climb inside a giant metallic bird and go up thousands of feet in the air."

Flanders clearly didn't like that logic. He leaned forward in his seat and said, "Are you trying to tell me that you actually believe some kind of prehistoric monster somehow made it into Lake Michigan and decided to kill a couple of boaters?"

Newt sat up and alerted on Flanders at the change in his tone and body language. Flanders sank back in his seat and scowled, forcing me to suppress a smile.

I had to confess, I enjoyed his discomfort a little, so I didn't tell him that the injuries to Will and Oliver were inconsistent with the more popular theories of what these creatures most likely would have been if they did exist. Will and Oliver both had marks that appeared to have been made from grinding teeth, like molars. But the plesiosaurs had sharp teeth, rip-and-tear canines designed to catch and kill their food. If plesiosaurs had somehow survived millions of years like the coelacanth, would their teeth have evolved into grinding molars? It didn't make sense, given the fish that I assumed would have been their primary food source, but then, lots of things about the case didn't make sense.

Oddly enough, that made it more appealing to me.

CHAPTER 4

⌐

The boat began to slow as we neared the end of Boyer Bluff, which rose to our right, and Flanders pointed toward a narrow strip of shoreline.

"This is where we found Will's body. He was over there at the base of the bluff, about three feet up from the waterline, facedown."

The area where the body was found was easy to spot, thanks to some stakes with the tattered remains of police tape on them, the yellow-and-black strips fluttering in the morning breeze. It was an isolated spot, not easily accessible from land, as the shoreline disappeared and became sheer cliff face several feet from the site in both directions. A few moments ago, we had passed a stairway attached to the cliffside that gave a homeowner access to one section of beach. But those stairs were barely visible from here and the house atop the cliff was set back in among the trees without a line of sight to where we were.

"Not easily observable or accessible from shore," I said.

"Tell me about it," Flanders said with a roll of his eyes.

"Is it okay if I go ashore?"

Flanders nodded. "We can take the dinghy."

"No need." I took off my top and slipped out of my shorts, leaving me in the bathing suit I'd put on that morning. I kept my sneakers on since the lake bottom and the shore were composed of rocks, making barefoot travel awkward and painful.

"You can't swim over there," Flanders said, aghast.

"Yes, I can. I'm a strong swimmer. I swim ten times this distance many mornings."

"But the water here is only about seventy degrees," he said.

"Refreshing!"

Haggerty looked amused. Flanders did not. He stared at me, mouth agape, and then started to take his shirt off.

"Fine. I'll go with you."

"Don't be ridiculous," I said, patting Newt on the head. "Stay here. I'll probably need help getting Newt back into the boat."

Flanders looked at my dog. "You're taking him with you?"

"Of course."

Newt let forth with a low growl, subtle but with a hint of menace, should anyone suggest otherwise.

Flanders shook his head, looking at me like I was crazy, then like I was the most trying person he'd ever encountered. He might have been right on both counts.

I slipped over the side and down into the water. Seconds later, Newt entered the water with a bit less aplomb, but then the two of us were swimming toward shore. The waters were relatively calm—I wouldn't have attempted the swim had they been otherwise—and I approached from an angle some feet to the east of where the body had been.

"The evidence guys are done with the site," Flanders hollered. "They just haven't come back to take up the tape. Feel free to explore it."

I reached a spot where I was able to touch bottom and clambered out of the water. I walked with Newt up to the perimeter of the stakes, watching as he sniffed the air and ground. He emitted a low growl and backed away from the spot and I wondered what had triggered that reaction. Was the fact that a dead body had been there reason enough? Or had he detected something else?

I put a hand on his head and reassured him. "It's okay, Newt."

He sat down and leaned into me, still facing the body site. I told him to stay and then I stepped inside the perimeter tape and squatted to get a better look at the ground. The waterline was only three feet away, but in terms of understanding how that body ended up there, it might as well have been three miles. While the water levels changed some with the seasons or with storms—though we hadn't had one of those for weeks—there wouldn't have been a significant change here in the time frame we were looking at. Tidal influences in the lakes were so minimal as to be nonexistent. That meant that the body had most likely been placed where it had been found. It hadn't just floated in on a tide.

Something niggled at my brain. I knew my Loch Ness history. One of the sighting reports had said that the creature made the water roil and churn before it finally disappeared beneath the surface, reportedly sending out waves that were big enough to have been caused by a steamer. It might have been hyperbole, but if it wasn't, could a wave like that have carried a body up onto the shore?

Another thought came to me. Would a Nessie-like creature have left the water to deposit the body there? Would its neck have been long enough to reach this spot without leaving the deeper water? I supposed it was possible but thought it unlikely. The creature would have had to hoist its body out of the water and onto the rock shelf that led to shore fifteen to twenty feet out in order to dump a human body where that one was found. I knew that some of the sightings of Nessie back in the 1930s involved people who claimed they witnessed the creature walking on legs as it made its way back to the water. But the plesiosaurs had four flipperlike appendages rather than legs, and they would have moved like seals on land. The odds of flippers evolving into legs on a creature that lived in the water for millions of years were slim to none. Of course, that assumed that the whole plesiosaur theory was correct.

I examined the shore between the body-drop spot and the water-line and saw what appeared to be drag marks, but Flanders had said kayakers had discovered the body and come ashore to check it. And then police and evidence techs had been there, as well.

I walked to the water and stared down at the lake bottom, study-ing the smooth stones, some of them apple sized, others as big as a cantaloupe. Wading out a few feet, I could see where the stones on the bottom appeared to have been pushed out, creating a hollow path to the shore as if something large *had* been there. I looked out at the water and saw Flanders and Haggerty watching me from the boat. A couple of kayakers paddled by behind them, eyeing us curiously. How easy would it have been to deposit a body there without being seen during that busy time of the year? I gave it even odds, unless it had happened during the night.

Newt whimpered, still staring at the spot where the body had been.

"Okay, buddy, we can go."

Out into the water we went, and minutes later, we were both back on the boat.

"Well?" Flanders said as Haggerty handed me a musty-smelling towel. "Thoughts?"

"I have some questions," I said, doing a quick dry off and slipping my clothes back on. "Both bodies were found early in the morning, right?"

"Yes."

"How wet were they?"

Flanders looked confused. "How *wet*?" he repeated.

"Were their clothes, hair, and bodies sopping wet, damp, somewhat dry, totally dry?"

Flanders gazed off over the water, his forehead wrinkling as he thought. "Will's clothes were saturated. Oliver Sykes was wearing a wet suit and it was dry along the exposed surface. The hair on both men was damp but not dripping. Skin where it was exposed was dry. No water droplets. They'd both clearly been where they were found for some time."

"Did you notice anything unusual, like any gelatinous or slimy substances on the clothes or the bodies?"

"No, nothing like that," Flanders said without hesitation.

"Do you know if what the men were wearing was swabbed for DNA?"

Flanders shook his head. "The medical examiner said it would be pointless after the amount of time they spent in the water."

"They'd still have the clothing, wouldn't they?"

He cocked his head to one side, looking a little annoyed. "Are you saying you think they should swab them for DNA?" he said in a dubious tone.

"What could it hurt?"

"The budget," Flanders shot back. "DNA testing isn't cheap, so we don't do it willy-nilly. We have to have a reasonable expectation for relevant results and a body that's been in the water isn't likely to have much in the way of surface DNA."

"Unless there was an animal of some sort that carried the bodies to where they were found," I countered.

Flanders sputtered for a few seconds as he struggled to respond, and his cheeks flooded red again. Haggerty, who was eavesdropping on our conversation, once again looked amused.

"I'll look into it," Flanders said finally. "But it will take weeks to get the results."

I had a strong sense that the DNA idea was going nowhere, so I moved on.

"One more thing," I said. "Those other pictures that were in the folder. Why didn't you tell me about them when we first talked?"

"I wanted you to see them without me setting any expectations."

"Where and when were they found?"

"The deer carcass was discovered about a week before Oliver Sykes went missing. It washed up near Schoolhouse Beach on Washington Island. The sturgeon was found floating not far from the ferry dock on Rock Island in late May. It might have slipped notice, but the DNR has been working to restore the sturgeon population, so they collected the body for examination."

"Did the ME compare the teeth impressions on those carcasses with the ones on the two men?"

Flanders nodded. "He said they were consistent in size and shape, and that the overall measurements of the bite found on the deer carcass matched the ones on the men's bodies."

Haggerty raised anchor and started the boat again. We rounded the bluff and headed down the other side, which led us into Washington Harbor and Schoolhouse Beach, a smooth limestone beach that is one of only five of its kind in the world. But we didn't go far before Haggerty stopped and I saw another spot onshore that was nearly identical to the first one: a small rock-strewn beach marked with stakes and police tape, and backed by sheer stone cliffs that were topped with thick groves of trees—isolated, hidden, and hard to access from land. I stared at the spot, imagining the body stretched out there on the sand with the towering bluff behind it. And then I looked toward Schoolhouse Beach, a popular spot for swimmers, picnickers, and sunbathers during the summer months.

I glanced at the device Haggerty had in the pilothouse that showed the depth of the surrounding water and a sonar display of the bottom. Once again, there was a shelf of rock that extended out, this time only about eight feet from shore with a water depth of five to six feet at the deepest point. Then there was a drop-off to seventy-four feet.

"Are you going for another swim?" Flanders asked me.

I shook my head. "No need. You can take me back now."

Flanders stared at me. "Something about this is bothering you," he said.

I nodded slowly, thinking. "It feels off to me. Why would an animal kill this way, crush another creature to death but not eat it? Animals aren't psychopathic or sociopathic the way humans are. They don't kill for pleasure and entertainment. Primarily, they kill to eat or to defend themselves. They might have discarded the men because they were too big and the clothing was off-putting, but why pass up the deer and the fish? Unless . . ." I gazed out over the water as another thought occurred to me.

"What?" Flanders said, leaning to put himself back in my line of sight. "Tell me."

I looked at him. "A mother's love," I said. "If there is a creature in the lake with offspring that these two men, the deer, and the fish got too close to, she might have killed to protect her children. And if that's the case, there will likely be more deaths to come."

CHAPTER 5

———

F landers looked disappointed as we motored back to Baileys Harbor, both of us once again seated at the back of the boat. I felt somehow responsible for his mood, though I wasn't sure why.

"You're new to this area, aren't you?" I asked him.

He nodded and gave me a coy smile. "I take it you saw the write-up about me in the paper a few months ago?"

I shook my head and his face fell. "I don't read the local rag much," I said by way of explanation. "It's just that most of the people who have lived here for any length of time, even most of the regular visitors who come back year after year, know about my store. Yet you seemed shocked by some of the content."

His smile turned sheepish. "I confess, I was caught a bit off guard. I thought it was a standard bookstore. Confronting a corpse first thing was a bit . . ." He shrugged.

"Yeah, I get it," I said with a smile. "But Henry brings in people, even if a lot of them are just lookie-loos. And he makes my store memorable."

Flanders chuckled. "No argument there." He tipped his head to one side, looking thoughtful. "Have you ever wondered about him? If he has family or descendants?"

"I actually sent a bit of him off for DNA analysis to a company that does that sort of thing. So far, no relatives have popped up that are closer than seventh or eighth cousins many times removed."

"What would you do if a close relative did pop up and wanted him to be buried properly, or wanted his body for their own use?" He looked appalled at the thought.

"I'd give Henry to them if I was sure of the claim, though it wouldn't be easy. I've become rather attached to the fellow."

Flanders gave me a dubious look, so I changed the subject. "How did you end up as the chief of police on Washington Island?"

"I relocated here from Colorado. The island was looking for a new chief of police and I needed a change of scenery."

Something dark slid over his face as he said that and I waited to see if he would elaborate, but he didn't. I wanted to pursue it, but I'm quite protective of my own dark secrets and figured if he wanted me to know, he'd tell me eventually.

"How did you end up with such a . . . unique bookstore?" he asked.

"I inherited it from my parents. Odds and Ends was their dream project, born out of their shared fascination for cryptozoology and anything in the world that was strange, bizarre, or unique. My father's family was quite wealthy—old shipping money—and he inherited a large sum at the age of eighteen, enough to ensure he'd never have to work a day in his life if he didn't do anything stupid. He used some of that inheritance to fund his passion for hunting cryptids. In fact, he was in the Mexican desert looking for Chupacabra when he met my mother."

"Chupa-who?"

"Chupacabra." I widened my eyes and, with a very dramatic voice, added, "The goat sucker. It's a mythical creature with vampiric habits blamed for the carcasses of goats and sheep found with all the blood drained from their bodies. Depending on whom you talk to, it might look like a demonic red-eyed kangaroo or a hairless dog with spines and huge teeth."

"Sounds charming."

"Not to mention questionable. No one has ever found one, and it's doubtful such a creature exists. One of the more popular theories, the one I think has the greatest likelihood of being right, posits that it's a wild dog with mange that rips the throats out of goats and sheep, causing them to bleed out." I shrugged. "Who knows? Anyway, my father was in Mexico investigating reports of a massive goat kill and that's when he met my mother."

"How romantic," Flanders said dryly.

I laughed. "It was for them. My parents were kindred spirits. They'd get giddy over finding a taxidermied two-headed cow, or Victorian-era death photos, or the skull of a hippopotamus. My father bought tons of oddities and eventually had so many that he got the idea of opening a store where he could display them, sell them, and purchase new ones that folks might bring to him. Sort of a pawn-shop for the weird and bizarre. And since he lived in Door County, a tourist mecca where kitschy shops have always been popular, he thought it would be a good fit. My mother brought her love of books and mysteries into the mix and, thirty-five years ago, they decided to combine their interests and open Odds and Ends. I think it may be the most unique mystery bookstore in the country, maybe the world."

"You'll get no argument from me on that front," Flanders said. "I suppose I should stop by one of these days and take the time to explore your inventory more thoroughly."

"You should. There's a story behind every piece we sell, some of them quite intriguing."

We fell into silent mode for several minutes and then Flanders asked, "So what's next on your end?"

"I need to look into some things."

"Can I ask what? Maybe I can help. Or maybe we've already looked into it."

"I doubt you've looked into any of what I have in mind. And I don't think you want to help me because it might mean doing some things that won't be strictly by the book, if you get my drift."

"Oh." Flanders gazed out over the water, his expression unsettled.

I waited to see if he would push the issue or perhaps decide not to work with me after all, but he did neither.

"You'll keep me informed?" he said.

"Of course."

The rest of our trip back was silent, and Newt and I hung over the side to stare into the water, though I'm not sure how much Newt could see. Occasionally I'd glance at the depth finder as it recorded anything from thirty-some feet to nearly a hundred fifty, depending on where we were. Had Nessie-type creatures been visiting these waters all along? Could they have been responsible for some of the hundreds of shipwrecks that had occurred in Death's Door?

I could feel my excitement building as I anticipated what I might be able to find, maybe even prove. But that raised the troubling question of what I should do with the truth once I knew what it was.

CHAPTER 6

———

When I returned to the store, Rita was surprised to see me back so soon. "I thought you might be gone all day," she said.

"I wasn't sure. It turned out to be a shorter trip than I anticipated. Things aren't making much sense to me, and I need answers to some complex questions."

"Anything I can help with?"

"Maybe." I gave her a rundown of the case Flanders had hired me for. "I need information on the currents around here. Do you know if any of your books from the old store might have that kind of information?"

Rita frowned and tucked one of a dozen stray white hairs into the messy bun atop her head. "Not that I can think of, but I know a fellow who studied the currents in these parts. He knows the area waters like the back of his hand."

"Perfect! Can you put me in touch with him?"

She bit her lower lip, looking doubtful. "Now, that's a good question," she said. "He's a bit . . . curmudgeonly and doesn't like people much, so I don't know if he'll talk to you." She shrugged. "I suppose it can't hurt to try."

"I can be quite charming when I want to be," I told her. "Give me his number and let me see what I can do."

Rita gave me a look of amused tolerance, one that said, *It's so cute how naive you young'uns can be.* "Oh, Marty doesn't have a phone," she said. "You'll have to go around to his place and knock, and then wait to see if he answers."

I didn't like the sound of that. "How is it he knows about local currents?" I asked, second-guessing whether this Marty person would be worth the trouble.

"He mapped them," Rita said. "He spent forty-plus years working for the USGS producing maps and hydrological studies of the waters in and around Door County."

"USGS?"

"The United States Geological Survey. It's a subagency of the Department of the Interior. They're tasked with studying the landscape of the country, its natural resources, and any natural hazards that threaten it. Marty was part of some specially funded study that focused on this area."

"And you know this Marty fellow how, exactly?"

"He used to come into our bookstore a lot. He and George would get to nattering like men can, you know, and Marty would talk about his work. He told George that he felt lucky, because his job was supposed to last for only five years, but it kept getting funded every year after that, so he was able to continue doing it." She paused, looking thoughtful. "I imagine it was kind of a lonely job, though I don't think

Marty had any family to speak of. If he did, he never mentioned them. I think that's why he doesn't take well to people."

"He lives alone, then?"

Rita nodded and looked up toward the ceiling, her eyes narrowing. "Though he did have a dog at one time, a big old mutt named Moose." She chuckled, shaking her head. "That dog humped anyone and anything he could. Marty would bring him into the store sometimes and damn if Moose wouldn't run straight over to George first thing, climb onto his leg, and start going to town. George would shake him off and then the dog would go find a chair or a rug or anything else he could use."

Rita smiled fondly at the memory for a few seconds before reality reared its ugly head and sobered her.

"You still miss George a lot, don't you?"

She nodded, her eyes moist. "We were married for forty-two years but some days it seems like it was a mere speck in time."

I stood by quietly and let her have her thoughts, wondering what it must have been like to be married to someone for that long. Two years ago, I'd had a close call when I discovered that the man who was my fiancé at the time was more interested in my money than in me. As a result, I have some trust issues. While I could easily imagine spending a lifetime with Newt, I didn't know anymore if I could do that with a person. It's one of nature's cruelest tricks that dogs have such short life spans. The mere thought of losing Newt made me tear up. The vet told me he was around a year old when he came to me last year, so hopefully we'll have at least ten to twelve more years together. But beyond that . . . I didn't want to think about it.

"It's been slow today. I can take you around to Marty's place now if you want," Rita offered, apparently finished with her trip down memory lane. "It's just down the road near Fish Creek. We can leave Devon in charge."

I thought about it for a nanosecond. "Yeah, let's do it. Let me give Devon the news and then I'll meet you out back by my car."

Rita looked delighted with the idea of escaping from the store for a while. She was a dedicated and knowledgeable employee, but I think the contents of my store sometimes gave her pause. She and her husband, George, had owned their rare-books store for over thirty years so she was no stranger to things old, dirty, and unique. And she was fine with things like the Victorian death photos and the antique medical instruments that were basically thinly disguised implements of torture. She was even okay with Henry. But I think stuff like the sculpture we had once that was made from pig intestines or the various insects and critters preserved in Lucite or resin gave her the heebie-jeebies.

Devon was behind the counter ringing up a balding, middle-aged man who had purchased an antique Ouija board, circa 1910. I thanked the customer warmly—that Ouija board was a pricey item—and watched as he exited the store, looking quite pleased with himself.

"Nice fellow. He said the Ouija board was a birthday gift for his mother," Devon told me. "He was quite excited about it and didn't even blink at the price. Apparently, his mother already has a crystal ball and holds séances on a regular basis. For a fee, of course," he clarified, shooting me a cynical look.

"Interesting," I said. "You're sure the charge went through?"

"Of course," Devon said, sounding insulted that I'd asked. He turned the store laptop toward me and showed me the transaction for one Mason Devereaux.

"Did he say where he was from?" I asked. "He might be a good repeat customer."

"His address came up as Washington Island. He said his mother lives in Mississippi, though he doesn't talk like he's from Mississippi," Devon said with a frown. "Devereaux is a popular name in that part of the country, though. Anyway, he seemed quite taken with the store and what we sell so, yeah, I think we'll see him again."

"That's good. Be sure and add his name to the mailing list."

"Already did, boss."

"You're such a brownnoser, Devon," Rita teased.

"Devon, since you're so efficient and all, would you mind watching the store for a bit? Rita and I need to go talk with someone about this case I'm working on with the police."

"Of course." Devon grinned broadly. He loved getting the place to himself.

"If things stay slow, maybe you could do some sleuthing for me," I suggested. I grabbed a pen and notepad from the counter and wrote down the names of the two victims Flanders had brought to me. "These guys both died while visiting up here, this one in June, this one a little over two weeks ago. See what you can find out about them on the internet and social media."

Devon rubbed his hands together. "I love creeping on people's pages. Anything specific you're looking for?"

"See if their paths crossed anywhere in any way. They probably didn't, but you never know. Maybe we'll get lucky."

I looked over at Newt where he was stretched out on the floor alongside the counter, and I made a slight sideways motion with my head. He understood immediately, got up, and padded over to the back door to wait for me. When I got to him, I looked down at his big brown eyes apologetically.

"You'll have to take the backseat for this one, buddy. Rita is coming along, and she gets to ride shotgun."

Newt let out a little doggy sigh, but when I opened the door, he went straight to the back door of my car. Driver's side, of course. He always wanted to be as close to me as possible. Rita, who knew my habits as well as any other human in my life, unclipped the short safety harness from the front passenger seat belt and handed it to me. I switched it to the driver's side backseat and clipped Newt into place.

"I should probably do the talking once we get there," Rita said, buckling herself in. "Marty is pushing eighty and he can be a bit . . . obstreperous at times." She shot me a sly sideways glance.

I smiled. "Obstreperous. Good one."

Rita returned the smile, did a little head bow, and said, "Thank you."

Rita and I both love words and we spend lots of our downtime at the store working crossword puzzles or playing Scrabble. We often insert obscure words into our everyday conversations in a faintly competitive way, trying to outdo each other.

"Anyway," Rita went on, "Marty can be difficult at times and not just because he's old. He's always had an odd personality."

"We can play it by ear," I told her as I started the car, not convinced that I needed her to talk for me.

After Rita gave me directions, we rode in companionable silence for several minutes. Then Rita said, "By the way, there's something else about Marty I neglected to mention."

I could tell from the tone in her voice that this revelation would be beyond obstreperousness.

"Marty collects things," Rita said. "*Lots* of things."

That last was said with heavy innuendo that, unfortunately, went right over my head.

"So do I," I said with a shrug.

"Yes, but you have a store and sell those things. Marty keeps them all. I delivered books to him several times over the years, and while I sometimes left them on his doorstep, I have seen the inside of his place a time or two. Marty's a hoarder."

"How bad?"

"A single-narrow-path-through-all-the-piles kind of bad," Rita said, wincing. "It's a disaster waiting to happen, and it wouldn't surprise me if Marty was found buried beneath one of his piles someday."

"Okay," I said slowly, thinking. "Maybe we can ask him to talk with us outside?"

"We can try. But be prepared to hold your breath either way. Based on the aromas that used to emanate from him when he came into our store and the way his place smelled . . . let's just say he tends to be quite . . . malodorous." She gave me a questioning look and said, "Too ordinary?"

"It is, rather, but I'll give you an A for effort."

As I turned onto the gravel drive leading to Marty's place per Rita's directions, I hoped the trip wouldn't turn out to be a waste of time. If nothing else, maybe Newt would get to enjoy the miasma of odors. Foul odors were among some of his favorite things in life.

How I wished I could say the same for myself.

CHAPTER 7

—

artin Showalter lived just outside of Fish Creek, on a bluff overlooking the bay waters. The view was spectacular, and Martin's piece of land was likely worth a bundle, but his dwelling was a mobile home parked on cinder blocks. It had clearly seen better days, as had the rusted old pickup truck parked beside it. In sharp contrast to this slow spread of neglect was the boat perched on a trailer behind the pickup. Its shiny fiberglass hull and twin outboard motors gleamed in the sunlight. It was obvious what mattered most to Marty.

I unhooked Newt and told him to heel. As soon as he hopped out, his nose was in the air, his nostrils flaring, but he stayed at my side. We walked up to a wooden block that served as a step to the entrance of the mobile home and Rita rapped loudly on the door.

After waiting a full two minutes, Rita knocked again, harder this time. Seconds later the door flew open, banging on the side of the mobile home and making me jump. In the doorway stood a slightly stooped, grizzled old man. He had a long gray beard that was tangled and yellowed in places, and the odors of stale cigarettes, urine, and something that might have been rotting food wafted out the door.

"Hold your damned horses!" he grumbled. "Why is everyone so frigging impatient these days?"

What little I could see over Marty's shoulders confirmed what Rita had told me. There was junk piled from floor to ceiling behind him: boxes, paper and plastic bags that contained who knew what, dishes, clothing, towels, small kitchen appliances, and books, with a small chair and table near the floor serving as a base.

Marty stared at Rita, and I saw recognition kick in as the anger in his yellowed eyes gradually softened. Then his gaze shifted to Newt and that old face cracked a smile, revealing lots of yellowed teeth. He hobbled out onto the wooden block and said, "Hello there, boy."

Newt surprised me by walking up and sniffing Marty's feet, which might simply have been Newt's way of enjoying an olfactory overload.

Marty eyed my dog with amusement and said, "What brings you out here, Rita?"

"This young lady is looking into some fellows who died in Death's Door recently. She needs information about currents in the area."

Marty finally tore his eyes from Newt and fixed them on me instead. "You a copper?"

"No, sir. But I've been hired to help them."

He scoffed and eyed me from head to toe. "As what?"

"A cryptozoologist."

Something in Marty's face shifted. He stared at me, his lips moving as if he were ruminating on my answer. "What's your name?"

"Oh, sorry. It's Morgan Carter."

That got a chuckle out of him for reasons I didn't comprehend. "Don't tell me. You're looking for a lake monster," he said.

I was impressed that Marty knew what a cryptozoologist was. "In a way," I admitted. "The police want to find out what's killed two men and some animals out on the water by crushing them in what appears to be a giant bite."

"Is that right?" Clearly, Marty was a skeptic, a good thing in my opinion. "And how do you think I can help with that?"

"I'm bothered by how and where these fellows' bodies were found. I don't have a good enough understanding of the local currents to know if the bodies could have traveled from where they presumably drowned, based on anecdotal evidence, to where they were found, but it feels wrong to me. I'm hoping you can help me discern if I'm right or just imagining things."

"I thought you said they were bit," Marty said. "Now you're saying they drowned. Which is it?"

"Both. It appears the men drowned, but they were also bitten by something with a mouth span of nearly twelve inches at or around the time of death."

Marty gave me a tired look that said this would be a waste of his time, time that, judging from his lifestyle and appearance, he didn't have a lot of left. I sent Newt a mental message, wanting him to cozy up a little more to Marty, sensing that my dog might have been key in gaining the man's cooperation. Newt glanced over his shoulder at me, and I gave him a subtle nod. With that, he put his front feet up on the wooden step and started licking Marty's hand. Having no idea how clean that hand was, I shuddered, but then I remembered that Newt had eaten and licked far grosser things in the past.

Marty gazed fondly at Newt and stroked his massive head. "He's a big fella, a lot like my Moose used to be."

His face contorted, and for a second, I thought he might cry. But then he gathered himself and looked at Rita.

"I was sorry to hear about George," he said.

"Thank you."

"You sold the store." Marty made it sound like an accusation rather than an observation.

"More like I gave it away," Rita grumbled. "Turned out, George wasn't so good at managing the money."

Marty nodded, looking thoughtful. "Sorry to hear that."

"Yes, well, fortunately, Morgan's parents gave me a job and bought enough of my book inventory to let me unload the store without declaring bankruptcy."

Marty digested this for several seconds and then said, "Let's go sit out back and we can have a chat."

Relieved that the issue of meeting outside had resolved itself so easily, we followed Marty around to the area behind his mobile home. It turned out to be much nicer than I expected. After seeing the squalor he lived in, I was expecting a junkyard mess. Instead, there was a small clearing in the heavily wooded parcel of land, and in that clearing sat four beautiful Adirondack chairs facing out over the bluff. Mingled with the scent of pine and the lingering aromas from Marty was a distinct odor of sawdust and paint.

"Did you build these?" I asked.

I expected him to say no, but he nodded. "I sell them. Give you a good price if you want one."

"I just might," I said, running an appreciative hand over the wide, flat arm of one of the chairs.

It was stained, giving the wood grain a slightly reddish hue, whereas the other three chairs were painted, two in a colonial blue shade and the third in a dark red.

"This is really beautiful," I said, eyeing the stained chair more closely. "I love the way you brought out the grain in the wood in this one. You do nice work."

"Thank you." Marty seemed genuinely humbled by the compliment.

I settled myself into the chair, sliding toward the back of it as I wondered how Marty could have built such lovely furniture, given what a mess his house was. Then I spied a shed out under the trees, nearly hidden in the shade. A trail of sawdust near the door told me that had to be his workshop. Rita sat in the chair next to me while Marty sat on her other side, looking delighted when Newt walked over and lay at his feet.

"Tell me where these fellows went into the water and where their bodies turned up," Marty said.

"First let me tell you about the animal carcasses," I told him. "A large sturgeon showed up floating in the water near the Rock Island ferry landing. Since there are efforts underway to try to restore the sturgeon populations, the DNR took an interest in the carcass and collected it for examination. They were surprised to see that the fish had apparently been crushed to death by something large that appeared to have bitten it. There were teeth marks on the fish's body, but the skin wasn't broken. All its insides had been crushed."

"Could have been caught between a jetty and a boat," Marty said. "Maybe stones made a pattern that looked like teeth. Nothing to get too excited about."

"I don't think anyone did until the deer carcass showed up," I said, and Marty's scraggly eyebrows shot up with interest. "It was found on shore in a small cove on Washington Island, near School-house Beach. It, too, had been crushed as if something large had grabbed it by its body and clamped down. And again, there were in-dentations and bruising that indicated teeth were involved."

"Any puncture wounds?" Marty asked, and I shook my head. "I don't suppose there's any way of knowing where these animals sus-tained their injuries initially," he mused.

"I don't think so."

"Deer can and do swim a long way," Marty said. "They've been known to swim a couple of miles, sometimes more. They swim from island to island in Death's Door all the time."

"That's true," Rita said. "I saw three of them swimming once when I was on the ferry."

Marty patted one of his knees and Newt dutifully sat up and rested his head there so Marty could pet him. The two of them looked quite content, and whatever else Marty was, he was okay in my book if Newt liked him.

"And our human victims?" Marty asked. "Where did they go into the water?"

"The first victim, Oliver Sykes, supposedly went kayaking along the northern coastline of Washington Island, taking off from School-house Beach back in June. By all accounts, he was a very skilled kay-aker and swimmer, and everyone thought he'd be fine on his own, but he never returned. His body washed up on the western side of Boyer Bluff two days later. Autopsy showed that he drowned, but he also had bite marks on his torso and most of his organs were crushed."

Marty frowned at that. "Did they find his kayak?" he asked.

"They did, in Green Bay, about a half mile west of Washington Island."

Marty frowned. "You said there were two victims?"

"Yes, the second one, Will Stokstad, was here on a fishing trip two weeks ago. He rented a small motorboat on Washington Island and there's some confusion as to where he went. He spoke to his wife on the phone the morning of the day he went missing, telling her he planned to go fish near Fisherman Shoal, though the boat rental shop thought he might have changed his plan and headed for the Rock Island Passage instead. His boat was found with most of his gear in it floating near Hedgehog Harbor. There was no sign of Stokstad until two days later, when his body was found on the eastern shore of Boyer Bluff on a small section of isolated beach."

Marty slowly shook his head. "I'll need to know the exact dates," he said. "There were some changes in the wind vectors during both months that resulted in a southeasterly wind for several days despite the prevailing southwest and northeast winds. I'll also have to consider temperature and the effect of the geography of the Niagara Escarpment since it runs right up through the middle of the peninsula and Washington Island. And then there're the warm waters of Green Bay flowing into and on top of the cold waters of Lake Michigan. That creates currents that change from month to month. We have bimodal winds and bimodal currents to consider here."

I must have looked dumbfounded, which I admittedly was, and Marty concluded with, "I need to look at some things before I can give you an answer. But for either victim's body or boat to show up where they did . . ." He shook his head again, more definitively this time. "Not likely."

Marty shifted his gaze to the woods and pulled at his beard with one hand while absentmindedly stroking Newt's head with the other. I watched him but said nothing, not wanting to disrupt his thought process.

Eventually he looked over at me. "Are you seriously thinking there might be some sort of creature out there that's doing this? Something along the lines of the Loch Ness Monster?"

"It's unlikely," I admitted, "but not impossible. Something created those bite marks."

Marty nodded but he looked unconvinced. "Maybe you have a rogue creature with a homicidal bent who strayed here from one of the deeper lakes," he said.

I saw a twinkle in his eye and realized he was having a bit of fun at my expense. "I assure you, I'm a skeptic at heart, Mr. Showalter."

"Like your parents?"

I stared at him.

"Hard to live in Door County all your life and not know about them," Marty said with a shrug, "though I came from a different side of the tracks than they did. Your dad was a Carter, and that family is well-known in these parts."

His presumptuousness annoyed me. I did my best to hide it and, eager to get back to the topic at hand, said, "Can you think of a plausible explanation for how the men's bodies ended up where they did?"

His face wrinkled in thought. "Again, I need to check some things. But my gut says something or someone had to have transported those bodies to the beaches where they ended up. And they were up on a beach, on dry land?"

I nodded.

"Wave action might have pushed them close to shore, but . . ." His voice trailed off.

"What?" I prompted.

"I've spent a lot of years on the waters around here, and I've seen plenty of people die in them. Bodies don't float when they drown because the lungs fill up with water and that makes them sink. If the water temperature is cold enough, those bodies may never come back up to the surface." He paused and pulled at his beard. "I suppose one explanation is that whatever bit them fellas carried them to the waters near the beaches where they were found."

"But why?" I said, a mostly rhetorical question. I was merely thinking aloud. "If the men weren't killed for food, why were they killed? It doesn't fit with typical animal behavior."

"Well, this ain't exactly a typical animal we're thinking about here, is it?" Marty said, arching those scraggly eyebrows. "I need to go to the beaches where these bodies were found, see them for myself."

I nodded. "I did that earlier today."

"Can you do it again tomorrow? Show me where they were? We can take my boat."

He wanted me to come along? I hadn't expected that. I looked at him, his body bent and crippled, and then I looked at his boat, all shiny and new and sparkly. I glanced over at Rita, who didn't look overly concerned with the idea.

"I go out on the water nearly every day," Marty said, reading my doubts. "You and the dog will be fine, I promise."

He punctuated his comment by patting Newt on the head. His automatic inclusion of Newt sealed the deal for me.

"Okay," I said, hoping the lake winds would help dissipate Marty's aromas. "When and where should we meet you?"

"How about the boat launch at the marina in Sister Bay?" he said. "Eight tomorrow morning?"

"We'll be there."

Rita and I drove back with all the windows down, relishing the fresh air. When we got to the store, Newt approached the back door ahead of us and whined. A ridge of fur rose down his spine and I shot

Rita a worried look as I unlocked the door and opened it, calling out to Devon.

"Devon? Are you in here?" No response.

Newt entered the store, crouched down, his nose sniffing the air anxiously. As soon as we reached the counter, I saw Devon. He was prostrate on the floor, either out cold or dead, a pool of blood near his head. I rushed over to him, relieved when I saw him move a hand.

"Call nine-one-one!" I hollered to Rita.

A closer look at the back of Devon's head revealed a gash that was oozing a steady flow of blood. I went to grab the roll of paper towels I kept in a cupboard by Henry's mummified body and was ripping off several sheets to use to try to stanch the flow of blood when I saw the note. It was pinned in place with a knife that was buried to the hilt in Henry's chest. Written on it in big capital letters was this:

BEWARE OF DEATH'S DOOR.

CHAPTER 8

The EMTs were checking Devon over and Rita was scouring the shelves to determine if any of our merchandise was missing when I saw Jon Flanders walk into the store.

"What are you doing here?" I asked. "I figured you'd be back on the island by now."

"I had some other business here on the peninsula to take care of, and when I heard the call on the radio, I came straightaway. Are you okay?"

"I'm fine. I wasn't even here when it happened."

Flanders glanced around the store but with his eyes raised toward the ceiling. "The sheriff over there said you don't have any security cameras in here?" There was an obvious tone of disbelief in his voice. "This is your home as well as your business, isn't it?"

"No, I don't, and yes, it is. As you might imagine, some of my customers have interests that other people might consider outside the realm of acceptable. Because of that, they tend to be a bit zealous about guarding their privacy. Cameras could cost me a lot of business."

Flanders cocked his head to one side and gave me a look of tolerant impatience.

"I considered putting some cameras up at the front and back entrances," I admitted, feeling an odd need to defend my reasoning. "But that's as far as I got, just thinking about it."

"Is cost a concern? Because if it is—"

"It's not," I said. I glanced around to see if anyone else was within earshot and then lowered my voice. "I inherited my father's estate when my parents died. I'm more than comfortable."

Flanders looked surprised. "You don't... I mean, the way you..."

"I don't act like a spoiled, entitled rich kid?" I finished for him. "I don't go around flaunting my wealth with a flashy car or live in a McMansion?"

Flanders flushed a vivid red, a trait I was finding more adorable every time it happened.

"Yes," he admitted with a sheepish grin. "You don't act rich."

"Stick with me long enough and you'll learn that I can," I told him. "If I want something bad enough and I think the only way I can get it is to throw my money around, I'll do it."

He looked intrigued. "I'd like to see that."

I wondered if he was flirting with me—it was hard for me to trust my own judgment in that arena anymore after being duped by my ex—and I couldn't decide how I felt about it if he was. He was attractive, seemed kind, and Newt liked him. Plus, he had a sense of humor—an absolute must in my department. But it was too soon.

The silence between us lasted a bit too long and our smiles started to look—and in my case, feel—awkward and forced. Flanders broke eye contact first, clearing his throat and looking around the store.

"Do you know if anything is missing?" he asked.

"Nothing obvious, but I haven't done an inventory."

"Cash in the register untouched?" he asked, and I nodded. "Sounds like the motive was intimidation, not robbery. I wonder if whoever did it knew you weren't here at the time, or if Devon's fate was meant to be yours."

Before I realized I was doing it, my hand reached up and gingerly probed my scalp in the area where Devon's gash was, imagining how it felt.

Flanders looked over at Devon, who had risen like Lazarus and was now sitting on Old Sparky, a wooden chair that had once been used for electrocutions at a prison in Texas. Devon was chatting with a freckled, redheaded female EMT who was securing a gauze bandage over his head wound. I walked over to see how he was doing, and Flanders followed.

"Are you okay?" I asked Devon.

"Hell of a headache, but other than that, I think I'm okay."

He winced as the EMT—Anne, according to her name tag— tightened the head bandage with a knot. I couldn't be sure, but it looked as if Anne might have given that knot an extra tug on purpose.

"You are *not* okay," she argued, and I got a sense those two had been having that debate prior to our approach. "You need stitches on that hard head of yours, and that goose egg you have means you should be seen and evaluated by a doctor so they can do a CT scan."

She finished the bandage and stepped back to admire her work. "You know, just to make sure you have a brain in there," she added sarcastically.

Devon grinned goofily at her, and I saw Anne return a hint of a smile. I felt certain those two would be seeing more of each other in the not-too-distant future.

"Can you tell me what you remember about what happened?" Flanders said to Devon.

Anne wandered off to talk to a coworker and Devon's eyes followed her, his expression that of a sad puppy. With a sigh, he finally shifted his attention back to us.

"I'd just finished ringing out a customer, and when she left, I thought the store was empty. I went over to reshelve a book that she'd decided not to buy, and just as I was placing it, I heard something behind me. I turned to see what it was, but before I could, my head exploded into bright stars. Next thing I knew, Morgan was leaning over me, telling me to wake up."

"Was this person already in the store?" I asked him.

Devon screwed his face up and then winced. "I'm not sure."

"Think," I prompted. "Did you hear the bell over the door ring?"

Devon perked up. "No. I'm sure I didn't. I would have looked toward the door immediately if I had. I'm like Pavlov's dog when it comes to that."

I shot a worried look at Flanders. "That means whoever it was had to have been in here prior to the attack. It's easy to hide back there in the bookshelves because they're so tall."

"Anything else?" Flanders asked Devon, who shook his head and gave an apologetic shrug.

"We need to get going," Anne said, returning to our group. "If you don't want to ride in the rig, someone should drive you and you'll need to sign a refusal form."

"How will I get back if I go in the ambulance?" Devon said, making a face.

I started to say that I would be more than happy to come and get him, or to take him there, for that matter, but Anne was faster on the draw.

"My shift ends in twenty minutes," she said. "If you want, I'll drive you back here once you're done. I have to come this way to go home."

While I might not have been able to discern what was going on between me and Flanders, I easily recognized the flirtation between Devon and Anne, even before Devon's face lit up like a happy puppy and he quickly said, "That would be great! Thanks!"

Once Devon was secured in the back of the ambulance, Flanders, Newt, and I retreated to the checkout counter.

"Can I reopen the store?" I asked Flanders. "There are some customers hanging out in the parking lot."

"I don't see why not," Flanders said, looking that way with a thoughtful expression. "But give me five minutes before you do. I want to check with the sheriff over there first since this is technically his case. And I'd like to snap some shots of the crowd."

I started to protest, worried that this invasion of privacy might scare off some of my customers, but Flanders raised a hand before I could utter my objection.

"I'll be discreet, but it's important. Perpetrators often hang around or return to the scene of the crime to try to keep tabs on the investigation. Whoever did this might be in that crowd out there." He let out an exasperated sigh and added, "Security cameras would have made this so much easier."

"I won't have them in my store," I insisted. "And even if I did have them out front, it wouldn't have helped unless whoever did it parked in the lot. There are plenty of other places nearby where someone could park and sneak back."

This was because my store is located on the northern edge of Sister Bay on a lane off Waters End Road. My closest neighbors are a parking lot and a grassy field on one side, and woods on the other. Across the road from my front door are more woods and, beyond that, a sprawling mansion of a home and the waters of Green Bay.

"I'm just glad you weren't here when this happened," Flanders said, deftly changing the subject. "Can I ask where you were?"

"Rita knows a guy who spent his life here studying the currents in Death's Door and the surrounding waters, so we went to chat with him, to see what he thought about where the bodies turned up."

"And?"

"It's a work in progress," I said vaguely. "He wants to go out on the water tomorrow and explore the locations where the men are presumed to have been when they died and where their bodies were subsequently found. I'm going with him."

Flanders looked troubled by that, but he said nothing.

"Do you think this episode with Devon was a random event, or might it be related to the thing you have me looking into?" I asked.

Flanders stared off across the room toward Henry, who looked none the worse for wear following his traumatic event. "You've not had other incidents like this before today, have you?"

"Can't say that I have."

He chewed his lower lip for a few seconds, still staring at Henry. "It seems mighty coincidental timing-wise, but the note was generic and vague enough that it would be easy to chalk it up to someone's twisted idea of a practical joke."

"If it was just the note," I said. "But bashing my employee over the head sends a more serious message, don't you think?"

He looked at me then, and a half smile softened the consternation on his face. "I agree. You need to be careful." He squatted down and

CHAPTER 9

—

The next morning—a Monday, meaning my store was closed—Newt and I arrived at the boat launch a few minutes before the agreed-upon time. Marty was already there, his boat in the water, and he welcomed us aboard with a come-on wave of his hand. I noted a light in his eyes that hadn't been there the day before and thought he was standing a little taller. His clothes and hair looked freshly washed and I realized that the miasmic odor that had clung to him yesterday was barely discernible. At first, I thought the smell was being dissipated by the morning breeze, but when I saw that Marty's beard had been trimmed and his hair washed, I realized he'd cleaned himself up for today. For some reason, that touched me.

"I like people who are timely," he said. He shifted his attention to Newt. "How are you doing this morning, big fella?"

Newt wagged his tail effusively, his butt wiggling in a happy dance. He leaned against Marty's leg and closed his eyes, a look of ecstasy on his face as the old man gave the top of his head a thorough scratch.

"There's a thermos of coffee and a couple of cups in the stern," Marty said, still smiling down at Newt even though I knew the comment was directed at me.

I'm a bit of a coffee addict and, if I'm honest with myself, also a bit of a coffee snob. I'd already downed a half cup that morning, but because I wasn't sure what kind of toilet facilities might be on the boat, I'd stopped there. More coffee did sound good, but then I remembered what Marty's mobile home had looked—and smelled—like. And what the coffee on the patrol boat yesterday had tasted like. Even if Marty's coffee was decent and there was a toilet on the boat, did I really want to go there?

"Thanks, but I think I'll pass," I said.

Marty's expression shifted ever so subtly, and I could tell my rejection of his offer bothered him on some level.

"It's just that coffee makes me have to pee all the time," I added, feeling a need to mitigate the situation. "Speaking of which, are there facilities on your boat?"

Marty gestured toward a small door to the left of his seat, which led into the bow of the boat. When I opened it, I discovered a cuddy cabin with a sleep area and a small chemical porta-potty. There were some pillows and blankets neatly folded at the far end of the bed, making me think the space got some use, yet it was surprisingly neat and odor free. Even the porta-potty looked clean, and while I'd have to hunch over to get my pants down since the cuddy cabin space wouldn't allow me to stand upright, just knowing there was a toilet I could use with some degree of privacy came as a huge source of relief to me. I'd find out later how difficult it could be to get one's pants down and pee while hunched over in the cuddy cabin of a boat that's motoring full out over waves several feet high, but at that moment, my ignorance was bliss.

"I keep a tidy ship," Marty said, blushing and not looking at me. "To be honest, I don't use the toilet much. I usually just pee over the side of the boat."

"Yeah, well, that's a bit difficult for me to do," I said, envisioning myself clinging to the rail while my bare ass hung out over the water. That, Dr. Freud, is the true reason for penis envy. "But this should work fine."

I closed the door to the cuddy cabin and then added, "Newt should be good for eight to ten hours. If we're out any longer than that . . ." I shrugged.

"Heck, he can lift a leg here if he needs to," Marty said dismissively. He patted the side rail. "This old gal has seen worse. I can just hose 'er down. And we might get a storm rolling in. Conditions are right. That will cut our time short."

I wondered what "worse" things the boat might have seen and then decided that some things are better left unknown and unimagined. With my toileting worries handily taken care of, I said, "Know what? I think I'll have a cup of that joe after all."

The pleased smile I saw on Marty's face made me glad I'd changed my mind, and the cups he provided were clean. What was more, the coffee was surprisingly good.

I didn't own a boat, but I'd spent a great deal of time on them and knew my way around the basics, so I helped get us underway by releasing the mooring lines. Then I settled in on the bench seat at the rear of the boat, with Newt at my feet and my hands wrapped around my mug of steaming coffee as Marty puttered us out of the marina.

"Looks like a great day," I said, gazing at the fluffy white clouds overhead as Marty steered us into the deeper bay waters.

"No such thing," he grumbled. "You should never get too comfortable in and around Death's Door. Things here change on a dime."

"Of course," I said, feeling a little insulted. I was only trying to set a mood and thought about saying so, but decided to let the matter go.

Marty kept us at a slow pace while he consulted a device that looked much like the one I'd seen in the patrol boat yesterday. It gave a readout of the water depth and speed, and a visual display of the bay bottom.

"Is that what you used for charting and studying the currents?" I asked, pointing to the device.

"Partially. I use sonar to identify underwater structures, geography, and aquatic life, but for the currents I used additional things, like a high-definition camera that tracked the flow and dispersal of dyes in the water, and a device that measured temperature variances and mapped out the thermoclines. I also had a device that could measure wind speed and direction, and oxygen concentrations in the water at different depths. For our purposes, I think the sonar is all we need."

"And what, exactly, are our purposes?" I asked, curious to see if he would mention the idea of a lake monster.

He gave me a sly look and said, "To see if we can find anything unusual. I want to examine the underwater terrain along those shorelines where the bodies were found. I also want to do some exploring north of Washington and Rock Islands where both these men supposedly met their demise."

He eyed the backpack I'd brought along, which was next to me on the bench seat. "Hope you came prepared for a full day."

"I brought along water and snacks for both of us," I said, nodding toward Newt.

We headed out of the bay and toward more open waters, circling around the west side of Washington Island. Half an hour later we reached the beach where Oliver Sykes's body had been found. I pointed out the remnants of police tape fluttering like the tattered remains of a yellow-and-black flag in the brisk morning breeze. Marty spent nearly an hour doing a back-and-forth grid pattern, watching his sonar display, while Newt and I relaxed in the morning sun, gently rocked by the waves. When we moved on to the second site, which was on the other side of the bluff, Marty offered up a brief geography lesson.

"Boyer Bluff is part of the Niagara Escarpment," he said. "The entire escarpment is more than six hundred fifty miles long and it's home to some of the best fruit-growing land in the country. It runs clear down into Illinois, up into Canada, and east to Niagara Falls. The falls, the mainland areas, and the islands and bluffs you see around these parts are the parts of the escarpment that sit above water, but it also runs below the water level, dipping and rising its way across lakes Michigan, Huron, and Ontario. The underwater geography of the escarpment is just one of the things that influences the currents. It's also the cause of many a shipwreck, thanks to the sudden cliff rises and shoals in the water. The wreck of the *Louisiana*, which went down more than one hundred years ago during the Great Storm of 1913, is right here in Washington Harbor, by Schoolhouse Beach. I'll show it to you."

As we moved deeper into Washington Harbor, I pointed out the location where Will Stokstad's body had been found. Marty motored up close to shore, looking concerned, one eye on his sonar screen.

"What position were these bodies in?" he asked me.

I described how both men had been found, toes to the water, heads to the cliff, Will on his back, Oliver on his stomach.

"Makes no sense," Marty grumbled. "None of it makes sense. The primary flow of the waters here is easterly. They can change if the prevailing winds do or if some weird weather hits, but for their bodies and their boats to have drifted west makes no sense at all."

"Meaning what?"

"Meaning either they didn't go where they said they were going or someone put those bodies there."

"Someone or something," I said.

Marty shot me a look but said nothing more. He did another criss-cross, watching the sonar screen, but this survey was briefer. Then he motored toward Schoolhouse Beach, stopping several hundred feet from the swimming area near a spot marked off by buoys and a dive flag.

"Come look at this," he said, pointing to his sonar screen.

I moved to the front and stood next to him, watching the screen. Seconds later, the outline of some boards came into view.

"That's part of the *Louisiana*," he said. "Her captain sought safe harbor from the storm of 1913 here, but the boat's anchor wouldn't take hold because of the high waves and seventy-mile-an-hour winds. She was eventually pushed aground. The men on board tried to ride out the storm on the ship, but come morning, the storm was still raging, and the hold was on fire. Forced to try to make land in their lifeboat amid gale winds, treacherous waves, and rock-strewn shores, the men's chances of getting to shore alive were slim to none."

Marty pointed toward a pile of wood vaguely shaped like a hull up on the shore. "That's another part of her over there," he said. "And the water's clear enough today, I think you can see her over the side."

I went to the railing and looked down into the water. After a moment I was able to make out planking and even some spots where rivets had been. Newt gazed down at the water with me, though I doubted he could see what I did.

"Wow, that's amazing," I said to Marty. "Thank you."

He beamed with the praise. Then he said, "I want to spend the rest of our time exploring the northern coast of the island and Rock Island Passage, if that's okay. It seems both men might have been in those waters when they suffered whatever calamitous event killed them."

"I'm fine. We're fine," I said, stroking Newt's big head.

I was impressed with Marty's use of the word "calamitous." All the books he had read over the years had likely given him an impressive vocabulary. "Calamitous" sounded like the kind of word Rita might have tossed at me.

Marty motored us out of the harbor and into the open waters of the passage between Washington Island and St. Martin Island, which was visible off in the distance to the north. He watched where we were going—one eye on that sonar screen most of the time—while I watched where we'd been or occasionally stared down into the watery depths, wondering if a giant lake creature lurked below. The warm sun and the motion of the boat eventually lulled Newt to sleep at my feet and I started to feel drowsy, too, so I helped myself to another cup of coffee from Marty's thermos to stay awake.

As we cruised along, Marty periodically pointed out rises and falls on the lake floor, and plenty of lake dwellers, though none of them were Nessie sized.

At one point, he gestured toward St. Martin Island and said, "Much of St. Martin is surrounded by rocky shoals that are nearly a mile wide in some spots." He pointed to an area up ahead. "Over there, those shoals extend down almost to Rock Island, creating a hazardous passage if you don't know where you're going. The water depth changes dramatically in one spot, rising from one hundred fifty feet to only seven over a very short distance."

"Have you been to St. Martin?" I asked, knowing that the island was uninhabited these days.

"I spent some time there back when I was charting these waters. I used to camp at the base of the old lighthouse."

"I'm surprised the federal government was willing to pay someone to do what you did for all those years," I said. "I guess Death's Door is more important than I realized."

Marty eyed me with a funny look, like he was measuring me for something. "I don't think it was part of the original plan for it to go on as long as it did," he said. He took in a deep breath and let it out in a long, slow sigh. "But thanks to your father, the project kept on long enough to keep me working on it for my entire career."

After a beat, I turned and stared at him, wondering if I'd misheard him. "Thanks to my father?" I echoed, expecting him to correct me by repeating what he'd really said, but he simply nodded. "I don't understand. What did my father have to do with it?"

"My job was funded by grants, lots of them," Marty said, staring at the sonar screen as he spoke. "The reason the work went on much longer than anyone originally planned was because the grants kept coming. Your daddy was the source of those grants."

"My father paid for someone to study the currents in Death's Door?" I said, a healthy dose of skepticism in my voice.

Marty glanced at me, then went back to staring at the sonar screen. "You never knew your paternal grandaddy, did you?"

"No. He and my grandmother both died before I was born, before my father met my mother, in fact. My grandmother had ovarian cancer and died in her early forties when my father was fourteen. And my grandfather died when my father was eighteen."

Marty nodded as if this was old news to him. "Do you know how your grandfather died?"

"I do," I said, though even as I uttered this, I realized that all I knew was what my father had told me, a one-sentence summary that

I now regurgitated for Marty. "He drowned when one of his ships went down in a storm."

"True enough," Marty said. "Your father was devastated by your grandfather's death, though his grief may have been mitigated some by the fact that he inherited enough money from the family shipping business to do whatever he wanted with his life."

If Marty resented my father for that, I didn't hear it in his tone. He said it matter-of-factly, as if reading it from a book. And what he had said was true. My father had become a very wealthy man at the age of eighteen, something he learned to stop apologizing for many years later. I hadn't yet reached that level of comfort with my wealth, and in general, I tried to hide it. I'd learned the hard way how money can twist and turn people.

"Do you know that the ship your grandfather was on went down in Death's Door?" Marty asked me.

"Of course," I said irritably, feeling churlish at the implication that he knew things about my family that I didn't.

Marty glanced back at me, eyeing me with amusement. Then he challenged my knowledge. "Can you tell me how it happened?"

I couldn't because my father had never discussed the details with me. I'd always assumed it was a subject too painful and I'd never been sufficiently motivated to dig into it on my own. Not wanting to admit my lack of knowledge to Marty, I simply didn't answer, and after a period of silence, he filled in the blanks.

"An unexpected storm developed, and it drove the ship onto one of the many shoals in Death's Door, damaging the hull. It was early December, and the ship went down fast, not giving many of the men aboard time to escape. The water temperature at that time of the year is often in the high thirties or low forties and your grandfather, along with many of the other men on the ship, died of hypothermia. Only three men survived by crawling onto an ice floe. According to their reports, your grandfather could have put himself ahead of them. After all, he owned the ship and was the boss of all the men on board. But instead, he helped the others to climb onto the ice first and then disappeared beneath the waves. Your grandfather died a hero."

I'd never heard any of that before and the fact that Marty knew it shamed and embarrassed me. Newt sensed my unease, and he got up and rested his big old head in my lap, looking up at me with those soulful, nearly blind dark eyes of his.

Marty continued, either oblivious to my discomfort or indifferent to it. "Your father discovered that your grandfather had funded the grants for the initial hydrological studies in Death's Door that the federal government was conducting back then, and he decided to continue funding it even though it was due to end a year after your grandfather's death. It benefited the family shipping business, of course, but I think it was your father's way of honoring your grandfather's memory. As it happened, it also funded my career, because he continued with the grants until I retired."

Much as I hated to admit it, that information surprised me. I'd always thought of my parents as open, honest, and forthcoming people who had shared things with me that other parents might not have shared with their kids. Our relationship had been a close one and they'd always treated me like an adult, never hiding harsh truths or showing a reluctance to tackle difficult topics. Or so I'd thought.

They had taken me with them on their cryptid hunts—trips that took us into the jungles of South America, the highlands of Scotland, the deserts of Africa, and the forests of Transylvania. I was one of the most world-traveled kids out there, though many of the places we visited weren't your typical vacation spots. Yet despite all that, it seemed my father had never shared that particular piece of his life with me. It not only surprised me; it hurt a little.

"We all have our secrets," Marty said, seeming to sense my consternation. "We humans need to keep some things for ourselves."

Something in the way he said that and the brief look of pain that flitted across his face told me that Marty had his own stash of secrets.

"What are yours, Marty?" I asked.

It was an impertinent question, one I'd had no business asking, and I regretted my words as soon as they left my lips. The utterance had been born from a petty need to strike back after Marty's revelations regarding my father.

Newt raised his head and stared at Marty when I asked my question, cocking his head to one side. Marty looked annoyed at first, but when he saw Newt, his expression softened. He turned back to stare at the sonar screen, and I thought he was simply going to ignore me, but after a few seconds, he spoke.

"I was married for a year, right after I finished college," he said, his voice so soft, I had to strain to hear him over the lapping of the waves and the idling of the engine. "My wife died during childbirth from a hemorrhage and our infant daughter was stillborn."

Good grief. As if I didn't feel bad enough for asking such a rude question in the first place. Hadn't Rita told me that Marty never married? She must not have known.

"Oh, Marty, that's just awful," I said. "I'm so sorry that happened to you."

No wonder he was a hoarder. Fate had robbed him of the most precious things in his life, making him cling desperately to everything else.

He glanced back at me, as if surprised by my empathy. Then his gaze shifted to something behind me, and a look of fear came over his face so fast, it made a shiver race down my spine.

Newt picked up on it, too, even though he likely couldn't see Marty's face or what it was Marty was looking at. Yet he sat up and looked around, suddenly alert, a small ridge of fur raised along his spine. I turned to see what was behind us, fully expecting to spot the long neck of a lake monster rising out of the water. But it was a monster of a different kind.

Off to the northwest, on the not-too-distant horizon, was a bank of thick gray fog being pushed ahead of a wall of dark, angry clouds that churned menacingly.

"Thought a squall might blow in today," Marty said, nodding knowingly. "It's moving fast. We best head in."

He steered the boat around to head back the way we had come but continued cruising at only a slightly faster pace, watching the sonar screen and occasionally glancing toward the approaching clouds.

I peered over the edge of the boat, searching for rising cliffs of rock, suddenly afraid of becoming one of the storied shipwrecks in the area. The water was too deep to see anything, and when I next glanced up toward the horizon, I was startled to see how close the clouds and fog had come. They were moving at a frightening speed, and since they were coming in from the northwest, we were headed straight for them. I knew storms in the area had a reputation for blowing in hard and fast, but I'd never seen one roll in while out on the water like this. It was terrifying.

Marty gave the clouds a wary glance and said, "That's it. Hang on. We're going back full speed." He was about to push the throttle lever forward when I saw him freeze, gaping at the sonar screen.

"What the hell?" he muttered.

I tried to see what he was seeing but the sun was behind us now, and it was hitting the screen in such a way that it obscured the display. A cold gust of wind blew over us, rustling my hair and making a new ridge of fur rise along Newt's back.

"What is it, Marty? Did you see something?"

He didn't answer me, so I stood and peered over the side of the boat, staring down into churning water. I saw two greenish yellow eyes looking up at me from the depths and felt the hair on my head and arms rise. The water around us began to roil wildly, making the boat buck, and I lost my balance, legs backpedaling and arms pinwheeling. I hit the seat on the opposite side and fell onto it. The combined effects of the coffee I'd had, the sight of those eyes in the water, and the fierce bobbing motion of the boat had nearly scared the piss out of me . . . literally.

I made a mad dash for the cuddy cabin and had just managed to get my pants down when Marty throttled up, sending me ass over teakettle toward the door of the cabin. Make that *bare* ass over teakettle. I hit my head on something hard enough that I saw stars as the door to the cabin flew open, leaving me stretched out on the threshold with my pants down around my ankles. I scrambled up as best I could and managed to get seated on the toilet before my bladder gave way.

When I was done and had my pants back up, I emerged from the cabin too mortified to look at Marty, and still struggling to keep my balance as the boat surged through the churning waters, bouncing over the waves, soaking me in the spray.

Even Newt turned his head away, as if he was embarrassed to be seen with me. Rain started to fall, and within seconds, it was pelting us. I felt the hairs on my arms and neck rise just as there was a big flash of light. A fogbank closed in around us as a deafening rumble of thunder rolled overhead.

"There's a vest in the seat beneath you," Marty hollered at me, his voice nearly carried away by the wind that had blown up. "And there's a flotation ring with a rope tied to it in there, too. You might want to attach it to Newt's collar, just in case." He looked at me then with a funny expression. "Your head is bleeding."

No sooner had he said this than I saw that the rainwater dripping from my curls had a distinct red tinge to it. Remembering the bang I'd taken to my head in the cabin, I reached up and probed around until I felt swollen tissue and the sting of an open, though thankfully small wound along my hairline.

"Here," Marty said, handing me a rag.

I took it and pressed it against my head with one hand to stanch the blood flow while I opened the seat to find the flotation devices Marty had mentioned, realizing in hindsight that we probably should have had them out, if not on, already. I hadn't anticipated any swimming today, but I should have at least brought Newt's flotation vest along, even if he didn't wear it the whole time. I found a vest for myself and pulled it out, dropping it on the floor. Under the vest there was a large self-inflating dinghy that I had to shove aside in order to get to the flotation ring beneath it. It took some maneuvering to free the ring, but eventually I got it out and attached one end of the nylon rope to Newt's collar. Then I put on my vest and slipped an arm through the ring.

The wind and rain mixed into a flurry of stinging, blinding drops that, when combined with the spray kicking up from our rapid flight across the water, left us soaking wet by the time we returned to the boat launch. Since we were already drenched, I offered to help Marty get his boat out of the water and back onto his trailer.

He considered my offer for several seconds and then shook his head. "Go home," he said.

He turned away but I stopped him. "What did you see out there?" I asked, hoping that my naked ass wasn't part of his answer.

He looked at me with a troubled expression and said, "I need to check on some things and then we'll talk. Go home, Morgan."

I considered pushing him but sensed it would do no good, so Newt and I trotted to my car, though why I felt the need to hurry was beyond me. We were already soaked to the bone. The rain was coming down so hard, I couldn't see more than a few feet in front of me. I had to sit in the parking lot for several minutes waiting for the condensation on the windshield to clear, even with the defrost blowing full blast. I used the time to examine my head wound in the rearview mirror, but the cut was buried beneath the heavy weight of my wet curls, and since it was no longer bleeding, I decided it was no big deal.

My windshield wipers struggled to keep up with the hard, driving downpour and I crawled along at a sedate pace, rarely making it above fifteen miles an hour. Fortunately, there was little other traffic on the roads—a lucky thing because a few minutes into our ride, I heard a loud pop, and the car began a rhythmic *thump-thump-thump-thump-thump*. I cursed aloud, making Newt whine.

"Damn it! Of all the times to get a flat tire."

I limped the car onto a sand-covered bit of road that split in two, going to some newer homes in one direction and dead-ending in some trees in the other. Odds were no one would be coming up behind me, but just to be safe, I turned on my emergency flashers. I could have gotten out then and changed the tire. I knew how because not only had my father taught me; he'd made me change several of them over the years. But despite being wet through already, I had no desire to get out of the car and try to change a tire in a downpour.

I looked over at Newt in the passenger seat. "Nothing to do but wait it out, buddy," I said.

He rested his chin on my shoulder for a few seconds. Then he curled himself into a ball on the front seat next to me, resting his head

CHAPTER 10

‎—

The following morning, I filled in both Devon and Rita on my adventures with Marty as we did our opening preparations for the store. I paused partway through my story to take some ibuprofen because I had a nasty headache, most likely from the bump on my head. Both Devon and Rita were starting to look bored, but when I got to the part where I saw two glowing eyes rising through the water, I had their undivided attention.

"How exciting!" Rita said. "Do you think it was a lake monster?"

"I don't know what I saw," I told them, and Devon's shoulders sagged with disappointment. "There are many mysteries in our planet's watery depths that have yet to be discovered, so who knows? I wish Marty had told me what it was he saw on the sonar."

"Marty always was a close-to-the-vest kind of guy," Rita said with a shrug.

I saw Devon rub his head where the staples—not stitches—were from his encounter. "Maybe you should take it easy today, Devon," I suggested. "Rest up. Did the doctor say it was okay for you to come back to work so soon?"

"She didn't say I couldn't," he said with a shrug.

"Were you able to find anything for me on the two men who died?"

"Nothing yet, but I'm still looking. They both had extensive social media content."

"I'll tell you what. Why don't you use my office and spend the day digging around to see what you can find? Rita and I can handle the store for now. If things get too crazy, we'll holler at you."

Devon brightened. He loved nosing around in people's lives on the internet and he was quite good at it. "Happy to help, boss," he said with a snappy salute.

He spun around and headed for my office while Rita and I watched him with amusement.

"That boy is a bit odd," Rita said. "He doesn't seem to have a life outside of this store and whatever it is he does on those computers."

"That's why he's such a good fit here," I said with a wink. "Let's face it. This store and its contents are an acquired taste. Plus, I don't think you should count him out yet. I saw something spark between him and that EMT that was here yesterday. I think Devon's life might be about to get more interesting."

"Speaking of sparks," Rita said, giving me a sly eye, "is there something going on between you and Flatfoot Flanders?"

"Flatfoot Flanders?" I said, trying to act indignant, though I couldn't pull it off. The best I could manage was to bite back the laugh threatening to burst out of me.

Rita shrugged. "Well, he *is* a copper," she said as if that was all the explanation needed. "It's a rather . . . ubiquitous moniker for someone in his field of work, though perhaps a bit old-fashioned."

"Ubiquitous moniker," I repeated, nodding approvingly. "You're on a roll lately."

"And you're avoiding my question." She arched her eyebrows at me, looking out over the tops of her glasses.

"Chief Flanders and I have a business relationship."

"Again, avoiding the question. Looked to me like more than a business relationship."

"I barely know the man, Rita. And what do you mean? What did you see that makes you think it's something more?"

Rita rolled her eyes at me. "Give me a break, Morgan. I wasn't born yesterday."

With that vague nonexplanation, she wandered off to dust some items on the shelves.

It was a minute before nine o'clock, so I went to unlock the front door, wondering what it was that Rita thought she had seen. Had it been something in me? Or in him? Was it two-sided? I did think Flanders was a nice-looking fellow and our personalities appeared to mesh well, but it wasn't like we'd shared any long, heated glances in our few times together.

I was still pondering this issue an hour later when the bell over the door rang and the man in question entered the store.

"Chief Flanders," I said, a little rattled by his arrival. It was as if I'd summoned him with my thoughts. "What brings you back to my store?"

I saw Rita smirk and shot her a dirty look.

"Please, call me Jon," Flanders said. He proffered a shopping bag he was carrying. "And I'm here to install some security cameras."

I gave him an adamant shake of my head. "I thought I made it clear why I don't want any cameras in my store. My customers value their privacy, as do I."

"Don't put them in the store," Flanders said. "Put them outside. One at each entrance."

I frowned, unconvinced.

"If you value the safety of your staff, it's a must-have," Flanders said, seeing my reluctance. "Not to mention that you also live here and having a bit of security for your own benefit seems prudent."

He glanced over at Henry. "Let's face it," he went on, staring at the corpse. "Your store is bound to attract some oddballs."

I probably should have taken offense at that, but he had a point and I'd said the same thing myself to Rita earlier. Plus, I sensed a dogged determination in the man that told me efforts to refuse would be futile.

"Fine. You can leave them on the counter over there. What do I owe you?"

Flanders waved my question away. "Nothing. These were some freebies given to me by the company that makes them. They asked me to install them on my own house and convince a few others to try them out as part of a sales promo. I put some up at my place and the picture on them is decent. I just never got around to giving some to anyone else. Until now. They're good-quality cameras and the service that allows you to save a month's worth of footage at a time is free for the first year."

"Then thank you, I guess."

"Do you have a toolbox?"

"Of course. Why?"

"So I can put them up. All I really need is a drill and a screw-driver."

"You don't need to do that," I said, watching as Rita grinned from ear to ear and waggled her eyebrows suggestively behind him. When she clapped a hand over her heart and fluttered her eyelashes, I vowed to hide her flavored coffee creamer as punishment for her insolence.

"There's a toolbox in the storage area," Rita said, her demeanor returned to normal. "I'll show you."

She steered Flanders toward the back of the store, and after about ten minutes, I heard the whir of a drill biting into wood near the rear entrance. My feelings regarding the cameras were mixed. On the one hand, I felt a bit violated by their presence. They were an invasion of my privacy as well as that of my customers, though the fact that they were only by the doors mitigated this some. And how much privacy did I really have during store hours anyway? On the other hand, the cameras did offer a certain level of security on the heels of the nastiness that had happened the other day. While the cameras might not prevent something horrific from happening, they could provide evidence of how it went down. I realized they might also serve as a deterrent, but perhaps to regular customers as well as to potential criminals? Then there was the fact that Flatfoot Flanders apparently cared enough about my welfare to put them up. I was flattered by that, but also mildly discomfited, almost as much as I was by the fact that I now thought of Jon as Flatfoot Flanders.

He and Rita reappeared thirty minutes later and went to the front entrance. They messed around outside for a while, garnering the curiosity of the handful of customers who came in. When they returned, the job apparently done, Rita came behind the counter and shooed me away.

"Go to your office. Flatfoot Flanders wants to show you how to monitor your new cameras. He said you'll need your cell phone."

Devon was in my office using my laptop to do his research, and when he started to leave, I told him to stay.

"Devon is my go-to person when it comes to anything techy," I said to Flanders. "Show him whatever you're going to show me."

Over the next twenty minutes, Flanders downloaded the app for the cameras onto both my phone and Devon's, and then onto my laptop, creating an account for us with a username and password. Once that was done, the views afforded by both cameras suddenly appeared on my phone. The rear camera showed the gravel drive out back, my parked car, and the grassy area beyond, but the front one gave us a nice view of the road, the parking lot, and both sides of the main entrance. We watched as a customer—a regular who lived in Door County and collected oddities of his own—pulled into the lot, got out of his car, and walked into the store. He didn't appear to notice the camera at all.

"Okay," I said, "I'll admit this is kind of cool in a creepy, predatory sort of way."

"Cool?" Devon scoffed, giving me a doleful shake of his head. "You need to get with the times, Morgan. How about 'dope' or 'sick'?"

"I'm an old soul," I said with a smile.

"If you're worried about your customers' privacy, don't look at the camera feed unless something happens," Flanders said.

"Right." I shut down the app, and then, feeling awkward, I hit Devon up for a status update. "Have you found anything for me yet?"

Devon shook his head, frowning.

"Can I ask what it is you're looking for?" Flanders asked.

I liked the fact that he always asked permission rather than behaving all bossy and acting like I owed him something because I was working for him. I'd had other clients who had done that.

"I asked Devon to dig around online to see what he could find out about the two men who died. I thought they might share some things in common that would give me a clue as to what happened to them."

Flanders tilted his head and gave me a curious smile. "That sounds like an old-fashioned flatfoot approach," he said, and I damn near swallowed my own tongue, biting back my laugh. "I take it you're coming at this thing from a skeptic's angle with regard to the idea of a lake monster," he went on.

"I'm coming at it from an angle of science," I said. "That and connections. Things are all connected somehow, some way, and discovering what those connections are will likely get me to the answers I need."

"That's basic detecting one-oh-one," Flanders said, sounding oddly pleased.

"Well, if there are connections between these two men outside of the obvious ones of dying in a water accident in Door County and having crush injuries that look like a big bite, I can't find them," Devon said.

"There's got to be some connection," I said. "I'm just not certain what it is yet or how it all ties together."

"Are you looking at anything else?" Flanders asked.

"Of course. I'm exploring several avenues." I told him about my excursion the day before with Marty and how I felt certain he'd seen something on the sonar just before the storm forced us in. "I couldn't see the screen well, nor could I get him to tell me what he saw, but there was definitely something there."

I paused, hesitant to say anything more, and then decided to bite the bullet. "I saw something odd myself. When I looked over the side, I swear I saw two large glowing eyes rising up through the water toward me."

Flanders paled. "Really?"

"Do you think we actually have a monster of some sort in the lake?" Devon asked, wide-eyed.

"Too soon to tell. What I have so far are bits of data, but I need more. I'm going to visit Marty again this afternoon and ask him what it was he saw. I might even ask him to take me out again."

"Mind if I come with you?" Flanders asked.

Surely, I had no power to stop him. Flanders was the police chief on Washington Island and could probably go anywhere he wanted. Granted, this was the peninsula, and it was ruled by the county sheriffs, but still . . . One wouldn't think a police chief would need to ask permission. I liked that he had, though.

"I suppose so," I said, wondering how welcoming Marty might or might not be.

Flanders glanced at his watch. "Have you had lunch?" he asked. I shook my head. "How about I buy you lunch and then you can take me to Marty's place?"

Not only had the color returned to his face; he appeared to be blushing.

"Let's go Dutch treat," I suggested. "Unless you want me to expense the meal to your account on my final bill?"

"Dutch treat it is," he said without hesitation. "But I get to pick the place. Deal?"

"As long as there's an outside eating area or we get it to go, because Newt comes with me."

Newt was lying on the floor at my feet, head resting on his massive front paws. He looked up at me at the mention of his name and then looked over at Flanders as if he knew his fate was in the man's hands.

Flanders looked down at the dog, brow furrowed. "Newt. Right," he said, nodding slowly. "You drive a hard bargain, Morgan Carter."

"Those are my terms, Chief Flanders. Take them or leave them."

He grinned at that. "Okay. We'll make it a threesome. But in return, I have a favor to ask of you."

"What's that?"

"Would you *please* call me Jon instead of Chief Flanders?"

"I think I can manage that," I said with a smile. And then I spent the next ten minutes silently repeating his name over and over like a mantra, hoping it would replace Flatfoot Flanders in my mind before I accidentally blurted it out.

CHAPTER 11

—

Flanders drove—he'd come over on the ferry in his police car, an SUV—and Newt climbed into the backseat without hesitation. I sat in the front passenger seat and studied the laptop that Flatfoot... Jon had mounted to his dash.

"Do you use this computer when you're driving?" I asked.

"I do. I can run plates, pull up maps, locate addresses, look up warrants, that sort of thing."

"Seems dangerous," I said. "Like texting and driving."

"Practice makes perfect, and we have some useful keyboard shortcuts. I don't do it when the car is in motion unless I absolutely have to."

He drove us to Baileys Harbor and pulled into the parking lot of a bar across the street from the boat-launch site where he and Haggerty had met me a couple days earlier.

"Do you like bacon cheeseburgers?" he asked.

"I do."

"Fries okay?"

"Sure."

Jon beamed. "Good. I like a gal who isn't afraid to eat. What do you want on your burger?"

"Some lettuce and tomato. A thin slice of raw onion if they have it. That's it. No ketchup or mustard."

"A purist," he said, nodding appreciatively. "Should I get something for the big guy?" He nodded toward Newt in the backseat.

The fact that he thought of Newt touched me. "I'm sure he'd enjoy a basic burger with cheese," I said. "Thank you." I took a twenty and a ten from my pocket and handed them to him. "Use any extra for a tip."

He accepted the money graciously. "Why don't you and Newt go scout us out one of those picnic tables over at the boat-launch site while I go inside and order? I'll bring the food once it's ready."

"We can do that."

Newt and I crossed the street and I staked out a table with a nice harbor view. Jon arrived with our food about fifteen minutes later and handed me a large foam container, a lemonade, and a paper-wrapped burger.

"Hope the lemonade is okay," he said. "If not, I can go back and get you something else."

"It's fine."

After checking to make sure it wasn't too hot, I set Newt's burger on the ground atop the paper it had come wrapped in. No sooner had I let go of it than Newt gobbled it down so fast that he ate part of the wrapper. Then he sat and watched us eat, long strings of drool hanging from his mouth. I loved the beast, but his manners were truly appalling at times.

"I apologize for Newt," I said to Jon. "He usually comports himself with more dignity and restraint, but when it comes to food, he tends to lose all control."

"On the contrary," Jon said. "The fact that he's willing to sit there patiently and wait until he's fed shows remarkable restraint."

He grabbed one of his French fries and held it aloft in Newt's direction, giving me a questioning look. I nodded and he tossed the fry to Newt, who snatched it out of the air and swallowed it whole, flinging a string of drool in the process.

"Do you need to get back to the island soon?" I asked. "I gather you're on duty since you have a police vehicle with you."

"I've got my other full-time officer covering things for now, and we have a part-timer taking backup calls. I need to return to the island by four, but until then, I'm yours."

There was something a little too intimate in the way he uttered those last two words. It made me squirm in my seat and in my gut, and I wondered if I was being overly sensitive because, in general, I enjoyed Jon Flanders's company. He proved himself a good conversationalist, chatting about the weather, about how tourists could sometimes be annoying, about dogs, and about how many quality burgers he'd had in his life and where he'd had them. I did notice that he managed to avoid telling me much of anything about his personal life or past aside from the burger locations, neatly skirting around my questions with clever segues and diversions. Still, it all felt comfortable enough until we finished eating and Jon hit me with the underlying question that had been lurking beneath the surface of what had thus far been a comfortable, companionable conversation.

"What's your gut telling you? Is there some kind of monster in Lake Michigan?"

"At the moment my gut is telling me I'm stuffed to the gills," I said. "That was one of the best burgers I've ever had. I'll have to remember this place."

Jon smiled, but he looked at me intently, waiting, and I knew he wouldn't let the question go. I flashed back on those two glowing eyes I'd seen yesterday when looking over the side of Martin's boat. In addition to a sliver of fear, I'd experienced a thrill at the sight, a burgeoning hope that maybe, just maybe, I'd finally found my proof. But the skeptic in me urged circumspection.

"I can't say yet," I said honestly. Seeing the disappointment on his face, I quickly added, "I'm certain there's something unusual in the water, something that isn't normally there, but just what that is, I don't yet know. I need more time."

"How much?"

I shrugged, wondering why he'd asked that question. Was it a money issue? Or something else? "Hard to say. Are you being pressured by someone on the matter?"

"Not about you, per se, but to get an answer of some sort, yes."

"Maybe our chat with Marty will get us some answers."

Jon nodded, though he looked doubtful. After gathering up the residue of our meal and disposing of it, we got back in the police car and drove to Marty's place. When we got there and I saw that his truck and boat were both gone, I felt disappointment tinged with a hint of resentment when I realized he'd probably gone back out on the water without me.

"Maybe he just went for a pleasure cruise," Jon suggested, reading my expression.

I shook my head. "No, he saw something yesterday on his sonar. I couldn't see the screen because of the way the sun was hitting it, but

I could tell it had him rattled. I'm betting he returned to that same spot to have another look." I let out a sigh of frustration and shook my head. "Damn, I wish he'd let me come along."

Jon looked around at the property, his forehead wrinkled in thought. "If you want, we can go back to Baileys Harbor and try to commandeer one of the patrol boats to see if we can find him."

I considered that. My curiosity was bursting at the seams, but I sensed that tracking Marty down with the cops in tow wouldn't sit well with him. It was a decision I'd come to regret.

"No, if Marty had wanted company, he would have let me know he was going out," I said. "Best to leave him to his own devices. He'll tell me if he finds something."

"You sure about that?"

I wasn't. "I am," I said, looking at my cell phone. "I should get back to the store. Thanks to that nifty security camera you installed, I can tell things are getting a bit crazy there."

"Your store is the very definition of 'crazy.'"

I winked at him. "That depends on your definition of 'normal.'"

We passed the boat launch in Sister Bay on the way, and I saw Marty's truck and trailer parked in the same spot it had been in yesterday. I pointed it out to Jon and then said, "Can you get me the names and contact information for the friends who came here with Oliver Sykes? And I'd like to talk to Stokstad's wife. Can you get me her contact info, too?"

Jon frowned, flexing his fingers on the steering wheel. "We've already talked to all of those people, and no one had anything useful to contribute."

I sensed he was being defensive, as if my desire to talk to these people was somehow an indictment of his own inquiries, a suggestion that the police work had somehow fallen short.

"I'm sure you were very thorough," I told him. "But I'm looking for information of a different nature."

"Like what?"

"I don't know yet," I said with a meager smile. "I want to know about offhanded things the victims might have said in passing or activities they might have done that seemed insignificant but also just a smidge out of character. I want to know what their hobbies and interests were when they were at home. I want to profile them, kind of like those FBI specialists do, but with a different focus. That's why I have Devon scouring their social media and online presence, to see what pages and groups they may have liked or visited or what connections they may have had to other people. Sometimes a seemingly insignificant detail can be surprisingly enlightening."

Jon considered that, and I waited.

"Okay," he said finally, "I'll get you the information, but you have to promise me you won't mention why you're asking or why I hired you. I don't want word of this getting out. If people find out we're looking for a lake monster that's trying to eat people, certain folks will have my head on a platter. The last thing anyone wants is a reason for people to stay away from Door County."

"Yes, sir, Chief Flanders!" I said in my best military voice, giving him a snappy salute. "I promise to be careful and discreet in my inquiries."

As if to reassure him of that, Newt leaned forward from the backseat and rested his head on Jon's shoulder. Newt had never done that with anyone other than me, and when I saw the corner of Jon's mouth curl into a smile, it triggered one of my own.

CHAPTER 12

———

The store was busy when we returned, and Devon had abandoned his research and come out of my office to help Rita. Jon called someone and arranged to have the contact information I'd requested forwarded to me via email. He waited to make sure the email came through before leaving, saying that he'd be in touch.

His absence left me with an odd sense of emptiness, a feeling of loss that confused me because I wasn't ready for a romantic relationship yet. Not that I hadn't had them before, or that I was naive or chaste. In fact, during my post-high-school years while traveling the world with my parents, I'd undergone a sexual awakening at the hands of a couple of generous and talented lovers: first Roberto and later Alexi.

But because of those travels, followed by college and more travel, I never established a steady, committed relationship until two and a half years ago. That was when David Johnson came into my life. My parents and I first met him when we were on a trip to Scotland on one of our many explorations of Loch Ness. David overheard our discussion while we were eating dinner in a pub one evening. He came over and introduced himself, telling us that he was a graduate from the University of Wisconsin with an MFA in creative writing and that he was in Scotland to investigate the history and lore surrounding Nessie for a book he was writing. Thanks to the shared interest and the gregarious nature of my parents, David became attached to us for the duration of our trip.

I fell fast and hard. David was charming, quixotic, terribly handsome, and an unapologetic flirt. Initially I saw him as an exciting fling for the two weeks I'd be in Scotland, but when I learned that he lived in Madison—only a four-hour drive away from home—I started thinking that fling could become something more permanent.

We spoke on the phone nearly every night, and David visited for long weekends whenever he could get time off from his part-time job at the university. Though he often stayed at a motel in Sister Bay— it was wintertime and rooms were cheap in the off-season—he also spent many a night on our couch. My parents were nearly as taken with him as I was.

Six months into our relationship, I rented a small house in Sister Bay for us, and David made plans to move to Door County. I paid the rent and other costs because David would have to quit his part-time job when he moved. He offered to help with the bills, saying that he had some money saved up and that his book had been picked up by a small press that was willing to buy more books from him once he finished the current one, but I refused, telling him I was happy to foot the bill for the time being so he could work on that book.

My father wasn't crazy about our plan; he was convinced that every man I dated was interested only in my money. In the past, he'd run background checks on anyone I saw more than twice. Just weeks before the trip to Scotland where we met David, Dad had turned up a DUI on a fellow I was seeing and really liked, and he confronted the guy with it. That invasion of my date's privacy, and the implication that I was too stupid or naive to be able to pick a decent person to date, pissed me off, particularly when the guy broke things off with me.

I had a terrible fight with my father over it and I finally told him that if he was going to continue doing background checks on every guy I tried to date that I'd simply stop bringing the fellows home or sharing any information about them. He relented then and said he wouldn't do it again unless I asked him to. I wasn't sure I believed him, but it was a détente of sorts and we moved on.

In early April, days before David and I were to move in together, my parents decided to take a trip to New Jersey to check out two recent cryptid sightings. They invited us along, and we flew there in my father's private plane—he had a pilot's license and often flew to places we visited in the US—and rented a car to take us to a motel at our first stop at the Jersey shore. Some local fishermen there were claiming they'd caught a sea monster, but it took only a matter of hours for Dad to determine that the rumor was drunken hyperbole. The "monster" was nothing more than a very large fish with a genetic defect that caused it to have three eyes and a tumor that vaguely resembled a human foot.

We spent the night there, and the next morning David shocked me and my parents by proposing to me on the beach during a chilly but beautiful morning sunrise, giving me a modest diamond to mark the occasion. Despite feeling it was too soon, I happily accepted, figuring we could simply make it a long engagement. The fact that I'd recently turned thirty and was keenly aware of my biological clock might have played a role in my decision.

While David and I celebrated with romantic walks on the beach and talks about the future, my parents went out and rented a luxury RV to use for the next leg of our trip. When they returned, my father called a guy and had him run a background check on David without telling me. The report he got back that evening verified a lot of the things David had told us—his degree from the U of Dub, his part-time job at the university, and his basic stats, like his date of birth, the names of his parents (whom he said he was estranged from), and his Social Security number. But it also revealed that David had a long-term online-gambling habit that had led to him declaring bankruptcy twice in the past ten years—the most recent time occurring not long before that fateful trip to Scotland. How anyone that strapped financially could have afforded a trip to Scotland should have been a clue that something more was up, but neither Dad nor his guy picked up on that. I think they felt that they had enough with what they'd found to that point and didn't need to dig any deeper. Maybe if there had been more time, or if I hadn't been so stubborn and impulsive, things would have been different.

We drove down to a campground in the Pine Barrens of New Jersey the next day—my parents in the RV, David and I following them in the car—to investigate reports of animals that had been found with their throats slashed, purportedly by a cryptid creature known as the Jersey Devil. Shortly after we arrived, my father complained of a bad case of indigestion, and he asked David to drive the car back into the nearest town to buy some antacid. I knew something was up when I offered to go with David, but my father asked me to stay and look at some of the reports about the dead animals to see what my take on them might be. As soon as David drove off, Dad took me aside, told me what he'd found, and said he was concerned that David's only interest in me was my money.

I was furious with him for reneging on his promise and potentially ruining yet another relationship for me. Our discussion quickly deteriorated into a screaming and yelling match with lots of gesticulations and finger-pointing, some of which was, unfortunately, witnessed by a couple—the only other people at the campground at the time—as they were departing. I didn't want to believe what my father was telling me, and I tried to convince him that he'd made a mistake, arguing that David Johnson was a common name and that I'd never once seen David gamble on anything.

Despite my vociferous protests, I think I knew deep down that my father was right. There'd been signs, like the way David locked his computer and wouldn't ever let me see what he was doing on it, stating that he didn't want anyone to read his book until he was done. Or the way he paid cash for everything, and there was precious little of that. Or the way he always changed the subject whenever I tried to get him talking about his past. But I'd been too caught up in the powerful field of David's extraordinary magnetism to care. I'd had my rosy future all planned out and now my father was destroying it.

To placate me, Dad agreed to at least confront David with what he'd found and see what David had to say for himself. We did that as soon as David returned with the antacid tablets, a couple of which I immediately took myself. David stayed cool and calm through the whole thing, appearing puzzled and surprised by the accusations rather than angry or defensive. Eventually he admitted to the gambling problem and bankruptcies with an embarrassed flush that turned his face beet red, but he swore he had it under control. He insisted he loved me and wasn't after my money.

I watched it all unfold through tear-filled eyes. Despite his pro-testations, I knew that my relationship with David was over, and life would never be the same. After an hour of soul-crushing, heart-wrenching arguments, I told everyone I needed some time to think. I asked David for the car keys, said that I'd be back before dark and that I'd pick us all up some dinner.

I drove aimlessly for a while, sobbing at intervals, swearing at other times, even laughing hysterically at one point. Eventually, my mind slipped into a protective task mode, shutting all the emotional stuff down for the time being. I found a deli and bought a rotisserie chicken and some side salads for our dinner.

It was just after five when I returned to the campground. The sun was low in the sky, the branches of the trees undulating in the wind, the long shadows they cast on the ground looking like giant menacing claws. I parked behind the RV and, since no one was outside, entered the vehicle. I smelled the blood first thing and dropped my bag of food. One of the salad containers burst open, spilling its vinegary contents, and that smell combined with the raw, meaty scent of blood made me gag.

I found my parents in the back bedroom. They were both dead, their throats slashed from ear to ear. I made futile, sobbing attempts to resuscitate them, shifting from one to the other, my tears mixing with the blood that hadn't yet soaked into the bed and carpeting around them.

David.

On weak, shaky legs, I searched the rest of the RV, leaving bloody handprints on the wall and some of the furnishings as I steadied myself. There was no sign of David and I shoved down the chilling thoughts trying to force their way to the top of my mind. I searched outside, calling to him, but my voice was swallowed up by the wind, carried off into the darkness of the surrounding woods. Had David been kidnapped? Killed somewhere else? Or had he . . . ?

The ideas that I was as naive and stupid as my father had thought and that I might have brought a killer into our lives were simply too much for my panicked, reeling mind to handle. One thought circled through my brain over and over, repeating like a stuck record and blocking out all other thought.

What have I done? What have I done?

Much of what followed was, and still is, a blur. I managed to call 911. There were police cars and ambulances, flashing red and blue lights, white searchlights and search parties. Then came the interrogations, the pushy, unrelenting press people, and nearly two weeks spent in a New Jersey motel while a detective questioned and shocked me daily with revelations of just how gullible I'd been.

David Johnson was a ghost. The fellow claiming to be him, the fellow I'd slept with (this still made me gag at times), the fellow I'd agreed to marry had stolen the identity of the real David Johnson, who did, indeed, have a bad gambling problem, two bankruptcies, and a job at the university that he'd lost right before he'd committed suicide seven months earlier. If only Dad's guy had found that obituary during his initial search, but the real David Johnson was from Florida and no obituary had appeared in any of the local papers. I learned that there was no university press planning to publish David's book; in fact, there was no book. Not surprisingly, the diamond in my engagement ring turned out to be a fake.

To make matters worse, there was no real proof that David—or the person pretending to be David—had even been at the campground. The couple who had left shortly after we arrived had been the only other people there. When they heard about the murders on the news, they let the police know that they had witnessed me and my father in a loud, intense, and demonstrative argument on the day they departed the campground. Unfortunately, they never saw David because he'd left to drive into town at my father's direction right after we arrived.

The house I'd rented for David and me in Sister Bay was in my name only. There were no fingerprints in the rental car except mine because David had worn gloves the entire time. He wore gloves a lot, claiming he had Raynaud's, a circulatory issue that caused chronically cold hands—oh, the power of hindsight. And when the police tried to find out where David had purchased the antacid tablets, there was no receipt, no identifying sticker on the bottle, and no credit card trail because he'd paid cash. Anything of David's that had been brought along on the trip was gone, and when the cops later tried to verify the existence of someone purporting to be David Johnson, no one at the motel at the Jersey shore could remember seeing him.

It didn't take long for the police to turn their attention to me, the bloodied sole survivor of the Carter family fortune and the only verifiable person there at the time of my parents' deaths. I had motive and opportunity, and when it was discovered that a knife was missing from the RV kitchen, a knife later found a few feet into the woods, covered with blood but no fingerprints, means were ascribed to me, as well. It didn't help that I could be heard muttering my mind mantra on the 911 call: "What have I done?"

Eventually I hired a lawyer and returned home to Door County, but the police in New Jersey let me know that I was still suspect number one. It was only when an unidentifiable set of fingerprints turned up in the RV (which the police argued could have been from anyone who had previously rented it or the company who managed it), and

Devon and Rita told the police that there had been a man in my life, that anyone gave me the benefit of the doubt. The entire ordeal had left me devastated, confused, afraid, and angry. I hired a private investigator to try to find David, but who he'd been in real life and where he was now remained a mystery. In addition to mourning the loss of my parents and dealing with the immense guilt I felt, I had the full-time day-to-day management of the store suddenly heaped upon my shoulders. In some ways, that was a blessing in disguise because it kept me busy and distracted, and Rita and Devon both did their best to help me get through it. But it wasn't until Newt dropped into my life that the real healing began. It had been a long, slow, one-day-at-a-time recovery since, and my narrowed emotional bandwidth had left no room for romantic relationships.

I realized that might finally be changing, however, because I felt a tiny thrill of anticipation when Jon Flanders called me just before six that evening. Unfortunately, my delight had a shorter life span than one of Newt's drool strings.

"I just got word from the Coast Guard that they found Martin Showalter's boat in the bay," Jon told me. "It was empty and adrift, and there's no sign of Martin anywhere."

"Oh, no," I said. "Do they think he fell overboard?"

"It isn't clear. They also found blood on the boat."

"Blood?" I echoed, hollow dread churning in my gut. "How much blood?" I braced for the answer.

After a moment's hesitation, Jon said, "A worrisome amount."

"Maybe he injured himself and someone picked him up and took him to get help," I suggested, desperate for a less devastating explanation. "Did you check his boat to see if it would run? Maybe he tried to work on the engine and cut himself."

"The engine turned over just fine. Keys were in the ignition. No one heard any Mayday calls and there were no reports of stranded or injured boaters from anyone else."

"Damn," I muttered.

"We've got patrol boats out looking for him, but it's going to be dark in an hour or so, and the chances of finding him tonight are slim. We'll keep a search going through the night, of course, but it's not looking good. I'm sorry, Morgan."

"You'll let me know if you find anything? No matter what it is? No matter when it is?" My request was met with silence, and I quickly added, "I promise I can handle it."

"I have no doubt of that based solely on the fact that you sleep above all that creepy stuff in your store every night."

"There's nothing here to be afraid of," I told him. "Besides, I have Newt."

"Good point." Silence stretched between us for several seconds and then he said, "Let me ask you something, Morgan. What are the chances . . . I mean . . . is it possible . . . Do you think—"

"That a lake monster could have attacked Marty in his boat and that's why he's missing and there's blood at the scene?"

"Yes," he said, sounding relieved that he hadn't had to utter the words himself.

"No."

"You sound mighty certain."

"I am. It just doesn't fit with any type of aquatic animal behavior I know. If he was in the water and got attacked, that would be one thing. But this isn't *Jaws*. The idea of something coming up out of the water onto his boat and pulling him overboard? I'm not buying it."

"Okay," he said. "I'll keep you posted."

I thanked him and, once our call was over, found myself wishing he'd call back. You know that adage about being careful what you wish for? Well, that thought would end up being proof of its veracity. It was around nine thirty, we had just closed the store, Devon and Rita had gone home, and I was sitting in my office adding up the day's receipts when Jon called me back.

"Morgan," he said, "This is going to sound a little, um, unfriendly, but it's not meant to be that way."

"O-kay," I said slowly, dread building. I braced for news that they'd found Marty's body.

"We have witnesses at the boat launch in Sister Bay who saw you and Marty getting on his boat and heading out yesterday, but we can't find a single person who saw you return."

"It was storming hard when we got back, raining sideways. There weren't any people out and about."

"We also can't find any witnesses who saw Marty go back out on the water today. But I do have people who say his truck and trailer are parked in the same spot as yesterday."

"Can't you track him by using GPS on the sonar thing he had in the boat?"

"We didn't find one," Jon said.

"Well, that settles one question," I said. "Lake monsters aren't in the habit of stealing sonar devices."

"What time did you get home yesterday?"

"It was at sunset, thereabouts. We came in a couple hours before that, during the storm, like I said. I had a flat on the way home and had to pull over and wait out the storm before changing it. I dozed off in the car for a couple of hours. Are you sure no one saw Marty go back out again this morning?"

"One of the folks who works in the restaurant down by the launch area said his truck and trailer never moved all night."

I remembered the look on Marty's face when he'd seen whatever it was that had appeared on his sonar screen. Had he simply waited out the storm and gone back out that same night? Based on what I'd seen in the cuddy cabin, I knew Marty sometimes slept in his boat.

I was about to suggest this scenario when Jon said, "Do you know of *anyone* who might have seen you come back last night?"

Up to that point, I'd thought Jon and I were thinking aloud, trying to figure out what had happened to Marty. But the emphasis he put on the word "anyone" gave me a flashback and made me realize what these questions were really about.

"Do you think *I* might have done something to Marty?" I said, appalled. I didn't wait for his answer. "You think I hurt him while we were out on his boat and then somehow made it back to shore?" I scoffed at the idea. "I'm a good swimmer, Jon, but not that good."

"The inflatable dinghy for his boat was missing. We found it on shore half an hour ago, near the boat landing. There was a rag in it with dried blood on it and dog hair stuck in the blood."

Tense silence crackled in the air between our phones. More flashbacks from two years ago washed over me as I tried to keep my response calm and reasoned.

"I hit my head on the ceiling of the cuddy cabin when we were out on the boat and got a cut. It wasn't bad enough to need stitches or anything like that, but it did bleed a decent amount. You know how head wounds do that."

"I don't recall seeing a head wound on you earlier today."

Had there been a hint of accusation in that comment? Anger flared white hot behind my eyes, but I snuffed it.

"It's hard to see," I explained calmly. "It's hidden by my hair, and it wasn't a big cut. Marty gave me a rag to use to stem the flow of blood.

I don't know how the rag ended up in the inflatable dinghy. Or how the dinghy got inflated for that matter." Something occurred to me then. "How do you know the dinghy belonged to Martin?"

"It had the name of his boat stenciled on it. The Coast Guard said they found a bloody fingerprint on the underside of a seat storage area on the boat. It won't be yours?"

I squeezed my eyes shut and cursed under my breath, feeling an all-too-familiar claustrophobic sense of dread. It felt like the walls of my office were closing in on me and I struggled to keep my breathing at a normal pace.

"The print is probably mine," I said, pleased with the controlled sound of my voice. "I had to open that storage area to get a vest and a flotation ring for Newt when the storm blew in. The ring was beneath the dinghy." I paused, still mildly exasperated. "Jon, why would I hurt Marty? What possible motive do I have?"

"You said Marty saw something in the water when you were out there. Maybe you didn't want to share the credit for a find if it turned out to be a lake monster."

Cold suspicion washed over me. "You've been talking to your uncle in New Jersey."

He sighed. "Not recently, but when I did talk to him, he told me about what happened to your parents."

"You mean what he *thinks* happened," I snapped. "Did he also tell you that he accused me of killing them? And that the real killer is still out there somewhere?"

Jon hesitated, taking his time before answering. "He told me the case was never solved."

Nice avoidance there, Jon. "Wow," I said, shaking my head, anger overpowering my rising panic. "I can't believe this."

"Morgan, I have to consider all—"

"I think we're done talking," I said, cutting him off. "Good night, Chief Flanders." I enunciated the title and name slowly, emphasizing each word, letting it distance me from him.

Newt, sensing that I was upset, came over and put his big head in my lap, looking up at me with pure unconditional love. I buried my face in the thick fur of his neck and let the tears I'd been holding back finally let go.

CHAPTER 13

———

A pall of heart heaviness still hung over me the next morning and I tried hard to keep my mind occupied with busy work: balancing the books, doing inventory, and shopping online for any new and unusual items I might be able to secure for the store.

Devon didn't help my mood any when he informed me that he couldn't find a single thing that Oliver Sykes and Will Stokstad had in common, save their similar ages, their apparent love of Door County, and the fact that they were male.

"I searched all of their social media and even did some dark web searches for their names, but nothing came up," he told me. "Sorry, Morgan."

"Thanks for trying."

He must have sensed my sullen mood because after a moment he said, "I'll take a second look just to be sure. Maybe something will pop up that I missed the first time around."

I nodded, though it was more of a reflexive response than a serious one, and since I spent a large part of the morning in my office on my computer doing the books, the inventory, and my searches, Devon was needed in the store proper to help Rita handle customers. The app that Jon Flanders had installed on my phone to monitor the security cameras kept dinging every time a customer came through the front door. I found it distracting initially, then annoying, and after an hour or so of dings, I dug into the settings and disabled the notifications.

Somewhere around lunchtime, Rita knocked on my office door and stuck her head in. "There's a young man by the name of Keith Olsen out here asking for you," she said.

"Did he say what he wants?"

Rita shook her head. "I asked, but all he said was that it was a personal matter."

I didn't feel like talking with anyone, but my curiosity was piqued. I stopped what I was doing and went out front to see what was up, hoping it wasn't a customer complaint. Maybe it would be a customer looking for a specific item that I didn't have in the store but might be able to find using my connections. I get three or four of those a year and they're always challenging and interesting, both in terms of what the people want and all the reasons I imagine for why they want it. Because I never ask.

With one such case, I did myself out of a potentially lucrative commission when a fellow came in and asked me if I could acquire the death mask of *L'Inconnue de la Seine*, a young woman of around sixteen who was found drowned in the Seine in the late 1880s. It was customary in those days to make a cast of a dead person's face for display if identification was unknown in hopes that someone would recognize it. This particular death mask achieved cultural significance and worldwide renown because of the mystery surrounding her apparent suicide and the girl's delicate beauty. When the coroner made a death mask of her face, controversy, gossip, and speculation followed. There was even a novel written in which the protagonist becomes obsessed with the death mask, leading to tragedy. Many copies of the mask were made, and perhaps the most well-known one was done by a toy maker who was asked to construct a mannequin for the purposes of teaching CPR. That's how it came to be that Resusci Anne bears the same countenance as the *L'Inconnue de la Seine*. My customer didn't know that, and once I explained it to him, he thanked me and dashed out of the store, no doubt with the intent of buying his own CPR training mannequin.

Today's visitor was asking for me for a completely different reason, however—one I never would have guessed. There were a lot of people in the store when I emerged from my office and Rita pointed him out to me with a nod. He didn't look familiar, and as I walked up to him, I couldn't help but be amused by the wide-eyed way he was surveying the items on my shelves.

"I'm Morgan Carter," I said when I got to him. "Can I help you with something?"

He swallowed hard. "I'm Keith Olsen. I have something for you."

He was empty-handed, a fact made obvious by his overwrought wringing of them. I stared at him, my eyebrows raised in question, waiting for him to elaborate further.

"It's from Martin Showalter," he said quickly as if speaking fast was a type of talisman.

His words instantly buoyed my spirits. "From Marty? He's okay, then?"

Keith's face furrowed in confusion and something else . . . fear, perhaps? He shrugged and said, "He was okay yesterday morning when he called and asked me to make this delivery. He wanted me to do it yesterday, but I got tied up at work."

"You saw him yesterday morning? You're sure of that?"

"No, ma'am, but I spoke to him on the phone," Keith said, giving me a wary look. "He told me he was out on the water and asked if I'd help him out by making a delivery for him."

"What's the delivery?"

"It's in my truck."

Keith spun around and beelined for the front door. I followed him, and as soon as I stepped outside, I saw what he had brought me. There in the back of a pickup was one of Marty's Adirondack chairs, the stained wood one I'd sat in and admired the other day.

"I had to go into his workshop to get it," Keith said. He reached into his shirt pocket and pulled out an envelope. "And this goes with it. It was taped to the chair, but I pulled it off, fearing it might fly off during the drive."

The envelope had my first name scrawled across it in a shaky hand. I opened it and pulled out a handwritten note scribbled out on paper with a brown stain in one corner. The message was straight-forward and simple:

Please accept this gift as my way of thanking your father for my job all those years. M

No signature, just that single capital letter M. I was touched, and my heart felt as if it were stuck in my throat. *Please be okay, Marty.*

"Want me to just set it out front here?" Keith asked.

I started to nod, but then changed my mind. "Actually, if you don't mind, I'd like to have it up there." I pointed above me to the balcony off my apartment, one of my favorite places to sit because it afforded me a small view of the bayside waters. "I'll get my employee Devon to help you."

Half an hour later, I settled into the chair and gazed out at the view, running my hands over the smooth finish on the wide arms. Tears threatened but I fought them back, unwilling to give in to those dark thoughts just yet. Marty would be okay, I told myself. He'd turn up with some crazy story about what had happened, and we'd all laugh about it.

My gut said otherwise, however, and after trying unsuccessfully to shut it up, I knew I needed to do something distracting and productive. I went back downstairs to my office and opened the email with the contact info for Oliver Sykes's friends and Will Stokstad's wife. My timing in requesting the contact information had been fortunate, because I doubted Jon would have passed it on to me after last night. I didn't know what his uncle had told him about me and the events surrounding my parents' deaths, but based on my own dealings with Detective Karl Swenson two years ago, I had a good idea. Clearly, Jon was having second thoughts about me, though at least he hadn't canceled my contract. Yet.

After thinking on it for a time, I decided to call Oliver's friends first, figuring they would be the easiest calls to make. While they had undoubtedly mourned their friend's death, their grief was not likely to be as acute as that of Will's wife.

Three of them answered my calls; the others went to voice mail, and I hung up without leaving any messages, figuring I would try again later. The three fellows I was able to reach all said essentially the same things: that Oliver was an experienced kayaker and swimmer, that he was the least likely of any of them to drown, and that it was a shocking and horrible thing that had happened. One of those three, a fellow named Tony, did offer up something interesting just as I was about to hang up.

"There was something off with Ollie during that whole trip."

"What do you mean?"

"Well, we've gone to Door County as a group several times in the past, and we generally all go out kayaking together. We have a few too many beers and a lot of laughs and all is good. But on this trip, Oliver kept wanting to go off on his own and making excuses for why he couldn't join us. On one of the days, he said he didn't feel well and wanted to stay at the house while the rest of us went out, but one of our kayaks sprang a leak and we headed back in after only being out for an hour or so, figuring we'd swap that kayak out for Ollie's. When we got back to the house, we discovered Ollie was gone. At first, we were worried that he'd had to go to an urgent care or something, but then we realized his kayak and all his gear was gone, too. We called him on his cell, but service is so dicey there, you know?"

I certainly did. The peninsula can be a challenge when it comes to cell service and Washington Island is even worse.

"Anyway, when he came back later that afternoon, he was surprised to find us there. He said he'd felt better and decided to go out after all. Then he disappeared into his room."

Tony paused and I stayed quiet, sensing there was more to come. I was right.

"This whole last trip, Ollie was different. There was something— I don't know—serious about him, super focused but not focused at all. You know what I mean?"

"Not sure I do, actually."

"Sorry. It's hard to explain. Ollie seemed distracted when we were all together, like he wasn't tuned in to us as a group. He always looked like he was trying to figure out some complex math problem in his head."

"Any idea why he was like that?"

"No, though I thought maybe he and Bess were having problems."

"Bess?"

"His live-in girlfriend. They've been together for nearly five years now and that's a long time for Ollie." Another pause. "*Was* a long time," he corrected, and I heard the grief in his voice as it hit him afresh. "Anyway," he went on, "Ollie used to be quite the player before he met Bess. She got him to settle down. I think he would have married her eventually."

A live-in girlfriend was as good as a wife when it came to observing changes or interests in someone. Maybe that girlfriend had picked up on something that Oliver's friends hadn't.

"Would you happen to have a phone number for Bess?" I asked.

"I don't, but her last name is Thornberg."

"Do you happen to know what she does for a living? Where she works?"

"She's some kind of medical administrator," Tony said. "Ollie told me she works at a hospital in Green Bay. Sorry. I don't remember the name of it."

"No problem. You've been very helpful, Tony. Thanks."

I disconnected the call, but before I tackled the grim task of calling Will's wife, I took the notes I'd jotted down about Bess Thornberg and carried them out to Devon.

"Could you please try to find me a cell number or an email address for this woman? This is what I know about her."

Devon looked at my notes and said, "Give me five minutes." He found her in three, including a cell number, a physical address, her employer, and an email address.

"You're a genius," I told him.

"I know."

He grinned broadly as he went back to work, and I found his good mood briefly infectious. After a few minutes of inner debate, which I recognized for what it really was—a stalling tactic—I called the grieving widow next, figuring it might be the tougher call emotionally, given that Will had left behind kids as well as a wife.

I expected a grief-stricken widow, someone still raw around the edges, but Janelle Stokstad surprised me.

"Mrs. Stokstad, my name is Morgan Carter and I'm helping the police here in Door County look into Will's death."

"What is there to look into?" she asked irritably. "He drowned, the damned fool. It was bound to happen sooner or later."

I was momentarily stunned into silence, unsure of what to say. As I struggled for a reasonable response, she hit me with her next barrage.

"Do you know how many times he ditched me, left me alone with these kids so he could go up to la-di-da Door County and fish? Like there aren't fish in the lakes closer to home? I never could figure out what was so special about Door County, other than the fact that it was far away. Maybe that's why he liked it. More distance between us."

"Mrs. Stokstad, I—"

"Don't call me that. Call me Janelle. Or Ms. Anderson. I'm taking back my maiden name. I was going to do it after the divorce, but now I don't have to wait."

I heard a crash and a distant screech from somewhere on her end as I contemplated the revelation that she and Will had planned to get a divorce. Then Janelle yelled so loud that I yanked the phone away from my head, fearful for my eardrums.

"Damn it! I told you kids not to climb up on the counters. Now look what you did!" This was punctuated by a heavy, irritated sigh. "Look, lady, I gotta go. Do yourself a favor and forget about Will. That's what I'm doing."

And just like that, the line went dead.

I set my phone down on my desk and stared at it, stunned by the exchange. Then I went out to the main part of the store, happy to find both Rita and Devon seated on stools behind the counter, Devon on his tablet, Rita reading a book. I needed clearer heads to help me parse this latest experience and I ran my conversation with Janelle Stokstad past them.

"Maybe she had him killed," Rita posed, her eyes growing big. "Heard about the first guy and decided to make it look like her husband went the same way."

I shook my head. "Too complicated. And critical details of the first death weren't made public, like the teeth impressions."

"Clearly there was no love lost between Will and his wife," Devon said.

"Did you pick up any hints of this animosity when you were doing your online research on Will?" I asked him.

He shook his head. "Though he did post that he prefers to go fishing alone."

"I would, too, if it got me away from a wife like his," Rita said. "Maybe it was his escape, his only chance for some peace and quiet."

"And look at how that turned out," I said.

CHAPTER 14

—

After my uncomfortable conversation with Janelle, I needed a break, so I stuck the phone number for Oliver's girlfriend, Bess, in my desk drawer. I called Jon Flanders to see if there was any update on Marty, but got his voice mail. I started to leave a message, but before I was finished, Jon was calling me back.

"Hi, Morgan, is everything okay?"

"That's what I was going to ask you. Any word on Martin?"

There was a pause before he answered, which I knew didn't bode well. "We haven't found him."

"Do you still think I had something to do with his disappearance?"

"I don't," he said without hesitation, making me feel better about things. "Some of the evidence does point a finger at you, but I'm satisfied with your explanations."

I sensed an unspoken *for now* in there but let it go. "Thank you.

And if it helps at all, this morning a young man by the name of Keith Olsen came to my store with one of Martin's Adirondack chairs in his truck. He said he spoke to Marty yesterday morning, when Marty called him and asked him to pick up the chair and bring it to me. So there's proof that Marty was alive and well yesterday morning."

"Do you have a phone number for this Keith Olsen?"

"I don't. But I'm guessing you can get a license number off his truck with that camera you installed in front of my store and track him down that way."

For the moment, at least, I was glad to have the cameras in place.

"You bought one of Marty's chairs?" Jon asked.

"No, it was a gift."

"Really?"

"Yes, really."

"Sounds like Marty was quite taken with you."

"That's a flattering thought, but I think it was more of a debt repayment."

I explained the history of my father and grandfather, their connections to Marty, and the contents of the note that had come with the chair.

When I was done, Jon said, "I'm curious. Did your parents ever look for a monster in our lake here? Or in any of the Great Lakes for that matter?"

"They did follow up on a report of something seen in Lake Superior once. That was when I was . . . oh . . . eight or nine, I think? All of the lakes have had reports of sightings at one time or another, but Superior's depth and its underwater caverns make it the one most likely to harbor a hitherto unknown specimen."

"I take it your parents didn't find anything?"

"Not that time, no."

A pregnant pause followed. "You mean they found things other times?"

"Relax," I said, chuckling. "They didn't find any monsters, per se, but on a trip to Lake Champlain once they did discover some underwater geographic features that could help explain why sightings of these lake creatures are so rare and why no one has ever found a dead one."

"Do tell," Jon said.

I opened my mouth to do just that, but before I could utter a word he said, "Wait. Why don't you tell me over dinner tonight?"

Now it was my turn to pause. "I don't know if we should do that."

"Sorry. I thought . . ." He let out a nervous laugh. "I don't know what I thought."

"You've hired me on as a consultant, and I don't want there to be any hints of impropriety there. It's hard enough in the cryptozoology field to come across as legitimate without having a bunch of salacious or suspicious rumors dogging me. I'm concerned about the optics."

"The optics?" He sounded like he was about to burst out laughing, which made me angry. "Morgan, there aren't many people who even know that I hired you, and the fact that I did should at least entitle me to an occasional update on the case, shouldn't it? And if we do that over dinner, what's the big deal?"

Now I felt stupid as well as angry. But there was no point in complicating things even more with emotions born out of misunderstandings.

"Fair enough," I said, swallowing down my doubts. "But I still can't do it tonight because I need to staff the store. Both Rita and Devon have the evening off."

"Oh. Of course."

I detected a hint of disappointment in his voice, and it heartened me.

"How about if I bring dinner to you at the store? We can eat there and chat."

I considered his offer. I did need to eat at some point, and that seemed a safer scenario, one less fraught with innuendo.

"I suppose we can do that," I said.

"Great! I'll be there at six."

And then he disconnected the call without so much as a goodbye. Perhaps to make sure I didn't have a chance to change my mind? This felt a little dangerous, a little too close to the fire I'd barely escaped from two years ago. What was I doing?

I looked over at Newt and said, "I might have screwed the pooch on this one, my friend."

His ears perked, and he let out a little *woof* of agreement. Or maybe it was a *woof* of disapproval over my choice of metaphor.

I took a moment to contemplate the complexity of human relationships, thinking that animals, even the cryptid ones, were so much easier.

Rita and Devon both took off at five, and Jon showed up at six o'clock sharp. Very timely, especially considering that he presumably had the ferry's schedule in the mix. He came bearing two large brown bags, which I soon discovered contained an assortment of items from a local Chinese restaurant.

"I wasn't sure what you liked, so I got a little of everything," he said with a goofy grin.

He wasn't kidding. There were more than twenty containers of food, everything from crab rangoon puffs and spring rolls to moo shu pork and two kinds of lo mein. There were no customers in the store when he arrived, and we carried the food into my office, where I kept a supply of paper plates and cups in a cabinet. I opted for the chopsticks that came with the meal while Jon went for a plastic fork.

"I never got the hang of those," he said, pointing at the chopsticks with his fork.

"I learned when I was a toddler," I told him. "In Japan. My parents were there—"

"Looking for a cryptid," he finished for me.

I smiled and nodded.

"What an unusual childhood you must have had. Did you enjoy it?"

I narrowed my eyes at him, chewing on a mouthful of broccoli and beef, wondering if he was asking out of mere curiosity or because of whatever his uncle had told him about what happened in New Jersey.

"I had no complaints," I told him. "I didn't want for anything, and I got to travel the world and see some amazing things."

"What about friends?" Jon asked. "It must have been hard to make friends with all the moving around and homeschooling."

I shrugged, partly as a stalling measure because I wasn't sure the making-friends thing was something I wanted to discuss and partly because my mouth was full of shrimp fried rice. Eventually, I decided to change the subject and thereby avoid an answer.

"I have a favor to ask of you," I said once I'd swallowed my rice. "I'm really worried about Marty, and I was wondering if you'd let me look around his place."

Jon eyed me skeptically.

I grinned. "Well, inside his place."

"I can't just let you into his house."

"Why not?"

"For one, we aren't certain something has happened to him and—"

"You found his boat abandoned with blood in it and you're not sure that something has happened to him?" I echoed, incredulous.

"We don't know that the blood is his," Jon said. "We know it's human and not fish blood, but we don't have anything to compare it to for Marty. Besides, even if we did, it takes weeks to get DNA back from the lab. What if the blood is someone else's? What if Marty hurt or killed someone on his boat and then went into hiding? He could be on the run, for all we know. If that is the case, I can't let you into his house, or anything else of his, and risk contaminating evidence."

"Marty isn't on the run," I said. "Has anyone been to his place since you and I were out there to make sure he's not inside injured or dying?"

"The local sheriff's department went there and knocked. No one answered the door."

"Well, if he's in there seriously hurt or injured, he might not be able to do that, right? He's a hoarder, you know. One of those piles in his house could have fallen over on him. He could be lying in there unconscious. Shouldn't you break in to check it out?"

"Without a warrant? No." No equivocation there. "And since his truck isn't there, it's unlikely he is."

Jon looked exasperated with me, but I wasn't ready to give in yet.

"You said his truck and trailer are still at the boat launch in Sister Bay. How far could he have gone without his boat or his wheels?"

"To Canada or Michigan in another boat, or anywhere if he was in another vehicle," Jon said without hesitation.

Damn. He had me there, and I think he knew it, because while I can't swear to it, I think he was biting back a self-satisfied smile.

"I'm sorry, Morgan, but for now we have to be patient and wait for something more to turn up."

Frustrated, I finally let the matter drop, at least as far as conversing with Jon was concerned. In my head, it was still very much at the forefront of my thoughts. It got busy after seven, and without Rita or Devon to help me, I didn't have much time for Jon. He kindly cleaned up the remains of our dinner, stuck a couple of containers in the fridge in my office—since it was a mini fridge, not everything would fit—and then he watched me hustle through a busy Wednesday evening.

It was also a successful evening, in terms of sales. I sold a seventeenth-century wallet made from tanned human skin, a collection of shrunken heads from an island in the South Pacific, a set of shark's teeth, a deformed cow fetus in a jar of formaldehyde, a 1910 vintage Houdini poster, and a crystal ball that was rumored to have once belonged to a Russian czar, though there was no provenance to prove that. I also sold thirteen mysteries, mostly current, new-release stuff, but also a couple of older books, including a 1935 edition of Agatha Christie's *The Mysterious Affair at Styles* that went for fifteen hundred bucks. Whatever was in the air those last two hours on Wednesday evening, it had people willing to plunk down some serious money for rare and oddball items.

While I didn't need the money, I loved seeing that kind of action in the place. Jon, on the other hand, sat behind the counter looking aghast at many of the purchases. It might have been a little too much for him because at nine, when I was ready to lock the doors and close for the night, he said he needed to get going and left. He seemed to be in a hurry, but whether it was to get somewhere or just get away from my store, I couldn't tell.

CHAPTER 15

—

That unusual Wednesday appetite for the macabre and weird should have been my first clue that things wouldn't go smoothly for me as I prepped for my after-hours excursion, but I was too excited and determined to think it through. After I closed out the register and locked the money and receipts away in the safe, Newt and I got in my car, and I drove out to Marty's place.

Marty's truck and trailer still weren't there, and the place felt empty and deserted. The woods loomed dark and mysterious all around the lot, and I left my car running with the headlights aimed toward the woods and the cliff beyond, which overlooked the bay. I reached into the glove box and took out a small pocket-sized flashlight I kept there, tested it to make sure the batteries hadn't given up the ghost, and stuffed it in my pants pocket. Then I donned the nitrile gloves I'd brought with me from the store, unhooked Newt, and got out of the car.

There was enough peripheral light from the headlights for me to easily see the door to Marty's mobile home, and I walked up to it and knocked several times as hard as I could. I kept staring at the woods as I waited between knocks and my eyes began playing tricks on me, making me see shifts in the shadows that looked like someone emerging from the dark density of the trees until I blinked them away. After three knocking attempts, I tried the knob and was surprised to find it turned easily. Upon closer inspection, I saw that the lock was damaged, dented with something like a pry bar just enough to keep the dead bolt from catching. Was that new? I tried to recall what the door had looked like when Rita and I had come before, but couldn't remember. Had it been like that when the police were there?

Newt sat at the base of the stairs, his ears pricked to the sounds of the night—owls hooting, leaves rustling, wind soughing through tree limbs. I told him to stay, and then I opened the door and went inside.

The smell hit me like a slap in the face, making me reel back. I realized, to my relief, that it wasn't the smell of rotting or decaying flesh but rather a rancid, sour smell like that of rotting food. It was the same smell I'd experienced the first time I'd been there, though on that occasion it hadn't been as in my face as it was now. I cupped a gloved hand over my nose and mouth, took a few steps deeper into the mess, and hollered for Marty. I was met with silence. Well, mostly silence. There was the sound of scurrying vermin off to my left and the relentless drip of a leaking faucet to my right. I flipped on a light.

If I hadn't seen the place a couple of days earlier, I might now have thought that it had been ransacked. Drawers were open with papers spilling out of them. Every surface was covered with bundled and rolled newspapers, envelopes, unopened junk mail, dirty dishes, boxes and cans of food, packages of toilet paper, dishrags, and paper towels. I pushed some of the papers around, looking for anything that might seem significant, but there was nothing of interest, save one rapidly scurrying and heart-stoppingly large cockroach. Given what the inside of Marty's trailer looked like, I found it hard to believe how neat and clean the cuddy cabin in his boat had been. Perhaps the boat was more of a home to him than this trailer.

After searching just enough to make sure Marty wasn't in there injured or dead, I bolted for the outside and gulped in lungfuls of the cedar-scented night air. I also smelled sawdust, and that lured me toward the shed, which served as Marty's workshop.

The shop area wasn't anything spectacular but it, like Marty's boat, was relatively clean and organized. The wood-plank floor near the door had been swept, though the floor at the back of the structure, where a table saw was located, was covered with sawdust. So were most of the surfaces. Despite this, saws, planes, sanders, and other tools were neatly hung on pegboards mounted on the sidewalls. Two unfinished chairs were partially assembled in the area near the door, and there were the subtle scents of stain, paint, and turpentine underlying the wood smells. A table, a chair, and a cot stood off to one side and the cot had a sheet, a pillow, and a blanket on it, suggesting that Marty slept in there sometimes. I walked over to the table and shuffled through the papers spread out there, but all I found were drawings of chairs and other pieces of furniture.

Newt had followed me into the building and had promptly switchbacked his way through the place with his nose to the ground. He returned to my side now with wood chips stuck to his nose and caught in his whiskers, his wagging tail stirring up a small dust-nado.

"Where are you, Marty?" I said to the air.

Newt cocked his head to one side and whimpered.

"I know, buddy," I said, clearing the wood chips from his face. "I'm worried about him, too."

I got back into the car and drove to the boat landing where I'd met Marty the other morning. His truck was still parked in the space it had been the morning I went out with him.

What did you see on your screen, Marty? Had he gone back out to that area in the Rock Island Passage and found it again?

I pulled into an empty parking space a couple rows back and grabbed the slim jim I had in my glove box, a tool my father had kept on hand because he was always having to help customers who had inadvertently locked their keys in their cars. For some reason, it seemed to happen to our customers more than it did anywhere else, if the claims of other Door County business owners could be believed, and I eventually came up with a theory as to why. Odds and Ends can be quite distracting when one first pulls up. Not only are there oddities inside the store, but often there are some outside, too. In fact, on nice days I drag Henry and his chair outside and park him beside the entrance, something my father used to do. My father's other favorite piece of outdoor decor was a coffin that was rumored to be from Transylvania. It was a simple black wooden affair, but it had a red velvet liner that caught one's eye and, when propped up outside, attracted a lot of attention. When Dad eventually sold the coffin—the fellow who bought it insisted on lying in it before he'd commit to the purchase—he started rotating other items to the entrance, though none proved quite as eye-catching as that coffin had been. It might have been these distracting items that led to people absentmindedly locking their keys in their cars so often.

The slim jim saw a fair amount of action during the busy tourist seasons back in my father's day. I still have to use it on occasion, though a lot of the newer vehicles are slim jim–proof and some cars won't let you lock your keys inside. Marty's truck was an older model that I was confident I could work with the device. After checking to make sure that the truck was locked and then checking my surroundings to make sure no one was watching me—the late hour and the cover of darkness helped—I slid the tool down inside the driver's side door between the window glass and the outside frame. Seconds later I had the lock undone and pulled the slim jim out. After one more look around, I opened the door and slid inside, leaving the door ajar and telling Newt to sit and stay.

There was a lingering odor in the truck's cab that I recognized as eau de Marty. Several papers were spread out on the front seat and across the dash, and I wondered if Marty had left them like that or if the police had sorted through them and left them all askew. Had they slim-jimmed their way into the truck the same way I had? I sifted through the papers and found electric bills, grocery coupons, store receipts, a pay stub for Marty's federal pension, and a receipt for a bank deposit that showed a balance of more than two hundred grand. It surprised me, given the way he lived, but then again, his lifestyle *was* relatively simple. He didn't have much to spend money on other than his boat, the materials he needed for making his chairs, and maybe a payment on the land where his trailer sat, though he might have owned it outright by now.

Marty was a mystery, a dichotomy of lifestyles and habits that intrigued me. I wanted to get to know him better. I'd always been drawn to quirky, odd people the same way I was driven to find quirky, odd creatures. Or maybe it was the other way around and I was the one who was odd and quirky. I shoved that idea aside. Sometimes it's not wise to dig too deep into one's own psyche.

I dug into the glove box and the visors in the truck instead. I found nothing of interest until I pulled down the driver's side visor. Tucked up there was a warped, torn-off piece of envelope bearing a postmark from four days ago. Written beneath that postmark in the same heavy, angular scrawl that I recognized from the note that had come with my Adirondack chair was one word: *Plymouth.*

CHAPTER 16

———

The postmark on that envelope was from Saturday and I had gone out on the boat with Marty on Monday before any mail delivery would have arrived. He presumably had gone back out in his boat after the storm, but he might have waited it out by sitting in his truck. The ink in the word "Plymouth" had run slightly, and it hadn't rained on Saturday or Sunday, leading me to believe that Marty had jotted it down with wet hands after our excursion and while waiting out the storm. Could it have something to do with whatever it was Marty had seen on his sonar screen?

When I got back home, I showered and then climbed into bed with my laptop, searching for any references I could find for the word "Plymouth." There were a lot of them; I got twenty-eight pages of results. The top ones that weren't business names were entries for the car models made by Chrysler, a city named Plymouth in Wisconsin, another in Michigan, a third in Minnesota, and, of course, the more famous Plymouth in Massachusetts. There wasn't much I could do with the car. If Marty had written down the word because he saw a Plymouth that was somehow relevant, all I could do was keep my eyes open for one in the area. There were other cities named Plymouth in the country, but I figured it made sense to start with the ones that were geographically close.

Given that, I began my online research with Plymouth, Wisconsin, and learned that the city touted itself as the Cheese Capital of the World, so much so that the phrase had been trademarked. Given that the city was home to four large processing facilities that provided ten to fifteen percent of the nation's cheese, I supposed they were entitled to the title.

I also learned that Plymouth, Wisconsin, was once called Hub City because it was a major center for wooden wheelwrighting—the making or repairing of wooden wheels—a trade not much in demand these days. What's more, Plymouth, Wisconsin, was named after its more famous Massachusetts namesake because the folks who settled the area were from New England and wanted a touch of home. It was all fascinating stuff, and while I made a mental note to plan a trip there sometime in the future, I couldn't find anything that seemed relevant to the situation at hand.

I moved on to the other two nearby Plymouths—Michigan and Minnesota—and came up equally disappointed. Then I allowed myself to get lost for nearly two hours reading about Plymouth Rock, the *Mayflower* Pilgrims, and the Plymouth colony, including a delightful assortment of ghostly tales involving both the settlers and the Native Americans. I even succumbed to the lure of a link that led me to someone selling what they claimed was the skull of an original settler with a lead ball embedded in it. There was a picture that got me excited at first, but upon closer inspection, it looked like something that had been epoxied together.

Some of the other links I followed led me to gruesome yet oddly fascinating stories born out of the many deaths that had occurred among the early settlers. One detailed how the survivors, knowing they were vastly outnumbered and fearful the natives might attack if they realized that, attempted to hide the truth by smoothing down the mounds of graves and planting seeds on top of them. The stories didn't say if the settlers ate the produce that grew out of these body gardens, and I decided I didn't really want to know.

There was also a story about a storm in 1735 that led to flooding, erosion, and a river of human remains washing down one of the streets, and another about a house that the courts ruled legally haunted in the eighteenth century. I could have spent the entire night going down delightfully creepy Google rabbit holes and it was a struggle to break free. Before I did, I ran across someone who was selling a young girl's shoe that they claimed had been found inside the wall of one of the haunted houses in Plymouth. The price was reasonable, and the item clearly looked like an old-style shoe, though I realized it might have been artificially aged. I did a quick bit of research and learned that the practice of hiding things inside the walls of houses built during the seventeenth and eighteenth centuries was common. They were called spiritual middens and the Brits and other Europeans had been doing it since the fourteenth century. The shoe would make a nice addition to my store's inventory, so I bought it, knowing that if it turned out to be fake, it wouldn't be the first time I'd been taken in. It would sell regardless. It had a creepy look and an intriguing story to go with it (one that I would, of course, embellish a bit) and that's what most of my customers wanted.

anything that might further alienate Jon, I opted not to answer her question, going for a diversion instead.

"I talked with several of Oliver's friends who went on the trip with him, and they said that he seemed preoccupied this time out, like he was focused on other things. Did he talk to you at all before he left about anything that he planned to do while he was there?"

"I wish," she said, hurt and anger apparent in her voice. "Trust me, Oliver was distracted long before he went on that trip."

She paused for a few seconds, sucked in a shuddering breath, and then blurted out, "I think he might have been having an affair."

Oh, geez. This was going to be more awkward than I'd imagined.

"I'm sorry," I said. "That really sucks. What makes you think that?" She didn't answer me right away, so I quickly added, "I ask only because I've had similar concerns myself with the guy I'm living with."

That was a lie since I wasn't seeing, much less living, with anyone, but I figured a shared sense of misery wouldn't hurt. Newt was curled on the floor at my feet, and I saw him raise his head, his ears pricked forward. I shook my head to let him know I wasn't referring to him and he settled his head back onto his paws.

"Oh, the usual things," Bess said wearily. "It's so easy to see it all in hindsight. Oliver lost his job a few months ago and he got depressed. Then he began spending more time away from home, claiming he was job hunting or going out with the guys for a drink. When he was home, he was on his computer constantly, again supposedly for the purposes of job hunting. But if I came into a room, he'd close his laptop so I couldn't see what he was doing. I overheard him on the phone talking to one of the guys on the trip before he left, and he was telling him how he was going to need some space while they were there and

not to be offended if he tried to go off on his own some of the time."
She paused and sighed. "I don't know if it was someone who lives in
Door County or if he arranged for her to be there at the same time so
they could hook up."

She sounded so sad and dejected, I felt heartsick for her, though
that was tempered by the excitement I felt over the fact that her revelations were providing me with another clue. If Oliver had had a secret girlfriend, had she somehow played a role in what had happened
to him?

"Bess, do you have any idea who this woman was?" I asked.

There was such a long pause I thought our call had been disconnected. "Bess? Are you still there?"

"I'm here. Sorry. It's just that when you asked me that, I realized
why you asked it. Clearly there was something about Oliver's death
that was unusual. Do you think this girl he was seeing did something
to him? Is she one of those black-widow women or something like
that?"

"No, no, no, Bess," I said, frantic to get her off that train of thought
before it ran completely off the rails. "That's not why I was asking
at all. I just thought that if he was meeting someone up here, she
might be able to shed some light on what he was doing and where he
went. Maybe she witnessed something or knows something about his
death that might help the police with their investigation."

Another pause followed, but this time I heard her breathing and
knew she was still on the line. I figured she was putting all the pieces
together the best she could and feared what she might come up with
in the end.

"Why is it again that the police are investigating Ollie's death?"
she asked.

There was a notable softening in her tone that, along with her use of Oliver's nickname, suggested she'd already forgiven him for his suspected transgression.

"It's just that where they found him didn't make a lot of sense because of where he put in and what he'd told his friends he was doing. He probably just changed his mind."

"Or he lied because he was going to meet with *her* and didn't want his friends to know," Bess grumbled, though the earlier anger I'd heard was gone from her voice. All that remained was sad resignation. And grief.

"Any idea who this 'her' might be?" I asked again.

"No, but I think she might live in Plymouth."

That got my attention. "Why is that?"

"Because I found it written on a scrap of paper that he'd torn up and tossed out. One piece of it slipped out of his hand and went under the table and he didn't see it. I picked it up later when I was sweeping and saw that it said 'Plymouth.'"

"That's all that was on the paper, just the word 'Plymouth'?"

"That's the only full word that was on it. There was a letter W after the word and the letter S before it. I figured the W was for 'Wisconsin.' I know a lot about Plymouth, Wisconsin, because my uncle works at one of the cheese-processing plants up there. I figured the S was part of an address, or maybe the last letter in her name."

"Bess, do you have Oliver's laptop?"

"No. I asked his mother if I could have it and she said it was collected by the police and never given back. I couldn't get into it anyway. He had it password protected, and I have no idea what his password was. I'm not proud of admitting this, but I did try several times to guess it before he left on the trip. That's another reason why I thought he might be having an affair. He'd never password protected his computer before."

"I'm really sorry you've had to go through all this," I told her. "I know how hard it must be for you. Thanks for talking to me, and if there's anything I can do for you, please don't hesitate to call."

After I gave her my cell number, she said, "I miss him so much."

I understood her grief. "I know."

"I hope whatever you discover makes you happy."

For a second, I thought she was referring to my hunt for the lake monster and I said, "I'm not sure which answer will make me happy."

"You're not married to your guy, are you?"

For a second, old anxieties and fear made my heart pound and little lights pulse in my peripheral vision. Then I remembered that all of that was in the past. Except for the fact that David had never been caught.

"No, not married, thank goodness," I said, once again grateful for the narrow escape I'd had.

"Good. I hope it works out for you."

Too late.

"Thanks for listening to me. It felt good to vent."

"Happy to oblige," I said. "We women have to stick together."

"Ain't that the truth!" She let out a pained laugh.

I laughed, too, but mine sounded forced. There was nothing about any of this that was remotely funny.

CHAPTER 17

After my call to Bess, I placed one to Jon Flanders.

"Hey, you must have ESP because I was just about to call you," he said when he answered.

"Are you saying you believe ESP exists?"

"I'm open to many things," he said in a mock creepy voice. "Have you ever looked into it?"

"Not me personally, but my parents did once."

"Of course, they did." His tone was teasing with a soupçon of sarcasm.

"I went along with them, though all I did was watch from the sidelines."

"What was the situation?"

"Someone wanted to know if a particular prognosticator was for real. The woman claimed she could read minds or rather receive thoughts from people, even when they weren't nearby."

"And who was it that wanted to know if she was for real?" Before I could answer, he said, "Wait. Let me guess. It was the adult child of some rich elderly person who was spending the child's inheritance on predictions."

The amusement in his voice made it clear he thought the situation had been farcical at best and a bad con at worst. I hated to burst his bubble. No, wait. That's not true. I didn't hate it at all.

"It was someone in the CIA."

My answer was met with several seconds of silence before Jon said, "The CIA?"

"Yep."

Another silence. Then: "You're yanking my chain now, aren't you?"

"I'm not. But you have to swear you'll never tell anyone. That's the deal. Not that anyone would believe you anyway. Heck, you don't believe it yourself."

"Yeah, well, I didn't believe in giant lake monsters either until a few weeks ago. Tell me."

"This woman named Sylvia claimed that she was picking up the thoughts of two foreign men who were plotting against the United States. She had visions of giant aerial bombs raining down on New York and Washington, DC. These thoughts also involved threats to attack our emergency systems and shut everything down. Sylvia put her visions in a letter addressed to the man who was president at that time and stated that she often received random thoughts like this, but never any so destructive or threatening. The date of her letter was August 23, 2001."

I paused, waiting to see if Jon would figure it out. He did quickly, which I liked. "And then 9/11 happened," he said.

"Yes. Sylvia's letter wasn't read until weeks after that. As you can imagine, letters to the president don't arrive on the actual president's desk very often, if at all. In fact, there's no way for me to know if he ever saw this one. Plus, there was the whole anthrax-in-the-mail scare that followed, slowing mail down even more. But when someone on the staff finally got and read Sylvia's letter, it was sent up some chain of command and the FBI showed up on her doorstep. They did an in-depth investigation into her, checking out all her contacts and acquaintances, interviewing neighbors and old school chums, digging through her computer files and every paper in her house. There wasn't a single connection they could find, or any hint of involvement with the culprits, though there were several people more than willing to label Sylvia as a kook. But given the perceived accuracy of her prediction, apparently someone in the CIA wanted to know if there was any way Sylvia was legit."

"Perceived accuracy?" Jon said, and I had to smile. He didn't miss much.

"Yes. It's easy to make the pieces fit in hindsight, particularly if you're looking for them. But Sylvia's prediction was based on common sense and logic. If a terrorist wanted to cause maximum disruption and chaos to our country, the two ideal primary targets are our financial center and our government. Most high school kids know that New York City and DC are the most likely terrorist locations for that very reason. There was a lot in Sylvia's prediction that was wrong. There were no aerial bombs raining down, but on the heels of 9/11, it was easy to interpret that statement in a way that fit what happened. And her comment about the disruption of the emergency systems—another commonly considered target for terrorists—was later interpreted to mean nine-one-one."

"Did Sylvia claim that was the meaning behind these thoughts?"

"Of course, she did. She capitalized on it right away. She took the stigma of the FBI visits and turned it into positive advertising, claiming that she was so good, the US government used her. She started traveling and doing these shows all over the country where she supposedly picked up the thoughts of people in the audience."

"Did your parents debunk her?"

"They did, as much as anyone could. They uncovered a host of hired helpers who mingled with the audiences before and during the shows, picking up bits of conversation that could then be used by Sylvia to claim she was reading someone's thoughts. They had tiny microphones, and Sylvia wore an earpiece that was virtually invisible. And again, if you watch these charlatans at work, you'll see that they're great at reading people's body language and facial expressions while they make vague generic guesses as to the meaning of the thoughts they've supposedly picked up. Sylvia was quite good, one of the best. But she wasn't good enough to fool my parents."

"Did they run her out of the business?"

"Heck no. There's an endless supply of gullible, desperate, and lonely people out there who are more than willing to plunk down their hard-earned cash in order to visit one of these frauds. Sylvia kept at it for another nine years after that. Then she had a stroke and lost her ability to speak. She spent the last five years of her life in a nursing home."

"That's kind of sad."

"I suppose, though it's hard for me to feel sorry for people like Sylvia who prey on people's vulnerabilities and weaknesses."

"Understandable. It seems we got sidetracked here. I'm guessing the life and times of Sylvia aren't the reason you called me."

"No, it's not. But first, I'm assuming there's no news regarding Marty since I haven't heard anything?"

There was an uncomfortably long hesitation before he said, "Sorry, no."

"Okay. Then I'm wondering if the police checked the GPS on whatever cars Will and Oliver were using when they were here."

"Checked it for what?"

"For where they went. Did they have GPS capabilities?"

"I think so. Both victims had newer model cars. Why?"

"I want to know if either of them drove to Plymouth, Wisconsin, recently, not necessarily while they were here in Door County but in the weeks or months before that."

More silence and my mind filled in the sound of wheels and cogs spinning inside of Jon's head as he tried to deduce the meaning behind my request. I could have filled him in and explained myself, but I was rather enjoying being one step ahead of him.

"Okay, I give," he said finally. "What's so special about Plymouth, Wisconsin?"

"Well, for one thing, they make a *lot* of cheese there. Did you know they are *the* Cheese Capital of the World?"

"I did not. And somehow, I don't think that has anything to do with why you're interested in the city of Plymouth, though I do love cheese. It's been one of the best things about my move here."

"I love cheese, too. We should go there sometime and check it out."

"It's a date," he said.

Another awkward silence followed wherein I suspect both of us were contemplating the hidden meaning behind his comment.

I cleared my throat and then told him about the piece of envelope I'd found in Marty's truck.

"You were in Marty's truck?" he said. He didn't sound at all happy about it.

"It was unlocked so it's not like it was a secure site or anything," I lied, hoping he wouldn't know if it had been or not. "I'm sure you or the local guys have already been in it, haven't you?"

He sighed and then cagily avoided answering my question. "Just because Marty wrote a word on a piece of paper doesn't mean it has any significance," he said.

"Except Oliver's girlfriend told me that she thought Oliver might have been having an affair, and recently, when she was sweeping in the room he used as an office, she found a torn piece of paper that also had the word 'Plymouth' written on it. No other words, but she said there was a W after the word and an S before it. She assumed the W meant 'Wisconsin' and deduced from that that the woman he was seeing was from there. I know it's not the greatest of connections but it's more than I had yesterday. So I was wondering if it would be possible to check the GPS on Oliver's car and see if he'd been to Plymouth. And maybe you could check his phone records to see if he called anyone from there? Then we could check the same things for Will to see if he has any connections to the city or maybe to this mystery woman."

I paused, a little out of breath from talking too fast, and said, "There has to be a connection between these two guys, don't you think?"

"Morgan, you're supposed to be finding out if there is a lake monster out there that could be responsible for these deaths, not doing police work. If either of the men had a cell phone with them, it's presumably at the bottom of the lake now, because no phones were ever found." He paused, sighing. "And I'll check to see if the lab can access the GPS in Oliver's car. But you need to leave the police work to the police. That's not what I'm paying you for. And if you're not careful, you could end up compromising the investigation. You need to stay in your lane."

"Stay in my lane? Is that some sort of lame police metaphor?"

"Morgan . . ." He sounded tired and cautious. But I wasn't ready to give in yet.

"I happen to think that finding a human cause for what happened to those guys, if there is one, *is* in my lane," I argued. "Can you tell me that the police have anything better in the way of clues?"

There followed a telltale silence, and I knew I had him, though it didn't give me quite the level of satisfaction I'd hoped for.

"I admit, what you uncovered might be useful," Jon said finally. "I spoke to Oliver's girlfriend myself back when it happened, and she didn't tell me she suspected him of having an affair."

"That's because you're a man," I told him. "And a cop. That's a bad combination for soliciting female confidences."

"Hunh. Maybe that's why . . ." He drifted off, not finishing the sentence, though I desperately wanted him to.

I started to prompt him but before I could, he said, "Reviewing any GPS history in the cars will take a while. I think they already have the phone records though, so that one should be easy."

"And their computers," I said. "Do you guys have their computers?"

"I think the sheriff's department has them," Jon said, "though they might have gone with the evidence techs to their lab. I don't have much storage for that kind of stuff on the island. I know they said Oliver's laptop was password protected and none of his relatives knew what the password was. I don't think anyone pursued it because it didn't seem relevant to what happened."

"Any way you could get ahold of Oliver's laptop and let Devon take a crack at it? The guy is a wonder when it comes to that kind of stuff."

"Why?"

"We can search through his emails and internet history to see if there's anything related to Plymouth."

Jon sighed. "I'll see what I can do, Morgan, but I think you're putting an awful lot of stock into something kind of random."

"I don't think it's random at all that both Oliver Sykes and Marty wrote down the word 'Plymouth.' Besides, do you have any better ideas?"

He did not and I mentally added a point to my column in the scoreboard I kept in my head.

CHAPTER 18

———

Those glowing eyes I'd seen in the water the other day were still haunting me and it was time for me to do my own research. I left Devon and Rita to handle things in the store and went upstairs to dig up information on lake monsters from the rather extensive resource library I had there. In addition to a variety of articles and books, my resources included personal notes, thoughts, and observations, both mine and those my parents had accumulated over the years.

My mother had homeschooled me, so it's no surprise, given the shared interests she and my father had, that my education had a strong emphasis on the animal sciences and mythology. It was probably a good thing I hadn't attended a regular school, because most people thought my parents were eccentric, weird, and, as one sweet British lady put it, "a bit daft." Their reputations often trickled down to me and that sometimes complicated my life. I did attend an expensive private boarding school for a year, I think to assuage some guilt my parents felt over my lack of a "normal" childhood, not that boarding schools provide that. Rich kids are just as mean and cliquey as public school kids—maybe more so—and even though my folks were members of the wealthy elite like most of the other parents at the private school, their unusual hobbies and interests were determined too "out there" for them to be included in any of the social outings or other gatherings attended by the rest of the "in" crowd. They weren't invited to parties, dinners, or nights out at the theater, and I wasn't invited to visit or spend any of the weekends or vacation times with any of my schoolmates like the other girls in my class were. Should anyone question my family's exclusion from the inner circle, one of the other parents would simply raise their eyebrows and say something like, "Go visit their store, Odds and Ends, and check out the inventory. Then get back to me."

I don't think anyone ever did—get back to anyone, that is. Several of them did come into the store, though, and they didn't just check out the inventory; they gaped, gawked, and gasped with looks that ranged from disgust and disdain to abject horror, though one or two stared at certain objects with curiosity and something akin to longing, not that they ever would have given in to their desires. Many of the parents who came in never made it past Henry, which might have hurt his feelings if he'd had any.

My parents might have seemed odd to those people, but given that those other parents spent hours on a golf course trying to hit a little white ball into a hole for fun, or dressing in uncomfortable clothes and mingling at various charity events while eating and drinking away lots of potential donation money, I don't think they had room to criticize. I'd much rather spend my day bouncing over the waves of Loch Ness or tromping up the side of a snowy mountain in search of a giant ape-man than doing any of those other things.

My parents weren't snubbed all the time. There were, and still are, plenty of like-minded people out there. While much of academia scoffs at the idea of crytpids, there are also some highly intelligent people who are at least open-minded enough to entertain the possibility that they exist. How can one not believe when looking at something like the coelacanth? It's not unreasonable to think that there might be living creatures out there that we haven't discovered yet, and the seas and lakes of the world—some of them with unreachable depths, underwater caves, and uncharted tunnels—are some of the last great unexplored places on our planet.

My parents dedicated a disproportionate amount of their time, effort, and money to the pursuit of Nessie and her ilk. That was because, to my way of thinking—and theirs—sea and lake "monsters" are the most likely of all the cryptids to exist. There are hundreds of stories, going back centuries, in which such creatures have been sighted and described with strikingly similar characteristics by people who lived on different continents and had no way of communicating with one another. There have been multiple sightings by rational, reasonable people who not only had nothing to gain by reporting what they saw, but who all too often ended up being ridiculed and derided.

Of course, the pendulum of belief swung both ways. There were plenty of hoaxers out there looking for notoriety or a chance to make a quick buck. And there was no escaping the fact that despite plenty of rational scientific theories about what these creatures might be and how they could have existed undiscovered for thousands, even millions of years, there was no definitive proof that they did. No bodies, or parts of bodies, have ever been discovered.

There was no denying that the odds of Nessie-like creatures existing were long, but I remained open to the possibility. I've always been a skeptic, however, and I knew that many of the reported sightings had much simpler and more sensible explanations. Water and light can play tricks on your eyes and mind. A bit of debris or a rogue wave can look like a humped sea serpent under the right conditions. How many times had my heart skipped a beat because my brain briefly interpreted something I saw as something I wanted to see rather than what was actually there?

I've always approached the hunt with my skeptic's point of view firmly in place, though after my glimpse of those glowing eyes in the lake the other day, on the heels of seeing the bite marks on the victims, I was struggling to keep my hopes in check. I needed to reassess, read over relevant notes my parents had jotted down over the years, and review some of the scientific articles hypothesizing the existence of such creatures.

In the apartment above the store was a room that my parents had used as an office. An antique wooden partners desk sat in the middle of it—a behemoth made from oak with drawers on both sides and a surface marred by scratches, glass rings, and tiny dents. I had many fond memories of watching my parents at that desk engaging in lively, sometimes heated debates with each other.

Back then, the top of the desk would have been covered with papers, books, magazines, and the beverage-filled glasses that had left those rings. Now its surface was clear of anything but dust, though this was in sharp contrast to the rest of the room, which was a disorganized-looking mess that somewhat resembled the inside of Marty's trailer, though without the ambient aromas. There were boxes overflowing with books; manila folders and envelopes stacked up against the walls, many of them leaking papers; four tall metal filing cabinets that I knew were full and whose tops were covered with more boxes and papers; three bookcases with books and papers and the odd tchotchke stuffed into every available nook and cranny; and pictures, maps, and posters hanging on all the walls. This office was its own encyclopedic library filled with everything and anything one might want to know about cryptids, mysticism, ESP, and other mysteries of life and death. Despite the disorganized appearance, I knew where most things were because I'd spent hours as a child exploring every square inch of the room and its contents.

After my parents died, I stopped using the room for the most part, only going in when I absolutely had to and then making quick work of it. The sight of that desk made me feel the loss of them all over again, and I tended to behave like an ostrich when it came to facing my grief.

That day's incursion into the hallowed hall was no different. I kept my eyes averted from the desk as I walked over to one of the filing cabinets and opened the top drawer. Information on sea and lake monsters was in the top three drawers, and I sifted through folders and papers, pulling some out, bypassing others. When I had what I wanted from the top drawer, I moved on to the other two drawers and did the same, building a pile on the floor. Finally, I went to one of the bookcases and, after a thoughtful perusal of the titles, removed five books.

I carried everything out to the living room in two trips, piling it all on the coffee table, where some of the folders slipped and slid onto the floor. Then I went downstairs and got my laptop from the store office and brought it up. My plan was to settle in on the couch to wade through it all, but then another idea came to me. I dragged the Adirondack chair that Marty had gifted to me into the living room, setting it on the other side of the coffee table and tossing a couple of throw pillows onto it. Finally, I made myself a cup of coffee, curled up in Marty's chair, and started reading.

I began with a quick review of the geography of the Great Lakes—particularly Superior, Huron, and Michigan—and some speculative articles regarding the geography we can't see, like certain caverns, particular areas of the lake bottoms, and what might lie beneath them. My parents had accumulated an impressive collection of these geographical studies and maps—some of them rendered by amateur geographers or laypeople, while others were professionally drafted from whatever modern-day technologies were available at the time.

Lake Superior lives up to its name as it's the largest and deepest of the lakes with an average depth of five hundred feet and a maximum depth of 1,335 feet. It is also the coldest of the lakes with a water temperature that rarely makes it into the fifties. Glacial activity during the Ice Age carved much of the area's topography and it also played a significant role in the creation of the lakes as well as the many underwater tunnels and caverns. Because of all these things, most of the scientific hypotheses regarding Nessie-type creatures in the Great Lakes list Superior as the most likely home base. When people drown in Lake Superior, the water temperature prevents the buildup of the bacteria that causes a dead body to swell with gas. As a result, the bodies often sink, never to be seen again. It's not a big step from that to an assumption that the bodies of any creatures living in those depths would do the same, thus explaining why one has never been found.

Sightings on a lake are harder to explain away than those at sea, because lakes aren't subject to the same tidal actions. They are, however, subject to something called "seiche," a word from the French that means "back-and-forth swaying." Seiche occurs because of the natural buildup of water on one side of a body of water, which then sloshes its way back toward the other side. It happens all the time because of the effects of wind, boats, wildlife, and other things, and while the resultant waves are generally small, they have been known to get big enough to capsize a ship, particularly when they are storm driven. Given that, it isn't much of a stretch to think that some of the reported sightings over the centuries have been optical illusions caused by seiche activity.

While Lake Superior might serve as home base for those creatures because of its size, depth, and the fact that it's the last of the lakes in a chain, all the lakes are interconnected and lead to the ocean, making it easy to envision these creatures migrating from one body of water to another. Some believe that Loch Ness, another deep glacial creation, has subterranean tunnels and caves that connect it to oceanic waters. The theory I personally favor suggests that Nessie lives in oceanic waters most of the time, in underground caverns that are hundreds, maybe thousands of feet deep. During certain times of the year when freshwater food sources that these creatures consider delicacies become plentiful, they swim through these underground highways and into the lakes to feed. That could have been when some of the more credible sightings have occurred.

With the Great Lakes, the ocean connection is more obvious as all the lakes are connected to one another and to the sea via the Saint Lawrence Seaway. While that would be a long and treacherous trek for a creature—particularly one rumored to be as large as Nessie—to take in modern times, ten thousand years ago, when glacial advance and retreat was shaping and forming the Great Lakes, those creatures could have ventured into the lake basins and then become trapped. Forced to adjust or die, they found ways to exist in their new, freshwater environment.

From that, one can conclude that while there is no absolute proof these creatures exist, there is also no scientific reason why they can't from an environmental and geographical perspective. It is this potential—something my mother called "plausible existability"—that drove my parents to keep searching. And it's what keeps me following in their footsteps.

After reviewing the literature and reassuring myself of plausible existability, I moved on to the science—the biology and zoology that are my areas of expertise—and the glowing eyes that I'd seen in the water. I'd been mulling over the significance of those glowing orbs ever since I saw them, trying to rationally explain them with the science I knew. There are creatures capable of bioluminescence—the ability to produce and emit light, like a firefly—as well as creatures capable of biofluorescence—the ability to absorb sunlight and then emit it back as a different color. Hundreds of animals, including humans, have eyes that can reflect light back in colors—witness the dreaded red-eye of photography—but there aren't many animals with eyes that glow like headlights. The fact that these had glowed supported my hypothesis that sea serpents, if they exist, most likely live in the deepest, darkest depths. While many denizens of the deepest waters are often blind or completely lacking eyes because the blackness around them makes the ability to see useless, the need to navigate through dark underwater tunnels might have triggered the evolutionary result of eyes that function like headlights. It made perfect sense.

Still, it was a hard sell. Most theorists have speculated that a form of inner sonar—much like the echolocation that bats, dolphins, and whales use—is the more likely method of navigation to have evolved, but glowing eyes weren't beyond the realm of possibilities. There are other examples of this in nature, such as the flashlight fish, which has pockets beneath its eyes filled with bioluminescent bacteria that can not only emit light but flash in communicative patterns.

It all added up to plausible existability.

Growing up, I'd seen how my parents changed whenever they caught the fever, watched as the excitement took them over and made them forget about everything else, including me at times. I didn't understand it then, but I came to. My glimpse of those two glowing eyes had been ever so brief and inconclusive, but it had triggered a fever inside me. Adding to it was my certainty that Marty had seen something at the same time. Had he gone out again to explore further? And had that exploration cost him his life? In all the sightings over the centuries, records or reports of lake monsters attacking people were incredibly rare and subject to skepticism and far more plausible explanations. So what had happened to Marty? And to Oliver Sykes and Will Stokstad?

That thought brought me to the part of the case that made me cast doubt on plausible existability. I looked at the collection of speculative papers I'd removed from the file cabinet, including several written by world-renowned zoologists and biologists, and one written five years earlier by a cryptid hunter with a questionable reputation. They all touted two main theories of what a Nessie-type creature might be: a surviving remnant of the prehistoric plesiosaurs assumed to have gone extinct millions of years ago, or a type of giant eel, most likely from the moray family.

I'd always favored the plesiosaur theory myself because the physical characteristics, as well as the described behaviors from sightings around the world and across the centuries, matched up better with the prehistoric creatures. There had been some reported land sightings, and if those were to be believed, the eel theory didn't fit. Plus, it made sense to me that a prehistoric creature assumed to be extinct might have survived by living in caverns and caves deep down in the waters, much like the coelacanth had.

Yet there was one thing that didn't fit either hypothesis: those tooth impressions. The bites appeared to have been inflicted by flat-surfaced molar teeth, the kind used for grinding rather than the tearing of flesh, yet both the eels and the plesiosaurs have, or had, sharp, flesh-tearing teeth. It was highly unlikely that the creatures, if they existed, were mammals, though I supposed they could have some biological similarities to whales. In fact, perhaps sightings of these creatures over the years had been of whales. But there were no whales I knew of that had teeth like the ones that made the bite impressions on Oliver and Will. The teeth of land mammals tend to be specialized, allowing them to catch prey and tear their food, and the teeth of the upper jaw generally mesh well with those of the lower jaw to facilitate chewing. Toothed whales have teeth that don't fit together because they don't chew; they swallow the prey they catch whole. Other species of whale have baleen rather than teeth, screens that filter water as they swim and capture tiny plankton and other organisms. The teeth of whatever had bitten those men appeared to be all molars, and that made no sense at all.

Even so, I felt the fever inside me climb.

CHAPTER 19

—

I awoke a little after six the next morning—my usual waking time no matter how late I stay up—after a night filled with dreams in which I swam alongside large, graceful plesiosaurs. I was still in Marty's Adirondack chair, the throw pillows haphazardly tucked here and there and the books, papers, and articles I'd been reading scattered around me on the floor. Newt was asleep at my feet atop a spilled pile of magazines, but as soon as I stirred, he was up and staring at me, tongue lolling, tail wagging, knowing that a walk was imminent. I patted him on the head, got out of the chair, stretched to work out some of the kinks from my awkward sleeping position, and headed for my bedroom, where I changed out of my clothes, slipped on a bathing suit, and then put my clothes back on.

I slipped Newt's flotation vest on him and he started dancing in front of me, trying unsuccessfully to contain his anticipation because he knew what the vest meant. I saw my cell phone on the coffee table and cursed to myself when I realized I'd forgotten to plug it in last night. Sure enough, the battery had only eight percent left on it, so I hooked it up to a charger on a side table. Newt watched me with tail-wagging impatience as I picked up my keys from this same table and slipped them into my pocket. When I grabbed the leash from where it hung on the coat tree beside the door, Newt lost the last of his restraint. He started jumping and twirling in circles, making excited whimpering noises. I stood to one side as he bolted past me and down the stairs, stopping at the door at the bottom. He whined as he waited for me to descend and undo the dead bolt, and then dashed through the open door, barreling through the store toward the back entrance. By the time I caught up to him and hooked the leash to his vest, he was a quivering mass of tensed muscles ready to spring.

"Let's go easy," I told him. "No ripping my arm out of its socket, okay?"

He wagged his tail and grinned at me. I undid the dead bolt and opened the door, bracing myself. Newt dashed outside, giving my arm a hearty yank, but I managed to hang on to both the leash and my arm. The back door automatically locked when it closed, but I gave the knob a quick check to be sure.

The first walk of the day was the only time Newt behaved like a maniac, and even then only when he knew we were going to the beach. It was as if being inside all night led to a buildup of energy that he simply couldn't contain. Once we were outside and he'd sniffed around the area behind the store, peed enough to mark the territory as still his, and had his morning poo, he was a fearless and eager explorer, pulling me toward the water.

Newt loved the beach with its myriad smells and the waves that washed up to his nose, carrying who knew what in its foam and bubbles. Sometimes he would try to bite the waves, but when the winds were strong and the waves big, he would charge into them as they crashed onto the shore, the sheer joy he experienced at doing that obvious on his face as he emerged from the water dripping wet. I loved the water as much as he did, and thanks to lessons I'd had as a child, I was a strong swimmer and diver. During a trip to Hawaii when I was a teenager, I'd even learned to free dive and could easily hold my breath for a full two minutes and change. The key, the free diver who taught me had said, was to hyperventilate beforehand.

When my father bought the warehouse that became the store and my apartment, it had come with an easement that provided access to the bay. That time of the year, the bay water was a comfortable eighty degrees, and as long as there were no algae blooms, Newt and I often started our days with a swim.

The water was clear, and after taking off my outer clothes and wading out to thigh-deep water, I plunged in, relishing the cool feel of it on my skin. I've always loved the water. Maybe being born on a boat in the middle of a Scottish loch had something to do with it, but lakes, rivers, ponds, and oceans have always had a strong pull for me.

I swam hard toward the middle of the bay, toward the Upper Peninsula of Michigan, Newt swimming beside me. Before Newt had come into my life, I used to swim out a lot farther, but because Newt insisted on being at my side even when swimming, I altered my routine when he started coming with me. We gradually worked up to a mile out and a mile back with him wearing his flotation vest, but that was where I'd set the limit. Newt was a good swimmer, but I didn't want to push him too hard.

After our swim, I sat on a log with Newt at my feet and stared out over that vast body of water, thinking about all the life teeming beneath those gentle waves. Then I tried to envision a giant creature swimming just under the surface, dark, menacing, and hostile, but this image was so contrary to what I'd always assumed such a creature would be that I immediately shook it off.

I returned to an earlier idea I'd had that might explain things better. Had a mother creature given birth in these waters and then been forced to protect her young from some real or perceived threat? Would the plesiosaurs of prehistoric times have attacked a human, had we coexisted back then? No way to be sure without a time machine and a rather dicey experiment, but again my gut said no. Their heads and mouths were small in comparison to their body size, their bite not that large. Could they have evolved into a creature with a larger head and bite? They could have, but that, too, felt wrong to me. Their regular food sources wouldn't have required it.

I felt like I was trying to solve a puzzle and all the pieces were there; they just weren't fitting together right. Or perhaps the pieces from one puzzle had gotten mixed in with another and I had to sort them into their proper, respective piles. I desperately wanted to talk it all out with someone who would understand the issues the way I did. But the only people I knew who could have done that were my parents, and they were gone.

The walk home was a somber one, and when I unlocked the back door and entered the store, I was struck with a wave of longing for my parents so intense that for a moment I felt like I couldn't breathe. Tears burned and then filled my eyes and Newt, sensing my emotional shift, sniffed at my hand, then pushed his head against it, forcing me to pet him. He turned around and did it again and the second time I let my fingers dig into his thick, soft fur. I sank to the floor and sobbed, my arms around Newt's shoulders, my face buried in his neck, my tears wetting his fur.

The grief flowed out of me in a way it never had in the two years since my parents' deaths. It was as if something had reached inside me and ripped the lid off the box where I'd kept the sadness locked away. I was all shuddering breaths, snotty sniffles, and flooding tears that I couldn't control because, once the box was opened, I couldn't push the emotions back into it. Newt pressed his warm body into mine, shoring me up with his strength while mine drained away. I don't know how long we stayed there on the floor, but when my sobs finally petered out, I felt so spent, I wasn't sure I could get back up to my apartment.

I managed it, Newt at my side the entire time, and when we reached the top, he looked up at me and whimpered. Those soulful brown eyes of his gave me strength and I patted him on the head and told him, "I'm okay, Newt. I promise. I'm okay."

I went to the kitchen and got him a treat. Then I showered, dressed, and fixed myself some toast and scrambled eggs for breakfast. The tasks helped to ground me, and by the time I sat down to eat, I felt better, stronger. My mind felt more focused, and I knew it was time to regroup. I needed to get back out on the water, even if it meant doing it on my own. Marty had seen something that day on his sonar screen, and I had seen those two glowing greenish yellow orbs. There was something in the water; of that, I was certain. I just had to figure out what.

It was a few minutes before opening time when I finished washing my dishes, so Newt and I went downstairs and I unlocked the front door. Devon was pulling into the lot, and I waved at him. He was scheduled to help me until Rita came in at four. The way he burst through the door with a big smile on his face, I could tell something was up. I got excited, thinking he had finally found a connection between the two victims.

"What's got you looking so chipper this morning?" I asked.

"My staples," he said with a big grin.

That wasn't the answer I'd been expecting. I stared at him with a look of confusion, and he clarified.

"Anne is coming to check my wound," he said, pointing to his head. "She said she'd be happy to come by and do it."

"I see," I said, smiling back. His enthusiasm and good mood were contagious and just what I needed to shake off the lingering bits of my earlier sorrow. "That's nice of her," I added with a sly wink. I didn't think the wound needed to be checked and suspected Anne was using it as an excuse to see Devon again.

"Isn't she great?" Devon said.

He didn't look like he needed an answer, and I didn't give him one, assuming the question was rhetorical. He went behind the counter and slipped his tablet—a constant accessory—onto one of the shelves below. Then he turned on the store laptop and, as it was booting up, grabbed a feather duster and proceeded to start dusting items on the shelves. This surprised and amused me because Devon had never dusted anything that I knew of in all the years he'd worked at the store. It was like watching a Disney movie.

"When is Anne coming?" I asked, amused.

"Around ten."

Great. That meant I had two hours of giddy Devon to deal with.

"Have you had a chance to look into the Plymouth thing?"

If Anne had made her offer to come by around the time I'd asked Devon to do that bit of research, I figured it was a lost cause, because he would have been incapable of focusing on anything else. I had to hope he'd had a chance to delve into it before Anne turned his brain into mush.

"I haven't done much yet," he admitted. "But I'll try to get to it today." He paused then, feather duster held aloft, a ponderous look on his face. "Actually, there was something I came across on Oliver's Facebook memorial page last night that I was going to mention to you, but now I can't recall what it was."

He shrugged, smiled at me, and said, "No worries. It will come to me eventually and I remember thinking it was a long shot anyway."

His casual indifference annoyed me a little, but I brushed it aside. Devon was always willing and eager to do any of the research I asked of him, and he was good at digging up the goods, so much so that I made a mental note to give him a raise. His inability to focus today because of his giddy anticipation was too adorable to watch.

If I thought Devon was cute in the anticipatory stage, it was nothing compared to how he was when Anne showed up. Generally, Devon was a quiet, introspective person, a man of few words and even fewer emotive moments. Yet the second he saw Anne walk through the front door, he started gushing and jabbering, spinning around in place like he meant to do something but forgot what it was a nanosecond later, muttering a constant stream of babble, much of it either inaudible or nonsensical.

Anne, who remained as cool as the proverbial cucumber, finally got him to sit down, though she never did get him to shut up. He talked about the weather, about the store, about some news article he'd read that morning, and at least he was making sense and speaking audibly by then. His verbal diarrhea was cut short once when Anne poked at a still tender area of his head, making him wince, but he wasn't paused for long.

I kept hoping Devon would take the next step and ask Anne out, but he didn't—whether from a lack of courage or simple distractedness, I couldn't tell. In the end, it didn't matter because Anne took the plunge.

"I got off duty two hours ago," she told him. "Are you free at all today? I'd love to challenge you to a game of miniature golf at Pirate's Cove. And maybe we could grab a bite to eat later."

Devon frowned and looked at me. "I have to—"

"He's done in an hour," I said, jumping in.

"Great!" Anne said, clapping her hands together. "Why don't you meet me at Pirate's Cove at noon?"

"Okay," Devon said, looking a little shell-shocked.

"See you then," Anne said, and with that, she left the store.

Devon gave me a curious look.

"It's not a problem," I assured him, thinking that he was concerned about the change in his schedule. "Call Rita and see if she can come in early. If not, I'll manage fine on my own until four."

"Okay." He seemed distracted. Then his eyes widened and he looked pleased suddenly, but not for the reason I'd assumed. "I just remembered what it was I found on the memorial page for Oliver Sykes," he said. "When Anne mentioned Pirate's Cove, it came to me. There was a fellow named James Cochran who wrote a note about how he hoped Oliver had finally found that treasure he was looking for. It got me to thinking that maybe Oliver was into treasure hunting on the shipwrecks."

Interesting. "Can you get me contact information for this Cochran fellow?" I asked.

"Can do. Give me a few minutes."

True to his word, he handed me a slip of paper a few minutes later with Mr. Cochran's email address and phone number.

"A phone number? That was quick. You're good," I said.

Devon gave me a one-shoulder shrug. "The guy's a car salesman. That's his work number."

"Got it. Call Rita, okay?"

He nodded and I went into my office, Newt on my heels, as usual, shut the door, and dialed Mr. Cochran's number.

"Miller Auto, Jim Cochran."

"Hi, Mr. Cochran. My name is Morgan and I'm wondering if you have a minute or two to talk to me about Oliver Sykes."

He hesitated, the silence broken by bits of static. "Ollie? Horrible thing that happened to him. Just horrible."

"How did you know him?"

"We were college roommates. Why? Are you a cop? Because you kind of sound like one."

"No, but I'm interested in some things about Oliver's death that are troublesome."

"What do you mean, 'troublesome'?"

I sighed. This guy was going to be work. "You wrote something on his Facebook memorial page about how you hoped he'd found the treasure he was looking for. Why did you write that?"

"It was all I could think of to put down. I hate those funeral things, but I felt like I had to put something in there. Why? Did Bess get upset over it?"

"Not that I know of. What treasure were you referring to?" As I asked that, something niggled at the back of my brain.

"Nothing in particular. It was just that Ollie loved the idea of trying to find buried treasure. Even when he was a kid. He told me that he used to dig holes in his backyards, looking for things, and his mother would get rightly pissed off because they lived in rental houses." He paused and chuckled. "The last time I saw him, he casually mentioned something about treasure in Door County and that one of these days he was going to score big. I didn't put much stock in it because he's been talking like that for years with nothing to show for it except for a few dirty coins and tiny baubles."

"Did he talk about treasure hunting a lot?"

"No. In fact, he'd always been rather secretive on the topic. I found out about it when we were in college because we shared an apartment, and I found his stash by accident one day."

"His stash?"

"Yeah, he had a collection of stuff: books he bought about various legendary lost treasures, maps, a metal detector, copies of obscure historical documents he apparently requested from the library, several compasses, and this disk-shaped thing that I had no idea what it was. It was something called an astrolabe, an ancient astronomical navigational instrument. He had it all stashed away in a duffel bag that he kept under his bed. I found it by accident because I had to make an emergency trip out of town and needed a suitcase. I knew he had that duffel under his bed because I saw it when I vacuumed. I figured it was either empty or filled with weights and gym stuff he never used, but when I pulled it out and opened it up, I found all these fascinating things inside. Ollie found me sitting on his bedroom floor with the contents of that duffel bag all around me, so he had to come clean and tell me about his passion for treasure hunting, though I could tell he wasn't happy about having to share with me. He swore me to absolute secrecy, and he was quite emphatic about it. I don't think even Bess knew."

"Interesting. Any idea what he did with his duffel bag full of stuff?"

"I would imagine he had it in his house somewhere. Or maybe in a storage unit? I don't honestly know. Maybe Bess would have an idea."

I thanked him, told him I was sorry for his loss, and ended the call. Then I gave Bess Thornberg another call.

CHAPTER 20

⎯

If Bess was surprised to hear from me again so soon, she didn't let on. "Do you have more questions about Oliver?" she said.

"I do. I'm wondering if you know anything about an old duffel bag he had? It might have been something he tried to hide."

"You mean like a go bag?"

"No, more of a storage bag for a hobby he had."

"Hobby?" Bess sounded dubious. "The only hobby Oliver had was kayaking, if you can call that a hobby."

"He doesn't have a duffel stashed away in a closet or under a bed? Or maybe he was using something else, like a box of some sort?"

There was a long pause and then Bess said, "Where is this coming from, Ms. Carver?"

"It's Carter, and please, call me Morgan. Sorry to sound so mysterious. I just finished talking to a friend of Oliver's, his old college roommate, Jim Cochran?"

"Did he loan Oliver a duffel bag?"

"No, he said Oliver had a secret hobby and that there was a duffel he used to keep under his bed that was filled with some of the items related to this hobby. I was just wondering if you knew about anything like that."

"Secret hobby?"

She laughed and it did give me pause, making me wonder if I was building something out of nothing.

"What kind of secret hobby?"

I figured I might as well tell her. Beating around the bush wasn't working. "Treasure hunting." I tossed it out there and waited for her reaction.

"Oh, that," she said with relief. "Yeah, he has some stuff from when he was a kid and used to think he could find buried treasures. He drew maps and had a small shovel and some books, I think. And an old metal detector. He found some arrowheads, coins, and stuff like that but no real treasure that I know of."

"Is that stuff there at your place?"

"Not anymore. Oliver has a small unit at a storage facility that he uses to store his kayaks in the winter. His mother lives here in Green Bay, and when she sold her house and downsized a couple of years ago, she made him come and get some old boxes he'd had stored there for years. He didn't want to toss the stuff out, but we didn't have room for any of it in our apartment, so he put the boxes in the storage unit. I'm pretty sure the duffel bag is there, too."

"Do you have the key to the unit?"

"I don't. Oliver had it on his key ring with all his other keys and I'm not sure where they ended up. The cops might have them. Or they might have given them to his mother."

"Do you know the name of the storage facility?"

"Um . . . I think it's called Safe Storage? I've only been there once, and I sat in the car while Oliver got something out of the unit. I know it's on University Avenue here in Green Bay."

"Do you know the number of his unit?"

"Sorry, no," she said apologetically.

"How did he pay for it? Might there be a bill somewhere that would have the unit number on it?"

"You know . . . hold on."

I heard her walking across her apartment, the floor squeaking beneath her feet, and then the rustling of some papers. There was a clunking sound—her cell phone getting dropped onto a surface, perhaps—and then the sound of drawers opening and closing and more papers shuffling.

I'd resigned myself to failure when she picked up her phone and said, "Got it. It's number fifty-nine. And I was right about the name of the place. It's called Safe Storage."

I jotted the information down. "Thank you, Bess. That's a huge help. Sorry to have bothered you again."

I was about to end the call when she said, "Morgan, what's this got to do with Oliver's death?"

"I don't know, Bess. Maybe nothing. I'm just following some random ideas to see if they flesh out into anything." *Like a lake monster.*

"Will you let me know if they do?"

"I will."

I ended the call and then placed one to Jon Flanders. I expected to get his voice mail but was surprised when he answered.

"Chief Flanders."

"Jon, hi. It's Morgan. Any word on Marty?"

"No, I'm afraid not. I promise, I'll let you know as soon as there's any news."

"Okay. I had another reason for calling. I really need to get my hands on Oliver Sykes's keys. Do you know if the family has them or if the sheriffs kept them?"

"There was a set of keys he left behind at the house he and his pals rented, meaning the sheriffs probably have them. Technically they're evidence, and until the case is solved and closed, they will remain evidence."

"Any chance you can borrow them for a spell?"

"Why?"

"And can you also take a ride with me to Green Bay?"

"Not unless you tell me why."

"Oliver Sykes has a storage unit there I want to poke around in. It's at a place called Safe Storage on University Avenue in Green Bay. Unit number fifty-nine. His girlfriend told me he had some things in it that might be helpful."

"Like what?"

"Treasure maps?" I said in a tone of voice that let him know I knew this answer sounded silly.

He sighed. "Tell me the rest."

"Can I do it on the ride there?"

"Why can't you tell me now?"

"I'm trying to save you money. I told you what my hourly rate is, and I can spend your money telling you everything now over the phone or do it when you'll be spending it anyway taking me there. Up to you."

He sighed again and I sensed a hint of irritation to it. "I can't leave here for another hour and with the ferry ride . . . I can be at your store by four. And we'll have to stop in Sturgeon Bay to sign out the keys from the evidence locker there."

This trip would mean leaving Rita alone to manage the store for a few hours, but I knew she could handle it.

"I'll tell you what," I said. "If you do this with me, I won't start the clock until we get to the address in Green Bay and I'll bill only for the time that we're actually at the storage facility. Fair enough?"

"You drive a hard bargain, Morgan Carter," he teased.

I scoffed at that. "If you think that's bad, just try to talk me down in price for some of the more unique items here at the store."

"Like I'd buy anything from your store," he said, scoffing right back at me.

"You hurt my feelings, Chief Flanders."

"Yeah, well, turnabout is fair play. See you in a few."

With that, he ended the call, leaving me to wonder what he'd meant by that comment. After pondering it for a few minutes, I went out to the main part of the store, delighted to see that Rita had arrived already, though I was also surprised to see that Devon was still working, helping a lady choose some mysteries from the bookshelves. Devon's a natural salesman and well-read, and of the handful of books he recommended to the woman, she chose three. Once the woman carried her books over to Rita, who was manning the cash register, I pulled Devon aside.

"I told you that you can take the rest of the day off."

"I was going to, but Anne called a little bit ago and said she was going to cover some extra hours for a coworker who just called in sick, so our date has been postponed. I figured I might as well stay and work. Hope that's okay."

"Of course." He looked disappointed, but I had something I thought might cheer him up a little. "It's not only okay, it's a huge help to me. Can you stay until closing?"

He shrugged. "Sure."

"And as long as you're here, I have a new project for you."

That earned me his trademark cockeyed smile. "You've been all over the map with this case, Morgan. I barely have time to finish one project and you've got me working on another one."

"I know. I'm sorry. I'll pay you a bonus for all your extra work. It's just that I keep thinking there has to be a connection between these two men and I can't find it."

"Do you want me to abandon the Plymouth search?" he asked.

"No, I'm convinced it means something. I don't think it's a coincidence that both Marty and Oliver Sykes wrote it down. But put it on a back burner and work on this new idea for now. Oliver Sykes had an interest in treasure hunting. It might be that it's just something left over from when he was a kid, but given where we are and where these deaths occurred—"

"You're interested in any treasure that might have gone down with some of the hundreds of ships in Death's Door?"

"Yes. The more obscure, the better. If Oliver Sykes was truly invested in treasure seeking, he wouldn't have gone after the common ones that everyone else knows about because those, if they existed, would have been found and well picked over by now. He'd have gone after something few, if any, people know about, or something that's been searched for and never found."

"Finding something like that online could be a challenge," Devon said. "I'll have to search through message boards and chat rooms."

Despite the negativity of his words, there was a definite hint of excitement in his voice.

"Do you know if Oliver participated in any of those?"

Devon shook his head. "No, but it's the proverbial needle in a haystack. Now, if I had his personal computer, that would be a different story."

"I'm going to work on that," I said. "But do what you can in the meantime."

When Jon Flanders finally walked into my store, it was nearly four thirty. I was pacing with impatience, making Newt and my employees anxious. My gut told me I was on the right track with this treasure idea but when I tried to come up with a summary for Jon of what I'd done and found out so far, it sounded thinner than the air atop Mount Everest. All my scientific instincts told me there was no lake monster, at least not one that was killing people, yet I had no way to prove it. It's next to impossible to prove that something doesn't exist. What I had to do instead was to prove that whatever was behind these deaths had nothing to do with any creatures living in the lakes. That meant some basic detective work, though not necessarily in the police sense of the term, but rather what most scientists do when they try to prove or disprove a hypothesis. Unfortunately, some of my detective work required the assistance of the police, and they are notoriously close to the vest when it comes to sharing information and evidence.

Jon had arrived in his personal vehicle rather than a police car, though they looked the same to me except this one lacked the light bar and emblems on the doors. I fetched the strap from my car and clipped Newt into a seat belt latch in the back and then I sat in the front passenger seat.

Once we were underway, Jon informed me that he had some good news and some bad news. "And before you ask, the bad news isn't about Marty. I don't have any news on that topic other than the fact that he's still missing."

"In that case, I'll take the bad news first," I said.

"I can't get Oliver Sykes's keys from the evidence locker."

"Why not?"

"Because they aren't there."

"Where are they?"

"I have no idea."

"Okay. What's the good news?"

"I made some calls, pulled a few strings, helped a couple of speeding tickets disappear, and voilà! I got a search warrant for the storage unit. Not an easy thing to do, mind you, since I have no idea what it is we're searching for. All we'll need are the bolt cutters I have in the back."

He looked over at me expectantly, clearly pleased with himself.

"Too bad those storage units don't use regular door locks," I said. "If they did, I could probably pick it."

Jon shook his head vigorously as if trying to rattle something loose inside his skull. Then he said, "I don't want to know how you can do that, nor do I want to hear anything more on the topic. And I don't want you to tell me if you have lockpicks on you—"

He paused and narrowed his eyes at me. I smiled enigmatically, making him shake his head again.

"Just . . . just . . . don't," he said, showing me a palm.

"Okay," I said, shrugging one shoulder. "What, exactly, are we looking for according to your search warrant?"

"Did Oliver's girlfriend happen to mention that he'd lost his job several months ago?"

I shot him an annoyed look. "I hate it when people answer a question with a question. And yes, she mentioned it. She said he'd been depressed and that he'd started spending a lot of time online and away from home, supposedly for job-hunting purposes, though she thinks he had a secret lover. Did you guys find any evidence of that?"

"Of another girlfriend?" Jon shook his head. "Not that our guys found. But he did have a lot of debt. And he also had a friend with some serious drug connections. I was able to convince the judge who gave me the warrant that Oliver's death might have been at the hands of drug dealers he owed money to."

"I see," I said, though to be honest things were a bit murky. "So . . . what is it we're looking for, then?"

"Logbooks, balance sheets, anything that might be a record of drugs bought, drugs sold, money owed and to whom. That will allow us to search through boxes if there are any."

"What about a duffel bag?"

"Sure." He shot me a curious look. "You want to tell me what it is we're really looking for?"

"I told you. Treasure maps." I paused and then in a meek voice added, "I think."

He shot me another look, that one incredulous. I gave him a cheesy smile, flashing lots of teeth, and he looked away, running a hand through his hair.

"Christ, Morgan. You'd better have something more than that or I'm turning this car around right now."

"Technically, I don't, though I'm hoping we'll find more than just maps. A friend of Oliver's from his college days told me that Oliver had a fixation on buried treasure ever since he was a kid. He kept an old duffel full of articles, maps, tools, and other paraphernalia related to it hidden under his bed, and when this friend found it by accident and asked him about it, he said he realized how serious Oliver was on the topic by the reaction he got. He was expecting something dismissive or fun, you know, like a childhood fantasy that held fond memories. But what he got instead was an intense discussion and a promise not to tell a soul about it. Oliver's girlfriend knew about his childhood interest but didn't think it was something he still did. She said his treasure-hunting stuff was in a duffel bag that he kept in this storage unit."

"You're thinking Oliver Sykes might have been onto some kind of sunken treasure in Death's Door or the waters around it," Jon said, his voice flat.

"Yes! Exactly."

We were currently at a red light and Jon turned his head slowly to stare at me, the lips of his broad mouth pinched into a thin, hard line. "Please tell me you're kidding, Morgan."

"No, I'm not."

"Sunken treasure? You dragged me down here and made me cash in some valuable favors for some theory about sunken treasure?"

A loud honk came from behind us, letting us know the light had turned green. Jon tromped on the gas and the car lurched forward, making Newt let out a small whimper in the backseat.

"Hey, easy," I said, reaching over the seat and giving Newt a reassuring scratch beneath his chin. "Don't hurt my dog."

The sigh that followed was Jon's loudest and longest yet. "Sorry," he said. "I didn't mean to hurt him. It's just that the horn startled me and I'm feeling quite . . . exasperated right now."

I stared at him, feeling a little bad that I'd upset him. But only a little. Putting on my best smile, I said, "Does this mean now is a bad time to ask you if I can have Oliver's laptop so Devon can look it over?"

That was the day I learned that Jon knew how to swear in French.

chance something probative does turn up and your fingerprints are all over it, I'll have a hard time explaining it."

I put the gloves on and went straight for the duffel bag. It was heavy, and when I unzipped it, I saw that it contained shovels, trowels, a pick, and a sieve that I assumed Oliver used to sift dirt. Or maybe to pan for gold. I considered pinching it, thinking it would make a good accessory for Henry, but then thought better of it. Newt was fascinated by the smells inside. He had his head practically buried in the bag. So much for the preservation of evidence. Surprisingly, Jon didn't object.

"I don't see any article or maps or anything like that in here," I said. "According to Oliver's friend, he had a lot of that kind of stuff in the duffel he had under his bed." I looked around at the other items in the unit. "Do you see another duffel anywhere?"

Jon moved a couple of boxes aside and then said, "Nope."

"We'll have to go through all these boxes," I said, grabbing the one closest to me.

It was sealed shut with some packing tape, so I stuck my hand in my pocket and took out my key ring, which has a small Swiss Army knife attached to it. It was something I used a lot when opening packages and boxes that came to my store.

"I'm not sure I understand how some treasure maps, even if they're real, would have anything to do with what happened to Oliver," Jon said as he watched me slice open my box.

"I'm not sure either, but something about it feels right. Given Oliver's apparent fascination with treasure hunting, doesn't it seem possible that he was onto some treasure that was sunken rather than buried? Maybe it had something to do with where he was when he was killed. Or even *why* he was killed."

CHAPTER 21

⌒

There wasn't any office to check in with at the storage facility. We found unit number fifty-nine in the third row of buildings and parked in front of it. There was a keyed padlock on the door, and after Jon retrieved the bolt cutter he'd brought along, he made fast work of the lock. He flipped the hasp off the loop and pushed the door open.

A quick glance at the ceiling told me there was no light inside and Jon must have figured it out at the same time because he came up with a small pocket-sized flashlight while I used the one on my phone. For a few seconds, our beams crisscrossed the interior of the unit, making it look like the star-studded red carpet at the launch of a big movie. Then mine settled on a large duffel bag propped up against the wall. I started to reach for it when Jon halted me with a hand on my shoulder. He handed me a pair of nitrile gloves.

"I need to treat this like an evidence scene," he said, "even if I don't think there's anything here that will be used in that way. If by

"If he was onto something related to the recent trip, isn't it more likely that he'd have had it at home or with him on the trip rather than tucked away in a storage unit?"

"Maybe," I said, shoving the first box, which was filled with old bank statements and tax-related stuff, aside. I grabbed a second one, the top of which was simply folded closed rather than taped. "Or maybe he wanted it to be somewhere safe and secure where no other eyes could see it."

I undid the flaps atop the second box. "And bingo!" I said, flashing a broad smile at Jon.

On top of the box's contents was a book about sunken treasures in the United States. I took it out and flipped through the pages to see if anything had been tucked inside. There was nothing there and I set it aside and moved on to the next item, a manila folder filled with printouts from various web pages detailing ships that had disappeared with treasure on board. Most of them appeared to be outside of the US, but another folder beneath it, stuffed with similar printouts, was about more local shipwrecks.

"Can I take this box of stuff with me?" I asked Jon.

He debated the question, his face contorting as he did so. It was comical to watch but I bit back my smile.

"I'll let you have it under one condition," he said finally.

Newt cocked his head sideways, staring at Jon as if he, too, were waiting for whatever edict was about to be handed down.

"We go through it together here and now to make sure there isn't anything worrisome in there."

I stared at him, eyebrows raised expectantly. "That's it?" I said after a pause, surprised.

"Yeah. Why? What were you expecting me to say?"

"I don't know," I said with a shrug. "I just thought there'd be more hoops to jump through. In fact, I was already debating how to get around them."

Jon frowned. "I thought we were a team."

"Oh, we are. As long as you do things my way." I winked at him and then gestured toward the box. "Shall we?"

We did a quick triage skim through the treasure box, and while some of the articles looked interesting, none of them leapt out at me as being relevant. There weren't any I could see that dealt with Death's Door or any of the surrounding areas, and most of the articles were about rumored treasures that were well known. I felt sure that if Oliver had been looking for treasure in the area, it would have been something more obscure. I set the box aside outside the unit.

"If you see anything you think might be related to Oliver's death, no matter how remote the connection might be, tell me before you do anything with it," Jon instructed as we went to work on the remaining boxes.

I nodded, pleased that he was allowing me to help at all.

There were fourteen boxes total, and by some unspoken agreement, we each took a side of the unit and tackled the boxes closest to us. Most of the ones I opened contained personal paperwork, job-related stuff, and old bills. Then I hit on a box that had envelopes filled with pictures. A quick examination of three of the envelopes' contents revealed black-and-white photos with yellowed borders of people I assumed were Oliver's family members. I was about to set the box aside as uninteresting for our purposes when I peeked into a fourth envelope and saw color pictures that had obviously been taken by someone in a kayak. I recognized several of them as scenic shots of the waters and islands in Death's Door. I glanced over at Jon and saw that he was busy going through a box of CDs. I stuck the envelope in the waist of my pants at my back and tugged the bottom of my shirt over it. I happened to glance at Newt and saw him watching me curiously. I sent him a mental message: *Don't judge.*

He sighed and then bent around and started licking his balls.

I glanced through the remaining envelopes, but there were no more scenic photos, just pictures of people, many of them older pics in black and white. As I closed the box, a question came to me.

"Jon, did you have a chance to check Will's and Oliver's phone records?"

"I did. No calls to any anyone associated with Plymouth, Wisconsin, for either one."

"I was also wondering if either of them might have had any pictures on their phones that might prove helpful. I don't suppose those are retrievable through the account like phone calls and texts are?"

"No, unless they were set up for automatic upload to a cloud. But that could take some time to figure out and even more time to retrieve."

"I'm going to call Devon and get his take on it. I'll put him on speaker so you can hear."

I called the store, and fortunately, Devon answered. "Hey, Devon, Chief Flanders and I were wondering if there's a way to retrieve photos that the victims might have taken with their phones. The phones themselves are lost, probably at the bottom of Lake Michigan, but we were wondering if the pictures could have been saved elsewhere."

"Sure," Devon said. "If the pictures were uploaded to a cloud automatically, I might be able to access them through a computer. But I'd need to know the person's account info, you know, usernames and passwords, plus what service was being used to access the cloud. And if they have an account with two-factor authentication turned on, I'd need access to their phone to get the six-digit code. No guarantees, but if you can get me either of the victims' computers, I can give it a try."

If I could have kissed Devon, I would have. He had given the perfect answer without any prompting from me.

"Yes," I said, shooting a slightly smug look toward Jon. "I've asked Chief Flanders if we can have Oliver's laptop to let you take a look at it, but he hasn't given me an answer."

Jon rolled his eyes, but a hint of a smile curled the corners of his mouth.

"Let me see if I can convince him," I said.

"He seems to like you a lot," Devon said. "Maybe if you offered him sexual favors, he'd be more inclined."

My eyes widened as I realized that I'd neglected to tell Devon that this call was on speaker. I spat out, "Thanks, Dev. Gotta go!" and disconnected as fast as I could. I was afraid to look over at Jon but something in me couldn't resist.

He was staring at me with this huge smug, know-it-all grin that made me blush. He folded his arms over his chest and leaned back against the unit's wall, head cocked to one side. Then he said, "Let the negotiations begin."

CHAPTER 22

———

J on had brought along a replacement combination-style lock for the door to Oliver's unit. He had set aside a couple of boxes containing financial records and he loaded these into the back of his car.

"Why are you taking those?" I asked.

"I need to show something for my search warrant," he said. "Financial records might at least reveal some unusual activity that could be related to an illegal drug business."

Twice I had to tuck the envelope I had in my pants back in to secure it, as it kept creeping up whenever I bent over. As I settled back into my seat in the car, it was pushed up once again and I barely had time to stuff it back into place before Jon got in.

Our return ride was silent for the first few minutes, but even though talking about my desire to get my hands on Oliver's computer now made my face flush hotter than a tin roof in the August heat, thanks to Devon's offhand comment, I was determined not to let the matter drop.

"Please let Devon have a crack at Oliver's laptop," I said.

"Our forensic guys can look it over the same way Devon can and determine if there's a cloud account," Jon argued. "If they find pictures, I can print them off and show them to you."

"Have these 'forensic guys'"—I made air quotes to go with the last two words—"done anything with Oliver's laptop yet?"

Jon let out another weary sigh, and when I glanced over at him, I saw his tongue was patrolling the inside of his cheek. I took that to be a sign of annoyance, but whether it was with me or with his "forensic guys," I couldn't tell.

"They looked at it," Jon said. "They saw that it was password protected and then didn't pursue it because it didn't seem relevant to the events at hand."

"Yeah, you told me that before. So why not let Devon have a crack at it? He can wear gloves and handle things in whatever way you say in order to protect it as evidence. You can even stand over his shoulder and watch what he does if you want."

I had no idea if Devon would allow that, but I was desperate and grabbing at straws.

"Let me think on it," Jon said, and I decided to let it go for the time being since this mild concession was at least some form of progress.

We rode in silence for the next twenty minutes until I realized that he'd veered off the main highway and was headed into Sturgeon Bay. He seemed to sense my question, negating my need to ask it.

"I want to drop these boxes off at the sheriff's department," he said. "They'll need to be marked and stored as evidence and they have more room for that than I do on the island."

We pulled into the parking lot of the sprawling Justice Center a few minutes later. It was a little after seven, but despite the late hour, the place was busy. In addition to housing the sheriff's department, the Justice Center was also home to the Door County Circuit Court, several victims' services offices, some lawyers' offices, and the county jail. I offered to carry one of the boxes in for Jon, but he stacked them up and hoisted them on his own.

"Thanks, but I got it. I'll be back out in a bit. It might take me a half hour or so. Maybe you can walk Newt while you wait."

His comments felt dismissive, but he had a valid point when it came to Newt. If I couldn't take him inside, I didn't want to leave him in the car in the late-summer heat, even if Jon was willing to leave it running with the air on. There were too many things that could go wrong. Instead, I leashed Newt up and walked him across the parking lot to a grassy area, where he proceeded to lift his leg and stake out several claims. I felt the envelope of pictures at my back, scratching me and threatening to fall out of my pants. After some adjustments, the situation was only mildly better, and I considered just taking the whole thing out and confessing to Jon what I'd done.

"How about this Jon Flanders fellow?" I asked Newt as he sniffed a bush and then lifted his leg for the umpteenth time. Newt looked at me and then went back to sniffing. "I mean, he seems really nice, doesn't he? But I don't know if I'm ready for a relationship again. I'm still raw and bleeding from the last one. And with Jon living on the island, it's going to be hard, though that distance might prove to be a good thing. It can help slow things down, you know?"

Newt looked at me again and then walked over and pushed his head against my hand.

"Morgan?" I hadn't realized Jon was back.

"Over here," I said, waving, and then Newt and I hurried over to the car.

Once we were settled inside, Newt leaned over the front seat and gave the side of Jon's face a sniff and a big lick.

"Good grief," Jon said, wiping a palm down his cheek. He sounded exasperated but he was smiling.

I looked at Newt, who was doggy grinning at me, tongue lolling. *I get it, You approve.* I reached back and gave him a scratch behind his ears.

"I signed out the laptop," Jon said once we were underway.

That was so unexpected, and he uttered it so nonchalantly, that the significance of it escaped me momentarily. When it did hit me, I clapped my hands with glee. "Will you let Devon take a look at it?"

"Under the right circumstances, yes. He'll have to do it the way I say, though."

"I'll make sure he does."

"I mean it, Morgan. You haven't shown yourself to be a great follower of rules so far."

Well, he had me there. I thought about the envelope of pictures still tucked away in the waist of my pants and looked away so he wouldn't see me blush. "I promise to try to behave."

If he noticed that I was only promising to try as opposed to actually doing it, he didn't let on.

After a brief period of silence, Jon said, "What really happened in New Jersey?"

Wow. That one came out of left field, and just when I was starting to feel a little good about things, too. I stalled, giving myself time to decide if I was ready to discuss this topic.

"What did your uncle tell you happened?"

He gave me a mocking look. "Answering a question with a question? You don't expect that to work on a cop, do you?"

"I expect it to give me some time to decide if I want to discuss the horrific and terrifying murder of my parents at the hands of someone who is still out there," I snapped back.

Jon's smug smile disappeared in a blink. "Sorry," he said. "I didn't mean to—"

"Did your uncle tell you that he thinks I killed them?" I heard the angry shrillness in my voice and apparently Jon did, too.

"Maybe now isn't the best time to discuss this," he said quietly.

"Maybe not," I snapped back.

Newt, sensing my rising level of anxiety, put his head over the seat, resting it on my left shoulder. The gesture instantly calmed me.

"I won't bring it up again," Jon said. "But if you ever want to talk about it, I'm willing to listen."

I said nothing, my head turned to the side window, watching the scenery go by.

"And for what it's worth, my uncle doesn't think you killed your parents."

"Yeah, well, he sure had a funny way of showing it."

"I think he was skeptical of your story in the beginning because of the evidence. All good cops have to keep an open mind when it comes to witness statements."

I said nothing, keeping my eyes focused out the side window.

"Aren't you worried that this guy might come back for you?"

"Not really," I said, a half-truth. "He has nothing to gain by killing me now and having me as a possible suspect took some of the pressure off him. Besides, if he'd wanted me dead, he could have waited until I came back to the campground and done me in the same way he did my parents."

"Have you—"

"I really don't want to discuss this now," I said, fighting back tears as flashes of terrifying, heartrending memories flitted through my mind. Damn Jon Flanders anyway!

The remainder of our trip was made in silence, a thick barrier of tension and emotion creating a seemingly impenetrable wall between us. When Jon pulled into my store parking lot, I got out without a word, happy to escape and thinking I was out of my mind to entertain the idea of a serious relationship again.

But as I let Newt out of the car, Jon said, "Mind if I come in for a bit? Or have I worn out my welcome with you? We can look over the stuff in the box and take a run at the laptop if Devon is here."

I'll say one thing for Jon Flanders; he knew my weak spot. It was a few minutes after eight and the store was still open for another hour. My stomach rumbled embarrassingly loud.

"Devon is here. Are you hungry? I can fix us something to eat," I said, a somewhat indirect answer to his question.

He looked immensely relieved, and I hoped he had a better poker face when he was questioning criminals because right now he was easier to read than a children's book.

"I'm ravenous," he said. "And I'm willing to cook, if you'll let me."

It seemed Jon Flanders knew more than one of my weak spots. I've always loved the idea of a man cooking for me. But I feared Jon was developing into an unexpected squall—a brewing storm that posed a deadly threat to my already bruised and battered heart, meaning he might well have been my own personal Porte des Morts.

Maybe it was time to batten down the hatches.

CHAPTER 23

There were several customers in the store, browsing. I found Devon and told him to come up to my apartment before he left for the night. Then I led Jon upstairs, Newt at our heels.

"This is home sweet home," I said, spreading my arms wide once we entered the apartment.

The building that housed the store had once been a warehouse. My father had converted the space, keeping the wide-open feel of the building as much as he could in the apartment upstairs. The bedrooms—two of them—were enclosed in their own space, as was the office, but the rest of the apartment was one big open area with the kitchen in the back corner. The living room and the dining area—identified solely by furniture and some area rugs—were along the front wall, where several large windows provided a view of the bay over the treetops. Dad had added French doors and a balcony off the front in order to take better advantage of that view. Separating the kitchen from the rest of the living area was a huge granite-topped island with seating for three along one side.

The apartment had been the perfect-sized living space for a family of three, but it was a lot of space for one girl and a dog. Yet despite its open airiness, it felt cozy to me, most likely because of all the memories it held. It was the only home I'd ever known, and it had always felt good to come back to it after my parents and I had been on trips that sometimes kept us away for as long as a year.

I watched Jon's face as he took it in, wondering what he thought of the decor. It reflected the offbeat and quirky tastes of my parents—though not as outré as the store downstairs—as well as some of their adventures. The furnishings, none of which matched, all had meaning.

"Most of the pieces in here came from places my parents traveled to," I told him. "They were chosen for comfort and personal appeal, but also because each one is reminiscent of a place they'd been."

I walked over and looked at the dining table, which was carved from walnut with a splotch of blue-tinted resin in the middle. "This represents Loch Ness," I explained. "If you look at Loch Ness from space, this is what you would see. And the six chairs around the table are all hand-carved African high backs from Cameroon, each one unique."

"Beautiful," Jon said.

He set the box and the laptop he'd carried in from the car on the island. Then he walked over and ran an appreciative hand over the back of one of the dining room chairs.

"The granite on that island came from South America," I told him. "I forget which country. And the barrel-stave stools are made from reclaimed whisky barrels from Scotland."

"And these?" Jon said, waving a hand in the general direction of the living room.

"Well, the sofa, which is one of my favorite places, is a Bali daybed made with a bamboo frame. The cover on the cushioned part is hand-dyed Indonesian fabric. My mother loved those red, purple, and orange tones. I think the throw pillows are from Indonesia, as well."

I turned and pointed at the lounge-style leather armchair across from the sofa. "That piece is a bit more mundane. It came from a club in New York City that was rumored to be haunted. When you sit in it, you sometimes get a whiff of cigar smoke mixed with bourbon. I suspect the smell is simply imbedded in the leather but who knows? And the chair next to it is the Adirondack chair that Marty had delivered to me."

My throat tightened at the thought, and I bent down and brushed a bit of dog hair off the glass-topped coffee table to give myself a moment. Then I segued into the next bit on my world tour of furniture by pointing to the table's base.

"That scrolled wrought iron bottom is from France," I said, "but the glass top, with the compass etched into it, came from Denmark. And this rug we're standing on? It's Australian sheepskin. The one in the dining room is a hand-knotted Himalayan from Nepal. In the room my parents used as an office, there's a wool rug from Iran that sits beneath a partner's desk made from rare cocobolo wood from Mexico."

"Wow," Jon said, looking overwhelmed but intrigued. "My place is furnished with pieces from Wally World."

I laughed. "I know it's a bit over the top but then my parents were kind of eccentric. And my father had enough money to buy or commission anything he or my mother wanted. They didn't flaunt their money in public and they were very philanthropic for causes they believed in. But this apartment was their sanctuary. They knew what they wanted and didn't hesitate to go after it."

Jon nodded and walked over to a table against the sidewall where there were several framed photos of my parents, taken over the years, some with me and two with just them alone. He took a moment to scan them all and then picked up one featuring all three of us that had been taken about ten years ago.

"That was in Iceland when my parents were hunting for the Lagarfljót worm, a serpentine creature rumored to live in a fresh-water, below-sea-level, glacial-fed lake."

Jon shot me a look I couldn't interpret. "Think we might have one of those in Lake Michigan?" he said.

"No."

Jon smiled and studied the picture some more. "You look like your father," he said. "And your mother . . . what a beautiful woman."

"Wow. I'm not sure how to take that," I said.

Jon set the picture down and looked over at me with a puzzled expression. Then it hit him.

"Oh, hell. I didn't mean to imply that you aren't beautiful, too, just that you have your father's eyes and coloring, and his curly hair." He was clearly horrified, his cheeks aflame.

I decided to let him off the hook. "I was teasing you. It's okay."

"I truly am sorry, Morgan," he said. "That came out all wrong."

Now it was my turn to be discomfited. I turned away to hide my reddening face and spoke over my shoulder to him. "You can make it up to me by fixing us dinner. The kitchen is all yours. Shall I give you a tour?"

To my surprise, he declined. "If you don't mind, I'd like to just poke around and figure it out on my own. I'll look at what you have in the way of food items and figure something out. I love doing that."

"Have at it," I said, and then I went over to Newt's food and water dishes, which were both empty, and took them into the small guest bathroom by the office entrance to clean them.

As I refilled and replaced Newt's bowls, I watched Jon with a subtle side-eye as he rummaged about in the kitchen, gathering things on the countertop next to the stove. I also felt the package of pictures that I still had tucked in the rear of my pants irritating me.

"Okay if I use these chicken breasts you have in the fridge?" he asked.

"Go for it. Feel free to use anything I have out there."

"I make a mean chicken parmigiana," he said. "Hope you like Italian."

"I'm not a picky eater and that sounds yummy."

I disappeared into my bedroom and removed the packet of pictures. After looking around the room for the best place to hide them, I settled on the drawer where I kept my pajamas and tucked the packet in between two folded sets. Then, to explain why I'd disappeared into my bedroom, I changed my top. It was stupid, really. Jon had no reason to be suspicious of me and I felt certain I was going overboard in my attempts to cover up my crime, but I'd learned my lessons during that last, fateful trip to New Jersey with my parents. Even the simplest, most ordinary act can prove fatal.

When I went back out to the main part of the apartment, Jon was busy at work in the kitchen, and I doubted he even knew I'd left the room.

"Mind if I look through the box of treasure-hunting stuff we took from Oliver's storage unit while you cook?" I asked him.

He frowned. "I don't suppose you have any gloves?"

"As a matter of fact, I do." I walked over to an antique Russian cabinet positioned along one wall in the dining area, opened a drawer, and pulled out a box of nitrile gloves. "I wear gloves a lot when looking at items that people send to me or bring me for the store. Some of that stuff can be a bit dicey."

"No doubt."

Already, the aromas of butter and garlic filled the room, making my stomach rumble embarrassingly loud. Newt raised his nose to the air, his nostrils flaring wildly. I went to the fridge, took out a bottle of Chardonnay, and held it up to Jon.

"I suppose red would be better with what you're cooking but this is all I have," I said. "Unless you want to crack open a rare vintage bottle of red wine purported to have come from Al Capone's stash in a house he owned in Milwaukee. It's rumored to be a century old."

"I like an aged wine but that might be pushing it," Jon said, looking like a kid staring down a plate of vegetables. "Besides, red wine tends to give me a headache."

"Me, too. Can I pour you a glass of the Chardonnay?"

"Sure. Thanks."

I opened the bottle, poured two glasses, and set his on the counter next to him. Then I carried mine into the living room and settled myself and the treasure box on the Indonesian daybed, which was big enough to sprawl on and spread stuff out on. When I had everything situated, I put on a pair of gloves and dug in.

There were several books in the box, all with variations on the title of the topmost one: *Hidden Treasures You Can Find!* A quick flip of the pages in each book revealed tales about lost treasures, including one intentionally planted by a millionaire who then provided obscure clues; the infamous D. B. Cooper case from the seventies; and historical legends like the Scepter of Dagobert, part of the French crown jewels that have supposedly been missing for more than 225 years.

I set the books aside and looked at the items beneath them, which included a handful of supposed treasure maps that I suspected were rip-offs Oliver had fallen for, and printouts of what I estimated to be well over a hundred emails and messages from various chat rooms and websites focused on treasure hunting. Resigned to reading them all, I started wading through them, hoping to find a reference to something local. I was only about a quarter of the way through the box when Jon announced that dinner was ready.

"Where should we eat?" he asked.

My parents and I had almost always eaten at the island. I typically ate in the living room.

"How about the dining room table?" I suggested, eager to avoid painful memories. Plus, I thought it might help keep things on a more formal level.

Jon found the cabinet holding my dishes and he carried over two plates and set them on the table. I got silverware and napkins while he put out the food he'd prepared: the chicken parm, a side of spaghetti and sauce, and a small salad with some sort of homemade lemony dressing.

As I served myself, delighting in the garlicky, cheesy aromas, Jon said, "I set aside a small amount of cooked chicken breast without any spices on it for Newt. Is it okay if I give it to him?"

Newt's ears pricked up at the mention of his name and he looked at me expectantly, as if he understood exactly what was in question here. I'm not sure whose heart was more won over by Jon's gesture, mine or my dog's.

"Of course," I said. "And thank you."

Newt gobbled his share of the meal down in a matter of seconds. I, on the other hand, intended to savor every bite of mine. The food was delicious, and I complimented the cook accordingly after only a few tastes.

"Tell me how you ended up here after Colorado," I said.

"I already did. I saw there was an opening, I was ready for a change, and I applied. They hired me."

"Yeah, you told me that part but not why you were ready for a change. For most people, a move that big follows some sort of life-altering event."

He put a forkful of chicken in his mouth, chewed on it, and stared at me, making no attempt to answer. I tried a different tack.

"Do you miss Colorado at all?"

That question he apparently deemed safe. He swallowed and swiped at his mouth with his napkin while nodding. "I do miss the mountains at times. There is such a majestic beauty to them and a sense of something powerful . . . almost magical."

I knew what he meant. While I'd lived all my life in Door County, where the highest elevation is only about eight hundred feet, I'd been around and even on mountains both in the US and abroad. Our sheer, rocky cliffs here are beautiful, but they can't compare to the majestic beauty of mountain ranges.

"Of course, the Great Lakes have their own magical qualities," Jon added. "And I quite like living on the water, even if that water is unforgivingly treacherous at times."

He paused, gazing out over the room though I sensed that whatever he was seeing in his mind wasn't anything in this building. "When I've been out on the water and looked down at some of the shipwrecks out there in Death's Door, it gives me a strange sense of history. I feel—I don't know—connected somehow to all those souls whose lives were lost on those ships."

He paused, silent for a moment, and then he blinked hard and looked at me, almost as if surprised to find himself seated at my table.

He smiled, looked down at his plate, and started twirling some spaghetti on his fork. "Does that make me sound strange and weird?"

"Not at all," I said. "I get it. I've felt the same thing. Sometimes I think there are threads that connect all living things on the planet, maybe even in the universe. And sometimes those threads affect our hearts and souls in ways we don't fully understand. It's part of why I love being a cryptozoologist. I believe there are other creatures out there that we haven't yet discovered because sometimes I can feel them. Here." I put my palm over my heart. "It's a sensation . . . a thrum deep in my chest, and sometimes it feels like it's tugging me toward something, though I don't always know what."

I paused and gave Jon a tentative smile. "Does that make *me* sound strange and weird?"

Jon rolled his lips inward and shook his head woefully. "You are certifiable, no doubt about it," he said, though I saw the twinkle in his eye and a crinkle at the corner of his mouth that told me he was teasing. "I think we're a good match."

That last bit gave me pause and Jon must have seen something in my face because then he said, "Uh-oh, what did I say?"

"Nothing." It came out too quick and with a distinct lack of conviction that even I could hear.

Jon set his fork down, put his elbows on the table, and laced his fingers together, staring at me over the top of his hands. "Morgan, I'm a single man with no romantic ties currently. I haven't been looking for any romantic connections, but I'm attracted to you, and I'd like to explore that at some point. I'm in no rush, but if I'd be wasting my time to do so, tell me now. I'm a big boy. I can take it."

I gave him a hesitant smile and then started playing with my spaghetti, swirling the pasta around on my plate. "I like you, Chief Flanders," I said, enunciating his title in a teasing way. "I'm attracted to you. But you need to understand something. Three somethings, really. One is that I can get quite absorbed in my work, to the point that it sometimes becomes all-encompassing. When that happens, I don't have the time or energy for anything else."

I paused, waiting to see if he would say anything, but he continued to look at me, his expression neutral, waiting.

"Two, I have trust issues because of my wealth and what happened in New Jersey. I can't tell you how many potential suitors have approached me solely because they were interested in my money."

"I'm not interested in your money," Jon said. Then he frowned. "Though I imagine every suitor you've ever had has said the same thing, making my claim meaningless. If it's any consolation, I have a job that comes with a whole truckload of trust issues, so I think we might be on even ground there. I suggest we play it by ear and see how things pan out."

I had to give him credit. His answers were spot-on perfect so far. I found myself warming to him, but an inner voice cautioned me.

"What's the third thing?" Jon asked.

I looked back at my plate again and resumed my study of creative art with pasta. "I think I may be . . . broken," I said. I didn't look at him, couldn't bring myself to, but I paused to see if he would comment. When he didn't, I continued. "My parents' deaths . . . there's more to the story than you probably realize. Things happened back then that . . . um, damaged something in me. It left me numb, unable to feel anything for a long time." I looked over at Newt and smiled. "Until this guy came into my life."

Newt got up and put his chin on my thigh, looking up at me with those big, soulful brown eyes. I set my fork down and stroked the soft fur atop his head. "I don't know if I'm ready to open myself up that way to anyone yet. Not sure I ever will be."

To Jon's credit, he didn't respond right away. I spared a quick glance at him at one point and saw that he looked thoughtful, contemplative. I liked that he typically didn't feel the need to fill a silence and jump right in with some pithy comment. But then it went on for so long that it felt uncomfortable. An interrogation technique, no doubt. His uncle had used it on me when he questioned me after the murder of my parents. One more reason I had trust issues when it came to Jon Flanders, but one I didn't feel obligated to share with him just yet.

"Aren't you going to say anything?" I said finally, unable to endure the silence any longer.

He was saved by the bell, or rather the knock that came on my apartment door.

CHAPTER 24

———

I answered the door and let Devon in.

"You said you wanted to see me," he said, stepping past me, tablet tucked under his arm.

"Yes, I do. We have Oliver's laptop and I've convinced Chief Flanders to let you have a crack at it. It's password protected, but I know you've managed to work around those kinds of things before."

"I figured that's what you wanted," Devon said, proffering the tablet. He looked over at Jon. "I saw you carrying a laptop that was bagged as evidence."

"You'd make a hell of a detective," Jon teased.

Devon laughed good-naturedly and headed for the island, where the laptop still sat.

"How long will it take you?" Jon asked him.

"Have your guys tried any passwords yet?"

"I don't think so," Jon said, slicing through the evidence tape on the bag with one of my kitchen knives. Then he put on gloves and slid the laptop and power cord out of the bag. "We didn't think it was that important in the beginning and no one has signed it out since it was collected, so I doubt it."

As Devon reached for the laptop, Jon stopped him. "Do you mind putting on some gloves?" he said. "It is evidence."

"Not at all."

I handed Devon a pair from the box I'd taken from the side cabinet, and once he had them on, Jon handed the device to him and plugged the power cord into a nearby outlet.

"Let's start by trying a couple of obvious passwords," Devon said, flexing his gloved fingers over the keyboard. "I did a little background check on our Mr. Sykes to obtain some of the pertinent dates and places he might have used."

His hands descended and his fingers flew over the keyboard while Jon and I stood behind him and watched. I tried to figure out what passwords he was trying but he was typing so fast, I couldn't make out most of the keys he was striking. I was about to say something to Jon when Devon said, "There we go."

I gaped at the laptop screen as Oliver's desktop appeared. "You're in already?" I said, astounded. "What was the password?"

"KayakKing. All one word with the first K's in each word a cap," Devon said. "It's a moniker he used on his social media a lot. Now that we're in here, do you want me to disable the password?"

Devon and I both looked at Jon, who appeared momentarily perplexed. "No, leave it," he said eventually. "As long as we know what it is, we should be okay."

"Okay," Devon said. "What would you like me to do first?"

"Check his emails," Jon said.

"Internet history," I said at the same time.

Devon raised his eyebrows at the two of us, waiting.

Jon's wide mouth narrowed into a thin line of resignation. "Do the internet history," he conceded. "It's more likely to produce something usable."

Devon launched one of the browsers—Oliver had three of them on the device—and checked the history, which produced several porn sites.

"I think we can move on from there," I said.

The second browser produced nothing. On the third attempt, we hit pay dirt. Or at least we found some potential. As Devon scrolled through the history, we saw several sites related to treasures and treasure hunting. Devon clicked on one and we saw a list of potential treasures that could still be found in the world. He clicked on another, and it produced an article detailing the top ten missing treasures yet to be found in the continental United States.

"This could take a while if we need to read all of these," Jon said.

"Go to that one," I said to Devon, pointing at one of the sites farther down in the list. "It says 'sunken treasures.'"

Devon opened the page and scrolled down.

"There!" I jabbed at the screen hard enough to make the images and typeface morph briefly. "That's about a sunken treasure rumored to be on or near Poverty Island." I saw the name Napoleon Bonaparte in the article and snapped my fingers. "Of course! I forgot about that one. Devon, can you print a couple of copies of that? Use the printer in my parents' office."

"Sure."

Five minutes later, Jon and I were both seated in the living room, me in Marty's chair, Jon on the couch, reading our respective printouts. Devon was reading it on the laptop.

The article highlighted a legendary treasure dating back to 1863 that was thought to have been lost near Poverty Island, a small, rocky bit of land in Lake Michigan off to the northeast. The first time I'd heard about it was when I was five years old. My parents were all abuzz over a TV show called *Unsolved Mysteries*, which was one of their favorites. A production company had come to the area to do a piece about the lost gold and the resultant episode was going to air that night. I have vague memories of watching it with my father, and hearing the story for the first time.

The legend claimed that in 1863, when the Civil War seemed to be turning in favor of the North, the cash-poor South asked France for help. Napoleon Bonaparte, who at the time was Napoleon III, the emperor of France, obliged by supposedly putting together five or more chests filled with gold bullion and coins that were estimated to be worth around four hundred million dollars today. France had a vested interest in seeing the South succeed because it relied heavily on Southern cotton. The plan was to send the chests down the Saint Lawrence River to Escanaba, Michigan, and then transfer them to a schooner on which they would eventually make their way south via the Illinois waterways and the Mississippi River. It was supposed to be very hush-hush, and all went well until the schooner carrying the gold was discovered and pursued in Lake Michigan. According to the legend, the crew didn't want to be caught with the gold and risk being arrested and tried for treason, so they chained the chests together and pushed them over the side, letting them sink to the bottom of the lake, perhaps in the vicinity of Poverty Island.

Skip ahead to the 1920s, when a freighter ran aground off the shores of Poverty Island. An anchor on one of the tugs that came to help free the freighter apparently snagged some wooden boxes that were chained together. But as the boxes got close to the surface, they broke free and sank again before anyone could find out what was in them.

Skip ahead again to the 1930s, when the son of the lighthouse keeper for Poverty Island claimed he watched a salvage boat work its way around the small island for three summers running. The boy knew about the gold legend and figured that was what the crew was looking for. When he saw the men rejoicing and celebrating on board the ship that third summer, he thought maybe they'd found it. But shortly after the celebration, one of the lake's infamous storms blew in, sinking the salvage boat.

Finally, there were the efforts of the crew from *Unsolved Mysteries*, though in the end, the gold, if it ever existed, remained undiscovered. There might have been another TV show or documentary that had been filmed some years back—I vaguely remembered hearing something about it at a chamber of commerce meeting—but once again, nothing ever came of it.

"Is there any indication that Oliver might have been looking around Poverty Island?" I asked Jon. "That seems like a crazy trip to make from Schoolhouse Beach in a kayak."

Jon shrugged. "You're right. That would be an insane trip to make in a kayak."

"Wouldn't he have to have equipment with him if he was going to be looking for a treasure like this one?" I posed. "Scuba gear or, at the least, sonar, like a fish-finder?"

"He might have had some of that with him," Jon said. "According to his friends, he had a large backpack that he took with him whenever he went out, but no one knew what it contained. It was apparently lost when he went overboard."

"You didn't tell me that before," I said, a hint of a whine in my voice.

"Sorry. It didn't seem relevant to the reason I hired you."

He had a point. "How far is it from Schoolhouse Beach to Poverty Island?" I asked.

After a couple of quick keystrokes, Devon said, "Fifteen point six miles, and that's if you go through the middle of St. Martin Island rather than around it. And going around it is a bit dicey because it has a shoal of rock extending out nearly a mile in most directions."

"More of an issue for a ship or boat than a kayak," I said. "But I can't see anyone going that far in a kayak in those waters. Seems like a fool's errand to me."

"Oliver *was* an experienced kayaker," Devon offered. "And he'd have attracted less attention in a kayak. He might have wanted to be as incognito as possible."

I shook my head. "That area has to have been explored hundreds of times. What could some guy in a kayak possibly know or find that more experienced divers, boaters, or salvagers couldn't?"

"Correct me if I'm wrong," Jon said, "because I haven't lived on the water all that long, but my understanding is that the storms this area is so well known for can sometimes stir things up to the point where items on the bottom that were once buried are then revealed."

"That's true," I conceded. "And if I remember right, there was a hell of a storm that blew through the area back in late May."

"You're right. There was," Jon said, snapping his fingers. "I remember because I had to answer a call for someone who was injured when a tree blew down. But even if Oliver found something, it doesn't explain what happened to him. Or the condition of his body."

"It does if there's a lake monster out there," Devon said. "Maybe

Oliver found one of those caves that are studded all along the coast-lines in this area. Maybe the gold was in there. And maybe some crea-ture was in there, as well."

Jon started to dismiss that idea with a laugh that made it clear he thought the idea nonsensical, but when he saw the look on my face, his smile rapidly disappeared.

"Is that possible?" he asked me.

"Possible? Of course. It's all possible," I said. "Probable? That's another question."

The three of us looked at one another, lost in our individual thoughts, until Jon said, "Let's see what else we can find on Oliver's computer."

For the next three hours, we dug through Oliver's private life via his computer and his box of treasure-related stuff. The box didn't of-fer much of interest, as its contents were mostly about land-based treasures. The computer, however, did offer up a few chat rooms ded-icated to treasure hunting that Oliver had bookmarked, though there was no way to know what conversations he might have had or with whom he'd had them.

"It's possible that the folks who visit these chat rooms regularly might not know that Oliver's dead," Devon said. "If you want, I could pretend to be him and see what I can find out."

That sounded like a great idea to me, but when I looked over at Jon to see if he approved, the frown on his face suggested otherwise.

"This isn't what you were hired to do," he said. "You're too far outside of your wheelhouse here, Morgan, stepping into investigative police work."

"Isn't that why you're here?" I asked him. "You hired me as a con-sultant to see if I could find out if the injuries inflicted on these two men's bodies could be from a lake creature, and that's what I'm doing.

Devon's cave theory is not outside the realm of possibilities. If we can get a better idea of exactly where Oliver went that day in his kayak, it might help me answer that question more definitively."

Jon made a face. "I don't know, Morgan."

"Couldn't you at least get the patrol boat from the other day and take me out to Poverty Island to have a look around?"

"Poverty Island is technically part of Michigan, not Wisconsin. It's outside of my jurisdiction."

"Does that mean we can't take a look?"

Jon blew out an exasperated breath, making his lips vibrate. "I'll have to check in the morning to see if Haggerty is available. But I can't leave the laptop with Devon. It's evidence and it has to stay with me the entire time it's out of the locker."

"I don't need it," Devon said. "I've bookmarked the sites Oliver was visiting on my tablet and I know what his IDs were."

Jon made that equivocating face again and I offered up an alternative, one I felt certain he wouldn't like.

"I can rent a boat to take me out to Poverty Island if you'd rather not be a party to that. I'll have a look out that way on my own. Of course, it would fall within the realm of what you hired me to do, so I'd have to pass that expense on to you."

Jon cocked his head and narrowed his eyes at me. Then he broke into a grin—the kind of grin that said he knew what I was up to.

"I'll call you in the morning and let you know if Haggerty is available to take us out," he said, deftly avoiding a direct response. He glanced at his watch. "I've missed the last ferry for the night, so I'm going to have to get in touch with my staff and let them know I'm not on the island. And then I need to find a place to stay. Any suggestions?"

"Why don't you stay here?" I offered.

A heavy silence filled the room and Devon was suddenly very focused on the laptop.

"I have a spare bedroom," I added quickly, lest there be any confusion as to the nature of my invitation.

"I don't have a change of clothes," Jon said.

"I still have some of my father's clothes," I told him. "You're about his size. I'm happy to lend you something."

"That wouldn't bother you?" he asked, and I appreciated his sensitivity on the matter.

"Not at all. I've been meaning to box them up and donate them to Goodwill for months now. I just never got around to it."

"It would save me a lot of time and trouble in the morning," he said. "If you're sure you don't mind."

"I'd enjoy the company."

"That's my cue to leave," Devon said, giving me a salacious wiggle of his eyebrows when Jon wasn't looking. I made a face at him. "I'm supposed to open in the morning with Rita."

"You can stay, too, Devon, if you want. I know from personal experience that my couch is quite comfy."

"Thanks, but I need to feed my cat," he said, closing the laptop and gathering up his tablet. "She gets vindictive if she doesn't get her breakfast and then she'll howl at me all night."

Jon laughed and blurted out, "Sounds like a girl I dated once." Then, seeming to realize what he'd said, he blushed from his hairline to his neck. "That's not as bad as it sounds," he said. "I'll explain it later."

Yes, you will.

CHAPTER 25

H owling girlfriends aside, Jon proved to be an easy houseguest and a near perfect fit for my father's clothes. We disappeared into our respective bedrooms—the "guest" bedroom was actually what had once been my parents' bedroom—after Devon left and I didn't hear a peep out of Jon until morning. When I came out of my room at my usual six o'clock waking time, I was greeted with the enticing aroma of fresh-brewed coffee. Jon was busy at the stove.

"I'm making cheese omelets and rye toast for breakfast," he said. "My way of saying thanks for putting me up for the night."

I don't normally eat breakfast first thing in the morning (I know, I know, most important meal of the day and all), but I didn't have the heart to tell Jon that, at least not yet. And to be honest, I *was* kind of hungry.

"Sounds good. I need to go let Newt out. I'll be right back."

I fixed myself a cup of coffee and carried it downstairs and through the store to the back door to let Newt outside. When I got back upstairs, Jon was on his cell phone, first talking to someone I assumed was one of his officers and then to Haggerty about going out in the patrol boat. He put two pieces of buttered rye toast on a plate next to a fluffy cheese omelet and set it in front of me while he was on the phone with Haggerty. From the sound of things, I deduced that we were on for our boat trip to Poverty Island at ten o'clock, something Jon confirmed once he disconnected the call.

"If it's okay with you, we can drive to Baileys Harbor in my car, and I'll bring you back here once we return," he said.

"That's fine, as long as Newt goes, too."

"Of course."

The way he said that, as if it was a given, warmed my heart. Judging from the enthusiastic thumping of Newt's tail, his heart was pleased, as well.

When we were done eating, I gave Jon a towel and a washcloth and told him he was welcome to use the shower in my bathroom if he wanted, but he said he'd be fine with a sink scrub. I offered him a razor, but he declined it, letting his blond stubble stay for the day. It was a good look on him.

After showering and rummaging around in the closet in my parents' office for something I'd need later in the day, I went downstairs to see to the opening of the store even though I trusted Rita and Devon to handle things on their own. I was a little concerned about whether Devon would make it on time, given the late hours he'd kept the night before, but he arrived minutes before opening time, raring to go.

Jon, Newt—his flotation vest on this time—and I were on the road at nine thirty, and we pulled up to the boat launch ten minutes early. Jon eyed the small duffel bag I'd brought along.

"Is that something for Newt?" he asked.

"Nope." I set the bag down and opened it, removing the device inside. "This is an underwater camera," I said, showing him the device, which looked like a mini yellow submarine. "It can go to a depth of one hundred and fifty feet and shoot four-K video or take pictures. The lens has nearly one hundred and eighty degrees of view and the device can swim in any direction using six thrusters that can be controlled remotely. My parents bought it to use for hunting underwater creatures and habitats. They only got to use it twice."

"Wow," Jon said, looking duly impressed. He held his hands out and I gave the camera to him. "It's so light. I thought it would be heavier," he said, hefting it a couple of times.

"It's around ten pounds, I think."

"Aren't you afraid you'll lose it down there?"

I reached into the bag and pulled out one end of a cable. "It has one hundred and sixty four feet of tether," I said. "And a pair of two-thousand-lumen lights for keeping track of things in those murky depths."

"It runs on a battery?"

I nodded. "I plugged it in last night to make sure it's fully charged. It should go for four, maybe five hours and has a max speed of three knots. It recharges pretty quickly."

"Well, this trip just got a whole lot more interesting," Jon said, eyeing the device with an eager glint in his eye. "My department could use one of these. Is it expensive?"

"I think it was around two grand."

He looked pleased with that answer. "I might be able to swing that in the next budget," he said. "I can't wait to see it in action. Wouldn't it be something if you were able to get proof of your creature's existence with it?"

"It would, but don't get your hopes up too high. The odds of finding Nessie here are long ones, I fear."

Jon frowned. "We can't call it Nessie, given where we are, can we?" he said. "And referring to it simply as 'the creature' seems too . . . generic. It needs its own name."

I couldn't help but be amused by his sudden investment in the possible existence of a lake monster. There was something endearingly childlike in his excitement.

"Well," I said, "when there have been sightings in other places, the creature has been named after that body of water. Nessie for Loch Ness, Champ for Lake Champlain, Chessie for Chesapeake Bay, and so on." Now it was my turn to frown. "Though that doesn't work for Ogopogo, given that its home is Lake Okanogan." I shrugged. "Anyway, we could call our creature Messy or Michie for Lake Michigan if you like. That last one is a name my mother used from time to time whenever there was a reported sighting. Though if such a creature does exist, I suspect it doesn't use Lake Michigan as its permanent home."

Jon considered this for a moment and then flashed what I can only describe as an evil grin. "What if we call it Chomp? That seems apt if perhaps a bit inappropriate."

I bit back a smile because, while I found his dark humor amusing, I was reluctant to show it. "Chief Flanders!" I said in my best chastising tone.

It was a tone Newt knew well and it got his attention. He gave Jon a look that said, *You're in the doghouse now, buddy!*

Fortunately, any further discussion on the topic was waylaid by the arrival of Haggerty and the boat. Jon helped him dock, and once we were onboard, Haggerty eyed the contents of my duffel with keen interest.

"I see we have toys for today's excursion," he said. "How delightful."

That was the most I'd ever heard from Haggerty, though he uttered the words in a monotone that belied the meaning of the final two. Even so, there was a hint of something in his eyes that made me suspect he really was secretly delighted. *Boys and their toys.*

We got underway after Haggerty and Newt reacquainted themselves. Haggerty made quick work of getting us past Death's Door, motoring around the eastern side of Detroit, Washington, and Rock islands and then cutting into the Rock Island Passage. We could see St. Martin Island off to the north, a now deserted isle though it had been occupied by lighthouse keepers in the past. Nowadays the lighthouse was automated, and while the old lighthouse keeper's cottage and the original lighthouse were still there, the cottage had long since fallen into disrepair and ruin.

As we drew closer to St. Martin, Haggerty slowed the boat down to a trolling speed. The treacherous shoals of rock that encircled the island lurked only a few feet below the surface in broad plateaus of stone that could ground a ship in a matter of minutes. Haggerty kept a close eye on his depth gauge and the sonar display, occasionally consulting a navigation chart that showed the water depths.

Since we were currently moving at a snail's pace, I said, "This might be a good spot to test out the camera. Give us a chance to play with the controls and get a feel for it."

Jon perked up visibly at the mention of "us" playing with the controls, and he nodded at Haggerty, who cut the engines back to an idle. As we bobbed along on the water, Jon and I spent several minutes testing the camera controls before letting it drop over the side. Once it was in the water, I steered it back and forth, up and down, side to side, getting a feel for it. Jon watched me with eager anticipation, licking his lips several times, and I knew he was itching to get a crack at it. His fingers were opening and closing, grasping at air even though his hands hung at his sides.

"Want to give it a try?" I said finally, putting him out of his misery.

He snatched the remote out of my hand so fast that Newt hopped up and came to my side, hackles raised.

"Sorry," Jon said, though I wasn't sure whom he was apologizing to, me or Newt. He had eyes only for the remote and its display screen.

"It's okay," I said to Newt, putting a hand on his head.

Haggerty came out of the pilothouse and peered at the image on the remote as Jon attempted to steer the device. "You want me to drop anchor here? Might make it easier."

"Yeah, why don't you?" Jon said. "At least for now."

Half an hour later, Jon had the device well under control and he got excited when he found a tiny underwater cave. It was an area where layers of rock deeper down had collapsed, creating a small void with a rock ceiling above. The opening extended back into the rock wall for several feet and there were a few fish hanging out in there. The clarity of the image and the ability to maneuver the camera just inside the void had Jon enthralled. Even Haggerty looked enthused.

"Let's bring it up and save the battery for looking around Poverty and Gull Islands," I said.

That elicited groans of disappointment from both men.

It didn't take long to reach Gull Island, as it sits in the shadow of St. Martin to the east on the Michigan side, and southwest of Poverty Island. Like St. Martin Island, it is surrounded by rocky shoals that extend around its entire circumference, covering a much bigger area than the island itself. At one point, the water depth rose rapidly to only a little over two feet, and then dropped just as dramatically to more than eighty.

For the next five hours, we slowly circled the tiny island, expanding out with each round and drawing ever closer to Poverty Island. We stopped at various points to launch the camera and explore the depths beneath when Haggerty saw something of interest on his sonar display, but all we found was lots of trash that had been dumped: tires, a rusted and broken motorcycle (which sparked a lively discussion on how it had come to be there, including lots of speculative suggestions involving Evel Knievel), an open steel drum, cinder blocks, and lots of timber, whether from wrecks or nature it was sometimes hard to tell. We did discover the remains of three boats. One was a metal rowboat, one was a speedboat missing part of its hull, and the third was the planks and boards of a hull from an older ship that had likely been there for decades, maybe longer.

"Well, this has been fun, but I think it's time to call it a day," Jon said when the battery life on the camera was down to almost nothing. "I have things I need to catch up on. Maybe we'll have better luck another time."

"To be honest, I doubt it," I said. "If there was gold down there, it isn't there any longer. Too many people know about the legend and I'm sure these waters have been thoroughly searched already. Plus, I find it hard to believe that Oliver would have come this far in his kayak, no matter how experienced he was."

Haggerty stood by listening to us but said nothing. When I was done talking, he arched his rather shaggy eyebrows at Jon, who merely nodded. Five minutes later, we were on our way back to Baileys Harbor. It was a silent trip with nary a word spoken. Once we docked, I took Newt for a quick walk to let him relieve himself and then I waited next to Jon's car for my ride back.

Seeing the somber expression on Jon's face once we were in his car and underway, I said, "Sorry this didn't pan out."

He looked surprised. "Why are you apologizing to me?" he said. "You're the one whose expectations weren't met."

"You mean because we didn't find Chomp?"

He gave me a nod and half a smile.

"I never expected to. I was thinking we'd be far more likely to find something that led us back to Oliver, but in hindsight that was a silly notion. Like I said earlier, I can't believe he would have kayaked all that way, particularly if he was looking for gold. He would have been the most ill-equipped treasure hunter ever and he struck me as someone too smart for that."

"Yeah, you're probably right," Jon said. "I doubt he came out here with an underwater camera." He smiled and sighed. "I have to admit, that thing is a lot of fun."

"Yeah, my parents loved gadgets, particularly anything they thought might help them hunt for cryptids." I shook my head and chuckled. "A few of them are quite bizarre. I'll have to show you some of the things in their collection one of these days. You might look at me differently once you see what the people who raised me thought was fun."

"I look at you differently now," he said with a wink. "It's one of the reasons I like you."

We rode the rest of the way in companionable silence except for Jon's offer to stop somewhere and get us something to eat.

"I've got stuff in my apartment for sandwiches," I said.

He smiled. "I know. I saw all your stores last night while I was fixing dinner. But I don't want to overstay my welcome."

"Nonsense. It's the least I can do after you cooked me dinner last night."

"Okay. It's a date."

Scary words, those. Jon Flanders was slowly tipping open the door on the closed part of my life. I resisted an urge to slam it shut again.

CHAPTER 26

As soon as we arrived back at the store, Jon got a call. He stepped outside for some privacy and looked disappointed when he came back inside.

"Change of plans," he said. "I need to head back to the island."

"Is everything okay?"

"Yeah, just some administrative stuff I need to tend to," he said vaguely. "I'll be in touch."

And just like that, he was gone, leaving that door on my life only slightly ajar.

I felt disappointed but my spirits got a boost when Devon waved me over to the counter with an excited look on his face.

"What's up?" I asked.

"I think I might have found something about the name 'Plymouth.'"

That perked me up.

"I got to thinking about shipwrecks and treasure," Devon went on, tapping away on his tablet. "And I came across a ship named *Plymouth* that sank in the area. It was referred to as the SS *Plymouth* and it sailed in Lake Michigan to ports in Wisconsin. That means it might have been printed with an S in front of the name and a W behind the name."

"Did it have any treasure on board?" I asked.

He shook his head. "Not that I could find, but it has an interesting history of shipments and owners that might have served as a disguise for something else." He gave me a suggestive arch of his eyebrows. "I sent you a link to some informational sites on it. Read them over and see what you think."

"Thanks, Devon."

"I'm not done," he said, grinning broadly. "I also found out something about Oliver Sykes."

"Really?"

"Don't know how relevant it is to what you're doing, but I think he may have been having an affair with someone who lives in the area. I didn't pick up on the clues at first because of the way they communicated. They're friends on Facebook, and Oliver would post something on the site whenever he was planning to come up for a visit, asking if anyone had any suggestions for a new place where he could eat or a good tackle shop or an area deli or bookstore or craft store. Quite a few people typically answered him, not surprising, given that most of his friends are Wisconsin based and most folks in the state have visited Door County at some point. But there was one woman, Sadie Hoffman, who never once failed to answer him and did so with oddly detailed replies that always had time references in them, like this one." He swiped at his tablet screen and then started to read.

"This was her response to Oliver's last inquiry in June asking if there was a place where he could get his car serviced while he was staying in Sister Bay. Sadie suggested a mechanic's shop in Sister Bay and then added that if he was going to be stranded while his car was being worked on, there was a nice place to eat within walking distance called the Waterfront Restaurant. Then she said that she'd had her own car serviced by this mechanic the year before and after dropping it off at eight in the morning she had it back an hour later."

Devon swiped at the screen again. "And here's another one, from earlier in June. Oliver wrote a post asking where the best fried fish could be found. Sadie answered with the name of a place on Washington Island, stating that she'd had lunch there not long ago and they had a great bar in addition to fabulous food. Then she writes that she arrived at noon with the intention to grab a bite and run but between the food, the drink, the view, and the ambience, she ended up staying for nearly three hours." Devon looked up at me, eyebrows raised.

"I don't know, Devon. I don't see it. What makes you think these are coded messages between these two as opposed to replies from some woman who is a chronic oversharer?"

"My gut," he says. "I think her replies were telling him where they could meet and how much time they had to be together. Did I mention that Sadie happens to be married?"

I frowned, not wanting to believe that Oliver was having an affair. Yes, Bess had said she suspected as much, but I'd liked her and didn't want to think that Oliver had been cheating on her.

"And did I also mention that her husband owns a shop on Washington Island that rents boats and diving equipment?"

Now he had my attention. Something clicked in my head, and I felt a tiny thrill of excitement. "Okay, send me Sadie's info," I said. "I'll give her a call."

I thought on that for a minute and then said, "Or maybe I'll pay her a visit instead. If she's married and desperate to keep her husband from finding out about her affair with Oliver, it might give me some leverage to get her to talk."

"Whatever works," Devon said, sticking his tablet on a shelf under the counter. "I should probably get back to work. Rita's been giving me the eye for the past hour."

"If Rita gives you a hard time, just let me know," I said. "And thanks for everything. You've been a big help. I'm going to go check out this latest info you sent me, but if you guys need help, just holler."

Back in my apartment, once again curled up with my pillows in Marty's Adirondack chair, I started wading through the links Devon had sent that led to information about the SS *Plymouth*. Built and launched in 1854, the cargo steamship *Plymouth* had had a diverse career on the Great Lakes up until it sank during the infamous storm of November 1913. It measured a little over 212 feet in length, generally had a crew of seven men, and a varied shipping manifest. The ship's history included several accidents, numerous owners, and an eventual conversion to a three-masted schooner. The first accident happened only a year and a half into its life when it ran up on a reef in Lake Michigan near Racine, Wisconsin. She was refloated and returned to service that time, but there was another, more serious accident just shy of a year later. Near the Manitou Islands in Lake Michigan, she collided with a three-masted barge headed for Oswego, New York, an accident that quickly sank the barge. In September of 1859, the *Plymouth* was caught in a gale, again in Lake Michigan, that resulted in the death of one of the crew members. Later, the ship ran aground in Lake Erie during the Civil War and was refloated a month later.

The conversion to a three-masted schooner in 1884 came with a change in ownership and cargo, and the *Plymouth* became part of the lumber trade. She was grounded twice more after that, in 1887 and 1888, both times in Lake Superior, and both times getting successfully refloated. Her final death knell occurred in November 1913, during what many consider the most disastrous storm to ever visit the Great Lakes. It was a furious squall marked by heavy snow, freezing winds, and mountainous waves that claimed more than 250 lives and a total of twelve vessels, though the *Plymouth* was the only ship lost on Lake Michigan.

During that storm, the SS *Plymouth* was carrying a load of cedar logs and being towed by a tug. The tugboat captain realized that neither ship was making any progress as the waves grew in intensity, and that they were at risk of foundering. He made the decision to tow the *Plymouth* to the safest place he could get to, which was at Gull Island, the same place Jon and I had been earlier. Once there, the tow captain cut the *Plymouth* loose and took off to seek shelter and repairs elsewhere. The presumed plan was for the *Plymouth* to drop anchor and wait out the storm with her crew of seven, which included Captain Alex Larson, and an eighth passenger, a federal marshal named Christopher Keenan, who was on the ship because of some pending litigation regarding ownership.

When the tugboat returned to Gull Island two days later, there was no sign of the *Plymouth* or her crew. It was presumed she sank there in the storm, though to date the actual wreckage had never been found. Marshal Keenan turned up, however. His body washed ashore in Manistee, Michigan, several days later. Eleven days after the *Plymouth* had been abandoned at Gull Island, a bottle with a note from Keenan was found that confirmed what everyone had feared: that the ship had gone down with everyone on board after withstanding the full force of the storm for more than forty hours.

While the history of the ship was both fascinating and tragic, there wasn't a hint of anything valuable being aboard the *Plymouth* at any point in its fifty-nine years of service, at least not treasure-hunting valuable. But the place where it was assumed to have gone down wasn't far from where the rumored gold chests were thought to have been sunk. Was it possible the *Plymouth* had ended up on top of the gold chests? Was that what Oliver had been looking for? It made a kind of sense and helped explain why both Marty and Oliver might have written the word down.

Thoughts of Marty made my chest tighten and I ran a hand over the smooth, cool surface of the flat arm of his chair. Much as I wanted to believe that he was safe out there somewhere, the odds of that being the case grew slimmer with each passing hour. In the short time I'd known the guy, he'd somehow managed to worm his way into my heart, and now I not only missed him, I felt responsible for whatever had happened to him. He never would have gone out there looking if I hadn't gone to him for help.

I'm not a religious person, but as I slipped into bed that night, I did say a little prayer for Martin Showalter, just in case anyone or anything out there might be listening.

CHAPTER 27

⁓

The next morning, I worked the store with Rita until Devon came in at noon. Then I told him where I was going, and Newt and I headed out. I had to catch a ferry over to Washington Island, and late August is a very busy time in Door County as everyone tries to squeeze in a last-minute vacation before school starts and the weather turns cold. I had to wait nearly an hour in the queue before I got on a boat. Once I was on the island, I drove to the address Devon had given me for Sadie Hoffman, a route that took me right past the police department, a small, rather nondescript building.

The shop was located along the northern shore of the island, not far from the pier for the passenger ferry that took folks to Rock Island, a popular hiking, boating, and camping destination. No cars or bikes were allowed on Rock Island, though plenty of folks got there via motorboats, canoes, and kayaks, making the location of Sadie Hoffman's shop an ideal one.

I pulled into a parking lot in front of a two-story building, which I quickly ascertained was much like my store, with a business on the ground level and living accommodations on the upper floor. There was one other car in the lot with two kayaks bungeed on top of it, and there were racks of canoes and kayaks stacked up on both sides of the building. Just off to the side of the lot was a large shade tree, and I looped Newt's leash around the trunk. Behind the building I could see a boathouse along with several smaller-sized motorboats that were tied up to a pier.

"Stay here and I'll be right back, okay?" I said to Newt.

He wagged his tail, gave my hand a lick, and then sat obediently.

Inside the shop, a man stood behind a long counter, talking to two women dressed and ready for a day of kayaking with their flotation vests and waterproof backpacks, a pair of binoculars hanging from each of their necks. The man was tall, muscular, bald, and tattooed, and I pegged him as in his mid-thirties. Despite a somewhat intimidating appearance, his voice was mellifluous and hypnotizing as he described various kayaking destinations to the women and pointed out some spots on one of the charts under glass on the countertop.

While waiting for them to finish, I browsed the rest of the shop. The walls were covered with maps and charts, and there were racks and shelves around the perimeter containing safety equipment, backpacks, fanny packs, lanterns, flotation devices, oars, clothing, water shoes, and an assortment of dehydrated meals. In the middle of the store was a display containing a canoe and two kayaks surrounding a well-equipped campsite.

The women had lots of questions, so I wandered toward a small window in one corner of the back wall. Down on the pier I saw a woman hosing down a kayak. She matched the driver's license picture Devon had sent me in the info about Sadie Hoffman, so I left the shop and headed down there, untying Newt as I went.

When I reached the pier, Sadie Hoffman was struggling to slide the kayak onto one of the top shelves of a rack of metal bars. She was off-center with her grip, and as a result, one end of the kayak kept tipping down and catching on the shelf below. I dropped Newt's leash and hurried over to grab the wayward end of the kayak.

"Let me give you a hand with that," I said.

"Oh, thanks."

She made no pretense at independence, nor did she try to shoo away my assistance. In seconds we had the kayak on the shelf, and she was wiping her hands on the sides of her shorts.

"Thanks. I appreciate the help," she said with a smile.

I saw that one of her eyes was bruised, though she'd tried to hide it with makeup.

"Is there something I can help you with?"

"Perhaps," I said. "I'm here to talk to you about Oliver Sykes."

Her smile disappeared faster than a drop of rain on the surface of the lake. "Who?" she said, looking away quickly and feigning ignorance.

"You know he's dead, don't you?"

She looked back at me, and at that moment, her eyes appeared nearly as big as those glowing ones I'd seen in the water the other day.

"What do you want?" she hissed with a wary glance up the hill toward the shop.

"I told you. I want to talk about Oliver. You two were having an affair, weren't you?"

She stared at me then, her head twitching to the side a couple of times as if she thought she hadn't heard me right. Her gaze drifted toward the ground for a few seconds and then lifted back to engage mine. She started to say something, but then clamped her mouth closed.

"I'm trying to figure out what happened to Oliver," I said in my best pleading voice.

"I have no idea what you're talking about," she said.

She started up along the side of the building toward the storefront, but I touched her arm as she passed me, and she stopped.

"Please," I said. "If you cared about him at all, you'll talk to me."

She hesitated. I saw it in her face. She wanted to talk but something was holding her back. Fear. When she finally turned and smiled at me, I thought she was going to come clean. Boy, was I wrong.

"If you value your own life, much less mine, you will walk away, mind your own damned business, and leave this alone."

The words, despite their stark and dire warning, were uttered in a sweet, almost singsongy tone, though she kept her voice low enough that no one else could hear it. She shot another wary glance toward the store and then continued up along the side of the building.

As I watched her go, I caught movement in one of the back windows and saw the face of the bald man who had been in the store. His narrowed eyes followed Sadie's progress with an intensity that sent a chill down my spine. Once Sadie had disappeared, I called to Newt, who was busy exploring the shoreline, and returned to my car. A window on the sidewall of the shop was open, and as I passed beneath it, I heard Baldy inside talking to Sadie.

"What the hell was that all about?" he asked in a decidedly unfriendly tone.

"Nothing," Sadie said.

I heard a slight shakiness in her voice and wondered if Baldy heard it, too.

"The lady wanted to know if we provided any guided tours. I sent her on to Shoreline Tours."

"Did you wash that kayak down good this time?" Baldy asked.

"It's as clean as it's going to get," she said with tired impatience.

"You best watch your tone, or I'll slap some more sense into you."

That was all I needed to hear. I hurried to my car and left. As I drove back to my store, I wondered what would have happened to Sadie if Baldy had gotten wind of the true reason behind my visit. Most likely she would have come away with a second black eye to match the first one. Or worse.

I despised bullies like Baldy and considered telling Jon about him, but then thought otherwise. Getting the police involved willy-nilly might set Baldy off and make him do something to Sadie. The safe way to handle the situation, assuming Sadie even wanted it handled, was to come up with a well-thought-out plan first with plenty of contingencies.

I got luckier with the ferry back to the mainland, only having to wait for about fifteen minutes. The store wasn't busy, and Devon was sitting behind the counter working on his tablet.

"Come up with anything new for me?" I asked him.

He shook his head, his face scrunched up in disappointment. Rita, who had just finished ringing up the only customer in the store, said, "He's been tapping away on that thing for hours, trying to find some connection between your victims."

"There isn't one," he said, pouting. "It has to be about the ship."

"But the SS *Plymouth* wasn't carrying any treasure or anything of great worth, for that matter. Just a bunch of cedar. Unless there was some secret cargo we don't know about."

Rita cocked her head to one side and scratched just above her ear with the pen she was holding. "You're looking for treasure?" she said.

I nodded. "We thought Oliver Sykes might have gotten a clue as to the location of Napoleon's lost gold. Are you familiar with that story?"

"Of course," Rita said. "Can't live in these parts as long as I have and not know about it. Not that it's real. Too many people have looked for it without finding it. Makes me think it either doesn't exist or it didn't get tossed anywhere near where the rumors say." She paused, looking thoughtful. "Why are you looking at the SS *Plymouth*?"

"Marty wrote down the word 'Plymouth' on a slip of paper I found in his truck. And Oliver Sykes's girlfriend said she found the word 'Plymouth' on a piece of torn paper in his office at their home. It seems like too much of a coincidence that both men would have written it down. But we can't seem to find any connection between the towns of Plymouth and our victims. Oliver Sykes had an interest in treasure hunting, and that got me to thinking about sunken treasures, but that hasn't panned out either. I even went out to both Poverty and Gull islands with Jon and looked around underwater with my submersible camera to see if we could find anything. I thought maybe the wreck of the SS *Plymouth* might have been on top of Napoleon's gold or something like that. But again, no luck."

Rita stared off into space with narrowed eyes and dug at that spot above her ear with the pen again, pulling loose dozens of hairs that sprung out from her head in a half halo of curls. "Of course not," she said. "Others have looked over the years and never found it. But you know . . . I might have an idea about that. Let me do a little digging."

Rita disappeared into the book section of the store while Devon went back to tapping on his tablet. I went to my office and shut the door to work on some of the bookkeeping duties, but I wasn't at it more than twenty minutes when Rita burst in without her usual warning knock. She was carrying a book, an old one, the cover worn and stained, the pages yellowed. She set it on my desk and carefully opened it.

Jabbing a finger toward the page, she said, "Drop everything, Morgan! I think I know where the gold might be!"

CHAPTER 28

⸺

R ita wasn't known for flights of fancy or unjustified bouts of giddy enthusiasm, so her obvious excitement had my undivided attention.

"When you started talking about the SS *Plymouth* and Gull Island," she said, her eyes bright, "I remembered something. My husband, George, bless his boring old soul, loved to collect old mariners' diaries. Many of them were written on paper and showed their age, making them barely legible. But a few, like the ones in here, were collected by an enterprising independent publisher who found, bought, and begged for sailors' notes, had them typeset, printed, bound, and published in book form. Most of the stories are boring tales about life at sea and gossip that circulated among the sailors. That kind of stuff fascinated George; he used to read excerpts to me all the time, assuming I'd be as entranced with them as he was. Some of them were interesting, but most were rather dry, paranoid, and misogynistic. A few of the writings were more fanciful and talked about legends and things like mermaids, but those were rarities. Still, I indulged George when he wanted to read them aloud to me because he clearly enjoyed them so much. It was something he and Marty bonded over. Marty liked those old sailing stories, too, and sometimes, when he'd come into our bookstore, George would share some of the passages with him."

I had no idea where Rita was going with this and waited with barely contained impatience for her to get to the damned point. Assuming she had one.

"Anyway, when you were talking about the SS *Plymouth* and how everyone thought it sank at Gull Island, it reminded me of this collection George had and one of the stories in it. Because of George's interest in her, I actually know quite a bit about the *Plymouth*."

"Thanks to Devon, so do I," I told her. "It's a sad story, and an all-too-common one when it comes to these waters. But I don't see how it relates."

"Read this," Rita said, pointing to a paragraph in the open book she'd set down in front of me. "It's a secondhand tale, a story told at a bar. No way to know if it's true or not. But if it is . . ."

She gnawed at the side of her thumbnail, her eyes bright and eager. I swear she looked ten years younger.

I took the book, noting its age and the small alarm tag on it, a necessary evil given its five-hundred-dollar price tag. The cover was flimsy, the pages thin and yellowed. Handling the book delicately, I read the selection Rita had pointed out, a recitation of a story told to the author in 1939:

The old man was a hundred if he was a day, and he ordered a shot of whiskey that he tossed back without hesitation, slam-

*ming the shot glass down on the bar and then ordering another.
His skin was terribly wrinkled and sallow, and tiny burst blood
vessels marked his cheeks and nose, an indication of a life lived
in the elements perhaps, or maybe a life lived with too much
alcohol. Later I realized it was probably both. His hands were
arthritic but also calloused, and when he saw me staring at
them, he turned them over, palms up and said, "These are a
sailor's hands." That got us to talking about sailing and ships,
and how many of them had sunk in Death's Door.*

I brought up the tragic story of the Plymouth *because a
distant relative of mine had died on that ship's final voyage.
But when I summarized the story, the old fellow looked at me
with a rheumy but sardonic eye and said I shouldn't believe
everything I heard. I asked what he meant, and he said that if
the* Plymouth *sank where the tug abandoned it, how come the
wreck was never found there?*

*Then he proceeded to tell me a story about a young fellow
back in 1913 who washed ashore on the northeastern corner of
Washington Island on the heels of that bedeviled storm. The
lad was in rough shape—hypothermic, coughing with pneumo-
nia, and waterlogged—and he died a few hours later, but not
before sharing a fantastic tale.*

*According to the old man, this young fellow claimed that
he was a crew member on the* Plymouth *and that the captain, a
man named Alex Larson, had decided to move the ship mere
hours after it had been abandoned by the tug. It was getting
battered hard where they were, and he figured they'd stand a
better chance out on the open waters. They pulled up anchor
and let the waves take them, and at first, they drifted south
around the eastern end of St. Martin Island toward Rock Is-*

*land. But the storm worsened, and they got caught in a trough,
a dangerous situation that can sink a ship in a mild storm,
much less one with cyclonic waves coming at them from every
direction. The wind and waves started pushing the barge toward Rock Island with frightening speed, and as land drew
closer, the crew tried desperately to drop anchor several times
to keep from running aground. But the anchor failed to catch
until they were so close to Rock Island's northern coast that
they could make out individual trees. Then, miraculously, the
anchor caught. Or so they thought. Yet the boat continued to
drift. Thinking they had snagged on another shipwreck, the
crew pulled up the anchor, surprised to find a wooden chest
trailing a rope of thick, heavy chain snagged on the anchor.
The chest broke apart and thousands of gold pieces rained
down into the water. The chain soon followed, slipping off the
anchor as the storm started tearing the ship apart. This fellow
and one other crew member tried to make for Rock Island in a
lifeboat. But their boat sank, and the second crew member disappeared, presumably drowned. This young fellow managed
to make it to shore on Washington Island, but after being battered and beaten by the storm waters, frozen, and nearly
drowned, he died a short time after telling his wild tale. It's
presumed that the others on the ship—the captain, four other
crew members, and Deputy Marshal Keenan—went down with
the* Plymouth *when it sank.*

When I finished reading, I looked up at Rita. "You think the gold
is somewhere in the Rock Island Passage rather than up near Poverty
Island?"

She shrugged, grinning. Much of her hair had sprung loose of its bun and strands of it floated around her head, making her look a little crazy. "It's not beyond possibility, is it?" she said, eyes wide. "What if this fellow's story was true? What if the gold is there in the Rock Island Passage and the *Plymouth* sank on top of it?"

"If it was, why didn't someone follow up on it back when this book first came out?"

"For one thing, look at the date of publication," Rita said.

I flipped back and looked at the copyright page. " 'December 1, 1941,' " I read aloud. "Six days before Pearl Harbor."

Rita nodded. "I suspect people's minds were otherwise occupied then and stayed that way for several years. Plus, this book was published by a small family-owned local press that went out of business months after the book came out because the three sons and the father who ran the business all went to fight in the war. I have no idea how many copies might have been printed, but I doubt many of them sold. Most likely they were returned and destroyed. George found this copy at an estate sale, and it had been in the attic of the fellow who owned it for several decades. I doubt anyone else has read it. There's also an issue of veracity. If you read on, you'll see that the fellow relaying this story chalked it up to the hallucinations of a dying man."

I thought about it all for a few seconds. "The wreck of the *Plymouth* has never been found, right?"

Rita shook her head.

"Okay. This is good stuff, Rita. Thanks."

"You're welcome. Just know, if you find the gold, I'm going to demand a finder's fee."

Before I could comment on that, Devon poked his head into my office. "There's a lady out here who wants to talk to you. She said it's about Oliver Sykes."

CHAPTER 29

―

Curious, I went out to the main store area, surprised to see Sadie Hoffman standing there.

"Hello again," I said.

She glanced over her shoulder, her hands wringing nervously. "Is there somewhere private we can talk?"

"Sure. Let's go into my office."

I turned and led the way, not bothering to look back to see if she was following. Or packing. Or if her husband might have been trailing along. I had Newt at my side, as usual. When I stepped into my office, Newt followed and sat beside me as I stood behind my desk.

Sadie walked in and looked warily at Newt. "Does he go everywhere with you?"

"Pretty much. Please, have a seat."

She walked over to the other chair and perched herself on the front edge of it, clutching the purse slung over her shoulder as if she thought I might try to steal it. I reached over and shut the door, then settled into my own chair. I leaned forward, arms on top of my desk, and looked at the woman, waiting.

"I'm sorry about yesterday," she said.

"I get it. Your husband is an abuser."

If she was shocked by my bluntness or by the fact that I'd figured out her deep, dark secret already, she didn't show it. She hung her head, whether in shame or to think, I couldn't tell.

"Were you having an affair with Oliver Sykes?"

Her head snapped up. "No. We never . . ." She let out an exasperated sigh and let her head fall back, looking at the ceiling. "Oliver was a kind, decent man who loved his girlfriend and made it clear to me that he wasn't interested in any kind of romantic relationship."

"Did he have any reason to think you were?"

She looked back down at the floor. "I kissed him. Just once. I'd arranged to meet him at a coffee shop by the Piggly Wiggly, supposedly to show him some things on a map. After the kiss, he kindly explained he wasn't interested in anything like that. To be honest, neither was I, at least not for romantic purposes. I was stupidly looking for my knight in shining armor, someone who could rescue me from T.J. and the life I seem to be stuck in with him."

"Why don't you just walk away?"

"It's not that simple. T.J. has control of all the money. I have nothing. The car, the shop, the inventory, all of it is in his name only, passed down from his father. The shop is a family-owned business and T.J. inherited it before we met and got married, so there are no guarantees I'd even get half of anything. I need money if I'm going to run, and I need to go far away, establish a new identity, find a place to live. . . ." She paused to catch her breath. "None of that stuff comes cheap. That's one of the reasons I wanted to believe in Oliver's theories about the gold."

"You were hoping to strike it rich so you could get away," I said with dawning understanding.

She nodded. "I really thought Oliver was onto something. He said he'd found a book here in your store that was a collection of old mariners' tales. It was an antique and expensive, so he couldn't afford to buy it, but he flipped through it and found this story about some fellow who claimed to have seen the gold close to Rock Island after his ship, the *Plymouth*, had been blown there in the storm of 1913."

I gaped at her, realizing that Oliver must have read the same excerpt from the book Rita had just shown me.

"Oliver thought the gold was in a spot that no one knew about. If he did find it, he was afraid someone else would try to claim it and it would get tied up in the courts or in disputes between countries claiming ownership, so he wanted to bring it up slowly and only a little at a time. He was certified as a diver, but he needed diving equipment, someone to watch while he dived, and someone to help him hide the stuff if he found it."

"Speaking of which, how did you find me tonight? I never told you who I was when I came to your place earlier."

"I've been in your store before. I love mystery novels and I've come in a few times to pick up something to read for myself. And I admit I find some of your other inventory rather fascinating." She gave me a wan smile. "Anyway, you waited on me once and I've seen you in the store on other occasions, so I knew who you were when you showed up today."

"How did you and Oliver meet initially?" I asked. "At your store?"

She shook her head. "We met in an online chat room for people who hunt for hidden and lost treasures. I talked about it more than I did it, but that kind of stuff has always intrigued me. Any kind of mystery, right?" She shrugged and chuckled.

"One night, Oliver and I got to chatting online and I was telling him how I'd been researching wrecks in Death's Door, and he said he was doing the same thing. We went into a private room then so we could compare notes. When he found out my husband owned a boat-rental and dive shop, he said we needed to meet in person. I knew T.J. wouldn't approve, so we arranged to meet at a coffee shop in Sister Bay on a day when I typically go to the mainland anyway for supplies. We spent an hour talking, looking at maps, comparing notes.... It was exhilarating, so full of promise." She smiled briefly but then her sadness returned.

"We met maybe a half dozen times over the past year, and during those visits, we came up with a plan to look for that gold. I offered to provide a small motorboat and the necessary diving equipment, and Oliver was going to do the actual diving while I served as his lookout. He wanted me to be his dive buddy, but I'm not certified. I went through the PADI training and tried a dive once because T.J. was insistent on the matter, but it didn't go well. I panicked and I have no desire to try again."

She shuddered at the thought. "I'm claustrophobic and superstitious. Too many people have died in the water around here. If I ran across an underwater skeleton or something like that, I'd probably have a heart attack."

I smiled, even as I was thinking what a great find an underwater skeleton would have been for the store. "So did you and Oliver ever go out?"

She nodded slowly, folding her arms over her chest in a way that made her appear to be shrinking. Her upper teeth raked over her lower lip, which was raw from being chewed.

When I saw terror flit across her face, I knew we were finally getting to the meat of things. "Tell me what happened," I prompted gently.

She didn't speak right away, and I waited. There was a faraway look in her eyes that told me she was remembering something that had happened in the past, something that, judging from her expression and body language, had terrified her.

"We went out three different times," she said finally, her voice soft, distant, and oddly childlike. "T.J. does dives with customer groups on Mondays during the summer, and we employ college students who work the store during their summer breaks in exchange for free equipment. Oliver and I went out on three consecutive Mondays in June. The first two times were a bust, but on the third try, Oliver came up all excited because he'd found a gold coin."

My heart skipped a beat and I wondered if I'd heard her right. "He found a gold coin?"

She nodded. "It was a gold ten-franc French coin with Napoleon's image on it. Oliver was beyond excited. He said it was proof that Napoleon's gold was down there."

"Do you still have it?"

She shook her head. "Oliver tried to flip it into the boat, but it hit the edge and fell back into the water. He said it was no big deal because there would likely be more where that came from and then he went back down."

She shot me a heart-wrenching look—a mixture of fear, regret, and sadness—before turning her focus to her hands, where she was busy destroying a cuticle. "He never came back up again," she said, her voice barely audible.

"What did you do?" I asked, trying to imagine the fear and helplessness she must have felt.

"I waited a long time without moving the boat. That was the one thing Oliver always insisted upon, that I not move the boat. But after hours passed and I knew something bad must have happened, this speedboat came in fast toward me. I had fishing lines in the water—that was my cover in case anyone wondered what I was doing just sitting out there in a boat—and I started reeling them in. Something about that boat gave me a bad feeling. There was a man driving it and he got up really close to my boat and just stared at me. I waved and smiled at him, and just as I was securing the last fishing line, I hollered over to him that something must have scared all the fish away." She paused, swallowing hard. "I said it in a joking way, you know? But after I said it, he smiled at me in a way that gave me chills. I started up the engine and left."

"How awful."

She nodded slowly, waging war against her cuticle again. "Two days later, Oliver turned up dead over by Boyer Bluff."

"Oliver was found in a wet suit, barefoot, with no diving equipment of any type on or around him," I told her. "No tanks, no buoyancy device, no mask or flippers, nothing. Did you ever get any of the equipment back?"

She shook her head. "Fortunately, I handle the inventory for the store, so I was able to hide the loss from T.J. Typically I'd charge the cost of lost equipment to the person's credit card, but I hadn't charged Oliver anything because I didn't want T.J. to know what we were doing. As it was, I panicked when I realized Oliver's kayak was sitting on our beach. I debated just leaving it there, but it had identifying information on it and I didn't want any investigations that might crop up to lead back to us. So, I tied it up to one of our speedboats one afternoon when T.J. was out and hauled it over to the area around Boyer Bluff. Then I just set it adrift."

She leaned back in her chair and closed her eyes, her brow furrowing. "At first, I was just so sad that Oliver had died, but then I started thinking about that gold coin and wondering if there was some other way to go after it. My hopes had been so high that I was finally getting my ticket out, you know?"

She lowered her head and looked at me, her body rigid and tense as if she thought I might reach across my desk and strike her at any moment. After a few seconds, her body sagged and she said, "You must think I'm a terrible person."

"Not at all. I think you're a woman who is trapped in a horrible situation that you're desperate to escape. Seeing that escape so close and then losing it must have been awful."

She smiled at me gratefully, tears welling in her eyes. "It *was* awful," she said, a hitch in her voice. "But that wasn't the last of it."

"What do you mean?"

She took in a deep, shuddering breath before continuing. "Well, I was considering logging back in to that chat room where I'd initially met Oliver, to see if I could hook up with someone else there and maybe make another similar arrangement, when the guy from the speedboat walked into our store."

"Yikes! That must have been scary."

"It was. I tried to tell myself that he was just a random customer, but when he looked at me, I knew he remembered me from that day on the water. He gave me that same creepy smile. I was afraid he was going to say something in front of T.J. and then I'd have to explain myself, but then he started asking a bunch of questions about who we'd rented diving equipment to recently. T.J. told him we didn't give out customer names, not that Oliver's name would have been on any list, and that pissed the guy off. In the end he left, but I've been afraid ever since that he or someone else would come back and hurt or kill us."

"I take it that hasn't happened," I said with a wry smile.

"Not yet," Sadie said with dead seriousness. "I know I can't prove anything, but I can't shake the feeling that the guy in the boat had something to do with Oliver's death. It's made me even more paranoid than usual. Coming here, I made a bunch of unnecessary turns just to make sure no one was following me."

She glanced at her watch and shifted nervously. "I need to go so I can catch the last ferry back to the island."

I eyed her for a moment and then said, "Sadie, is it safe to assume that if you had the money to escape from T.J. and start over somewhere, you would go?"

"Of course."

I smiled at her and said, "Well, then, we have some planning to do."

CHAPTER 30

———

The next morning—a Monday, so the store was closed—I loaded my tethered remote-control underwater camera into the car, along with a backpack of food and drink for both me and Newt. We caught the first ferry of the day to Washington Island, and I drove us to Sadie and T.J.'s rental shop. Sadie was with another customer when I arrived, and she made a point of looking past me as if we'd never talked, so I did my business with T.J. I arranged to rent some fishing gear and a sixteen-foot outboard motorboat with a higher-end fish-finder. I also bought a navigation map that showed approximate water depths and the locations of all the known wrecks and other water hazards. T.J. gave me a quick lesson on how to use and read the fish-finder, and then said that Sadie would provide me with a lesson on the boat's engine and handling. I showed my boating-safety certification card, signed a waiver, and forked over a hefty deposit on my credit card.

"Next time, call ahead with what you want so we can have it waiting for you," T.J. advised me with a hint of a scowl.

"I'll be sure to do that," I said with a smile.

If that was the way he treated all of his customers, he'd be out of business soon.

After fetching both my and Newt's flotation vests from the car and putting them on, we headed down to the boathouse behind the store. By the time Sadie came down with the key, I'd studied the map carefully, marking several spots that might be near where Oliver had found that gold coin. I left the map open when Sadie arrived, and while ostensibly giving me an orientation to the boat, she pointed to the precise spot where she'd anchored when she last saw Oliver.

"Good luck," she said. "This boat is easy to manage, and her draft is only two feet. Just turn the key and she should start right up. As long as you don't drive it up onto a shore, you should be fine. And FYI, you can take a snapshot of the screen on the fish-finder if you want, in case you see anything interesting. Just use this button and it will save it to the SD card. Watch out for the wrecks and shallows."

"Got it. Thanks."

Moments later I motored out along the western coast of Rock Island into the Rock Island Passage. It was a beautiful day, without a cloud in the sky, and the weather report predicted more of the same through tomorrow. The waters were calm, and the fish-finder didn't have any problems visualizing things, identifying several schools of fish that swam beneath us and providing a clear view of the lake bed as it rose and fell. I got excited at one point by a big blip on the screen until I realized the device was simply reading a large, closely packed school of fish as one big creature.

When I reached the general area Sadie had indicated to me, I turned off the engine, closed my eyes, and leaned back in my seat for a minute, letting the sunlight warm my face and shoulders. Then I sat up, consulted my navigation chart, and checked my surroundings. I was close to the state border between Michigan and Wisconsin that ran through Rock Island Passage, close enough that I couldn't be sure which state I was officially in. Off in the distance to the north, I could see St. Martin Island, and between me and it, there was a hardworking tugboat pulling three barges through the waters, a slow-moving nautical train. It reminded me of the tragic story behind the SS *Plymouth* and I hoped it wasn't an omen.

To the south was the northwestern tip of Rock Island, a rocky bluff with a craggy, uneven face that hinted of hidden caves and crashing waves. The bluff rose well over a hundred feet from a beach of large rounded stones, most of them bigger than a fist. Above the bluff, peeking out above the tree line, I could see the light tower of the old Pottawatomie Lighthouse—first operated in 1836, making it the oldest lighthouse in Wisconsin and on Lake Michigan—and the much plainer, newer light—little more than a metal tower—that stood close by. While it undoubtedly did the job, I hated the newer lighthouse, which wasn't a house at all. I mourned the loss of older lighthouses like Pottawatomie. There was something magical and romantic about them.

As I prepared my underwater camera, Newt peered over the edge, staring into the water, cocking his head from one side to the other, his ears pricking every so often when a rogue wave broke over the bow. According to the readout on my fish-finder, the water here was just over one hundred feet deep. While I didn't know what kind of PADI certifications Oliver might have had, I'd done the classes and had a basic certification. One hundred feet was considered the safe limit for most dives. Had he gone beyond that to find his gold coin?

Once I had the camera ready, I lowered it into the water, and watching the screen on the remote control, I began a slow reconnaissance of the area, moving back and forth in a gridlike pattern. I saw some fish, though nothing overly large, and after half an hour or so, I brought the camera in, started the engine, and slowly paralleled Rock Island's coast to the east while simultaneously edging a little closer to St. Martin. I knew from my navigation chart that the lake bottom rose off the southern tip of St. Martin, where the rocky shoals that surrounded the island extended south for a couple of miles like a clawing finger. I was puttering along about two miles out from Rock Island, watching the water depth change dramatically, once going from 128 feet to thirteen in a matter of seconds.

I was close to the spot where Marty and I had been last week, so I turned the engine off and let the boat slowly drift while I again prepped the underwater camera. I kept a wary eye on my depth reading, which ranged between thirty and eighty feet. I was about to launch the camera when Newt began sniffing the air and growling. He peered over the side of the boat into the water—though what he could have seen with those nearly blind eyes of his was beyond me—and growled again. Then he suddenly turned and hurried over to me, shoving his head into my lap, clearly anxious. I stroked him and told him it was okay. Then I slipped out of my seat and went over to where he'd been peering into the water to look for myself. I didn't see anything out of the ordinary, but the fish-finder began beeping loud and long, an indication of something big down there. I glanced at the image on the screen and froze, fear and excitement racing through me. The shape of the image moving across the screen was much too large to be any ordinary fish one might find in these waters. It had a large round body and extending out from either end was a long appendage... like a plesiosaur's neck and tail.

The water around me began to roil and churn, creating waves

that rocked the boat. The image on the fish-finder screen appeared to be directly beneath me and I hit the button to save a screenshot. When I looked over the side again, I was startled to see two greenish yellow eyes, the same ones I'd seen when I was out with Marty, rising toward me at a frightening speed. I made a mad, drunken dash back to my seat, turned the key to start the engine, and cursed as it coughed and belched. It caught just as something hit the bottom of the boat hard. The boat tipped sharply to the right, and before I could grab anything, I was flung over the side and into the chilly waters. The shock made me gasp and I sucked in a mouthful of lake water. Then my head smashed into something hard. The water around me filled with bright little stars for a second and then everything went dark.

I slowly became aware of my body moving through water. I felt lighter than normal, buoyant, but also chilled to the bone. Something pulled and chafed at my neck and armpits, and above my head, I could hear heavy breathing and grunting. Sunlight made the insides of my eyelids look red, and when I opened them, the bright light was blinding. I tried to roll over, but something got in my way. Turning my head to the side, I saw Newt with the loose end of the strap from my flotation vest caught firmly between his teeth. He was swimming for all he was worth, dragging me with him.

I reached over and patted him on his back. "I'm okay, Newt. Let go."

He did so and I was able to roll over and start treading water. I saw the cliffs of Rock Island off in the distance one way, and the low profile of St. Martin Island much farther in the distance the other way. I didn't see the boat at all. Easy choice.

"Okay, buddy," I said to Newt, who was paddling about in a small circle near me. "It's just another morning swim, albeit in colder water. Okay?"

He must have understood because he turned and headed for Rock Island. I did the same, head down, stroke after stroke, looking every so often to make sure he was with me and to check on my progress. As often happens with distance swims like that, it seemed as if I were swimming in place and the cliffs of Rock Island refused to get closer. But eventually the cliffs loomed higher, their details became more visible, and I knew I was making progress. When I finally felt my kicking feet brush the bottom, I gave it a few more strokes and then stopped, turning to sit in about two feet of water atop a bottom covered with large stones. Newt, panting hard, was able to stand next to me, the water lapping at the bottom of his stomach. After a moment, he whined at me.

"Yeah, yeah, okay," I said, forcing myself into a standing position.

It wasn't easy. The stones beneath my feet shifted and rolled, making each step a wobbly one, my head throbbed, and the trees jutting out of the craggy stone bluff I saw ten feet in front of me swam crazily. Drizzles of red water sluiced down over my right eye and there was a distinctive stinging sensation about a handbreadth above my right ear. I reached up and felt my scalp, discovering a gash about three inches long. I closed my eyes for a second but that just made things swim even more inside my head, so I quickly reopened them and checked Newt to make sure he was okay.

He wagged his tail excitedly as I ran my hands over his head and body, removing the flotation vest to make sure there were no injuries hiding beneath it. Once I was sure he was okay, I put the vest back on him and patted him on the head.

"You did good, boy. Really good. Thanks."

Tongue lolling, Newt wagged his tail even harder, flinging water drops every which way, his entire butt moving from side to side in a delighted doggy dance.

I remembered being tossed out of the boat a second after I got the engine started, but as I scanned the water, I couldn't see any vessels out there at all, not even the tug train I'd seen earlier. I wondered if my boat had motored off somewhere or sunk. Either way, I figured I'd be making an unplanned, hefty payment to T.J. and Sadie's store in the not-too-distant future.

Shifting my focus to land, I looked around, unsure where on the island we were. My parents had brought me to Rock Island to camp in a tent for a week when I was about ten, but I hadn't been back since. Realizing that I should have paid more attention to the island part of the map earlier, I debated which way to go. The thought *Right is wrong* popped into my head, though I had no idea where it came from. Despite that, I decided to heed it, turn left, and head clockwise around the island.

"Let's start walking," I said to Newt.

I took a few tentative steps, the stones beneath my feet rolling precariously. Bloody water continued to run into my eye but, aside from swiping it away, there was little I could do about it. At least the wound was oozing rather than gushing or squirting. I'd be okay, assuming my whack on the head hadn't caused something more severe, like a brain bleed, but I did feel a little woozy and that worried me.

Newt and I trudged along for a while, him in the lead. We navigated driftwood and downed trees, sheer cliff faces and thick tree lines that forced us to wade back out into the cold water at times to get around them, and an endless supply of those lovely but damnable rounded stones, which threatened to make me turn an ankle with nearly every step.

After we walked for about half an hour, the landscape changed from rocky cliffs to a mix of rock and dirt with tree-lined slopes. I heard distant laughter coming from somewhere above us, beyond the thick growth of trees. Buoyed by that, I stepped up my stride, and after I rounded a tiny jut of land, my heart leapt at the sight of a beach with a stretch of sand between the water's edge and the rock-strewn high-water mark. I knew where I was.

Sensing my improved mood, Newt ran about, sniffing at deadwood and a rotting fish carcass, wading out into the shallows, and rolling in the sand. After walking the length of the sandy beach, we were forced up onto a trail when the trees once again blocked our passage and we passed signs pointing to campsites. Minutes later we entered a wide-open area with several structures: a stone wall, picnic tables, a pagoda, a boathouse, and, best of all . . . a toilet!

After beelining for the toilet and ignoring wide-eyed stares from the few people we passed along the way, I made my way toward what was known as the Viking Boathouse, a testament to Icelandic immigrant Chester Thordarson—a wealthy inventor and electrical engineer who had once owned the island and used it as a vacation retreat—and his fascination with things old and mythical. The boathouse had a lower level with two huge stone arches rising out of the water, each one big enough to allow a large yacht through. The upper level, a museum, contained numerous artifacts and pieces of historical interest, many with a Nordic connection. The most important fact about the boathouse for me was that it marked the landing for the ferry to Washington Island.

I found a docent by the door to the boathouse's main level and asked if I might impose upon her to make a call for me to Chief Jon Flanders on Washington Island to let him know I was there and needed help. The help part must have been obvious given the bloodstains on my face and shirt, not to mention the gaping wound on my head. She made the call without hesitation, contacting the police station on Washington Island and eventually getting transferred to Jon, eyeing me warily the entire time. She switched the call to speaker—I'm guessing she didn't want me handling her phone with my bloody hands—and I explained to Jon what had happened and that Newt and I were going to need passage on the ferry to Washington Island.

"Why didn't you tell me you were going back out?" Jon chastised me after I finished my tale.

Feeling cross and tired, I said, "We can discuss that later. Right now this nice lady would probably like to have her phone back so she can continue with her job, and I think I might need some stitches in my scalp. Can you help me or not?"

That last came out harsher than I'd intended, but after a pause, Jon said, "Of course. I'll let the captain know to give you passage and I'll meet you at the landing on my side."

With that, the call ended, and the docent gave me an uh-oh look, her eyebrows raised.

"Thanks for your help," I told her, and then Newt and I left to go await the arrival of the next ferry.

We walked down a jetty and I sat atop a concrete pony wall that separated the pier area from yet another rock-covered beach, Newt at my feet. I had no idea when the next ferry would arrive or even what time it was, though judging from the location of the sun overhead, I guessed it was early afternoon.

My head ached something fierce, and as I replayed the events of the day in my mind, the pain worsened—painful memories in the most literal sense. At one point I closed my eyes and massaged the bridge of my nose. The image of those eyes rushing up through the water flashed through my brain, a dizzyingly frightful memory. I opened my eyes and had to brace myself to keep from falling off the wall. My heart pounded erratically inside my chest and Newt whimpered at my feet, sensing something was wrong. I took a deep breath, blew it out slowly, and reached down to give Newt a reassuring pat on the head.

Had those glowing eyes been the last thing Marty had seen? Even as this question came to me, I realized that it meant accepting the idea that Marty was dead. It left a heaviness in my heart that made me even more determined to get to the bottom of this mystery.

A small crowd began to assemble on the jetty, some standing around, others sitting or leaning against the wall like me. I took that as a sign that the ferry would be coming soon, and I kept glancing out over the water toward Washington Island—easily visible from here—hoping to catch sight of it. Most of the other people eyed me and Newt with guarded surreptitious looks, though others stared at us outright. I could only imagine what they thought when they saw my dried blood, head wound, and still-damp clothing. One man eyed me with disgust and made a comment about how dogs were supposed to be leashed and I should be ticketed for letting my "beast" run free. Given that Newt was sitting by the wall right next to me and hadn't moved, I thought his comment rude and unfounded.

"You're right, sir," I said with a tired smile. "I was in a boat that capsized, and my dog and I washed up on shore here a bit ago, but if you could go fetch his leash from the bottom of the lake, I'd sure appreciate it."

A woman leaning against the wall on the opposite side of Newt snorted a laugh. The man shot me an angry look as red crept up his neck and onto his face. With a harrumph he spun around and stormed out onto the far end of the pier. I envisioned going over there and pushing him into the water, and imagining the act made me feel a little better. If I'm honest, following through with the act would have left me feeling a *lot* better, at least for a short while, though the long-term consequences might not have been so great.

I felt the stare of the woman who had laughed and looked over at her. She was slender and fit-looking, well tanned, dressed in hiking shorts and boots with a backpack at her feet. I pegged her as in her mid- to late forties.

"Were you really in a boat that sank?" she asked.

"I'm not sure if it sank," I told her. "We got thrown overboard when something from below hit us. The engine was running at the time, so who knows what happened to the boat? All I know is that Newt and I ended up on the other side of the island here."

"Your dog got thrown overboard, too?"

I nodded.

"You have a nasty cut on your head," she said, eyeing my scalp with a grimace.

"I know." I reached up reflexively and touched the area. "I was knocked out. When I came to, Newt was pulling me through the water."

"What a good boy!" she said in a typical pet-speak tone of voice.

Newt wagged his tail, tongue lolling.

She bent down and picked up her backpack. After unzipping a section and rummaging around, she said, "Are you hungry?" and offered me a granola bar.

"Oh, my gosh, yes, thank you!" I said, taking the bar.

"I have some beef jerky in here. Can I give some to your hero dog?"

"That would be very kind. Thank you."

She took out a piece of beef jerky and held it aloft, a pensive expression on her face.

"Go easy, Newt," I said.

She lowered the jerky toward him, looking tense and ready to snatch her hand back at a moment's notice. Newt sniffed the jerky and then gently took it from her, his upper lip twitching with the effort.

"Wow, he's a sweetheart, isn't he?" the woman said.

"Yes, he is."

"If you need a ride when we get to Washington Island, I'd be happy to take you somewhere."

"Thank you very much but not necessary," I said, genuinely touched by her concern and generosity. "You've been so kind already and I think I've got someone meeting me."

"I'll hang a bit until you're sure," she said.

As we waited for the ferry, I chatted some more with my kind benefactor. I learned that her name was Jeanette Terwilliger, that she lived in Green Bay, that she'd just lost her husband to cancer, and that her only child, a son, had planned to go to college next year but had to postpone because of money concerns related to the cost of her husband's medical care and a lack of insurance.

"Caleb had his heart set on Northwestern," Jeanette said of her son. "But he didn't get any of the scholarships he applied for and I just can't swing it right now. I tried to convince him to go to the local community college for a couple of years and then reevaluate things, but he said he wants to take some time to gain some life experience." She flashed me a meager smile and scoffed. "As if I'd believe that. I know he's staying to try to help me get back on my feet financially."

"He sounds like a good son."

"He is." She smiled again and that one looked a little more genuine. "Do you have kids?"

I shook my head.

"Caleb is my one and only, and I'm dreading when he's gone but I want him to live his own life. He's off for two weeks with a friend who has a small camper. They're driving out to Yellowstone and back, so at least he's getting in a little fun this summer." She paused, sighing. "The house felt awfully lonely, so I came up here to hike the island. It always restores me."

By the time I parted company with Jeanette Terwilliger on the Washington Island side of the ferry route, I knew enough about her to know that Devon would be able to find her. And when he did, I would repay her kindness to me and Newt with an anonymous scholarship for her son and a payoff of her husband's medical bills. My father raised me with the belief that people who have a lot of money should try to do good with it, and it was a credo he lived by. I try to honor his memory by doing the same.

CHAPTER 31

As promised, Jon was waiting for us on the other side, standing outside his car, and I gave Jeanette Terwilliger a grateful wave goodbye.

When Jon saw me, he went all saucer-eyed, mouth hanging open. "Good Lord, woman!" he said. "You look awful!"

"Thanks," I said, laughing. "And take my advice. Don't ever play poker. You'd suck at it."

That got him to clamp his mouth shut.

"I'm going to need some stitches," I said. "Are there any medical services here on the island?"

"Of course. Where's your car?"

"It's in the parking lot of the boat shop on Old Indian Point Road."

"Can you drive?"

"I'm not sure, to be honest. I'm feeling a little woozy, but I don't know how much of that is from the head wound and how much is because I haven't had anything to eat all day except a granola bar. All my food is either still on the boat I rented or it got tossed overboard when Newt and I did."

"Speaking of which, I think your boat has been found. Someone reported seeing an apparently empty one adrift over by Washington Harbor about an hour ago. The Coast Guard was looking into it."

"Well, that's good. At least I won't have to buy the shop a new one."

"Yeah. Right. Let's get you looked at."

The closest ER was in Sturgeon Bay, so Jon drove me to a clinic on the island while I filled him in on more details from Newt's and my adventure. He didn't say much, but the scowl on his face told me he wasn't pleased with what he heard.

At the clinic, I was able to see a doctor after a brief wait. Jon stayed outside with Newt, who was none too happy at being separated from me. I was none too happy at seeing what I looked like when I glanced in the mirror in my room at the clinic. My curls sprouted out around the top and sides of my head like a crop of brown-and-red broccoli. Dried blood smears ran down and across parts of my face: my eyelids, my cheeks, my nose, my chin. I looked like something out of a horror movie. No wonder people had been staring at me.

"That's a right nasty gash you got there," the doctor said when she came in.

By then I'd used paper towels and a sink in the room to wipe away some of the blood on my face.

The doctor's name was Maggie Holland, and she was lovely, with poker-straight red hair and big blue eyes. She smelled faintly of roses with an underlying tinge of astringent—probably alcohol—and she had a deep, calming voice. Her touch, however, left something to be desired as she probed my wound with jabbing fingers that felt twice as big as they looked, after which she made me bend over a sink so she could scrub the area. After towel-drying my hair, she numbed me up, the needle jabs making me see stars and get so light-headed, I had to lie down. It got better once the medicine took effect, and Dr. Holland closed my wound with calm, speedy efficiency—not with the stitches I'd expected, but with staples from a stapler that looked scarily like the one on my desk at home.

"Those can come out in seven days," she said once she was done. "It requires a special tool to remove them, so you'll need to go to a doctor's office or urgent care. You can shower and wash your hair, but don't scrub hard around the area of the wound and be careful not to snag the staples. It should heal just fine. You're lucky you have such thick curly hair because the wound barely shows, not even the small area I had to shave."

"You shaved my head?" I said, feeling around with my fingers. The staples felt hard and cold.

"Just a tiny spot. Are you up-to-date on your tetanus?"

I was and told her so. One advantage of all the traveling I did with my parents was that I was always up-to-date on my vaccinations.

"Okay. Just let me finish my neuro exam and then we can get you on your way, assuming you pass, of course."

She hammered my reflexes, shone a light in my eyes and ears, listened to my lungs, checked my vision, and asked me if I had any numbness or tingling anywhere. I didn't.

"You're going to be fine," she said finally with a smile. "It sounds like you were very lucky, but that doesn't mean you can start playing hard just yet. You've most likely sustained a small concussion, so don't be surprised if you feel a little dizzy, nauseated, or foggy for the next week or two. Rest and plenty of fluids should fix you right up."

I thanked her for getting me in on such short notice, and then I went outside to find Jon hanging around near the entrance to the clinic. Newt nearly bowled me over when he saw me, yanking the leash Jon had fashioned from a rope in his car clean out of his hand.

"I thought he was going to drag me into the building," Jon said. "He does *not* like being away from you."

"I know. Thanks for hanging on to him."

"Are you okay to drive now?"

"I think so," I said, nodding. "Just a headache, is all. A bite to eat and a cup of coffee will fix me right up."

"I know just the place."

Jon drove us to a small sandwich shop where we ordered sandwiches and coffee to go. We settled in at a picnic table in a small nearby park to eat.

Once I'd downed most of my sandwich—I shared it with Newt—Jon asked me to once again tell him what had happened. I did, adding in details that I hadn't mentioned earlier, including the glowing greenish yellow eyes. Admitting to that still sounded too crazy to my own ears, so I could only imagine what it sounded like to someone else's.

"You're sure something hit your boat from beneath?" he said when I was done. "Sometimes when you're out there bobbing about on the lake, those waves can really toss a boat around."

"I'm positive," I told him. "I saw it on the fish-finder. I don't know what it was, just that it was big. And I got proof. I saved the screenshot."

Jon frowned. "How far out were you when it happened?"

"I was southwest of that long arm of shoals that extends down from St. Martin Island," I said.

"That's nearly two miles out from Rock Island," he said. "You're damned lucky you didn't drown. You must be a good swimmer."

"I am. Newt and I swim together a lot. Part of the credit goes to him, because I was knocked out cold initially, and he pulled me through the water toward shore."

Newt thumped his tail at the mention of his name and grinned up at us from where he was lying alongside our table.

Jon stared at him with newfound respect for a few seconds before turning his attention back to me. "By the way, I have some good news and some bad news for you."

"Give me the good news."

"I got a call while you were in the doctor's office. The Coast Guard managed to get someone onto your boat and bring it to shore. They figured out what shop it came from and they're taking it back there now. Apparently, it was none the worse for wear, so if something hit you out there, it didn't do any serious damage."

If something hit me? I frowned at him, miffed that, apparently, he harbored a certain amount of skepticism regarding my story. "What's the bad news?"

"There was nothing in the boat," he said. "Not your pack, not your camera, not even the expensive fish-finder the rental shop had installed on the boat. That's unfortunate because that model has memory storage that would have allowed us to go back to exactly where you were when this incident happened. I'm guessing the pack and camera went overboard when you did. The fish-finder is a bit more puzzling since it was attached to a mounting post on the boat, but if it was jarred hard enough, I suppose it could have gone over the side, too."

Not bloody likely.

I must have been making an ugly face because Jon said, "Are you okay, Morgan?"

"I'm fine. I'm just pissed, is all. Losing that fish-finder means losing my proof of what I saw. It all seems a little too convenient, doesn't it?"

Jon said nothing, which said everything.

I let out an exasperated sigh. "This whole situation is starting to give me the heebie-jeebies."

"Big words coming from a woman who lives with a corpse."

That made me smile. "Touché."

"You can quit if you want."

I shook my head. "I'm not a quitter. There's something out there. I saw it on the fish-finder. It was big and had two long appendages, just like the neck and tail on a plesiosaur."

"Maybe it was a school of fish packed together in such a way that it looked like a big creature with a long neck and tail."

"I considered that," I said. "But that doesn't explain those glowing eyes I saw rushing up toward me in the water right before something hit the boat so hard, it tossed me out. And this isn't the first time I've seen them."

Jon's brow folded into a scowl. "Tell me."

I told him about seeing those eyes right before Marty revved up the engines on his boat. When I was done, I leaned back, puffed my cheeks out with a sigh, and went to run a hand through my hair, stopping short when I felt my stapled wound. The numbing medication was wearing off.

Jon's cell phone rang, and after glancing at the screen, he gave me an apologetic look and took the call. I couldn't hear who was on the other end, and Jon's only commentary was the occasional grunt and one "I see" before he said thanks and disconnected the call.

"Your boat is back at the shop where you rented it. They said they'd probably have to charge you for repairs and for the missing sonar device."

"Of course," I said, exhaustion kicking in.

By silent agreement we cleared up our meal detritus and walked back to his car. The drive to T.J. and Sadie's store took all of three minutes.

"Are you sure you're okay to drive?" Jon asked as he pulled in next to my car.

"I am."

"Do you need passage for the ferry ride back to the mainland? I can arrange it for you."

"I'm good. I bought a round-trip ticket. It's in the car."

"Okay, then. Call me if you need anything. Don't push yourself too hard because you think you have something to prove."

I turned and stared at him, annoyed. "You think I think I have something to prove?"

He sighed and stared out the windshield. "That came out wrong. Sorry."

"Just what is it you think I have to prove?" I asked, unwilling to let it drop.

He looked at me, his blue eyes dark. "I like you, Morgan. A lot. I don't want to see anything happen to you, okay?"

After opening and closing my mouth like a fish a few times because I kept coming up with and then rapidly discarding smart-assed responses, I simply said, "Okay."

I got out of his car, let Newt out of the back, and quickly got into my own car before anyone in the shop might see me and come outside. I would happily pay for any damages related to my boat rental, but I simply didn't have the energy or emotional bandwidth to deal with the drama attached to Sadie and T.J. Besides, it was probably best to let Sadie carry out the plan we'd discussed. My showing up might set T.J. off.

I thought Jon might follow me to the Detroit Harbor ferry landing, but he was gone before I'd even backed out of the parking lot. Luck was with me as I pulled up only five minutes before the ferry arrived, and even though I was in a long line of waiting vehicles, a line that rapidly grew behind me in the five minutes I waited, my car was the last one allowed on the current boat.

I got out of the car with Newt and climbed up to one of the upper decks. As the ferry left port, I stood at the rail, watching the tip of Detroit Island slip away and the lighthouses on Plum Island come into view as we navigated through Death's Door. I thought about all the ships that had gone down in these waters over the centuries, all the lives that had been lost, including that of my paternal grandfather. While my adventure hadn't occurred in Death's Door, per se, today I'd nearly become one of those deadly statistics. And that not only made me mad; it made me singularly determined to figure out what the hell was going on.

CHAPTER 32

—

When I got back home, I was surprised to see Rita's car in the lot, given that the store was closed. I came in through the back and found Rita standing behind the counter.

"You get your butt over here, young lady," she said as soon as she saw me.

She stepped out and hurried toward me lest I try to ignore her command. When she got to me, she took hold of one of my arms and eyed my head with curiosity and worry.

"Flatfoot Flanders called and said you got tossed from a boat."

"Yeah, something from below hit my rental, tipping it enough that I was thrown out."

"What's all this about?" she said, releasing her grip on my arm and making a circular motion around my head with her finger. "Are you trying to become a redhead?"

I reached up and gingerly touched the spot where the staples were. The numbing medication had worn off completely and my scalp was throbbing. "Not sure what I hit, but I hit it hard," I told her with a meager smile. "I've got staples up there."

"First, Devon, now you," Rita grumbled. "This had better not be the start of a trend. I don't need a crack on my head."

"I don't think anything could penetrate that thick hair of yours," I told her. "That bun is like a shield of armor."

Rita seemed to like that. She smiled and tucked one of the ever-present errant strands up into that huge mess of a bun. I wondered if she ever took it down or if she washed it that way. It had a definite look of permanence to it.

I reached back with one hand and massaged my neck, which was currently throbbing as much as, if not more than, my head. Now that I knew I was safe and at home, I felt overcome with fatigue.

"As much fun as this hardheadedness discussion is, I need to shower," I said. "And then I could use some rest. I'm exhausted."

"Of course," Rita said, grabbing me by the shoulders and turning me around to face the stairs to my apartment. She gave me a little push in the right direction. "Devon and I will be here in the morning to open back up. You sleep as long as you like."

I cast a grateful smile at her over one shoulder and then dutifully went upstairs, Newt at my heels. I still felt chilled to the bone, and I stood beneath the hot spray of my shower until the water turned cool, basking in the heat of it. When I was done, I donned some yoga pants, a T-shirt, and a fluffy robe. Feeling somewhat rejuvenated, I settled in on my wide, comfortable couch, intending to look through some more of the articles and papers I'd pulled from my parents' files the other day. It didn't take long for my eyelids to grow heavy, and I set aside the paper I was reading and curled up into a ball, closing my eyes.

The next thing I knew, someone was knocking on my door. I sat up and saw that it was dark outside.

"Who is it?" I hollered, rubbing the sleep out of my eyes.

"It's Rita. I know I said we wouldn't bother you, but I got a call from that copper fellow Flatfoot Flanders, and he insists he needs to speak to you. He said he tried your cell phone, but it went straight to voice mail, and then he realized you probably lost your phone in the boating incident."

He was right about that. Most likely my cell phone was sitting on the bottom of Lake Michigan. I made a mental note to get a replacement as soon as possible.

"Are you okay, Morgan?"

"I'm fine." This was a bit of a lie. My head felt foggy, and I had to pee something fierce. "I'm sorry you had to come here, Rita. I need to go to the bathroom and then I'll come down and call him back on the store landline. Thanks so much for coming all the way out here."

I hoped my comments had sounded final without being rude. The last thing I needed right now was Rita asking me a bunch of questions. Much as I adored the woman, she could be trying at times. But I didn't want to alienate her either, especially not after the kindness she'd shown me that day.

After trying to shake off the fog in my head, I went to the toilet and emptied my bladder while Newt sat and watched, making me wonder idly why it is that dogs feel the need to accompany us to the bathroom. Is it because we're so often present when they do their business? Feeling a little better after that meager act, I went downstairs to the store. Rita was nowhere in sight, and while I breathed a sigh of relief, I also experienced a twinge of guilt. I glanced at the clock on the wall and saw that it was nearly nine thirty.

I dug Jon's business card out of my desk drawer and was about to dial when the phone rang, making me jump. I grabbed the handset and said, "Hello?"

Jon's voice, soft and concerned, said, "Hey, Morgan, Rita said you were going to use the store landline, so I thought I'd call it. Sorry to bother you but I wanted to make sure you're okay."

That was it? I got dragged out of my pleasant, dreamless slumber and came downstairs to the store for that?

"That's sweet of you," I said, immediately wishing I could take it back and reword it to something a little less . . . oogy. "I'm fine," I added quickly.

"You need to get a new cell phone," he said. "Is there a better number where I can reach you in the meantime?"

"The store line is it for now."

"Okay." He sounded disappointed. "I have an update for you."

I hoped it would be good news, maybe even news about Marty. But it was neither.

"I went out to the marina and examined that boat you rented myself. It's in dry dock now, so I was able to get a good look at the damage to the underside. I don't know what it was that hit you, but it transferred gray paint onto the boat."

"Paint?"

"Yep. Most likely gray marine paint. I'm going to send a sample to the lab to have it analyzed. Should have a definitive answer in a day or two."

"Are you sure the paint wasn't there beforehand?"

"I asked the shop owners. Turns out, that boat is their newest one, and they swear it was pristine when they got it. The only people who used it before you were the shop owners themselves."

"Interesting."

I considered this. What kind of creature leaves behind paint marks? Easy answer: none. Whatever I'd encountered out there, it hadn't been a living creature, at least not on the outside. It had to have been a submersible of some kind and I said as much to Jon.

"I agree. I'll see what I can find out about equipment like that being used in the area."

"Jon, were there any paint marks similar to this on Marty's boat?"

"Sorry, no," he said.

"Speaking of which, I don't suppose there's any news on that front?"

"Sorry, no," he said again.

Silence filled the air between us until I felt compelled to say something. "Does the police department have a dive team?"

"We have divers that we can call on. Why?"

"I'm not sure yet. I'll let you know."

"Morgan, is there someone who can stay with you tonight to make sure you're okay? You whacked your head pretty hard."

"I'm fine."

After a pregnant pause, he said, "I can come and stay the night if you want. I can boat over to Sister Bay. I'll sleep on your couch."

"It's kind of you to offer but I'm really fine. The doctor did a thorough neurological exam on me. I'm just tired. And I'm not alone. I have Newt and Henry."

"Henry?" I waited a beat, knowing he'd get there. "Oh, right. Henry. Very funny."

"Let's talk tomorrow," I said.

"Okay, but don't hesitate to call me if you need anything. Anytime, day or night, got it?"

"Got it. Thanks."

"Good night, Morgan."

"Good night, Jon."

Despite feeling tired, I was too jazzed now to go back to sleep. Instead, I went upstairs to the apartment, got on my laptop, and ordered another remote-controlled, motorized underwater camera. Then I started researching Napoleon's rumored gold. I found all manner of speculative posts on some dodgy websites, but there were a few that made sense and got me to thinking. One suggested that Napoleon's gold had been dumped near Poverty Island as the rumors had said, but then the chain connecting the trunks had been snagged by a ship's anchor during a storm and the entire mess had been dragged to a new location. But the area where Oliver had been looking, according to Sadie, was miles from Poverty Island. Could something as heavy as chests full of gold have been dragged that far by an anchor? Maybe in a fierce storm like the infamous one of 1913?

Then I found several stories that said the gold was in a boxcar on the lake bottom rather than in wooden chests. One historian claimed the gold wasn't even in Lake Michigan, but rather in Lake Erie.

My brain was too muddled to sort it all out and I eventually set the laptop aside and went into my bedroom to get ready for bed. When I opened my pajama drawer, I saw the pictures I'd taken from Oliver's storage unit. I'd forgotten about them. I sat down on the bed and started sifting through them. Most were scenic shots of coastlines and landmasses, presumably taken from where Oliver had kayaked, and I recognized that most of the shots were in the general area I'd been in earlier. Then I came across some photos that were taken underwater, most likely with one of those specialized disposable cameras you can buy in drugstores, gift shops, and tourist meccas.

I looked through the photos carefully, examining the underwater shapes and the occasional fish. And then I came to a photo that showed a structure of some sort, much of it covered with plant growth. On that structure, faded with time and erosion but still legible thanks to the cold freshwater depths of the lake, I could just make out the remnants of the first three letters in a word: a P, an L, and a Y.

My heart pounded with excitement. Oliver had found the SS *Plymouth*! It had to be that ship. If the location of the *Plymouth* according to the seaman's diary was true, might not his tale about the sighting of the gold also be true? Had Oliver not only found the wreck of a ship that had been missing for over a hundred years but also the legendary gold stash that Napoleon had sent to help the South? And had he died as a result?

I thought about calling Jon back to tell him what I'd discovered, but then I looked at my watch, saw that it was one in the morning, and decided it could wait. Besides, I was going to have to confess to copping the envelope of pictures and keeping it from him, and I was in no rush to do that.

CHAPTER 33

—

I slept in fits and turns, in part because of the excitement I couldn't quell and in part because of my earlier nap. At a little after six in the morning, I got up, feeling bleary-eyed but not sleepy. I pulled on shorts and a fresh T-shirt, slipped my spare key into my pocket, and made a cup of coffee that I then carried downstairs so I could let Newt out to do his morning thing. When I opened the back door, Newt dashed outside and trotted over to his favorite bush, where he promptly lifted his leg. It amazed me that the bush was still alive, considering how many times Newt had christened it. I stepped outside, but before letting the door close behind me, I gave my shorts pocket a reassuring pat to make sure the key was in there. I'd locked myself out before and knew it was no fun. It would be even less so now, because I didn't have a cell phone to call Devon or Rita with so they could come and rescue me with their keys.

It was a beautiful morning, the air crisp with the first hints of autumn even though it was only late August. I sipped my coffee and watched as Newt zigzagged through the small field behind the store in search of mice, moles, and voles. He'd caught the critters a time or two, and had his vision been better, I suspect he'd have caught a whole lot more. As it was, he hunted by scent and kept his nose low to the ground as he scoured the field. After stopping to lift his leg a couple more times, he finally did a squat. I kept a roll of poop bags in an old coffee can next to a small trash receptacle out back for just this purpose, but when I went to grab a bag, I remembered that I'd used the last one and hadn't put out a new roll. I unlocked the door to go back inside, and Newt dashed past me. I grabbed a new roll of bags from a small cabinet by the door and told Newt to stay, tossing him a treat from a box on top of the cabinet. While Newt scarfed down his dog cookie, I went back outside, letting the door close and lock behind me.

After removing one of the bags from the roll, I dropped the rest into the coffee can and walked over to where Newt had done his business. As I bent down to pick it up, I felt a shift in the air near me that made my hackles rise. Newt's hackles must have been at attention, too, because I heard him growl and then bark from inside the store. Before I could holler out a reassurance to him or return to the door, I was hit by something big and knocked to the ground. A second later a hand gripped one of my arms and yanked me to my feet as a dark hood was pulled over my head. Just before the hood blocked my sight, I glimpsed a pair of white athletic shoes with bare legs above, and long black slacks with scuffed black shoes like a cop might wear. Something hard and cold jabbed into my ribs.

A low male voice spoke close to my ear, his breath hot even through the fabric of the hood. "I have a gun and I'll use it if you don't cooperate. Understand?"

"Yes," I hissed, adrenaline and fear making my breaths come so hard and fast that I sucked a little of the mask material in with each one. I nodded to cement my answer just in case my verbal response had been muffled by the cloth.

The hand on my arm turned me, nearly making me trip over my own feet, and then it urged me forward. Another slight turn and then I was shoved, my upper body landing hard on what felt like cheap carpet. Someone grabbed my feet, and my body was hoisted inside a vehicle of some kind. I heard a door slide shut and latch behind me, and another door somewhere near my head opened and closed. The engine of whatever vehicle I was in came to life, and we started moving.

Off in the distance, I heard Newt's frantic barking coming from inside the store. I wanted to cry for him. He didn't like being apart from me, and I could only imagine how upset and worried he was.

He wasn't the only one. What the hell was going on?

The hood over my head came off suddenly, and I had to blink several times at the unexpected onslaught of light. I pushed myself up into a sitting position and looked around. I was in the cargo area of a van, and I scooted back to the sidewall behind me. Across from me, sitting on the floor and leaning against the other sidewall, was a dark-haired, tanned man wearing a uniform and the scuffed shoes I'd briefly seen after the hood had been put over my head. I studied the uniform, trying to figure out where this cop was from and then saw his badge. He wasn't a regular cop; he was a warden with the DNR, the Department of Natural Resources, the agency responsible for the enforcement of fishing and hunting licenses. He saw me staring at him and his hand moved in his lap, drawing my attention to the pistol he held there.

"You would do good to behave because if you don't, this will be your end," he said.

The fact that he'd removed my hood and let me see his face suggested that my end was coming regardless. They just needed a good place to dump my body.

"We're going to be at the marina in a minute," the man went on, "and you're going to board our boat like a good little girl. Understand?"

I nodded. Maybe that was why they'd removed my hood. They couldn't very well walk a hooded person through the marina and onto a boat without attracting attention. Getting on a boat also answered the question of where they planned to dump my body. The deep, cold waters of Lake Michigan would provide the perfect solution, particularly if they weighted me down. I squeezed my eyes closed, hoping like hell that they would kill me before they dumped me overboard. A gunshot sounded like a much nicer way to die than rapidly sinking to the lake bottom and drowning.

"Can I ask where you're taking me?" I asked DNR Guy, suppressing a shiver.

"You'll know soon enough. Behave and you'll be fine."

I didn't believe that for a second, yet I let his words cheer me for the briefest instant. Then reality kicked in. This was no time for complacency. If I didn't think of something soon, odds were I'd be dead before lunchtime. A thought came to me then, and before I had a chance to calculate the wisdom of what I was about to say, the words burst out of me.

"You killed Marty, didn't you?"

"That grizzled old fool with the nice boat?" he scoffed. "Got a bit too nosy for his own good, that one." He paused, looking thoughtful. "The old guy was tougher than he looked, though. I'll give him that. I had to shoot him and use his dinghy to divert attention away from where his boat would be found. Shooting him kept us from using him as monster fodder."

"Monster fodder?"

DNR Guy stared at me for a moment and a cold reptilian smile crept over his face. "Never mind," he said. "You'll figure it out soon enough."

I had most of it figured out already. My subconscious mind had known the truth of it for a while, even if I had clung to the hope of finding a real lake monster for longer than I should have. I decided to test the waters.

"You found Napoleon's gold, didn't you?"

The look of surprise on DNR Guy's face, the rapid disappearance of that hideous smile was all the answer I needed.

In the periphery of my vision, I saw the guy up front turn around and shoot a look at DNR Guy. The driver was blond, blue eyed, tanned, and muscular. I pegged him as being in his thirties. Something about the look on his face as he stared at DNR Guy made me continue with my revelations.

"The gold was beneath the wreck of the SS *Plymouth*, wasn't it?" I said, deciding to go for broke. "In the Rock Island Passage. Who would have thought to look for it there? No one, that's who, because the last known location for the *Plymouth* was miles from there. But her captain decided to risk the storm rather than stay where they'd been abandoned by the tugboat, and she ended up sinking near Rock Island. And she sank right on top of Napoleon's gold, didn't she? Four hundred million dollars' worth of gold."

DNR Guy's poker face was terrible. He struggled to conceal his surprise, but it wasn't his reaction I was interested in just then. The driver shot another look at DNR Guy, his own shock apparent on his face.

"Is she right?" he asked DNR Guy, slamming on the brakes when he finally looked forward again, making me nearly topple over sideways.

"Don't worry about it," DNR Guy said. "You'll be paid well for your services."

"You're using some kind of submersible to get at the gold, aren't you?" I said. "Where are you storing it?"

DNR Guy glared at me and whispered, "You've just sealed your fate, missy."

That grin returned, reptilian and cold, but before he or I could say anything more, the van came to a stop.

"We're here," Driver Guy said.

DNR Guy brandished his gun one last time, just in case I'd forgotten about it. Then he draped a beach towel over his arm and hand, hiding the weapon.

"Behave or I'll shoot you where you stand. Don't think I won't. Our boat is at the ready, and by the time anyone reacts to the shooting, we'll be halfway to Canada and well on our way to disappearing."

I believed him.

When the van door slid open, I scooted out and followed Driver Guy, while DNR Guy fell into step behind me. We boarded a boat a little bigger than Marty's, and once we were on board, DNR Guy dropped the towel and tucked the gun into the waist of his pants. Then he removed a zip tie from a tackle box and secured my wrists behind me before pushing me down onto one of the padded benches at the back. A quick look around the boat revealed a rack of scuba tanks secured to one side with bungee cords and a high-end sonar device attached to the ceiling in the pilothouse. This boat was rigged for some serious underwater work.

The zip tie was uncomfortably tight, and I twisted my hands in a futile effort to relieve the pinch of it. In doing so, the side of my hand scraped up against a tiny but sharp protuberance on one of the boat's interior metal braces. I winced as I felt it slice into my skin; then I froze, realizing what a stroke of luck it might be.

DNR Guy sat across from me, while Driver Guy started the engine and motored us out of the marina. The boat bobbed its way over the waves, giving me the perfect cover, and I began rubbing the zip tie against that sharp little point, going up and down with the motion of the boat. Though I thought I was being subtle, I didn't like the way DNR Guy kept looking at me. I needed to distract him.

"Why all this ridiculous subterfuge with a fake lake monster? Why not just claim the gold and bring it up?" I asked him.

"Do you have any idea what a hassle that would cause?" he said, leaning toward me, his voice low. He glanced toward Driver Guy, probably to make sure he couldn't hear him. "There'd be claims and lawsuits lasting Lord knows how many years. It's not a finders-keepers game and four hundred mil is a lot of money. France and America could both have claims. Descendants of the ship it was on might have claims. Shipping companies, ecological societies, and museums would all get in the fight. I've seen it happen before with other sunken treasures. It would get tied up in the courts for years." He paused, shaking his head, his lips compressed in a determined line. "Nope. I've come too far to deal with that. That gold is mine. Half of it anyway."

"Only half?"

Something shifted in his eyes, and he leaned back with an awkward, halfhearted shrug. "Technically, I could claim it all, since I'm the one who found it, but I had to partner with someone that could fund the retrieval. It's harder than it looks, particularly if we want to do it in a way that avoids attracting attention."

"Well, it seems you failed on that account," I said, "though the deer and fish carcasses were a nice touch."

He smiled.

"How did you know about my involvement?" I asked. "I mean, aside from Marty, I thought I was way under the radar. Did you figure it out when I hit upon the spot you were working in yesterday?"

He laughed, shaking his head. "We knew about your so-called involvement from the moment that dumb-ass Flanders guy thought about hiring you. We tried to talk him out of it, even threatened to file a complaint if he used police funds to pay for it, but he was determined. Used his own money even."

I tucked that little revelation away for later consideration. Now that we were far enough out from shore, Driver Guy increased our speed, steering us through Green Bay and toward the western side of Washington Island and Lake Michigan. The waves grew choppier once we cleared Gills Rock and entered Death's Door, and that enabled me to work a little harder on the zip tie, though my movements were also less precise. I prayed that the little metal defect wouldn't break off, knowing that with every minute that went by, with every mile of water we covered, time was running out. I had a plan, albeit a desperate one, and when the boat sped up even more as we came abreast of Washington Island, I picked up the pace of my sawing motion, taking care to move only my hands and wrists and not my upper arms. At the same time, I started breathing fast and shallow, hoping that if DNR Guy noticed it, he'd chalk it up to panic, which wouldn't have been a totally wrong assumption. I had no doubt those guys intended to kill me, and that scared the hell out of me.

DNR Guy was staring at me again, so I stirred things up some more.

"How much of the four hundred million are *you* getting?" I yelled at Driver Guy.

"Shut up!" DNR Guy seethed, shooting another worried glance in Driver Guy's direction.

I kept at my rapid breathing and sawing, my growing panic making the first part easy and making me not care anymore if DNR Guy saw my arms moving.

"What makes you think your fate won't be the same as mine?" I went on, yelling at Driver Guy. "He just told me that he's splitting that four hundred million fifty-fifty with whoever's financing this gig. That doesn't leave much for you, does it?"

"I told you to shut the hell up!" DNR Guy shouted, taking his gun from the waist of his pants and aiming it in my direction.

"Okay, okay," I said, hyperventilating even more, as much out of fear as from any planned attempt at escape.

I squirmed, sawing frantically at my restraint, feeling the stickiness of blood on my hands. Panicked that time was running out, I strained my arms to add tension on the tie. I squirmed some more as if trying to get comfortable and turned my head away from DNR Guy and the gun, looking out the back of the boat instead.

What I saw made my heart skip a beat and I blinked hard, unsure if I was imagining things. Once I was convinced it was real, I said, "Oh, look."

It wasn't a planned utterance, but it came at a timely moment because the zip tie broke just as DNR Guy looked that way. I desperately wanted to shake and move my hands to get my circulation going again, but I gripped the broken zip tie and kept my arms behind me, buying every second I had.

"Better not shoot me now," I said, jutting my chin toward the boat behind us. "You've got witnesses."

Driver Guy turned to look, throttling down the engine in the process. It was now or never. I stood and flung myself over the side into the water.

I was prepared for the cold shock of it that time, though the water there was warmer than the water I'd been dumped into yesterday. The bay waters can reach temperatures in the eighties at the peak of summer, and the spot we were currently in was one where bay and lake waters mixed. What I wasn't expecting was the impact. Even though Driver Guy had throttled down, the boat was still moving at a good clip, and I wasn't prepared for how unforgiving the water would be when I hit it.

I managed to stifle my gasp and not take in a mouthful of water, but only because the wind was knocked out of me. Momentarily stunned, I let my body sink into the cool depths of the water. Then I had an image of a bullet zipping a path through that water and into my heart, and it spurred me to action.

I rolled into a prone position and swam deeper for a few seconds, stroking and kicking as hard as I could. When I thought I was deep enough, I paused and looked up, seeing the undulating glint of sunlight on the surface waves above. The boat's wake was visible in the patterns, and after orienting myself in what I hoped was the right direction, I swam as hard as I could while beginning a slow ascent with each stroke.

The hyperventilation I'd done beforehand would give me about two minutes before I had to surface. I listened for the sounds of both boat engines—one moving away, the other moving closer—and aimed for the approaching boat. When I finally burst through on the surface, my lungs were screaming for air.

I gulped in a couple of quick breaths in case I had to go down again, and spun myself around in the water, trying to rapidly assess my situation. The approaching boat was coming at me at a frightening speed, and I realized they likely couldn't see me in the water. DNR Guy's boat was moving away fast, headed toward Boyer Bluff. Making a run for it.

I thrust my arms into the air and waved, yelling as loud as I could at the oncoming boat. I couldn't do it for long, though, because having my arms in the air impaired my ability to tread water. Every time I tried to wave, I sank. The boat showed no sign of slowing, and as it drew closer, I saw a Coast Guard insignia on its side. I waved my arms and yelled some more, kicking my legs as hard as I could not only to keep from sinking but to propel myself a little higher out of the water. A quick look around eased my panic because I saw that the coast of Washington Island was only a mile or so away—an easy swim if the Coast Guard boat passed me by.

After one more hard kick, wave, and holler, the patrol boat finally began to slow, and I saw someone on board waving back at me. Relieved, I lowered my arms and treaded water as the boat circled around me. Someone tossed out a flotation ring, and I swam to it, then let them pull me in.

I was nearly to the boat when I realized that the person pulling on that rope was Jon Flanders.

CHAPTER 34

———

"Boy, am I glad to see you," I said to Jon as two young men lifted me out of the water and onto the boat. Seconds later a foil blanket was draped over my shoulders. I pulled it close around me, grateful for the warmth.

"Are you okay?" Jon asked.

I looked toward Boyer Bluff and saw no sign of DNR Guy's boat. "I am now. How did you end up here?"

Jon did that thing where he turned red from his neck up to his forehead. "The cameras I installed at your store. I have the feeds on my phone from when I set them up. This morning I got an initial notification of someone at your back door. I figured it was you letting Newt out like you do each morning and I ignored it. But then I got a second notification for the same thing and that got me curious, so I checked it out. I saw it was you going back outside with a roll of bags, and I was about to close the view when I saw those guys charge at you."

"You've been spying on me with the cameras?" I said.

He blushed and started to stammer but I stopped him by adding, "Thank goodness."

Then I leaned over and gave him a quick peck on the cheek. I wouldn't have thought the man could have turned redder than he was, but he proved me wrong.

"I couldn't see where they took you once you went off camera," Jon said, looking away to hide his painfully obvious embarrassment. It was kind of adorable. "But I knew there were other cameras along the roads, including the one on your front door. I saw a van that came out from the side of your building, and from there I was able to track it to the marina using CCTV cameras around town. I couldn't get to the mainland fast enough to step in, and the nearest sheriff's deputy there was forty minutes away, but I was able to see the boat you boarded. I called the Coast Guard and got them to come through Death's Door to see if the boat went that way. They didn't see it, and I met them at the marina in Detroit Harbor. That's when we saw the boat go by, toward Boyer Bluff, so we took off after them."

"Thank you," I said. "Poor Newt must be losing his mind."

Jon nodded. "I could hear him on both cameras barking up a storm."

A panicked thought came to me. "What time is it?"

"Seven thirty-two," Jon said, glancing at his watch.

"I need to call Rita and let her know what's up with Newt."

"First, tell me what the hell is going on with those guys in the boat?" Jon said.

I shook my head. "I need to call Rita first. If I don't cue her in, Newt might bolt when she opens the store."

"Morgan, you were kidnapped and—"

"I need to call Rita *now*!"

Jon let his head loll back and he stared up at the sky for a moment. Then, after letting out a weighty sigh, he took his phone from his pocket and handed it to me.

Rita was burning with curiosity about what was going on, but she accepted my sense of urgency and resigned herself to the bare minimum of facts. She also promised to look after Newt. When I was done, I handed Jon's phone back to him. We were bobbing in the water, not going anywhere, and the two Coast Guard guys were standing by, just watching and listening.

"Shouldn't you go after those guys in the boat?" I asked Jon. "I'm pretty sure they were going to kill me and dump my body overboard."

"We won't catch them now. My guess is they're on their way to Canada to try their human-trafficking techniques there."

"Human trafficking?" I said, shaking my head, thoroughly confused. "What are you talking about? They weren't human traffickers. They're murderers who found Napoleon's gold and are desperately trying to hide it while they squirrel it away. They killed Oliver Sykes. Marty, too. That one guy shot him. They're the explanation behind why you hired me."

Jon blinked several times, staring at me as he processed that. The two Coast Guard fellows straightened up, suddenly more interested in what was going on.

"Those guys came after me because I got too close to their secret yesterday when I was dumped out of my boat. I saw them or at least the submersible they're using to bring the gold up. It's just off the coast of Rock Island, underneath the wreck of the *Plymouth*."

"You know all this . . . how?" Jon asked, looking skeptical.

"DNR Guy told me."

"DNR Guy?" Jon said.

I gave him an exasperated look. "That's what I called the guy with the gun because I didn't know his name. He was wearing a DNR uniform. I can give you descriptions for both men. You need to go after them. Believe me, they aren't headed for Canada, at least not yet. Not until they finish getting their gold."

I'd allowed the foil blanket to fall off my shoulders while I was talking and a chill came over me, making me shiver.

"Take me into shore," Jon said to the Coast Guard guys. "I need to get her someplace warm. And get on the radio to see if anyone can spot that boat."

The throttle was pushed forward, and within a matter of minutes, we were pulling into Detroit Harbor.

"Thanks, guys," Jon said to the Coast Guard fellows. "I've got it from here. Appreciate your help."

The guys nodded and watched us disembark before heading out again. Jon steered me down the pier to a parking area, where I saw his police cruiser.

"If it's okay with you, I'm going to take you to my place to get you some dry clothes while I take care of some business. I need to talk to you some more about what happened. Besides, the next ferry to the mainland isn't for another forty minutes."

I nodded, feeling the morning chill more acutely now that I was up and moving with my wet clothes on. It felt better once we were inside his car and out of the wind. Jon cranked the heat up to full blast, but the drive was a short one and the car never had a chance to warm up much. He drove along the western coast of the island on Green Bay Road for a couple of miles and then headed inland briefly before turning onto a gravel drive.

Jon's house was at the end of that gravel drive on a small hill surrounded by trees, including several apple trees laden with fruit. The cleared area near the house held a garden that was enclosed inside a tall, gated chicken wire fence—there are lots of hungry deer in these parts—and I saw squash, pumpkins, lettuce, radishes, peas, and beans growing inside. The house, a sprawling ranch style with lots of tall windows, looked like new construction.

"Nice spot," I said as Jon stopped in front of a three-car garage, which I assumed held his personal vehicle. What else might he have in there? A boat, perhaps?

He shifted the police car into park and turned off the engine.

"Thanks. I've got almost six acres and a beach-access road along with fifty feet of shoreline about a tenth of a mile from here. There are some hair-raising iron stairs built into the cliff leading down to my tiny piece of beach, but I have a pier there, where I can keep a small boat without having to pay a slip fee to a marina. Come on inside and I'll give you the nickel tour."

Wrapping the foil blanket tight around me, I followed him onto a long front porch and waited as he unlocked the door. The house smelled wonderful inside, a mix of cinnamon and other spices I couldn't quite nail down. It was surprisingly neat for a bachelor pad, and the furnishings all looked new and well cared for. I wondered how much of it he'd brought with him from Colorado and how much he'd bought new. Moving onto an island isn't easy, what with the constraints imposed by the ferry schedules and the space limitations on the boats. I vaguely remembered Jon making a comment about his furniture coming from Wally World the first time he saw my apartment, but this stuff was clearly higher end than that.

He led me past a living room that had a wood-burning fireplace, two leather chairs, and a leather couch, and stopped at the doorway to a bathroom.

"There are towels in the cabinet there," he said, pointing to a built-in cupboard on one wall. "I'll grab you some clothes of mine. They'll be too big but at least they'll be dry."

He disappeared into another room and returned a moment later with a T-shirt, a pair of drawstring sweatpants, and some heavy wool socks.

"You should drink something warm. Would you prefer coffee or tea?" he asked.

"Coffee, please. Thanks." I took the clothes from him and shut the door.

I peeled out of my wet clothes, dried my hair the best I could, and, after a quick wipe down, pulled on the clothes he'd given me. While the shirt and pants were loose and baggy, the socks fit like a glove and felt wonderful on my freezing-cold feet. Carrying my wet clothes and shoes back out to the kitchen, I found Jon sliding a cup of coffee toward me on the counter. He nodded at a square baking pan with a lid on it.

"That's some coffee cake I baked yesterday. Feel free to help yourself. The washer and dryer are through there," he said, pointing to a door off the kitchen.

I went into the laundry room, tossed my wet clothes in the washer, and started it on a speed cycle. The key to my place, which had miraculously stayed in the pocket of my shorts, I put on top of the washer.

When I came back into the kitchen, Jon said, "I just got a call from the Coast Guard. They found the boat those guys had you on abandoned over near Jackson Harbor. I'm going to head over there and have a look. Will you be okay here for an hour or so? I'll drive you back to the ferry and your store once I'm freed up, but I really want to get a look at this boat while the evidence is fresh."

Part of me wanted to go with him; another part of me desperately wanted to get back to Newt, knowing he had to be anxious without me there. Still another part of me felt exhausted and surprisingly cozy in my warm, oversized clothes, holding a hot mug of coffee, which I'd given a passing grade to with my first sip. And I knew Rita and Devon would take care of Newt until I could get home.

"If you're okay with me staying here alone in your house, I'm okay with it," I said.

"Of course. Call me if anything comes up."

"I don't have a phone," I reminded him.

"Right. Well ... no worries. I shouldn't be too long."

As soon as Jon went out the door, I checked out the crumb-topped coffee cake, which smelled divine. I cut myself a healthy piece and carried it and my coffee into the living room. The house was eerily quiet with only the faint hum of the washer to be heard, so I turned on the TV and flipped channels to a cable news station. Then I curled up on the couch, pulling a thick, soft throw over me.

I considered my surroundings, figuring the house and its acreage must have been worth at least half a million dollars on today's market. Most of the furnishings appeared to be new. The washer and dryer looked brand-new. The kitchen had high-end solid-surface countertops and solid wood cabinetry. How had Jon, someone who had supposedly made a policeman's salary prior to moving here, managed to afford a place like this? And what had DNR Guy said about the money I'd been paid? That Jon had paid for it out of his own pocket. A thousand bucks in cash. How was it he had that kind of money just lying around?

Past insecurities reared their ugly heads, and I felt the first vestiges of panic rise in my chest. I mean, what did I really know about Jon Flanders? Not much, I realized. He was stingy with information about his past life and relatively new to the area. Yet he possessed an uncomfortable amount of knowledge about me and my past and had connections to all that awful business in New Jersey. *And* he was spying on me!

Presumably he would have had to undergo a thorough and extensive background check in order to get a police chief's job, even for a force as small as that one, but I knew how easy it was to hide things and deceive people if someone put their mind to it. Look what David had managed to do. Was I being naive and gullible? Again?

I gobbled down my coffee cake and then got up from the couch to carry my dish to the kitchen sink. From there, I explored the house some more, looking for a home office or a desk with a computer. I found what was obviously the master bedroom, a guest bedroom, and then a third door that was locked. Why would anyone lock a door inside their own house? Was it because I was there? Was Jon hiding something he didn't want me to see?

I heard the faint sound of a tune playing and realized my wash was done. I went into the laundry room and switched my clothes from the washer to the dryer. Then I went back to that locked door. Warning bells niggled at the back of my brain, and after checking the most obvious places I could think of for a key, I took a closer look at the lock. It was a basic door-handle lock, the kind with a button to turn on the other side, not a dead bolt.

"Okay," I said. "This should be easy pickings."

I went back into the kitchen and retrieved a dinner knife from the silverware drawer. Carrying it back to the door, I went to work, trying to spring the latch enough to get the door open, trying to do so carefully so as not to damage the wood trim and leave evidence of my attempts.

I was diligently manipulating the knife when a loud knocking came from somewhere behind me, making me nearly jump out of my skin. My first thought was that it had been the washer trying to spin with an unbalanced load, but then I remembered that I'd already put my clothes in the dryer. The knocking came again, urgent and loud, and I realized someone was at the front door.

I shoved the knife into the pocket of my sweatpants and went to the door. A woman in a sheriff's uniform and a baseball-style cap stood on the porch.

"Are you Morgan Carter?" she asked.

"I am."

"Chief Flanders sent me to pick you up and take you to a safe location. We need to hurry."

"Why? What's going on?"

"He didn't give me specifics, ma'am. Just said I was to get you to the other location as quickly as possible."

She held a cell phone in one hand and kept her head bent, staring at it. I tried to see what was on the screen, but the sun and the angle were wrong. With her free hand she did a come-on gesture at me, the rather large diamond on her finger catching the sunlight.

"Let's move!" she said, her tone urgent and demanding.

Without another thought, I stepped outside and pulled the door closed behind me. Belatedly I wondered if I should have locked it but by then I was already halfway across the yard to a plain dark-blue sedan parked alongside the house.

"Get in the backseat," the officer commanded. "And keep your head down."

Now I was spooked. What the hell had happened? Had DNR Guy and his pal somehow gotten away and decided to come after me? As I opened the back door to the car, climbed in, and stretched out on the seat, I wondered how they had known where I was. Had they recognized Jon in the Coast Guard boat?

As I grabbed the armrest and pulled the back door closed behind me, something niggled in my brain, a warning bell that told me something was off. The officer got in, started the car, pulled a fast U-turn, and then fishtailed out to the road. I saw that even though the car we were in wasn't marked as an official police vehicle, there was a metal grid separating me from the front seat. I wanted to sit up to see where we were going and what might be around us, but I was afraid to. Were there armed men out there looking for me?

As I hunkered down in the back, trying to make sense of it all, something underneath the front driver's seat caught my eye. I reached down, grabbed an edge of it, and pulled it out. I cursed to myself, knowing then that I was not only an idiot, I was also in some serious trouble. Again.

It was a purple-and-orange athletic shoe, an exact match for the one that had remained on Will Stokstad's dead foot.

CHAPTER 35

—

I did sit up then, but all I could see was a tree-lined dirt road in front of me and clouds of roiling dust behind. Through the grate, I saw the officer's eyes meet mine in the rearview mirror. Except I felt certain at that point that she wasn't really a police officer.

I glanced around for anything I might use as a weapon and that was when I noticed the lack of handles on the insides of the back doors. There was no way for me to open them, effectively trapping me in the backseat until someone opened the doors from the outside. My captor might not have been a real cop, but that car had features like a real police vehicle. I knew because I'd ridden in one before, just two years earlier, when my parents had been murdered.

Was my captor armed? I turned my head sideways, leaned into the grate, and studied her waist. She was wearing a belt, but I couldn't see any weapon on it. Nor could I see the front of her uniform fully. I tried to remember what she'd looked like when I'd answered the door.

While I didn't recall seeing a weapon, I also knew that I hadn't been totally focused. Between my guilt over my attempted break-in to Jon's locked room and the sense of urgency I felt from what the woman had told me, my brain hadn't been concentrating on what it should have been. I mentally slapped myself for not realizing sooner that something was off. Then I tried to figure out what to do next.

"Where are you taking me?"

My question was answered with stony silence—she didn't even look in the mirror again—and I decided to use whatever time I had left coming up with a plan for my escape. I sat back in my seat, and as my arms fell to my sides, I felt something hard in my right pocket. That was when I remembered the dinner knife. It wasn't sharp, but it did have some small serrations on one side. My eyes wandered back down to the floor and the heel of Will's shoe sticking out from beneath the seat. If I removed the shoelace, maybe I could create a garotte with it and the knife. The woman driving the car wasn't big. I had a couple of inches and several pounds on her, and she'd have to let me out of the car eventually.

I tried to imagine what I'd have to do. It wouldn't be easy to get into the position I'd need to make use of a garotte. Still, the more options I had, the better. I was about to reach down and grab the shoe, when my captor brought the car to a stop. Up ahead I saw a small cabin nestled in a clearing, and beyond that, through the trees, I could see light sparkling on water. The woman turned the car's engine off, got out, and walked up to the cabin, disappearing inside. I briefly considered trying to kick out one of the car windows and attempting an escape on foot, but before I could even change position, the woman emerged from the cabin accompanied by a man. I was now outnumbered.

As they drew closer, I realized I knew the man. He was the fellow who had bought the antique Ouija board in my store a week earlier. I didn't know his first name but recalled Devon saying that his last name was Devereaux.

The duo walked up to the driver's side of the car and Devereaux looked in the window at me. He sighed and showed me the gun he held. With the other hand, he opened the back door of the car.

"Out," he said, waving his gun hand.

I got out and stood next to the car as the woman got back in it and drove away.

"What is this about?" I asked, trying to play dumb. Bad move.

"Do you think I'm an idiot?" Devereaux said irritably. "Roger already told me what you told him, so I know you've figured out what we're doing. And now, thanks to you, we've had to abandon one of our boats, which should be burning into oblivion out on the water as we speak. All unfortunate circumstances for you, I'm afraid."

He shook his head and tsked me. Then he gestured toward the cabin with his gun hand. "Let's go."

So much for my hope that the guys who had kidnapped me had been captured. "Who is Roger?" I asked over my shoulder. "Is he the DNR guy?"

"I got Roger a job with the DNR, yes. He's my nephew." He let out an annoyed breath and then added, "On my wife's side."

"Hey, I have no skin in this game," I said, stopping near the back corner of the cabin where a gas generator was humming away. I turned to face him on legs that shook. "I was hired on as a consultant solely to rule in or out the presence of a lake monster. I can safely rule that out now, and I'm happy to write up a report that says so. What you do with your gold and your shipwreck is no business of mine."

It was a statement born of desperation, one that had little hope of working, though I decided to juice up my offer a bit, figuring it couldn't hurt.

"Though if you find any interesting pieces down there on your wreck or trinkets amongst your gold that would fit in with my store's inventory, I'd be happy to make you an offer. Just let me know what you have." I was babbling, talking too much and too fast, but I felt helpless to stop myself. "I've got money. Lots of it. I'd pay handsomely. You don't even have to sell me anything. I'll just pay you. I'm sure we can work something out."

He scoffed, shaking his head woefully. "I don't need your money," he said. "You don't have any idea who I am, do you?"

"I know you've been a customer of mine, Mr. Devereaux."

His eyebrows arched up in surprise when I said his name. "Good memory."

"I make a point of remembering my customers. Do you really have a mother in Mississippi who holds séances?"

He looked mildly impressed with my ability to resurrect this tidbit about him, maybe because I hadn't been the person who waited on him.

"As a matter of fact, I do," he said, "though holding séances is just what she does to amuse her friends. Most of her talents these days are reserved for more sophisticated situations, like exorcisms, tarot card readings, and ghost hunting." He straightened up a bit and stuck his chin out. "I'm not ashamed to admit that I come from a long line of well-established con men and women dating back to the early 1900s. It's how our family made their millions initially, and my mom is old-school, still practicing the family's earliest talents. She does quite well with it, though most of the family money nowadays comes from land we own and our riverboat casinos. I was pitching a lake boat casino here, thinking it would be a good idea, albeit rather seasonal. But then I found the gold and put things on hold."

"You think you can steal Napoleon's gold?"

"It's not stealing. I found it. That makes it mine. Besides, Napoleon has no use for it these days." He chuckled at his own joke.

"Roger said he was the one who found the gold."

"A technicality," Devereaux said with an equivocating waggle of his hand. "He found it with *my* equipment in a spot where *I* told him to look. Hell, that's the only reason I brought him up here from Florida."

"Ownership aside, you're murdering people."

"Yes, well, it's not like we went out of our way to kill anyone. If Mr. Sykes had simply minded his own business, he'd still be alive. But he happened upon our sub while he was scuba diving on our site. The mechanical arms are quite adept once you get the hang of operating them. We were able to rob Mr. Sykes of his gear while keeping him below, and unfortunately, he drowned."

I understood now why Oliver had been found barefoot. They wouldn't have wanted to leave his body with any hint of scuba gear, because that might have directed authorities to start looking into other things. So his fins, tanks, respirator, and buoyancy device had all been removed.

"As for the second fellow, it was the storm that did him in. I mean, it wasn't our fault that he got knocked out of his boat, even if our sub did come up beneath it rather quickly. Of course, once he saw the sub, his fate was sealed. We couldn't have him spreading tales, now, could we?"

"The ME said Will Stokstad drowned."

"Yes, he did," Devereaux said mockingly. "With a little help from our sub. We had to use one of the mechanical grips to grab his arm and hold him beneath the surface." He paused and frowned. "That resulted in a bit of an unexpected problem," he added. "Because then we had to figure out a way to hide the mark left by our grasping claw." Will's body had demonstrated a crush injury on his arm as well as on his torso. Was this why? Had they crushed his arm the same way they did his torso in an attempt to hide the marks left behind by a submersible clamp?

"What about Martin Showalter?" I said, my voice breaking slightly as I said his name. "Roger murdered him in cold blood."

"Again, if he'd just minded his own business . . ." He shrugged. "A minor glitch in our plan, that's all. Things would have been fine if Flanders hadn't gotten that crazy idea to hire you. He's one of those cops with a more modern way of thinking when it comes to a police department's relationship to the community. He's all about transparency and open communication, community involvement . . . yada, yada, yada." He rolled his eyes. "As soon as that Sykes guy's body showed up, Flanders decided he wanted to involve key people—he called us stakeholders—in the decision-making process. I was a part of that group, since I'm a big contributor to the island in many ways and own more than twenty rental properties here. As a local DNR warden, Roger was also included." He sighed, shaking his head in disappointment. "Damn if the group didn't decide we should keep the information about the nature of the injuries from public knowledge. I wasn't too happy about that. I wanted the word to get out."

"To scare off the tourists."

"Of course. The last thing we needed was more nosy people poking around."

His cavalier attitude angered me. I wanted to keep him talking even though I feared all I was doing was postponing the inevitable, so I decided to play to his ego some more.

"I'm impressed that you found Napoleon's gold. People have been looking for that for more than a hundred and fifty years. How did you figure it out?"

He shrugged. "Honestly? It was a bit of a lucky accident. I've been diving in these waters for years and I used to travel to Florida every winter. Roger got me into cave diving down there. I started exploring around this area a couple of years ago because these islands are full of undiscovered caves. Last year, I discovered an underwater tunnel on the north side of Rock Island and decided to explore it. Imagine my delight when I discovered a decent-sized cave that sits above the waterline only twenty feet in. I think the tunnel provided above-water access to the cave thousands of years ago because I found some ancient tools carved out of animal bones in there, evidence of early man.

"Last fall, Roger got laid off and came up here because I knew I could get him a job with the DNR. We were using scuba jets to examine a search grid around the tunnel entrance, thinking we might find more artifacts. I was off skimming along the coastline, and while I was doing that, Roger was exploring some wood debris that turned out to be remains from the long-lost *Plymouth*. He got excited when he realized what ship it was, and then he saw something glimmer and discovered a gold brick."

"Napoleon's gold," I said, a statement, not a question. "Estimated to be worth around four hundred million."

He nodded. "Sounds like you've done your homework." He sucked in a deep breath and let it out slowly. "Unfortunately, our find happened late in the fall, and by the time we found a reliably private way to have the gold brick verified as being from the stash Napoleon sent during the Civil War, winter had arrived, so we couldn't dive anymore. We tried ice diving, but a good portion of the wreckage, and presumably the gold, is resting at the bottom of an underwater cliff that drops down nearly one hundred and thirty feet. We were forced to wait, and I used that time to strategize. I realized that diving wasn't the most practical way to retrieve the gold, so I bought the submersible and had some very specific alterations made to it."

"You designed it to resemble a Loch Ness Monster," I said. "Not the greatest deterrent. Rumors of a Loch Ness Monster in these waters could attract people rather than scare them away."

His chin jutted out and a hint of a scowl came over his face with my criticism. "Which is why Roger came up with the brilliant idea to create victims with the fish and deer carcasses. The human victims that followed weren't planned, but they were effective. And if I've learned anything over the years, it's that you need to seize the moments when they happen."

I had to respect the brilliance of Devereaux's scheme, awful as it was. "You gave the submersible an appendage that resembles a long neck and another that resembles a tail," I said. "And glowing eyes. All to make it look like a lake monster. It seems I'm not the only one who has done her homework."

He smiled, clearly pleased. "Yes, it was a stroke of brilliance, if I do say so myself. There are two headlights that can be dimmed or brightened, and I had them made to look like eyes. And the appendages, as you call them, are fully retractable mechanical arms that are operable from inside the sub, which can hold two men at a time. The gold is heavy, and it's a slow, cumbersome process: digging to find it beneath pieces of the shipwreck or the muddy bottom, and then transporting what we do find to a secret location. I have to say, the guy I ordered the sub from did a magnificent job of retrofitting the thing. It wasn't cheap, but it will be well worth the expense if I get four hundred million in gold in return."

"How did you manage to hide delivery of a vessel like that?"

"Ironically, it followed much the same route that was taken by Napoleon's gold, transported on a semi through Canada and then on a ship into Lake Michigan. We simply offloaded it from the ship out in the middle of the lake. That was the sub's maiden voyage. Once it was in the water, the cave I found made a perfect hiding spot. The tunnel leading into it serves as a natural airlock and it and the cave are both big enough for the submersible. Roger and I dive into the cave, man the sub, do our thing, and then return to the cave."

"I don't understand," I said, shaking my head. "If you're already as well off as you claim, why go through all this?"

"It's not about the money," he said, his tone mocking. "It's about the thrill of the hunt, the prestige of finding a long-lost treasure that so many others have looked for and failed to find, though I daresay Roger wouldn't agree. His side of the family hasn't been as successful in finding ways to make money without ending up in jail."

"It would seem you're having the same problem. You've murdered three people."

"Soon to be a fourth," he said with horrifying delight. Seeing the terror on my face, he sobered and said, "Yes, well, I admit I did underestimate the determination of the tourists who come here, and I think I underestimated you, too. Flanders assured us that you would get to the bottom of what was going on, but I calculated it as a long shot. I tried to scare you off, but clearly that didn't work."

"That's why you came into my store, isn't it? To check me out?"

He shrugged, looking pleased with himself. "In part, though my mother will truly love that Ouija board. My main reason for coming to your store was to make sure you didn't have any security cameras. You know, to make sure no one saw me leave you that little warning that you chose to ignore."

"The note?" I said, remembering the attack on Devon.

He cocked his head to one side and smiled. "Come on now. Admit it. The delivery method was quite clever of me, wasn't it?"

I didn't answer; I just glared at him.

"Where were you when I came back, by the way? I expected my message to be delivered a bit more personally. I had to settle for your employee instead. That was rather rude of you."

"You're insane," I said, appalled.

"Whatever," he said dismissively. "I think we're done with the chitchat. Let's go inside."

A shiver shook me as I stepped over the threshold and into the cabin, in part because it was cold in there, but also because I was keenly aware of that gun aimed at my back. The interior of the cabin was basic and rustic with no furniture, no curtains on the two grimy windows, and a dirt floor. Electrical cords snaked along the walls and the floor leading to two bare-bulb lights that hung from the ceiling. The light they emitted was dismal, but Devereaux left the cabin door open, allowing some daylight inside. It helped to highlight the only other thing in the room.

It took me a moment to figure out what the hell it was, between the carved wooden base, the hydraulic pistons, and the giant lid. It resembled one of those large presses that dry cleaners use. Or a giant coffin.

"Impressive, isn't it?" Devereaux said as I stared at the structure. "I'm quite proud of the design. It turned out larger than I'd initially intended, given that it was meant to be used on animals, but that proved to be a lucky mistake because, in the end, we needed it to be big enough for people."

I stepped closer and studied the underside of the raised wooden lid. Part of it had been carved in a pattern that resembled teeth—

crushing, molar-type teeth—and it appeared to mesh with a similar pattern carved into the top surface of the base. It was a pattern I'd seen before, in the bruises and indentations left behind in the dead flesh of two men.

It seemed I'd found my lake monster after all.

CHAPTER 36

—

You built this bizarre contraption to mimic the bite of a giant lake monster?" I said.

I'd never admit it, but I was impressed with this guy's ingenuity. Too bad it was being wasted on something twisted, illegal, and deadly.

"Wood carving is another hobby of mine," he said, chin jutting, pride evident in his voice.

"So many hobbies. Where do you find the time?" I taunted.

I half expected to feel that bullet smash into me from behind any second. But then Devereaux said, "You are about to become intimately acquainted with my little invention. How sad, yet ironic, for the monster hunter to be killed by one," he said with mock regret, thereby returning the taunt. "If only you'd minded your own business."

What he said, not to mention the madness I could hear in his voice, terrified me. But it also provided me with a fleeting moment of relief. He couldn't very well shoot me and pass that off as an attack by a lake monster. If he intended to make me look like one more of Chomp's victims, he'd have to find another way to kill me. That was when the terror returned. Was he planning to simply crush me to death in that thing? If so, I wasn't going down without a fight. I'd rather be shot than die by being slowly crushed to death. I needed to keep stalling for time and try to come up with a way out of this.

"Who was that woman who drove me here?"

"That was my wife, Ginger. I knew you'd seen me before and wouldn't be likely to go anywhere with me, so she was happy to help. She'll do anything necessary to protect the lifestyle she's become accustomed to."

"How did you know where I was?"

"Police scanner. I heard that Flanders had plucked you out of the water, and then the call about the boat that Roger had to abandon. I followed Flanders after the Coast Guard dropped you off and figured he'd want to go check out the abandoned boat, leaving you at his place. Ginger had the police uniform from a Halloween gig we did two years ago. I had one of those black-and-white jail outfits and I was supposed to go as her prisoner. I bought the police car at an auction to make it all the more authentic. I even found some blue lights to attach to the roof." He looked away and smiled. "That was a fun party."

"Jon has security cameras installed at his place. He's bound to know that your wife came and got me."

Devereaux scowled at me for bringing him out of his momentary reverie. "Oh, I know about the cameras," he said. "I'm not worried. Jon Flanders has never actually met Ginger and she wore a baseball cap to hide her face. I told her to make sure she kept her head down and to park the car on the side of the house, out of sight of the cameras. Plus, I took the plates off the car."

I cursed under my breath.

Devereaux cocked his head to one side and gave me a questioning look. "There is one thing I haven't figured out," he said. "How did Flanders know to come after Roger and you in the boat? I can't figure out how he copped onto that so fast. Did he give you a tracker of some sort?"

I shook my head and now it was my turn to smile. "He saw the abduction on my security camera, and he was able to track Roger using CCTV."

Devereaux looked askance. "I checked your store for cameras when I bought the Ouija board, remember? And I looked again just to make sure when I paid your employee that fun little visit. You don't have any security cameras."

"I do now, thanks to you and your *fun little visit*. Jon Flanders installed them the very next day."

"Hunh," Devereaux said, scowling. Then he shrugged. "Oh, well, can't be helped now. Best get on with things."

I watched him tuck the gun into the waistband at the back of his pants. Panic made me start to tremble, and I fingered the outside of the pocket that held the dinner knife, willing myself to stay controlled. I didn't know exactly how Devereaux planned to kill me, but he'd probably have to get up close. I flashed back to the human anatomy class I'd taken in college and thought about soft tissue points that might be susceptible to the plunge of a dull knife. I'd need to find a way to distract Devereaux to give myself as much of an advantage as possible. After turning slightly so that the knife pocket was away from Devereaux, I slipped my hand inside and gripped the knife handle firmly. Then I turned back to face Devereaux, my eyes growing big. I looked past him toward the door, surprised and confused by what I saw.

"What are you doing here?" I said.

Devereaux burst out laughing. "What kind of an idiot do you take me for?" he said.

Thinking fast, I said, "The kind of idiot who thinks he can get away with another murder." I nodded toward his monster teeth contraption. "That getup you built is so amateurish. You didn't fool anyone. If you'd really done your homework, you would have known that a lake creature like that would have tearing teeth, not grinding teeth. No one ever believed there was a lake monster out there."

The smile on Devereaux's face morphed into an angry scowl. "Flanders did," he retorted. "That's why the idiot wanted to hire you. How that man got the chief's position is beyond me. He's as gullible as they come."

"Not as gullible as you think," Jon said from where he stood behind Devereaux. He lifted the gun from the back of Devereaux's waistband and tossed it out the open door. "That's my gun you feel poking into your back," he said. "Hands behind your head."

The startled look on Devereaux's face was well worth the price of admission. He slowly raised his hands and placed them behind his head, allowing me to finally relax.

For a whole millisecond.

Devereaux moved so unexpectedly that it took my brain several seconds to process what was happening. I watched as he spun around with amazing speed and grace, and then I saw Jon's gun go flying off to the side and skitter out of reach beneath the contraption. The two men struggled, and at first it appeared that Jon was going to restrain Devereaux easily, but then Devereaux swung a leg toward Jon and the next thing I knew both men were on the dirt floor rolling around and grunting. Devereaux managed to get on top and straddle Jon, using his thighs to pin Jon's arms to his side. He outweighed Jon by at least forty pounds, and despite Jon's wild, bucking attempts to get loose, he could barely move. Then Devereaux started punching.

I reacted with pure instinct. Pulling the knife from my pocket, I lunged at Devereaux, snaking the fingers of my free hand through his hair, gripping tight, and yanking his head back. Then I used my other hand to dig the serrated edge of the dinner knife into the side of his neck. Devereaux froze.

"One move and I will slash open the side of your neck and let you bleed to death right here," I said.

I dug those tiny serrations in a little deeper to emphasize my point, even though I had doubts that the knife would cut him at all.

Jon finally wriggled out from beneath Devereaux and scurried around to my side. He grabbed Devereaux's arms and yanked them back, tying his wrists together with a zip tie. Poetic justice. When that was done, I released my hold on Devereaux and walked around to stand in front of him, the knife still in my hand.

Devereaux looked at the knife, then at me. "Are you kidding me?" he growled, shaking his head. "A goddamned dinner knife? Son of a bitch!"

"Happy to do my part," I said.

I walked over and knelt in front of Devereaux's contraption while Jon yanked the man to his feet. I reached underneath and used the knife to fish Jon's gun out. Picking it up, I blew some dirt off it and walked over to hand it to Jon, who examined and then holstered it.

"Would you mind collecting that one for me, too?" Jon asked, nodding toward the gun he'd tossed out the door.

As I went to get it, I heard Devereaux ask Jon, "How the hell did you find this place?"

"Your wife, Ginger, was quite forthcoming once I informed her that one of you was going to prison for a very long time, and if she'd like to start cooperating in preparation for turning state's evidence and maybe working out a deal, she should do so right away and tell me where she took Morgan. She's outside in my car waiting for you. I'm sure she'd be happy to fill you in on the specifics."

Devereaux looked confused. "But how did you know to go after Ginger? She assured me she was careful to keep her face away from your security cameras. And you've never met her. You don't even know what she looks like."

"Oh, but I do," Jon said. "You see, you once complained to me about how your wife had an insatiable taste for diamonds that no amount of jewelry seemed able to quench. To prove your point, you showed me a picture of her and the giant diamond in her engagement ring. That rock was quite memorable, and it showed up on my cameras clear as day, even catching the sun and reflecting a brief flash of light. So while your wife didn't show her face to my cameras, that ring was a dead giveaway." He paused and looked over at the contraption against the wall.

"Meet Chomp," I said with a grin.

Jon winced. "Did you build that thing?" he asked Devereaux.

The man's chin jutted. "I did. You probably don't know this about me, but I have a degree in engineering and own several patents."

I rolled my eyes. "Are those patents for other machines designed to steal from or murder people?"

He shot Jon a look of irritation. "She's so annoying," he said. "I don't know why you insisted on hiring her. This whole thing would have been a lot simpler if she'd never gotten involved."

Jon grinned, making Devereaux frown. "She figured it all out," Jon told him.

"Whatever," Devereaux said irritably. Then, in his best patronizing tone, he added, "I'm not going to give up my claim on the gold."

"We'll see about that," Jon said. "In the meantime, this gullible idiot is about to place you under arrest. Mason Devereaux, you have the right to remain silent..."

While Jon recited the Miranda warning to Devereaux, I went back outside and walked down toward the beach. There was a small pier there, one of those kinds that can easily be taken apart and pulled out of the water. Currently attached to that pier was a small boat with several tarps and scuba tanks in the back of it. I wondered if those tarps had been used to conceal the bodies of the men Devereaux had killed and maimed with his Chomp machine. I also wondered how much gold he'd found so far, and how much of a legal battle would ensue over it. Would it go international?

Sadly, the people most likely to benefit the most from the gold's discovery would be the lawyers hired to handle the inevitable legal battles. It was enough to make Napoleon turn over in his grave.

CHAPTER 37

⁓

Jon had one of his officers come to collect Mason and Ginger, after he arranged for some Door County sheriffs to meet the island ferry on the peninsula side and escort the couple to their new home at the county jail in Sturgeon Bay. After I told Jon about the shoe I'd found under the seat in Ginger's police car, he called and instructed his other officer to get the state's crime unit to come and assist with the evidence collection both at the Devereaux house and at the burned boat that Roger had used. It was a little nerve-racking to learn that Roger was still on the loose, but Jon assured me they'd find him. Then he drove me back to his place, where I was able to get back into my cleaned and dried clothes.

"Thanks again for your help earlier," he said when I emerged from the bathroom. "You may have saved my life."

"My pleasure."

"I am curious about one thing, though. How did you happen to have one of my knives in your possession?"

I hesitated, not wanting to admit the truth, but unable to come up with a plausible lie in such short order. "I'm ashamed to admit it, but I was trying to jimmy the lock on that room over there," I said, pointing toward the third bedroom. "It seems odd to have a locked door inside your home if you live alone."

"All you had to do was ask," he said.

He walked over, removed a key ring from his pocket, and unlocked the door. "It's my home office. I keep a lot of confidential files in there, plus case notes and other stuff that I wouldn't want other people's eyes on."

After giving the room a quick once-over—it looked like any other home office space—I gave him a questioning look. "But you live alone, don't you? How many people are in your house who might wander into your office?"

"I did leave you here alone," he pointed out. He had me there. "But locking it is just a habit." He raked his teeth over his lower lip. "There's something you should probably know about me."

I braced myself for something I wouldn't want to hear. Was he a player? Did he have a parade of girlfriends traipsing through the place on a regular basis? Or worse, one special girlfriend who spent a lot of time there? I hadn't seen evidence of a regular female visitor, but then I hadn't looked for it either. I'd been too busy trying to break into his office.

"I was married," he said.

Okay. I hadn't seen that one coming.

"You're divorced?" I asked, trying to make it sound casual but knowing I failed.

He shook his head, and for a brief second, my heart sank. Then he added, "I'm a widower."

Oh, geez.

"My wife and three-year-old son were killed in an accident in Colorado three years ago," he said, making me feel like a reprehensible heel. "My son was riding his tricycle at a park and a garbage truck driver lost control, went up over the curb, through the grass, and hit him. My wife saw the truck coming and tried to save our son, but they both ended up dead."

"Oh, my God!" I said, clapping an open hand to my chest, where I felt a sudden physical ache. "How awful."

"Yeah, and to top it off, the truck driver was drunk. Turned out, he had a history of driving drunk on the job and had been reprimanded several times but still allowed to drive."

"Good God, Jon. I'm so sorry." I reached over and put a hand on his arm. My eyes burned with unshed tears.

"Anyway, I got into the habit of locking my home office because of them . . . well, mostly because of Bjorn. I was a homicide detective in Colorado. Not only did I keep files in there with pictures that I wouldn't want either of them to see, it was also where I kept my gun."

"I am so, so sorry," I said again, feeling like the worst human being ever. Well, except for Devereaux and his stupid nephew.

"It's okay," Jon said with a sad attempt at a smile.

"No, it's not! It is *not* okay," I insisted. "I'm a complete and utter ass. I've been the victim of nosy people myself and should've known better. I should have respected your privacy. I don't know what got into me."

He smiled. "Apology accepted."

"If I'd known, I wouldn't have made such an ass out of myself.

You should have told me, though I don't imagine you want to talk about it much." I paused, biting my lower lip. "Do you?"

A droll smile flitted across his face. "I don't mind so much anymore. Took me a while to get there, though. And it's not the sort of thing one brings up early in a relationship, particularly a business one."

Ouch. That was a slap in the face. Was that all I was to him? A business relationship?

"The job has helped me a lot," he went on. "It keeps me busy."

"I imagine the change of scenery has helped, too," I said.

He nodded. "It was fortuitous that I got this job, I think. I didn't need it because I received a hefty settlement from the garbage company, though I'd give it all back in a heartbeat if I could have Bjorn and Natalie back again. I considered selling my house and just traveling, but then I saw the posting for the chief's job here and thought it sounded perfect: small, kind of isolated, not a lot of people to have to deal with. To be honest, I was kind of surprised I got it. I wasn't all that qualified, and I heard there were quite a few applicants."

"It was meant to be," I said, understanding now how he'd managed to afford this house and pay for my services out of his own pocket. My concerns about him had been completely unfounded, and I felt ashamed for some of the doubts and assumptions I'd entertained about him.

He pulled the door to his home office closed and locked it. "We should get going," he said, glancing at his watch. "The next ferry leaves in fifteen minutes and poor Newt is probably beside himself. If it's okay with you, I've arranged for someone I know and trust to meet you at the ferry landing on the other side and drive you to your store. I'd do it myself, but I have a ton of things to attend to here, as you might well imagine."

"If you let me call Rita, I can have her come and pick me up. Devon can handle the store for half an hour by himself."

"I don't know," Jon said with an exaggerated grimace as he handed me his phone. "Look what happened the last time you left Devon in charge by himself."

He had a point, but I made the call anyway. Not surprisingly, Rita was full of questions, which I told her would have to wait because if we were going to get to the ferry in time, we had to leave now. Jon used the lights on his police car after making me promise not to tell anyone about this abuse of his authority, and we arrived with five minutes to spare.

After paying for my ticket, Jon said, "I'll be in touch."

Thinking I was dismissed, I turned to walk to the ferry, but he grabbed my arm and pulled me back.

"Thanks again for saving my life, Morgan." He leaned in and gave me a quick kiss on the lips before turning around and heading back to his car.

I replayed that moment in my head a thousand times during the half-hour ferry ride to Northport. By the time I reached the other side, I was convinced that our relationship wasn't just business after all, and the thought made me smile even as I reminded myself that neither of us was ready for anything new.

Rita was a little crazy when she met me. She peppered me with questions all the way back to the store, some of which I answered and some of which I skirted around.

Then she gave me a sly look and said, "You're obfuscating. You need to be more loquacious."

"A twofer," I said, duly impressed. I was too tired to think of a comeback. "You're the winner today, hands down."

When I walked into the store, Newt was a lot crazy, whimpering, whining, and sniffing me all over, jumping up to lick my face, even grabbing the leg of my pants in his teeth at one point and dragging me toward the door to my apartment.

That night he slept in my bed with me, something he almost never did. He's always preferred the floor. Whether for its cooler temperatures or because of some alpha-dog instinct he has, I don't know. Whatever his reason for breaking protocol that night, I was grateful, and I spooned him all night long.

that might be in the area wouldn't be any easier, thanks to the water depth and the size of the debris field.

The gold bars were valued at around thirty grand, a far cry from the four hundred million Devereaux had hoped to find. Though efforts were made to keep the discovery of the gold's supposed location a secret, word got out and treasure hunters, thrill seekers, and lookie-loos showed up in short order. The number of boats that could be seen in the Rock Island Passage on any given day increased tenfold. The water surrounding the area was declared off limits to divers, but that didn't stop the occasional industrious and creative treasure hunter from trying to get to the site. So far, no more gold had been found—at least none that anyone admitted to.

Devereaux's wife turned state's evidence in exchange for a lighter sentence. I was glad they didn't offer her immunity, though the five years she did get seemed like too little to me. I can't shake the feeling that Devereaux found more gold than he admitted to and that he has it hidden away somewhere. Or perhaps he already sold it and has the cash stored in an offshore account. If so, he won't be enjoying it anytime soon, thanks to a sentence of life without the possibility of parole. But if Ginger has access to her husband's hidden treasures—if there are any—she might be able to live out the rest of her life quite comfortably.

Roger was caught the day after he kidnapped me, though the driver of the boat remained at large. Roger denied killing anyone at first, claiming it was his uncle Mason who had done all the murdering. But in the end he confessed to shooting Marty and to operating the arm that grabbed Will Stokstad and held him under the water until he drowned. Those confessions were part of a plea deal that got him a sentence of life but with the possibility of parole after twenty-five years.

Roger told the authorities that Mason Devereaux weighted down Marty's body and dumped it in the lake. The area where that supposedly happened was in water over a hundred feet deep in Lake Michigan, and I know that means Marty's body will most likely never be found. Perhaps that should have saddened me, but it didn't. I felt Marty would have liked knowing that his final resting place was in the waters he spent his life on and knew so well.

When she was ready, I gave Sadie Hoffman the money she needed to escape from her husband and her marriage, and Jon and I helped her make the arrangements. She was grateful to the point of crying tears of relief, and she promised to pay the money back. I told her that instead, if she had the money in the future, she should pay it forward to some other woman who needed it. Knowing that the restraining order she took out on her husband was about as useful as the paper it was printed on, I also gave her some contacts on the sly—folks I knew she could use to set up a new identity if she wanted to. And so it was that on a sunny morning in late September, Sadie Hoffman went to the mainland to shop for some items that T.J. wanted, and she never returned.

The final thing I did after things settled down was call Bess Thornberg and let her know that Oliver hadn't been cheating on her.

"He *was* keeping a secret from you," I told her. "But it wasn't another woman. In fact, the woman who was helping him said that he hoped to score a find that would allow him to buy you the kind of engagement ring you deserved so he could propose."

That made Bess cry so hard that she had to hang up on me.

Jon Flanders and I had dinner a couple of weeks after Devereaux's arrest, and I gave him back the money he'd paid me for my consulting fee.

"I don't need it," he'd told me.

"Neither do I."

"You earned it."

I shook my head. "It was never my intention to keep it. Charging an up-front fee is merely my way of testing people's commitment to what they want me to do. Or what they think they want me to do."

After a few seconds of thought, Jon took the envelope and stuffed it in a pocket. "Okay, I give," he said. "I'll donate it to a worthy cause."

Jon and I were taking things slow. That was easy to do, given that we were separated by Death's Door and limited by ferry schedules and our respective jobs. Neither of us was eager to get super serious too fast, and all we'd done so far was share some meals together. There was possibility there, for sure, but for now I was content with the way things were. Our relationship was building up a slow heat on the romantic front, but Jon turned up the flame when it came to contract work for me as a cryptozoologist. Thanks to him, I've just been consulted to help with some mysterious deaths up near the Apostle Islands that some believe might have been caused by a Sasquatch. I do love the hunt.

There are still many unanswered questions regarding Napoleon's gold, but the discovery of the final resting place of the SS *Plymouth* and her crew was good news for the descendants of those who died and the historians who kept track of the Great Lakes' dead. Would we eventually find human remains down there? It was possible. But it had been more than a century since the ship sank, and the frigid fresh waters of the Great Lakes are notorious for not giving up their dead.

Though the *Plymouth* sank in the Rock Island Passage and not in Porte des Morts proper, I can't help but think that the curse of Death's Door is still very much alive now that the souls of Oliver Sykes, Will Stokstad, and Martin Showalter have been added to the area's watery graveyard.

As for whether large creatures resembling a plesiosaur call those haunted depths home, who knows? I haven't found one yet, but I continue to hang my hopes on plausible existability.

AUTHOR'S NOTE

This is a work of fiction that plays on some factual history. The location of Napoleon's rumored gold—if it even exists—and the final resting place of the SS *Plymouth* are two of the greatest mysteries in the world today. Both remain unsolved as I write this, though the world gets smaller every day and either one or both might be found at any time. While I have no reason to think that either of them is located where they are found in this book, my research indicates that it's possible, and possibilities are the backbone of fiction.

There are lots of caves in the area of Death's Door and the Rock Island Passage, and the geography of the Niagara Escarpment as it rises and plummets its way through the area is such that underwater tunnels and undiscovered caves are not only a distinct possibility, but a high probability. While my conclusion for the final resting place of the SS *Plymouth* is fictitious, the infamous storm that caused her demise was all too real. I hope that someone will eventually find her for the sake of the descendants of those who perished and all the others who died during the horrific storm of 1913.

ACKNOWLEDGMENTS

My first thank-you goes to Captain Jim Robinson of the Shoreline Charters, LLC, located in Gills Rock in beautiful Door County, Wisconsin. This man's comprehensive knowledge of the area, his charming personality, and his skill as a captain were invaluable to me. Captain Robbo, I honestly wouldn't have been able to tell this tale half as well without your help. Your willingness to explore the possibilities with me made it all come together. I am indebted to you and your crew. Thank you, too, to your lovely wife for helping me coordinate things. I hope to see you again soon if you haven't yet retired to Florida. A special thank-you goes to my new editors at Berkley: the incomparable and wise Jenn Snyder, and she of the wonderful laugh, Michelle Vega. (I've never had so much fun on a phone interview!)

I also need to thank my extraordinary agent, Adam Chromy, for his patience in dealing with me, his excellent negotiating skills, and his willingness to tell me when something sucks. Thanks to you (and Jamie) for hanging in there with me over the years.

A nod and many hugs to my family for their understanding and patience when I pass on social outings and other events because of my need to write, and for being some of my greatest cheerleaders. I love all of you! And finally, thank you to all the readers out there who have stuck by me over the years, and who promote and support me through book buys, reviews, and word of mouth. It's thanks to you that I get to keep doing this job I love so much. I am forever indebted.

Keep reading for an excerpt of

DEATH IN THE DARK WOODS

The next Monster Hunter Mystery from Annelise Ryan

I looked up as the bell above the door to my store, Odds and Ends, jingled to announce a new arrival. A blond, blue-eyed fellow in a police uniform entered and I immediately broke into a big smile at the sight of him.

"Jon! Hello!" I hurried over to greet him—my dog, Newt, close on my heels.

"Hello, Morgan," he said. A mini tornado of red, brown, and yellow leaves swirled in behind him, carried on a gust of brisk fall air before the door closed. He did a quick surveil of my store, taking in the customers browsing the aisles. It was mid-October and Mother Nature was flaunting her colors, a vibrant, vivid display known to draw tons of leaf peepers to the area. Lots of visitors meant lots of shoppers for the store. If only all shoppers equated to buyers.

"This is a surprise," I said.

It was. Mostly. Jon Flanders was the Chief of Police for Washington Island, which is located off the tip of the Door County peninsula here in Wisconsin. While I'm quite fond of Jon and have seen him several times over the past few weeks, his unexpected arrival unsettled me a little. I mean, it wasn't as if he decided to drop in because he was in the neighborhood. Getting to my store in Sister Bay required him to take a half-hour-long ferry ride and then do a bit of driving. Plus, he was in his uniform, suggesting he might be here on official business.

Newt was clearly glad to see him. He walked up and pushed his massive head into Jon's hand while wagging his tail hard enough to threaten inventory on some nearby shelves.

"Looks like business is booming." Jon said with an approving nod, stroking Newt's head.

"It is. What brings you by today?"

He turned his attention back to me and, for a moment, his eyes warmed, his expression softening. Then he got all serious and businesslike. "I want you to meet a DNR warden by the name of Charlie Aberdeen who should be here in a few minutes."

"Okay," I said slowly, trying to parse this out. "Can I ask why you want me to meet a DNR warden?"

He winked at me, and I saw a wicked gleam in his eyes. "You'll see," he said vaguely. "I rather enjoy keeping you in suspense for now, though I will let you know Charlie is driving down here from Bayfield and wants to hire you. If you decide to take the job, I'm hoping you'll do it pro bono. Money is an issue."

"Hire me? You mean as a cryptozoologist?"

Jon nodded.

While I own Odds and Ends—a combination mystery bookstore and oddities vendor—I also do work on the side searching for cryptids, creatures thought to exist despite there being no proof. Jon and

I met a couple of months ago when he hired me to look for a Loch Ness–type monster in Lake Michigan after a couple of mysterious deaths had occurred.

His pro bono request wasn't a big deal. I don't search for cryptids to make money; I do it because I love it and to continue the work my parents did in the field. Jon knew this, though he hadn't known it when he first hired me. I find a willingness to pay can sometimes be a good indicator of sincerity and motive when someone wants to hire me. I'm a cynic at heart, and I approach my cryptid searches from a position of science and reality, not speculation and rumor. There are hucksters out there claiming to be cryptozoologists, and I'm always eager to distinguish myself from them.

"I only charge people to determine their level of commitment and seriousness," I reminded Jon. "A recommendation from you serves the same purpose, assuming I decide to take the case."

"Oh, you'll take it," he said with a knowing grin, managing to both annoy and intrigue me. "Assuming Charlie's willing to trust you."

That gave me pause. "What do you mean?"

Jon's mouth twitched. "Charlie has already dealt with a fellow claiming to be a cryptozoologist and things didn't go well. Apparently, the fellow sounded all excited at first, but after they discussed plans for him to come to the area and help out, the money game began."

"He wanted cash up front," I said nodding. I'd heard of similar scams before.

"Yep. The DNR and the local law enforcement agencies want nothing to do with this, so Charlie offered to pay this guy a small fee. It wasn't going to be nearly enough. First, he wanted roundtrip airfare from Connecticut, a rental car, accommodations once he got to Bayfield, and an agreement to pay an hourly fee. Then he asked for a bunch of expensive equipment, a local guide, and a large upfront deposit."

This MO sounded familiar. "Do you happen to know this guy's name?"

"The last name is Baumann. I think his first name was . . ." His face scrunched up in thought and he tapped the side of his head a few times. "Herman? No, that wasn't it, but it was something like that."

"Hans," I said.

Jon snapped his fingers, getting Newt's attention. "Yes, that's it! Do you know him?"

"I'm afraid I do, mostly by reputation. I only met him once, about five years ago on a trip with my parents, but I've followed him and his antics online for years. He's a shyster. If there's a way to bilk gullible folks out of their money, he'll find it."

"Good thing Charlie ditched him then," Jon said. He focused more fully on Newt, who had been whining for attention ever since the first head scratch. Jon reached down—he didn't have to go far since Newt stands more than two feet at the shoulder—and sandwiched Newt's head between both hands, giving him a good, hard rub. "How ya doing, Newt, old boy?"

Newt, who is not just big but also nearly blind, wagged his tail so hard he brushed a display of shrunken heads—fake ones, the real one I had was in a glass case elsewhere in the store—off a nearby shelf. I quickly picked them up and replaced them after telling Newt to sit so his swishing tail disturbed only dust rather than the merchandise.

I had just returned the scattered heads to their rightful spots when the bell over the door tinkled, and a woman walked in. She was pretty with a pale, flawless complexion; shiny black hair with bangs; and huge blue eyes rimmed with thick, dark lashes. I pegged her as in her late twenties, maybe early thirties. She was dressed in boots, blue jeans, a khaki shirt, and a vest with an embroidered patch from the Department of Natural Resources on the right shoulder. A name tag on her shirt read C. Aberdeen.

Charlie was a woman? I did a fast mental adjustment in my head, feeling strangely disoriented.

Jon waved at her, and she smiled as soon as she saw him, making a dimple in her right cheek deepen. She started toward him but then her gaze shifted inexorably to Henry, and she stopped, staring in astonishment. Henry is a mummified corpse that typically sits on a chair along the edge of the book section of the store near the entrance. He's our unofficial mascot and greeter, though he tends toward the taciturn. Currently, he was suspended on a wheeled pole to make it look like he was standing, something we do with him every year in preparation for Halloween.

C. Aberdeen pointed and said, "Is that—"

"Real?" Jon finished for her. "It is. Meet Henry."

She moved closer to get a better look—Henry was wearing a large, floppy hat set at a jaunty angle to hide some of his face since he was missing his nose. Seeing how curious she was, I decided to enlighten her and offered up an abbreviated version of Henry's history.

"Rumor has it that Henry was a forty-niner who went west to look for gold and eventually headed up to Alaska. Unfortunately, he fell into a crevasse in the ice up there, died, and became mummified. He's had some travels since and ended up here when my father bought him."

Warden Aberdeen looked at me with a surprisingly whimsical smile, and then did a quick surveil of my place. "I wondered what a store called Odds and Ends might be about," she said, zeroing in on three eerie-looking African masks I had hanging on one wall. "I don't think I ever would have guessed."

"The store was my parents' idea. They were both fascinated by anything weird, unusual, or strange in the world, and they collected oddities during their travels. My mother was also an avid mystery reader, so she decided to dedicate part of the store to books. Those would be the 'ends' in Odds and Ends since someone always dies in a mystery."

"Ah, I get it," she said. "Very clever. Such a unique place." Her gaze settled on Jon, and she smiled warmly. "You look just like your picture. Nice to meet you in real life."

Jon returned her smile and extended a hand for her to shake. "You look younger in real life than you do in your pictures," he said. Their hands clasped and they did a token shake while Warden Aberdeen beamed at Jon. The amount of time the two spent eyeing one another made me a tad uncomfortable. Finally, she shifted her gaze to Newt, who was obediently sitting at my side. "May I?" she asked, pointing toward him.

"Of course." I was pleased and impressed she showed no fear of Newt. He's a sweetheart, but he can look and seem intimidating at times. Plus, I find dogs are a good barometer for people and their personalities.

Warden Aberdeen—Charlie, I reminded myself, though my prior association of a man with the name was proving hard to shake— walked over to Newt, bent down, and stroked his giant head. Newt closed his eyes in momentary ecstasy and then gave her a big, wet kiss up one side of her face. I thought she might rear back from Newt's slobbery display of gratitude, but instead she let out the most delightful, heartfelt laugh before returning the gesture by kissing Newt's muzzle.

She straightened and cocked her head to one side. "I apologize for my manners. I imagine you must be Morgan Carter. I'm Charlotte Aberdeen, but everyone calls me Charlie."

She extended a hand, which I shook. "Pleasure to meet you. And this slobbery fellow is Newt," I said, nodding toward my dog, who was gazing up at Charlie with blatant adoration. "Let's go upstairs to my apartment so we can talk."

I looked toward the counter where one of my employees, Devon Thibodeaux, was checking out customers. He appeared busy, so I looked for my other employee, Rita Bosworth, who's always easy to spot thanks to her rhinestone-studded eyeglass chain and a tall, lanky frame topped off with a messy bun of snow-white hair. I caught Rita's eye—she was always tuned in to me, it seemed—and pointed toward the ceiling. She nodded and I turned back to Jon and Charlie.

"Follow me." I led them through the store displays to a locked door and, once I opened it, upstairs to my apartment, the place I'd called home my entire life even though I hadn't spent much time in it.

"Oh, wow!" Charlie said as we emerged on the upper floor. She did a slow spin, taking in the large open area that made up my living room, dining area, and kitchen. Bright, cheery daylight streamed in through the tall windows on the front wall, bathing everything with a warm, inviting glow. The décor was eclectic and colorful, filled with items my parents had bought during their travels around the world. There was no theme to the furnishings, no attempt at a color scheme, or any real organization to any of it, yet it all seemed to work, the colors blending or complimenting each other, the unrelated items fitting together in a welcoming and cozy way.

"Yeah, that was my reaction, too, the first time I saw it," Jon said. He looked over at me and smiled.

Feeling a little embarrassed, I said, "Charlie, have a seat in the living room. Can I get you something to drink? I have lemonade, or I can fix you a cup of coffee or tea if you like. I also have a few beers in the fridge, if you'd prefer."

"I'd love a cup of coffee," Charlie said, wandering into the living room and running her fingers appreciatively over the arm of my Adirondack chair. "Black is fine."

"Jon?"

"Coffee sounds good to me, too."

I saw the two of them exchange warm smiles and turned away to focus on my coffee machine. "Three coffees, coming up," I said, hoping I sounded more chipper than I felt.

I set a pot of coffee to brewing while talking over my shoulder to Charlie, telling her where the various pieces in the house had come from. I'd covered the dining room and most of the living room pieces, and was explaining how the Adirondack chair she'd just been admiring had been a gift from someone I'd met during a recent case I'd done with Jon.

"Exquisite craftmanship," Charlie observed, giving the chair arm an appreciative stroke.

I started to reply but was overcome with emotion that made the words stick in my throat. That chair had sentimental meaning for me. To cover, I busied myself setting cookies out on a plate, along with cream and sugar for the coffee.

Charlie, oblivious to my emotional strangling, filled the void. "Yes, Jon mentioned the two of you recently worked together on a case. He said you're a cryptozoologist? What a fascinating field of work."

"Yes, I am; and it is," I managed, grateful for the change of subject. "I'm always on the hunt for the latest cryptid."

"I take it Bigfoot qualifies?" Charlie said without missing a beat.

I looked at her, intrigued. "It does." I held up a finger. "Hold that thought."

The coffee was done brewing, and I poured three mugs and added them to the tray with the other items, carrying it all into the living room and setting it on my glass-topped coffee table. Jon and Charlie each took a mug, Jon adding sugar to his—the man had a sweet tooth—and I took the remaining mug after adding a dollop of cream. Since Charlie had settled into the Adirondack chair and Jon had chosen the leather armchair next to it, I sat across from them on the Bali daybed that served as my sofa, the cushions and pillows of which were covered with hand-dyed Indonesian fabrics in purple, orange, and red, colors that will always remind me of my mother.

I was ready to give Charlie my undivided attention. "Okay, tell me why you're here."

Charlie had just bitten into a cookie, so it was her turn to hold up a finger. She chewed and swallowed, licking at a few errant crumbs on her lips before taking a sip of coffee.

"I'm here because there's something strange going on in the Chequamegon-Nicolet National Forest," she said finally. "We've had some Bigfoot sightings in the area, a couple of which have been rather . . . disturbing."

I shrugged. "There are always Bigfoot sightings in heavily forested areas. Hundreds of them every year all over the country. Heck, all over the world. It's nothing new."

Charlie shot a worried look toward Jon, and he gave her an encouraging go-ahead nod. Charlie squared her shoulders and swallowed hard, as if to brace herself before she spoke. "It's true, we certainly have our share of Bigfoot sightings up north, but this was more than just a sighting. One of them may have torn a man apart."

She dumped the words out there and they sobered the atmosphere faster than an AA meeting. I narrowed my eyes at her. "Can you be more specific?"

Charlie grimaced. "I can, but it's not pretty."

Author photo by H. Claire Photography

Annelise Ryan is the *USA Today* bestselling author of multiple mystery series, including the Mattie Winston Mysteries. A retired ER nurse, she now writes full-time from her Wisconsin home.

CONNECT ONLINE

AnneliseRyan.com

🐦 Ryan_Annelise

❶ AuthorAnneliseRyan

Ready to find
your next great read?

Let us help.

Visit prh.com/nextread